Also by C. K. Harewood

Under Cover of Darkness

Lies and Desperate Measures

The Empire Club Murders

Echoes of a Murder

Death of a Blackbird

A Killing for Christmas

A Kiss for a Killing

Ashes & Ink

SIXPENCE
for a
SLAUGHTER

C.K. Harewood

ISBN (Hardback): 978-1-912968-65-7

ISBN (Paperback): 978-1-912968-64-0

ISBN (eBOOK): 978-1-912968-63-3

1

Wednesday, 15th October 1930

Silver light flickered across Roy Grainger's pudgy face as he surveyed the auditorium of the Regal Picture Palace. He allowed himself a small smile, pleased now the panic was over.

The day had been going well until the late afternoon show when the final reel of *The Broadway Melody* got mangled in the machine ten minutes before the end of the picture. Grainger had had to refund the grumbling patrons and then scramble to find another film to show for the evening trade. He'd telephoned around the local cinemas to see if he could borrow a recent release but to no avail. So, he'd resorted to searching the old stock racks in the projection room, much to the chagrin of Ivor Topling, the projectionist, who complained he messed up his film tins. Together, they'd dug out an old Chaplin picture, and Grainger had pasted a 'CANCELLED' banner over *The Broadway Melody* poster on the front of the cinema. And then he'd had the unenviable job of rooting through all the junk in the alley, thrown out a few years before and never cleared away, searching desperately for a Chaplin film poster that hadn't been reduced to pulp.

It had turned out all right in the end, he thought, as he ran his eyes over the seats. The house was about a third full, a big improvement on recent weeks when the films had been playing to an almost empty auditorium. His pleasure had diminished when he'd overheard a few patrons say they'd tried to get in at the Majestic in Craynebrook only to be turned away because the house was full. That was what the Regal had become, Grainger mused. A second choice. A last resort. Oh, how he wished he had the Majestic to manage. Then he'd show the bosses what he could really do. The Majestic seated two hundred and fifty, and he'd fill it every night, he was sure of it. He'd have the latest films as soon as they came over from America, and all the big star vehicles, too, not the third-rate pictures he had to show starring actors no one had ever heard of.

Grainger sighed as he toed the carpet at his feet, catching the rim of his sole in a hole that was just one of many. The Majestic wasn't a fleapit like the Regal, either. It didn't have damp in the walls or dodgy plumbing in the lavatories. It didn't have plaster falling off the ceiling or carpeting fit only for the rubbish heap. The basic refurbishment of the Regal two years earlier hadn't included replacing the carpet, the owners of the cinema deeming it good for another five years at least. But when the lights were on, it was all too obvious how frayed and filthy it was. Even the pattern was disappearing beneath the dirt. It smelt too, especially when it was damp, and he'd taken to spraying eau de toilette around the auditorium before opening in an effort to disguise the smell. He shook his head, remembering the telephone conversation the week before when he'd asked for the carpet to be replaced. 'There's no money for new carpets, Grainger,' his boss had told him. 'Especially not with the takings down this last quarter.'

'That's not my fault,' Grainger had felt like saying, but held his tongue, knowing he'd only land himself in the muck if he told his boss the truth as to why the takings were down. It wasn't just that the Regal was most people's second choice of cinema. The takings were also down because kids had been letting their friends in through the side door when the staff weren't looking, so it could be that as many as five children had been getting in for the price of one. He'd soon put a stop to this thievery, ordering the staff to be on the lookout for kids trying it on. But now that the kids knew they couldn't get in free, they were turning their backs on the Regal completely and going over to Craynebrook where they could see the latest films. Time was when Grainger could fill the Regal all day long on a Saturday with children, but those days were long gone.

His mood didn't improve as he contemplated what the absence of the usherette in the auditorium would do for the night's takings. Lucy Simpson had telephoned fifteen minutes before the doors opened to say she was ill and couldn't come in to work. Grainger had done his best to be sympathetic as the young woman coughed and spluttered down the line, but all he could think of was how few choco-lates and cigarettes were likely to sell without Lucy's persuasive smile and patter. The cinema needed all the extra money it could get, and she usually managed to empty her tray by the end of the evening, topping up the cinema's coffers considerably. He hoped Lucy would be well enough to return to work tomorrow.

Grainger pulled open one of the auditorium doors by its brass handle and stepped out into the foyer. He tutted in annoyance when he saw it was empty, and with a deter-mined jutting forward of his shoulders, made his way into the private area of the cinema. Yanking open the door to the staffroom, Grainger glared at a man in a doorman's coat slouching in a low armchair. A cigarette jutted out from the corner of his mouth, and he barely looked up from the horse-racing periodical he was reading. A dark-haired woman dressed in a plain blouse and checked skirt stirred a cup of tea at a small wobbly table and looked at Grainger enquiringly.

'I thought so,' Grainger said, nodding vigorously as his fists curled on his hips. 'I've told you two about this before. You're not to leave the foyer unattended.'

'But the picture's started, Mr Grainger,' Rita Amstell protested with a careless shrug of her shoulders.

'That's no excuse. Customers could still come in.'

George Cordell puffed out a cloud of smoke and turned a page in his magazine. 'No one comes in this late.'

His nonchalance infuriated Grainger. 'It's this kind of laxity which meant those brats could let their friends in for free. Do you have any idea how much money was lost through that little caper of theirs?'

George didn't know and didn't care. 'They can't do that anymore, not now the side door's locked. And anyone coming in the front is going to pay for their ticket.'

'Even so,' Grainger sighed, the inclination of his head acknowledging the truth of this, 'I'd appreciate it if you would return to your posts.' He gestured towards the door.

'All right, Mr Grainger,' George smiled. 'When I've finished my smoke.'

Grainger glared at him, aware of Rita trying to hide a smile behind her teacup. 'Very well. But don't take too long about it.' He turned on his heel and strode out, knowing, just knowing, they were laughing at him behind his back.

He thundered up the foyer stairs to his office, but halted on the landing outside the Projection Room door and sniffed. With an annoyed pursing of his thin lips, he threw the door open.

'Good grief!' he cried, waving his hand in front of his face. 'How many times must I tell you, you cannot smoke in here?'

A scrawny man in his early forties twisted on his stool beside one of the two projector machines that took up most of the room. 'It's just the one, Mr Grainger,' Ivor Topling said, showing him his smouldering cigarette.

'I don't care if it's one or a hundred. Don't you realise how dangerous a naked flame is in here? What does that say?' Grainger pointed to the words painted in red block capitals on the wall above the projector windows. 'No Smoking. That's not there just for fun, Ivor. The celluloid is highly flammable. Just one little spark and the whole place could go up in flames.'

'There's no need to worry about that. I'm very careful.'

'You can never be careful enough. If I catch you smoking in here again, you'll be out. Is that clear? There's plenty who would be glad of this job, I can tell you.'

'It won't happen again, Mr Grainger,' Ivor said resignedly and nodded at the nearest machine. 'The reel will need changing in a minute. I better get it ready.'

'Yes, you better had.' Grainger gave one last demonstrative wave of his hand to clear the smoke, tugged his suit jacket down in a show of annoyance and left the projection room, closing the door behind him and climbing the last few stairs up to his office.

Sitting down at his desk, Grainger took a letter out from the top drawer, set it down on the blotter and studied it with unease. He had been wondering how to respond to it for most of the day, ever since it had arrived that morning. What could he say to the writer? Grainger wondered unhappily. He understood the difficulty his friend was in –

he didn't imagine it was easy to face unexpected unemployment – and although he didn't like to let a friend down, he was at a loss as to how he could help. There weren't any vacancies at the Regal, and though he may threaten Ivor with the sack, there was no denying the projectionist was very good at his job and that he'd be difficult to replace with someone as experienced with the machines. There was nothing for it; he had to reply saying he was sorry but there was nothing he could do.

Grainger took a pad of writing paper from his drawer and picked up his fountain pen, slowly unscrewing the cap as he considered how to begin. He decided on the usual pleasantries, then moved on to the meat of the matter.

> *You have my sincerest sympathies for the predicament you find yourself in and I wish I could be of some help. But unfortunately, I have no vacancies, nor am likely to have. And besides, for a man of your undoubted talents, I'm sure you will be able to find much more suitable work elsewhere. As my wife is always saying to me, something will turn up.*

Grainger nibbled the end of his pen. He supposed that would be enough – he didn't want the letter to be a long one – but he ought to make a propitiatory gesture, soften the blow, so to speak. A thought struck him, and he set his pen to the paper once more.

> *But I do want to do what I can for you, so from now on, wherever you want to sit in the*

Grainger signed his name with a flourish, blotted the ink, folded the page, and stuffed it into an envelope. Adding the address, he set it aside for posting later.

He nodded in satisfaction. It was done, and now he thought about it, he'd been more than generous, especially with the takings being down. Grainger reached for his pipe and lit it, listening to the muffled sounds of the film's musical accompaniment coming through the carpeted floorboards.

Reverend Bertram Laing threw the prayer books he had gathered from the empty pews into the cardboard box at his feet and turned to stare out of the heavy oak door of his church.

His dark eyes narrowed as they fixed on the buildings on the opposite side of the high street. In the public house on the corner, he could make out the figures of men and women through the coloured glass windows, and even this far away, he could hear the murmur of their voices, smell faintly the alcohol they drank and the smoke from their cigarettes. And next door to the pub was the cinema, its frontage boasting colourful posters of the current and upcoming attractions.

Laing shook his head in disgust as he remembered the poster he had seen that morning. Two cowboys pointing guns at each other while a young woman with flushed cheeks and ruby red lips clasped another man to her ample breasts. That such images of licentiousness and violence should be on public display where any child could see them was reprehensible and morally irresponsible, and yet no one but him seemed to bat an eyelid. He'd written to the cinema's manager, insisting the posters be taken down, but he'd not received a reply and the posters remained obstinately in place.

A cheer went up, jerking Laing's attention back to the public house. He saw a man bent over double, vomiting into the gutter, while his friends clapped in approval. Laing's disgust grew, and he gripped the edge of the door, his nails digging into the wood.

'I'm all done, reverend,' a voice said behind him, and he turned to see Dennis Hillman, the churchwarden, pulling on his overcoat. 'Everything's away.'

Laing nodded. 'Thank you, Mr Hillman.' He returned his gaze to the view out of the door.

'Is something the matter?' Dennis asked.

'Look over there,' Laing said, waving his hand at the pub. 'Such despicable behaviour.'

Dennis joined Laing at the door. 'Yes, it is. But what can one do? Men will drink to excess if they have a mind to.'

'Indeed, they will. Which is why men like us should take a stand against such attitudes.'

Dennis gave a feeble smile. 'I'm afraid I'm not a taking a stand kind of man, reverend.'

'Nonsense, Mr Hillman. It only takes a little backbone. A little determination. It is my own determination to show society the error of its ways that led me to begin writing my book.'

'Oh, yes, your book. How is it coming along?'

'Slowly, I'm afraid. The more I write and research, the more licentiousness and sin I realise I must expose.'

'You should get someone to help you with the research. Couldn't that girl who helped with the typing look up things for you?'

Laing shook his head. 'I'm afraid she is no longer interested in assisting me. Yes, the youth of today are extremely unreliable. And yet, they are England's future. It does not bode well. It does not bode well at all.' He turned away from the door. 'So few of them even bother to come to church. This is not a large church, is it, Mr Hillman? Yet is it ever full? How many were here for the service tonight? Nine? Ten?'

'I counted eleven. But midweek services are never that well attended.'

'No, they're not. And do you know why, Mr Hillman? Because they've been seduced, lured away by alcohol, drugs and sex. The cinema and the public house are two prime examples of everything that is wrong with society today.'

'I think it's because of the war,' Dennis said, wiping his cold nose with his handkerchief. 'I know it was a while ago now, but people haven't forgotten what they went through back then. I suppose they want a little fun.'

'And what of God, Mr Hillman? Where is He in this fun-filled world of yours?'

'He's still here, reverend.' Dennis gestured at the pews. 'He'll always be here. And people do come to church.'

'Oh yes, they come. On a Sunday, when it is expected of them and eyebrows would be raised by their neighbours if they didn't. But do they come willingly? No, they do not. And on other days, they don't come at all. My church should be full for every service, but how often am I speaking to an empty house?'

'It was the war,' Dennis insisted despairingly. 'It was hard to believe in a god who could put people through so much horror. They lost their faith.'

'So, I should be thankful for the flock I have, is that it?' Laing shot back angrily. 'I should simply accept England has become a godless nation and there is nothing to be done about it? I must accept the people of Foxhall Green now worship a new god, one that extols the virtues of drink and violence and the lusts of the flesh? I must accept the cinema is more compelling than myself or God? Films that show criminal gangs gunning down their rivals. Indiscriminate murder. Greed. Women flaunting their bodies and abusing the sanctity of marriage. How can I make people understand the wretched influence these films are having?'

Dennis edged towards the door. 'I'm sure that when your book is published, it will open people's eyes.'

Laing shook his head. 'I fear it will take much more than a book to do that, Mr Hillman. What society needs is a short, sharp shock.' He turned at the sound of heels on the flagstones. 'Ah, there you are, my dear.'

A smartly dressed, dark-haired woman had come out of the vestry. Behind her came another woman of similar middle age, patting her blond curls in place beneath her hat.

'Yes, here we are,' Violet Laing said, pulling on lavender-coloured gloves, 'and ready to go.' She glanced at Dennis halfway out of the door. 'Why, Mr Hillman! Aren't you coming with us to the funfair? I made Bertram promise he would take me. And Mrs Wildsmith,' she gestured at the blond woman, 'is meeting her husband and son there. So, we'll make a very merry party.'

'No, thank you, Mrs Laing,' Dennis said. 'Mother will be expecting me.'

'Surely, your mother will be all right for an hour or two?'

'I'd rather get back to her. She worries. Good evening.'

'What a funny man he is,' Violet said, watching Dennis hurry away.

'Mr Wildsmith and Lewis are already at the funfair, are they?' Laing raised an eyebrow at Lydia Wildsmith. 'That explains why they weren't at my service tonight.'

Lydia gave him an apologetic smile. 'Lewis so wanted to go to the fair, reverend. And we couldn't let him go on his own.'

'What nonsense!' Violet said. 'Lewis isn't a child. Why, he's how old now?'

'He's eighteen,' Lydia said. 'But a very young eighteen, Mrs Laing. Lewis is quite an innocent.'

Violet's eyebrows rose. 'Not all that innocent, from what I've heard.'

'My dear,' Laing said reprovingly. 'Mrs Wildsmith doesn't want to be reminded of that.'

'No. Indeed, I don't,' Lydia said, and snapped her handbag shut. 'Shall we go? Herbert will be wondering where I am.'

Dennis pushed the dishcloth into the bottom of the glass, twisting it to get into the sides, and stared at the road outside the bungalow's kitchen window. There was the man from No. 23 walking his wife's Pekinese, Mr Robertson returning home from the train station having caught the 5:59 from Holborn, and a boy kicking a football against the fence of the bungalow opposite.

Dennis's throat tightened. He squinted behind his round spectacles at the boy and relaxed when he saw it was young Ollie from No. 4 and not the other. He rinsed the glass under the cold water tap, set it on the draining board and wiped his hands on the tea towel.

The sardines under the grill were smoking and he hastily drew out the pan, wincing at the very nearly charred bodies. He flicked them onto the toast with a shrug. His mother didn't mind her sardines well done. Setting the plate on a tray, Dennis added the salt and pepper pots and left the kitchen, kicking open the door of his mother's bedroom.

'Here you are, Mother,' Dennis said, setting the tray down on Agnes's lap. 'They're a little well done, but you don't mind, do you?'

'No, I don't mind,' Agnes said, buttoning up her bedjacket. She picked up the salt and sprinkled it liberally over the sardines.

'Not too much,' Dennis chided. 'You'll be drinking all night.'

'Don't fuss,' she said, setting the salt down on the tray with a thump. 'You were late tonight.'

'I got caught by Reverend Laing. He wanted to moan about the state of society again.'

'Does that man ever stop?'

'No, I don't think he does. And then his wife went on at me to go to the funfair with them.'

'You should have gone with them. It would have done you good.'

'I had to get you your tea.'

'I've told you, Dennis, you don't need to worry about me. I can manage.'

'No, you can't, Mother. And anyway, I didn't want to go to the funfair.'

Agnes shook her head, then eyed her son suspiciously. 'Where's your tea?'

'I had mine in the kitchen,' Dennis said, turning away to twitch the eiderdown straight.

'Don't tell fibs. You haven't eaten, have you?'

'I'm not hungry, Mother.'

'Dennis,' she sighed, 'you've got to eat. You'll waste away to nothing, the way you're going.'

'I don't have much of an appetite these days.'

'Your clothes are hanging off you.'

'Mother,' he snapped. 'You've told me not to fuss, so don't you.'

'I'm just worried about you.' She set down her knife and fork. 'I'm not daft, Dennis. I know you're not right. I hear you in the night.'

'Mother, please.'

'You're crying in your sleep—'

'I know I am,' he yelled at her. 'You don't have to tell me.' Her startled face pained him. Dennis groaned and fell down onto the bed beside her, his head in his hands. 'Sorry. I didn't mean to shout.'

Agnes patted his shoulder. 'What's all this about?' she asked gently.

He sighed. 'It's the nightmares. They've come back, and they're worse than before. Honestly, Mother, they seem so real. It's as if it's happening all over again. I'm walking along and then I hear him breathing behind me. But in the dreams, instead of him hitting me before I can see him, I turn and I do see him, and he's...he's... oh, I can't describe what he looks like, but it's horrible.' He shook his head.

'But you were all right for a while. Why have they started up again?'

He shrugged. 'I don't know.'

'Is it work?' Agnes suggested. 'Have you heard about your job?'

'Work has been on my mind,' Dennis admitted. 'I've been worrying how we would cope. But I meant to tell you. I was told today my job's safe, so we're all right. I just wish the management would let everyone else know. People keep asking me whether they're going to be made redundant. As if Head Office tells me anything! I tell them I don't know, but they keep on. And then there's the Scouts, and that wretched boy, Frankie Ashe. I wish I'd never let him join, the trouble he's caused me. Truth be told, I'm thinking of giving it all up.'

'But you love the Scouts!'

'I used to love it.'

Agnes grabbed his chin and forced his head around to face her. 'Now you listen to me, Dennis. You are not giving up the Scouts. I'm not having some little sod forcing you out of doing something you love. God knows, you haven't got anything else. What's this boy's address? I'll write to his parents and get them round here. I'll tell them they've got to control their son.'

'His parents aren't interested. I told his mother that if Frankie didn't behave, I'd expel him, and she sent his father round to the church hall. He said he'd give me what for if I expelled his son. I'm not a fighter, Mother, you know that. I can't stand up to a man like that. I can't stand up to anyone. So, there's nothing we can do. I just have to grin and bear the little brat.' He shrugged. 'Or I leave.'

Agnes sighed. 'Well, don't make any decision in a hurry. Let's see what happens. But I want you to see the doctor again. You ask for some stronger sleeping draughts. Promise me you will.'

Dennis nodded. 'All right, Mother. I promise.'

The bright lights and noise of the funfair were making Herbert's head ache. He took off his spectacles and pinched the bridge of his nose to ease the pain. It didn't work, and he replaced his spectacles with a sigh.

'Do you want some, Daddy?' Lewis Wildsmith waggled his candy floss beneath Herbert's nose.

'No, thank you,' Herbert said, pushing his hand away. 'And finish it before your mother gets here. You know she doesn't like you eating that rubbish.'

'I'm almost done.' Lewis pulled the last strand of the sugary pink cloud from the stick and folded it into his mouth. They passed a waste bin and he tossed the stick into it. 'I want to go on the ghost train. Can we?'

'I don't think so,' Herbert said, thinking the last thing he wanted was ghouls and skeletons jumping out at him. 'How about the merry-go-round? That's fu—' He broke off and came to a halt, his stomach tightening as he saw who was walking their way.

'What is it?' Lewis asked, stopping too, and following his father's gaze. His mouth pursed and he turned away. 'Let's go the other way,' he said.

Herbert would have agreed, but it was too late; Lucy Simpson had seen them. She grinned and sashayed over to them, dragging the man whose arm she held along behind her.

'Well, hello,' she said, her wide mouth spreading to show off a row of imperfect teeth. She ran the tip of her tongue over her plump bottom lip. 'Fancy seeing you here. Does Mummy know you're out this late, Lewis?'

'Leave him alone, Lucy,' Herbert said. 'Shouldn't you be at work?'

'Oh, I called in sick,' Lucy said airily and tugged her male companion closer. 'David wanted to bring me here.'

David was about twenty-five, Herbert guessed, and good-looking, but he was also more than a little drunk if the blankness in his expression was anything to go by. 'And he seems to be enjoying it immensely,' he said, his voice thick with sarcasm.

Lucy bristled. 'David's in films. He's going to get me a test.'

'What's a test?' Lewis asked.

'A film test, dummy. I'm going to be in pictures.'

'Hollywood?'

'Maybe,' she preened.

'Only if you're any good,' David said, poking a finger into the dimple in Lucy's cheek.

She smacked his hand away. 'Oh, but I am.' Lucy glared at Herbert. 'You believe I'm good in front of the camera, don't you, Herbert?'

Herbert's jaw tightened at the familiarity. 'Come along, Lewis,' he said, taking hold of his son's elbow and pulling him away.

'Be seeing you, boys,' Lucy sing-songed after them.

'Don't look at her,' Herbert ordered as Lewis turned to watch Lucy walking away.

'Who's that man with her?' he asked.

'It doesn't matter who he is.'

'But why did she come with him? I would have brought her here if that's what she wanted.'

Herbert rounded on him. 'Now, you listen to me, Lewis. You've been told before that you're not to have anything more to do with Lucy.'

Lewis nodded glumly. 'I know, Daddy. Sorry.'

'That's all right. But just you remember that. And don't mention Lucy to your mother when she gets here. She doesn't need to know we ran into her.'

'I won't say a word. Promise.'

Herbert sighed at his son's dejection, wishing he hadn't spoken so harshly. 'Come on,' he said, determined to cheer Lewis up. 'Let's find the shooting gallery. What do you say?'

Lewis brightened. 'I'll beat you this time.'

'I don't think so,' Herbert grinned.

'I bet you I will. You haven't seen me practising after Scouts. Even Mr Hillman says I'm the best he's ever seen.'

'Well, come on, then. What are we waiting for?'

They moved off, but halted and searched the crowd when a voice hallooed them.

'It's Mummy,' Lewis cried, and waved frantically.

Lydia waved back and came over. 'There you are. We've been looking all over for you.'

'Who's we?' Herbert asked, getting his answer as the Laings joined them. He hid his irritation behind a polite smile. 'Good evening, reverend. Mrs Laing. I didn't think a fair would be your idea of an evening out?'

'My wife expressed a desire to attend,' Laing explained stiffly.

'I certainly did,' Violet said with a smile. 'Do you know, Mr Wildsmith, if Bertram had his way, we wouldn't go anywhere except to church?'

Herbert nodded, then gestured at Lewis, who was tugging his arm impatiently. 'We were just off to find the shooting gallery. Lewis thinks he has a chance of beating me.'

'Oh, we passed the gallery on the way here,' Violet said, and pointed back the way they had come.

'Then if you'll excuse us.' Herbert made to step around them, but Violet put out a gloved hand to stop him.

'Bertram would like to have a go. Wouldn't you, dear?'

'Oh, Violet, I haven't shot a rifle in years,' Laing protested.

'I'm sure it's just like riding a bicycle. And you were a good shot. You never forget. Come on.' She led Laing away, gesturing for the Wildsmiths to follow.

'Don't let him take over,' Lydia whispered to Herbert. 'You know how touchy Lewis is when he wants to win.'

'I'll do my best,' Herbert replied.

There was no one else at the shooting range when they arrived. The three men paid their pennies and each picked up an air rifle from the counter, pressing the butts into their shoulders and taking aim at the yellow metal ducks moving from left to right across the far end of the range.

They had paid for five shots each. Laing went first,

hitting three out of five ducks and setting down the rifle with a rueful smile at his wife. Lewis went next, hitting all five ducks. Then it was Herbert's turn. He hit four ducks in a row and met his son's eye. He winked, then squeezed the trigger and the pellet struck the wall behind the row of ducks.

'You missed!' Lewis cried. 'That means I won. I won! I won! Did you see, Daddy? I hit all five and you only hit four.'

'I saw,' Herbert said, smiling at Lydia as he laid down the rifle. She smiled back, knowing he'd missed the last duck on purpose.

The owner of the shooting gallery began reloading all three air rifles.

'I want to go again,' Lewis declared, and held his hand out for some more coins.

Herbert's expression hardened. The funfair had already swallowed too much of his money. 'Once is enough.'

Lewis stamped his foot. 'But I want another go.'

'Oh, let him have another go, Herbert,' Lydia said.

'I'm not made of money, Lydia,' he snapped.

'Here. Allow me.' Laing dug into his pocket and drew out a fistful of coins.

Lewis reached to take the coins, but Herbert grabbed his wrist and thrust it away. 'I can pay for my son, reverend, thank you very much.'

'As you wish,' Laing said stiffly, and dropped the coins back into his pocket as he gave his wife a pointed look.

Lewis suddenly cried out in pain and rubbed the back of his neck.

'What is it, darling?' Lydia asked.

'Something hit me,' he said, and turned. 'It was him!'

The others followed his pointing finger to see Frankie Ashe standing twenty feet away with two of his friends.

'Look. It's Loony Lewis,' Frankie laughed. 'What's up, Loony?'

'You shut up!' Lewis yelled and took a step towards him, but Herbert held him back.

'You behave yourself, Frankie Ashe,' Laing ordered.

'You going to make me?' Frankie stuck his tongue out at the vicar.

Laing opened his mouth to reply, but Violet tugged at his arm. 'Don't lower yourself, Bertram,' she said, and they turned their backs on the boys.

Frankie and his friends began chanting 'Loony Lewis' and making rude gestures. Lewis, his face red with rage, turned back to the counter and snatched up the nearest air rifle.

'I'll show you,' he declared and aimed the rifle at Frankie's head.

'Lewis, no!' Herbert cried, and grabbed the barrel of the rifle, yanking it away. But Lewis had already squeezed the trigger, and the pellet shot out, thudding into the earth an inch from Frankie's feet.

The boys stopped their chanting. Frankie's eyes widened at Lewis. The shot had surprised him, but he recovered quickly. 'Missed,' he cried triumphantly.

'I won't a second time.' Lewis aimed again, but Herbert tore the rifle out of his son's hands.

'That's enough, Lewis.' He turned to face Frankie. 'You better get out of here before I give you a clip around the ear.'

Frankie seemed inclined to fight. He raised his fists, but then changed his mind and stuck out his tongue once more before jerking his head at his friends. 'Come on. Let's go,' he said, and they followed him, disappearing into the crowd.

Herbert turned to Lewis. 'What were you thinking? You could have hurt him.'

'I wanted to hurt him,' Lewis protested. 'He threw a stone at me.'

'I know he did. But you can't go around shooting at people.' Herbert put the air rifle back down on the counter.

'You going to pay for that shot?' the gallery owner asked.

Herbert was minded to argue, but he didn't want any more trouble. He fished in his pocket for a penny and pressed it into the owner's waiting palm.

'That son of yours wants his head looking at,' the man said. 'He could have killed that boy.'

'He didn't though, did he?' Herbert shot back, and turned away, only to catch Laing's disapproving eye.

'Mr Wildsmith,' Laing said. 'If I could have a word.' He stepped aside, forcing Herbert to do the same. 'You really do need to have a word with Lewis about his temper. That's not the first time I've seen him lose it.'

'He's fine,' Herbert insisted irritably. 'It's just that boy is so provoking. He's always bullying Lewis.'

Laing nodded. 'I know he is. I've seen him at the Scouts with Lewis and I've had run-ins with the boy myself. But Lewis must learn to keep his temper under control. You may not always be around to stop him from going too far.'

'Thank you for your concern, reverend, but I know how to look after my son. Come, Lydia. Lewis.' He snatched at both their hands. 'It's time we were getting home.'

Frankie Ashe kicked a pebble along the pavement, watching as it skidded over the stones. He was alone, his friends having left him an hour ago at the funfair when their money ran out. He hadn't had any left either, but Frankie had been in no hurry to go home and so had wandered around the fair until it closed. But now, there really was nowhere else to go but home.

Frankie turned into his road and walked towards his house, dragging his feet, deliberately scuffing the toes on the paving stones, even though he knew his mother would scold him for it. He opened his front door, and his small chest tightened as he saw the coat hanging on the newel post. Snores coming from the front room told him his father was home, and he put his foot tentatively on the bottom step of the stairs. They creaked loudly, and he held his breath as the snoring stopped.

'Frankie? That you?'

'Yes, Dad.'

'Come in here.'

'I'm going to bed.'

'Come here.'

Frankie dragged himself away from the stairs, moving only as far as the doorway where he would be out of his father's reach.

Pete Ashe was slouched in the armchair, his long legs stretched out in front of him. He stared at Frankie through bleary eyes. 'Where you been?' he growled.

'At the funfair with my mates.'

'This late? Your mother's been worried.'

'But I told her where I was going.'

'Don't answer me back. And I don't care what you told her. I wanted you here hours ago to get me fags. I'm out.'

'You could have got them yourself,' Frankie retorted before he could stop himself.

His father's eyes hardened. 'What did you say to me?'

'Nothing, Dad,' Frankie said, backing away.

'Come here.' Pete pointed to a spot on the carpet beside his chair.

Frankie knew it would be worse for him if he didn't do as his father said, so he obeyed, preparing himself for the blow he knew was coming. Pete struck him on his left ear, making it ring. Frankie cried out and clutched the side of his head.

A woman appeared in the doorway. 'Frankie? What's the matter?'

Frankie ran back to the doorway where his mother now stood and threw himself against her.

Alison cradled him, pressing his head against her breast, and glared at her husband. 'What did you do?'

'He was cheeking me. I won't have it.'

'You didn't have to hit him.' She turned Frankie's face up to her. 'Does it hurt, Frankie?' He nodded, and she bent and kissed his forehead.

'Give over with all that kissing and cooing,' Pete said. 'I don't want him turned into a sissy. He's enough of a mummy's boy as it is.'

'Don't call him that, Pete.'

'Don't you answer me back,' Pete warned, jumping up from his chair and looming over her. 'Or you'll get a slap as well. Now, get out of the way. I'm going to bed.'

Alison backed away, still holding Frankie to her. Frankie watched his father stamp up the stairs and heard the bedroom door slam. He lifted his head and poked his tongue out at the ceiling.

'Don't do that, Frankie,' Alison snapped. 'Why do you always have to make him angry?'

'I didn't say nothing,' Frankie protested. 'What did he have to come home for? Why can't he stay away?'

Alison sighed and pushed him away. 'I know, Frankie. I like it when it's just you and me, too. But he is your father. Now, get up to bed. You've got school in the morning.'

She turned and returned to the kitchen. Frankie watched her go, wanting to say sorry he'd upset her, but she had closed the door and it was too late. He tiptoed up the stairs to his room and got into bed. Squeezing his eyes shut, he mouthed a prayer that his father would go back on the road soon and never come back.

2

Friday, 17th October 1930

Detective Inspector Matthew Stannard signed his name at the bottom of the report and murmured, 'And that, with any luck, will see Mr Dewson go away for at least seven years.' He closed the file and handed it back to Detective Constable Samuel Rudd. 'Is that it?'

'Yes, sir, that was the last one,' Rudd nodded. 'There's nothing more for you to do.'

Matthew screwed the cap back on his pen and dropped it into the tray on his desk. 'It'll make a change to be able to forget all this for a couple of days.'

'When was the last time you took some leave, sir?'

'Do you know, it's been so long, I can't remember.'

'I suppose it has been all go since you got here.'

'That's an understatement, Rudd. Still, as long as it stays quiet for the next two days.'

Matthew rose and took his hat and coat down from the stand. He studied the young man, who was looking a little nervous. Rudd had only recently joined CID from Uniform, replacing DC Gary Pinder. It was unusual for an officer to make the move to CID and remain at the same station, but Matthew had persuaded Superintendent Mullinger to make Rudd a special case, feeling he owed the young man for the beating Wilfred Gadd had given him during the Blackbird Farm murder case. He knew Rudd had long wanted to be in CID, but knew too the new DC was still finding his feet and was not looking forward to being without Matthew's guiding hand for the weekend.

'If you have any problems over the next few days, just ask one of the others,' Matthew told him. 'There's nothing wrong with not knowing what to do. Better to ask than do it wrong.'

'Yes, sir,' Rudd said uncertainly.

'You'll be fine.' Matthew glanced across the office at the mess that was DI Lund's desk: the ashtray overflowing with dog-ends and ash, the plate with smears of jam on it, the teacup with its grey dregs and the In tray spilling over with paperwork. 'Is DI Lund due back? I thought I would see him before I go.'

'He was called up to the Super as soon as he came back from court.' Rudd grimaced. 'I don't think Mr Mullinger was too happy.'

Matthew made no comment. Everyone in the station had heard what had happened at the court that afternoon. Lund had been called to give a statement for the prosecution and it hadn't gone well. He'd made so many mistakes in his testimony that the defence had torn him to shreds and the case had been dismissed. The victim broke down and had to be dragged away by the court stewards. Her father had spat in Lund's face, and the prosecution barrister threatened to make a formal complaint against him, claiming the inspector hadn't been fit to be in the witness box.

Matthew could believe it. Never a fine figure of a man,

Lund had deteriorated sharply over the last month. His weight had ballooned so much his creased shirts were straining at the buttons and the waistband of his trousers had become hidden beneath the overhang of his belly. He looked dreadful, too. The colour of his skin varied between grey and deep red, and his cheeks were scarred with razor cuts as if he had been shaving in the dark with a blunt blade. Matthew suspected the dark rings around Lund's bloodshot eyes were the result of too little sleep and too much booze.

Just then, the main office door opened and Lund waddled in, head down, cigarette hanging from his mouth. He glared at Matthew as he entered their office, not even acknowledging Rudd's presence.

'You still here?' he muttered, falling down into his chair as Rudd ducked out. 'Thought you'd be long gone.'

'I was just on my way out,' Matthew said.

Lund grunted and rested his cigarette on the ashtray. 'I suppose you heard?'

'Heard what?'

Lund made a face, not believing Matthew's pretence of innocence. 'My balls-up at the court. Old Mouldy just hauled me over the coals for it.'

'I did hear, yes. Bad luck.'

'Story of my life. The prosecution has made a complaint. Said I was drunk.' Lund yanked open his drawer and took out a hip flask. He unscrewed the cap and took a long swig.

'Maybe he has a point.' Matthew raised his eyebrows at the flask.

Lund drained the contents. 'Maybe he did.' He tossed the flask onto his desk, his eyes daring Matthew to make another sarcastic remark.

'You remember I'm on leave this weekend?' Matthew

said instead. 'I don't think you'll be bothered with anything of mine. But if you do, there's nothing that can't wait. Leave it till Monday when I'm back.'

'You bet I will, sunshine,' Lund muttered, reaching for his cigarette. 'Well, go on, get out of here before the telephone rings and you get lumbered with something.'

Matthew put his hat on his head. 'I'll see you Monday, Lund.'

He got a grunt in reply.

'You've got my new address?' Matthew asked Rudd as he passed through the main office to the door. 'Just in case?'

'Yes, sir, we've got it,' Rudd said. 'Good luck with the move.'

'Thanks. See you on Monday.'

Matthew left the CID office, casting a glance back at Lund as his fellow inspector took a second hip flask from his desk drawer and raised it to his lips.

Matthew opened his front door, and it suddenly struck him that he was doing it for the last time. He had never been fond of his flat – it had merely been somewhere to eat and sleep – and the knowledge he would never have to come back to this place filled him with pleasure.

He made his way to the bedroom to change out of his suit, his mind on how much he still had to do. Matthew hadn't had a chance to do any packing, and he had a busy night ahead if he was to be ready to leave early the next morning.

Matthew stepped inside his bedroom, expecting to see his cat curled up on the bed, but she wasn't there. Disappointed, for he always looked forward to a cuddle with Bella when he came home, he turned back towards the doorway to call for her.

But the cry stuck in his throat. A cold sweat coated his body. Someone was standing behind the bedroom door. He staggered backwards as a hand reached out for him.

'Mattie!' his sister cried and went to him, grabbing his arms. 'What's the matter? Mattie, for God's sake. Tell me what's wrong.'

'Nothing.' Trembling, he pulled out of her grasp and turned away to the window. 'It's nothing.'

'Don't give me that,' Pat said. 'You turned as white as a sheet.'

'I just—' Matthew broke off. His face screwing up in vexation, he thumped his forehead against the cold glass, trying to knock some sense into his head. 'For a second there, I thought you were him.'

'Who—?' she began, then realised who her brother meant. 'But Gadd's in prison, Mattie.'

'I know, I know. But it all came back. Him standing there, the cosh in his hand. Just leave me be a minute, Pat. I'll be all right.'

Matthew sat down on the end of his bed and put his head in his hands, feeling a fool. He knew Wilfred Gadd couldn't have been standing behind his door, but knowing that didn't make any difference. Knowing Gadd was locked up and destined to hang in a few weeks' time hadn't stopped the nightmares, hadn't stopped him from waking up in the middle of the night in a sweat, scrabbling for the switch on his bedside lamp to make sure he was alone. It hadn't stopped Matthew from wondering if someone was lying in wait for him almost every time he came home.

'I had no idea you've been like this,' Pat said, a tremor in her voice, and Matthew knew he'd scared her.

'I'm fine,' he said. 'It was just a shock, that's all. I didn't know you were here. Don't tell Georgie. Or Mum. I don't want them worrying over nothing.'

Claws tapped on floorboards, and a moment later, Bella jumped up onto the bed. Matthew grabbed her and pressed his face into her fur, feeling the soothing rumble of her purr against his cheek. When he put her down on his lap and looked up, Pat was watching him with concern etched into every line of her face. 'Did you bring any boxes with you?' he asked, wanting her to forget what had happened.

She nodded. 'A few. I notice you haven't packed anything yet.'

'I haven't had the time. Is Georgie still coming over?'

'He came with me, but he's popped out to get us some fish and chips. I expect he'll be back in a minute.' She turned and opened the wardrobe, and Matthew was relieved she was letting the incident drop. 'So, you're really not working this weekend?' she said, taking out a hanger.

'No,' Matthew said, pushing himself off the mattress. 'I'm on forty-eight hours' leave.'

Pat threw his grey flannel trousers on the bed. 'I've lost my bet, then. I was sure you'd end up working, and I bet Fred five shillings you'd leave everything to me and Georgie.' She tutted in annoyance as Bella meowed loudly. 'Is she crying for more food? I fed her as soon as I got here. She can't still be hungry.'

'She likes her grub,' Matthew said, bending down to stroke Bella's head.

'You're feeding her too much. She's got fat. And you can stop mucking about with her. We've got too much to do.' There was a knock on the door. 'Oh, who's that?'

'It'll be Georgie,' Matthew said, pulling his tie out of the knot.

'It can't be. I gave him the key.' Pat bustled out and a moment later, Matthew heard her cry of surprise as she opened the front door.

'Who is it?' Matthew hurried out of his bedroom in

alarm, but was brought up short to see his downstairs neighbour standing beside his sister. 'Mr Levitt!'

Mr Levitt shuffled his feet awkwardly. 'I just thought I'd
come up and say goodbye.'

Matthew was astonished. Mr Levitt coming up to his
flat, not to complain but to say goodbye? 'That's good of
you.'

Mr Levitt nodded in agreement. 'So, you're off then?'

'In the morning.'

'Where are you off to?'

'Halesden. It's closer to work.'

'A flat, is it? One of those new blocks?'

'Yes. A serviced flat.'

'Indoor lavvie?' Mr Levitt asked enviously.

'He's got an indoor everything,' Pat said proudly. 'All
mod cons in the kitchen. Electric fire in the sitting room.
Porter in the lobby.'

'Cor, it's all right for some, ain't it?' Mr Levitt rolled his
eyes. 'Well, I won't miss getting woken up in the middle of
the night by that bleeding telephone calling for you all the
time. So, that's something.' He sniffed. 'Well, I'll say
goodbye now in case I don't see you in the morning.' He
held out his hand, keeping his eyes on the floor.

Matthew took it, hoping he didn't look as surprised as
he felt. 'Goodbye,' he said.

'Well,' Pat grinned, closing the door after Mr Levitt had
gone. 'Wonders will never cease.'

Detective Sergeant Justin Denham stepped into his hall, his
nose wrinkling at the smell. Disinfectant, starch and an
underlying odour of excrement mingled with the damp and
steam that hung in the air. He closed his front door, trying

to remember a time when coming home hadn't been like this.

He was sure it wasn't all that long ago when he would come home and Mary would emerge from the kitchen with a smile on her face, hurry along the hall to give him a kiss and ask how his day had been. She would take his hat and coat and hang them on the hall stand, follow him into the front room and pour him a beer without even asking if he wanted one. Then Mary would tell him dinner wouldn't be long, and he'd put his feet up with the newspaper until she called him to the table. It could only have been a year ago, and yet it seemed an age.

And all because of the baby.

The house Mary had been so proud of when they moved in and had kept as clean and neat as a new pin was now in a constant state of disarray. A pram had a permanent home in the hall, always ready to trip Denham up when he came home late after a long day at the station. These days, when he sat down in his favourite chair, he would invariably sit upon a rattle or an empty baby bottle, or put his arm upon a muslin cloth soggy with milk puked up by the baby and discarded by Mary. Dust was left to build up on the furniture, and it could be weeks before Mary would take a mop to the kitchen floor. He wasn't allowed to listen to the wireless as loud as he liked anymore for fear of waking the baby, who always seemed to be sleeping when he wanted it on, and his meals were served either under-done or burnt because Mary hadn't kept an eye on the oven.

He'd known their lives would change when a baby came along, but he hadn't expected a baby to come along so soon or to be so disruptive. It wasn't just the state of the house that bothered him; it was the fact that he and Mary never seemed to have any time for each other anymore. No longer could they decide, on a whim, to go to the pictures or a dance. Even taking a walk in the park became a military exercise because the baby and pram had to go with them. They couldn't do anything anymore because of the baby.

All because of the baby.

'What time do you call this?' Mary called from the kitchen.

With a sigh, Denham hung up his hat and coat and wandered down the passage, leaning against the kitchen door frame and shoving his hands in his trouser pockets.

'I went to the pub after work,' Denham said, watching as Mary kneaded the dirty terry towelling nappies in the sink, the water tinged a light brown.

'Night out with the boys, was it?' she said, giving the nappies a vigorous plunging.

'It was just a couple of drinks. It's been a long day and I needed to unwind.' He suddenly thought enviously of Matthew, who didn't have a wife or a baby and didn't have to explain himself to anyone.

'Huh. *You've* had a long day.'

'I did say I might be late tonight.'

'Yes, you did, and I said it was fine. But I said it was fine because I thought you'd be working, not jollying it up with your mates.'

Denham knew this was an argument he couldn't win, so he said nothing and pulled out a chair from the kitchen table. It scraped noisily on the linoleum and he waited for Mary to give her usual scolding to be quiet, her eyes looking up at the ceiling meaningfully. But the reproach didn't come, surprising him, and he fell into the chair, staring at the shoulder blades that moved beneath her dress as she worked.

Mary wrung out the nappies and hung them over the wooden rods of the dryer, hauling on the rope to raise it to the ceiling. She wiped her hands on a tea towel and turned to him. 'Aren't you going to ask how my day has been?'

Denham toyed with the lid of the teapot sitting on the table. 'How has your day been?'

'Oh, thank you for asking. It's been exhausting. I could have done with your help this evening.'

'Help with what?'

'With all this.' She threw up her hands, gesturing at the nappies and the dirty pots and pans on the worktops.

'Oh, I see,' he said, his temper rising. 'You expect me to go to work all day, put up with all the rubbish I have to put up with, then come home and do the housework as well?'

'I'm asking you to pull your weight around the house, that's all.'

'The house is down to you, Mary.'

'You live here as well,' she cried. 'And it's not just the house. You could help with Ellie. She's your daughter, too, you know?'

'I know she is. But I don't think it's too much for a man to expect to come home and be able to put his feet up after a hard day's work.'

'I have hard days, too, Justin. When do I get to put my feet up?'

'For God's sake, Mary, you wanted the baby!' He regretted the words as soon as they were out of his mouth.

Mary stared at him in horror, her eyes brimming with tears. 'You didn't want her?' she whimpered.

'That's not what I said.'

'But it's what you meant.'

'No, it wasn't. I just would have liked to wait a bit longer before having kids, that's all. It's not as if we had to rush.'

Mary tugged a handkerchief out of her apron pocket and pressed it to her eyes.

'Mary, don't. Please. Let's not have a row.' He rose and moved towards her, arms outstretched.

But then the baby cried, loudly and insistently, from the nursery upstairs, and Mary shoved her handkerchief back into her pocket and turned away from him. 'You can go to her.'

Denham left the kitchen and climbed the stairs to the first floor, entering the small box room that served as the nursery. Ellie was standing up in her cot, her pudgy little hands gripping the edge of the bars, her face beetroot red as she bawled.

'All right, all right, you can shut up now. I'm here.'

Denham lifted his daughter out of the cot and held her against his chest, wincing as she screamed into his ear. He closed his eyes and wished he hadn't bothered to come home at all.

Ivor watched Lucy through the glass of the cinema entrance doors as she walked away. He waited until she turned the corner and was out of sight before hurrying up to the projection room.

With a rebellious air, he took out his cigarettes and lit one. 'Up yours, Mr Grainger,' he murmured, waving his hand to waft the smoke around. Fixing the cigarette in the corner of his mouth, he moved to the far wall, squeezing behind the metal racking that held the cinema's films in their round metal tins. Bending, he dragged a cardboard box out of the corner and carried it over to his stool by the projector and spent the next five minutes sorting the contents into piles, performing calculations in his head. If he got rid of everything, it would be a pretty good night. He'd have a nice wadge of notes in his pocket. Of course, he thought, his lips curling in irritation, he would have a lot more if it wasn't for Lucy.

He checked his wristwatch; time was getting on. Ivor replaced the items in the box and carried it down to the foyer, leaving it outside the auditorium doors before hurrying inside and down the aisle steps. He reached the side door, delving into his trouser pocket for the key and fitting it into the lock. A blast of cold air greeted him as he threw the door open, and he hurried down the alley to the gate that led onto the high street. He opened it, just an inch or two, and put his eye to the gap. A figure was crossing the road, heading his way, hat pulled low, head hunched down.

Ivor grinned. His first customer had arrived.

Lucy unbuttoned her uniform and wriggled out of it, tossing the dress onto her bed where it joined the red and gold-braided cap.

The cap made her smile. Mr Grainger had told her off about wearing it at an angle again. But she liked wearing it a little to the side; it set off her face better. Lucy had listened to his scolding and nodded at the right moments, but she had no intention of doing as he said. She'd wear her cap how she liked, and he could go whistle. And, she thought, her gaze going to the black-and-white pictures pinned above her bed, she would look even better in it once she had her new hairstyle. Clara Bow and Louise Brooks stared back at her out of the photographs, luminous, their perfect faces framed by their perfect bobs. That's how she was going to look. *This time next week*, she thought, *I'll look as good as them.*

She put her uniform and cap away in the wardrobe and turned to her dressing table. Her gaze settled on the bottle of perfume that was its latest addition. She unstoppered the bottle, applied a dab to each wrist and sniffed. Her eyes closed in pleasure. The smell was gorgeous, an expensive scent that would last all day, unlike the cheap eau de toilette she used to buy for herself.

Replacing the bottle on the dressing table, Lucy opened the middle drawer and took out the leather writing case her father had given her three years earlier for her birthday. Delving into the front pocket, she drew out a wad of banknotes, her mouth silently moving as she counted them. Satisfied with the number, and smiling at the thought of how many more she would have by the end of the following night, Lucy tucked the notes away in the pocket and returned the case to the drawer.

A light turned on in the house opposite, catching her attention. Lucy rose, looking over the top of her dressing-table mirror and across the back gardens to the bedroom directly opposite hers. Lewis was pacing his room, his hunched gait an indicator of his mood.

Lucy moved to the window. She was wondering how to get Lewis to notice her when there was a bang and her eyes dropped down to the back of his house. Herbert had come out of the kitchen door and was walking along the garden path. Lewis had also heard the bang and gone to his window to watch his father until Herbert disappeared inside his shed. Then Lewis looked up and saw Lucy.

She waved. Lewis didn't wave back, but kept his eyes on her. She held up a finger, telling him to stay where he was, and stepped away from the window. Positioning herself so he could see all of her body down to her thighs, she hooked a finger under the satin strap of her slip and, ever so slowly, pushed it over her shoulder. She did the same to the other strap. The fabric draped over her breasts, and she moved it down, an inch at a time, until her breasts were exposed to Lewis's gaze. She stayed still, letting him look, then pushed the slip down over her rounded hips and belly, holding it for a tantalising few seconds before letting it fall to pool around her feet. Next, she nudged her knickers off. Naked now, Lucy raised her arms above her head and moved her body sensuously.

As she moved, Lewis's bedroom door opened and Lydia entered the room. Lydia looked towards Lewis and the window, then Lucy saw her gaze fix on her. Her face signalling her outrage and disgust, Lucy watched as Lydia stormed across the room and yanked the curtains together, shutting off Lewis's view.

Lucy giggled. Poor Lewis. He was probably getting an earful from the silly old cow.

She moved to the bed and took her nightdress out from under the pillow, pulling it over her head with none of the coquetry with which she had undressed.

That had been fun, Lucy thought, as she climbed beneath the blankets.

Herbert closed the kitchen door and locked it. Moving to the sink, he washed his hands and looked over his shoulder at his wife sitting at the kitchen table.

'What's the matter?' he asked.

Lydia angrily tapped her cigarette out into the ashtray. 'She was doing it again.'

He grabbed the tea towel and dried his hands. 'Who was doing what?'

She narrowed her eyes at him. 'Don't pretend you don't know who I mean. Her over there.' Lydia jabbed her finger out of the window towards Lucy's bedroom window.

Herbert threw the tea towel on the counter. 'What was she doing?'

'Flaunting herself. Standing naked in front of the

window. Showing Lewis all she had and teasing him.' Lydia shook her head and took a drag of her cigarette. 'Lewis is very upset.'

Herbert pulled out a chair and sat down. 'Did he say so?'

'He doesn't need to say so. I know my son, Herbert. He's all worked up. Having a go at me, if you please. As if it's all my fault.' She shook her head at him. 'Something's got to be done about her. She's got to be made to stop, to leave him alone. That word you had with her did nothing.'

Herbert took out a cigarette from her packet and lit it. 'There's no reasoning with a girl like her. We'll just have to tell Lewis to stay away from her. I'll have a word with him before bed.'

'Oh, that's all we do,' she snapped, banging her hand on the table. 'Talk, talk, talk.'

'Then what else do you suggest, Lydia?' he cried angrily. 'Do you want to move? Take Lewis away from everything he's known and make him start somewhere new? You know he doesn't like change. That would upset him even more.'

'I don't know,' Lydia groaned. 'But we have to do something.'

3

Saturday, 18th October 1930

Bella lifted her head, ears pricked at the sound of the front door opening. She sat up, and Matthew, feeling her move away from his arm, propped himself up on his elbow and listened too.

'It's only me, Mattie,' his sister called as she banged the door shut.

Matthew slammed his head back into the pillow, his hand finding Bella's furry head. 'Time to get up, Bella,' he murmured, and she jumped off the bed and padded out.

'Hello, you,' he heard Pat say. 'Daddy still in bed, is he?' She came into the bedroom, Bella in her arms.

'Did you really just call me Daddy to the cat?' he asked.

'What else should I call you? This furry thing's a right little daddy's girl.' She frowned down at him. 'I thought you'd be up by now.'

Matthew grabbed his alarm clock from the bedside cabinet and peered blearily at it. 'It's only half-past six.'

'And you're usually up at all hours of the night, so half-six is nothing for you.'

39

Matthew threw back the blankets and sat up, running his hand over his head to flatten his wiry, dark-brown hair. He rubbed his knuckles into his eyes. 'You didn't say you'd be coming this early.'

'I want to get on,' she said, dropping Bella onto the bed. 'The sooner you're out of here, the sooner you'll be settled in your new place. So, come on. Get up.'

He waved her away. 'I'm not doing anything before I've had a cup of tea.'

'I'll put the kettle on and do you some breakfast.' Pat went out and he heard her banging about in his kitchen.

By the time Matthew had washed, shaved and dressed, his sister had tea in the pot, eggs boiling in a saucepan on the gas ring and a slice of toast under the grill.

He looked around for Bella, saw an empty saucer on the floor and the open window. 'You didn't feed Bella, did you?' he asked, alarmed.

'She was meowing at me for food.'

'And you let her out?'

'She had to do her business. What's the matter?' Pat cried as Matthew groaned and stuck his head out of the window, frantically looking left and right for Bella.

'She won't come back now she's been fed,' he said. 'I was going to lock her in.'

Pat tutted and waved away his concern. 'She'll be back by the time we're ready to go.' She buttered the toast, spooned the eggs into cups and handed him the plate. 'Eat your breakfast. I'll bring your tea in.'

Reluctantly, Matthew carried his breakfast to his sitting-room table. Pat followed, bringing in two mugs of tea, setting one down beside his plate and taking a mouthful from the other.

'Ooh, I needed that,' she said, closing her eyes in pleasure.

'Georgie's still coming, isn't he?' Matthew asked as he broke the shell with the back of a teaspoon.

'He's gone to fetch the van from Fred's mate. But it has to be back by noon, so we'll need to get a move on. As soon as you've finished eating, I'll get the kitchen things away.'

'That won't take five minutes, so stop hovering over me.' Matthew pushed out the other dining chair. 'Sit down and drink your tea.'

Pat obeyed, watching as he ate his breakfast. 'Once you've moved, you will still come round the pub, won't you?' she asked anxiously. 'No, don't roll your eyes at me, Mattie. Mum thinks because you'll be further away, she won't see you again. And I know she's always on at you to come round more, but she really is worried.'

'I come round when I can, Pat. I always will,' Matthew said. 'Me being in Halesden won't make any difference.'

'You promise?'

'I promise.'

'Good. I'll tell Mum so. And you'll be round soon? She hasn't seen you for ages.'

'She saw me three weeks ago,' Matthew protested. 'And I'll have to see. I'm busy.'

'Not all that busy if you can take time off. And I know for a fact you haven't had any big cases lately because you haven't been in the 'papers. Mum's moaning she hasn't had anything to put in her scrapbook.'

'Not every case I work on makes it into the newspapers,' Matthew said, scraping out the last of his egg. 'And besides, I've had enough of being in the news to last me a lifetime.'

He meant it. The last time his name had featured in a newspaper was when *The Chronicle* apologised for printing unsubstantiated accusations of sexual assault made against Matthew during the Blackbird Farm murder. Even though he had been vindicated and received many letters of support from the public, the whole affair had scarred him deeply. When he thought about how close he had come to losing his job, not to mention his reputation, it still made his blood run cold.

Pat nodded understandingly. 'When I think what that cow did, I'd like to wring her neck. Telling all those lies about you.'

'Can we not go over all that again, Pat?' Matthew asked wearily.

'All right,' Pat held up her hands. 'I won't say another word. You finished?' She took his plate away without waiting for an answer as there came a knock on the door. 'That'll be Georgie. You let him in. I'll wash up. And then we'll start getting your things in the van.'

'I've got the van,' Georgie said, holding up a metal keyring as Matthew opened the door. 'But we've only got it until midday. Mr Carey needs it back by then for his afternoon deliveries. Where's Pat?'

'Washing up.' Matthew made a face as he closed the door and lowered his voice. 'She let Bella out.'

Georgie's bright blue eyes widened in understanding. He was almost as fond of Bella as Matthew was. 'Will she come back before we have to leave?'

'I hope so.' Matthew went into the kitchen and leaned out of the window once more, whistling loudly, hoping Bella would appear.

'For gawd's sake, Mattie, stop fussing over that blooming cat,' Pat said irritably. 'Let's get on. Georgie, come with me. We'll start in the bedroom. You too, Mattie.'

Matthew took one last worried look out of the window, then followed after his brother and sister.

· · ·

Denham entered the CID office, stared down at his desk and swore.

DC Simon Barnes looked up from his typewriter. 'What's up?'

Denham pointed at the file sitting on his blotter. 'I gave Lund that case file last night for him to sign off and he's given it back to me with this.' He pulled out the slip of paper clipped to the buff-coloured file. '*Do it again. And do it properly this time.*' He screwed up the note and threw it in the bin. 'I did do it properly. I showed it to Stannard first and he said it was fine. If it's good enough for Stannard, it's good enough for Lund.' He fell into his chair with a loud sigh. 'Just look at him now.'

Barnes turned around. Through the partition window of the inspectors' office, he saw Lund slumped in his chair, head thrown back, mouth open, snoring. 'He better hope Old Mouldy doesn't catch him like that. He'll get hauled over the coals again.'

'It would serve him right,' Denham said. 'What is the matter with Lund lately? I didn't think it was possible for him to get any worse.'

'Maybe he's got problems at home?'

'Who hasn't? We've all got problems, but we don't all go around like him.'

'All right, Just,' Barnes said, surprised by the vehemence in his friend's voice. 'Calm down.'

'Don't tell me to calm down. I'm fed up with him.' Denham opened the file Lund had returned. 'And what am I supposed to do with this? There's nothing wrong with it.'

'Just leave it for an hour, make out you've worked on it, then give it back to him. He'll probably sign it off without another word.'

Denham shook his head in disgust. 'Bloody ridiculous,' he muttered.

Barnes watched Denham as he reread his report, wondering what was bothering his friend and doubting it was just Lund's behaviour of late. 'Let's just hope we have a quiet weekend, eh?' he said with a sympathetic smile. 'Then the inspector can stay snoring in there and not bother us until Stannard gets back.'

Mrs Simpson opened the bedroom door and entered. 'Will you be home for tea, Lucy?'

Lucy was sitting on the bed, rolling a stocking over her knee. 'Not tonight,' she said, fixing the stocking in place. 'I'm working late.'

'You're not doing extra shifts again? Oh Lucy, you'll wear yourself out.'

Lucy smiled as she moved to the wardrobe. 'I'm fine, Mum. And I want the money.'

'I don't know what for.' Mrs Simpson sat on the bed and watched her daughter take out her uniform. 'I'm sure you don't need to work so hard at that place. I can't think why you don't try for a place at the Majestic over in Crayne-brook. It's a much nicer cinema. I'm sure they'd be glad to have a girl like you.'

'I like the Regal,' Lucy insisted. 'Don't go on.'

Mrs Simpson held up her hands. 'I'm only saying.' She gave her daughter a sideways glance. 'I popped into the hair-dressers this morning. Sylvia says you've booked an appointment to have your hair done.'

'That's right. I have.'

'She said you want it all cut off. I told her she must have got that wrong.'

'No, she wasn't wrong. I'm having it bobbed.'

'But you'll look like a boy!'

Lucy laughed. 'With my figure?' She gestured at her

body, now encased in the uniform. The fabric clung to her curves, accentuating her hips and breasts. 'I don't think so, Mum.'

'You're putting on weight, Lucy. That's too tight,' Mrs Simpson said, nodding at the uniform. 'Your father won't like you having your hair cut short.'

'Dad doesn't have to like it. It's my hair and I'll do what I want with it.'

'Lucy!'

'It's only hair, Mum. Don't be so old-fashioned.'

'Jenny hasn't had her hair cut short,' Mrs Simpson said sulkily. 'I saw her the other day. She's kept it long.'

Lucy said nothing as she sat down at her dressing table and opened a pot of rouge, rubbing two spots onto her cheeks.

'Jenny hasn't been round for a while, has she?' Mrs Simpson went on. 'It's odd when I think about how you two used to be joined at the hip. You haven't had a falling out, have you?'

'No,' Lucy said, but there was a note of uncertainty in her voice. 'We've grown apart, that's all.'

'Oh, that's a shame. Jenny's such a nice girl.'

'Oh, yes, she's very nice.'

'Why do you say nice like that?'

'Because I'm fed up with nice, Mum,' Lucy snapped, slamming in the drawer so hard her dressing table shuddered. 'I'm not a little girl anymore. I wish you and Dad would realise that.'

'I don't see why growing up should make you so cruel.' Mrs Simpson rose and headed for the door. 'I don't know what's come over you these last few months, Lucy. I really don't.'

Lucy watched her mother leave in the dressing-table mirror and breathed a sigh of relief. It had irritated her to have Jenny brought up like that. What was it to anyone else if she'd outgrown her childhood friend? Children grew up. Adults moved on and people got left behind. It happened all the time.

She opened her compact and patted powder over her cheeks, angling her face in the mirror to ensure she covered every shiny spot. Bright red lipstick was applied next and blotted with a handkerchief.

Pinning up her hair took the most time, and Lucy wished she could have got an earlier appointment than next Thursday. She also wished her hair was black rather than light brown. Bobs looked so much better with black hair. Maybe she could dye it? She smiled at the idea. If her parents thought cutting her hair was risqué, what would they think about her dyeing it black? But then, she thought, the smile faltering a little, what would they think when...?

She shook the thought away. They wouldn't find out and if they did, so what? It was her life.

Lucy rose from the dressing table and reached into her wardrobe for her usherette's cap. She put it straight on her head, then bent her body to see what it looked like in the mirror. With an amused twist of her lips, she set it at an angle over the left side of her face.

There, she decided with a nod. That was better.

Dennis checked his wristwatch, then clapped his hands to get the boys' attention. 'All right, boys. That's all for today. Get the equipment together.'

He breathed a deep sigh of relief as the Scouts collected the bandages, safety pins and gauzes they had been using for their First Aid instruction. For the first time in ages, the Scout meeting had gone well. Frankie Ashe had turned up when the meeting was well underway; so late, in fact,

Dennis had hoped he wasn't coming at all. But Frankie turning up so late had meant the boy hadn't caused nearly as much disruption as usual and had only answered him back the once. Maybe the boy was learning to behave and there would be no need to give up the Scouts after all?

If only he could go back to how things had been before the attack. He'd been happy then; happy at work, happy as churchwarden, happy as Scout leader. But everything had gone wrong after he'd been hit on the head. There had been all the trouble at work, with no one knowing if they were going to lose their jobs. Being churchwarden had become a chore ever since Laing arrived and kept going on about society and how everyone was falling into a sink of depravity. And then the Scouts, the one thing in his life he truly loved, became tainted by the presence of a troublemaker in the shape of a twelve-year-old boy!

Dennis looked over at Lewis sitting in the corner of the church hall. The young man had been distant ever since Frankie had turned up that morning, even though the boy had mostly left Lewis alone. Lewis was watching the boys pack up the equipment, a surly expression clouding his face. Dennis went over to him.

'Are you all right, Lewis?' he asked.

Lewis looked down at his feet and shrugged.

'What's the matter?'

'Nothing.'

'Something's wrong. Tell me.'

Lewis tutted. 'I just wish it was like before. Before he came.'

Dennis didn't need to ask who 'he' was. 'I was wishing the exact same thing not a moment ago.'

'Then why don't you tell him to go?'

'It's not that simple, Lewis.'

'Yes, it is. You just tell him to go away and not to come back.'

'I tried that. I got a flea in my ear for my trouble.'

'But it's not fair. He's spoiling everything.'

'I know, I know.' Dennis patted Lewis's shoulder as the young man's hands curled into fists. 'If there was something I could do, I'd do it.'

He jumped at a sudden shout behind him. Dennis turned to see Frankie wrapping a crepe bandage around Timmy Lane's neck.

'Ashe,' Dennis yelled as Frankie wound the bandage tighter and Timmy's eyes bulged. 'Stop that at once!'

Frankie didn't stop.

Dennis rushed over to him. 'You heard me,' he said, tugging at Frankie's hands. 'Stop it!'

Frankie laughed and gave the bandage a savage jerk. Timmy's face was bright red and he scrabbled at his neck, trying to hook his fingers under the crepe.

'I said stop it!' Dennis cried.

'You gonna make me, Mummy's Boy?' Frankie jeered.

Rage erupted in Dennis. He grabbed Frankie's small neck with both hands and squeezed. It was Frankie's turn to go red, for his eyes to bulge. He pounded at Dennis's hands with his small fists, but Dennis was enjoying the look of terror on the boy's face too much to let go. He would hold on and on, until he'd squeezed the last breath out of the little brat's—

'Mr Hillman!'

Laing's stentorian voice destroyed the wonderful image Dennis had conjured. He released Frankie and shoved the boy away. Frankie fell on his backside, gasping for breath.

Dennis turned to Laing standing in the church hall doorway. 'I don't—' he began, but couldn't find the words to explain himself.

Frankie scrambled to his feet. 'You pig,' he yelled at Dennis, his voice croaky. 'You wait till I tell my dad what you did. He's going to get you. You just wait, you pig.' More obscenities spewed forth, foul words no child should know.

Laing crossed the hall in three strides, drew back his arm, and struck Frankie across the face. The boy tumbled to the ground, a hand held to his blazing cheek, tears flowing from his eyes.

'I will not have such language,' Laing roared at Frankie. 'You despicable child. Get out of my sight.'

'My dad'll get you, too.' Frankie got once more to his feet, his hand still cradling his cheek. 'You just wait. He's going to get both of you,' he promised, and ran out of the church hall.

Laing rounded on the other Scouts, who were huddled together, staring at him in terror. 'What are you looking at? All of you, go. Get out.'

They bolted from the hall. Only Timmy remained, the crepe bandage dangling from his neck. Laing unwrapped the bandage and tossed it on the floor. He waved Timmy away and the boy scurried out of the hall.

Laing turned to Dennis. 'That was not seemly behaviour for my churchwarden, Mr Hillman.'

'I don't know what came over me.' Dennis shuffled to a chair and fell into it. He put his head into his hands.

'It was brilliant,' Lewis said, a huge grin on his face. 'I thought you really were going to kill him.'

'I wanted to,' Dennis admitted. 'I was so angry. I wanted to kill him.'

'I wish you had. He's a rotter. You think so, too, don't you, Reverend Laing? I bet you wish he was dead after what he did to your window?'

'You should not say such things, Lewis,' Laing said, staring at Dennis disapprovingly.

'I don't see why not. You told me once brats like him were a – what did you call them? – a scourge upon the face of the earth and it was better if they hadn't been born.'

'Yes, well, maybe I did.' Laing waved his hand at the floor. 'You need to tidy this hall up, Mr Hillman. The WI have it at one o'clock.'

'Yes, yes, of course.' Dennis rose and began gathering up the scattered First Aid equipment.

'Help Mr Hillman, Lewis,' Laing said, and left.

'He did say that, you know?' Lewis muttered as he wound up the crepe bandage. 'And I don't care what he says. I bet he would have been very glad if you had strangled Frankie.'

'Shush, Lewis,' Dennis said. 'Reverend Laing is right. You mustn't say things like that. People will think you mean it.'

'I do mean it.' Lewis got to his feet, his arms full.

Dennis, likewise burdened, led him out of the church hall and across the grounds to the vestry, where all the Scout equipment was stored. When they entered, they found Laing at his desk, pen in hand, making corrections to a typed page, and he didn't bother to acknowledge the two men as they passed his desk and entered the storeroom.

The storeroom was lined with wooden shelving, upon which were various cardboard boxes, a collection of old vestments covered in dust and damaged prayer books. On the floor at the rear of the room was a large trunk, and Dennis unhooked a key from the top shelf of one of the wooden racks and handed it to Lewis.

Lewis bent and unlocked the trunk's padlock, throwing the lid open. Lifting out the six rifles used for the Scouts' marksmanship training, he dropped the bandages, gauzes and various ointments into the trunk. Replacing the rifles, he closed the lid. Locking the padlock, he returned the key to Dennis.

'Well, that's that,' Dennis said with a sigh. 'Come along, Lewis. Let's get out of Reverend Laing's way.'

'Just a moment, Mr Hillman,' Laing said. 'I'd like a word with Lewis.' He gestured for Lewis to take a seat by his desk.

Lewis hesitated, but with a resigned glance at Dennis, obeyed.

'I'll be off, then,' Dennis said. 'But I think I'll just take a look at the window in the church. Make sure the boards are holding.'

He left the vestry, a quick backward glance over his shoulder showing him the vicar and young man deep in conversation.

The morning hadn't gone well.

The bottoms had fallen out of two boxes, breaking some of the contents, and forcing a repacking of those items still intact. Matthew had cut his hand on a broken glass, not badly but it bled quite a bit, and all packing had to stop while cotton wool and plasters were found.

Then, when the van was full and the flat empty, and they were ready to leave, Matthew pointed out Bella had not yet returned. Pat's temper, kept under control this far, finally broke, and she said she didn't care a flying fig about the cat and they had to go. Matthew stated equally firmly they couldn't. A row ensued, which only ended when Georgie stepped in to say he would stay behind and find the errant feline. Matthew was reluctantly agreeing when a loud meow announced the return of Bella and everyone stopped shouting.

They all squeezed into Mr Carey's van, Matthew with

Bella in a box on his lap, Pat beside him and Georgie driving. Bella was sick five minutes into the journey, stinking out the van and causing yet more irritable words between Matthew and Pat. Everyone was very glad when the van pulled up outside Fairfax Court in Halesden.

Matthew's new flat was on the third floor. The lift wasn't large enough to take the furniture, so Matthew and Georgie had to hump it up the stairs, and by the time all the furniture was out of the van and in the flat, both men were sweating and swearing in equal measure.

'I've put Bella in the bathroom,' Pat declared as Matthew and Georgie collapsed on the settee. 'She'll probably piddle in the bath, but at least she won't be able to get out.' She glared at Matthew pointedly. 'I've found the kettle and cups. So, tea?'

'I could do with a beer after all that,' Matthew said, wiping the back of his neck with his handkerchief.

'We don't have any. So it's tea or nothing.' She bustled off into the kitchen, and Georgie left to return the van to Mr Carey.

Left alone, Matthew looked around his new sitting room. He noted with appreciation the freshly painted white coving and skirting board, the understated wallpaper, the brand new wall-to-wall carpet, the modern electric fire and its tiled surround, and thought of his old place with its peeling, decades-old wallpaper and chipped brown paint, and the wide cracks in the floorboards letting in draughts.

He smiled to himself as he considered he'd made the right decision in moving. His new flat already felt more like home than his old one ever had.

4

Timmy Lane took a quick glance around the auditorium, checked none of the adults were watching, then leaned back and lifted his legs to put his feet on the back of the seat in front. He knew he was being naughty, and he wouldn't have dared do it if his mother was there, but he was feeling a little rebellious after what had happened to him at the Scout meeting.

How he hated Frankie Ashe! He'd spoiled his morning, and now he might spoil his afternoon as well. For to Timmy's dismay, Frankie had come into the cinema with his friends, Paul and Martin, all of them like him, still in their Scout uniforms. If Timmy had known they were going to be at the cinema, he would have gone somewhere else, the park, maybe, and played on the swings. They'd come in just as the picture started and stomped down the aisle steps, taking seats near the front. Luckily, they hadn't seen Timmy, so he reckoned all he had to do was get out as soon as the picture ended and Frankie would never know he'd been there.

A girl giggled, and Timmy glanced over at the young woman sitting across the aisle. She was the usherette who

53

had sold him his humbugs at the start of the picture, and she was supposed to be walking down the aisles, selling chocolates and cigarettes, and standing at the back the rest of the time. But she'd left her tray at the top of the aisle steps where Timmy could just see it and dropped into a seat next to a young man. The man had his arm around her waist and their heads were together. Timmy made a face as he realised they were kissing. But then the young man grabbed her cap and threw it into the aisle where it came to rest on the edge of the step. The young woman giggled again.

Girls were so silly! Timmy turned his attention back to the film. It was a good picture. He enjoyed cowboy films, but only when there was a lot of fighting going on, and at the moment, the cowboy was wooing a schoolteacher, so his attention wandered once more. He took the pink and white striped paper bag out of his pocket and drew out a humbug. He rolled it around his mouth for a while, waiting for the Indians to come onto the big screen, when he saw a man striding down the aisle steps. Whoever he was, he had come in very late to watch the film; he'd missed the first half hour.

The man reached the bottom of the aisle steps, and Timmy expected him to take a seat in the front row. But he didn't. Instead, the man turned back to face the way he had come and took something out from inside his overcoat. Something long and heavy that he brought up to his shoulder.

The hairs on the back of Timmy's neck stood up. His heart banged in his chest. Timmy didn't know why, but he felt that something was very, very wrong.

Police Inspector Allan Oakenshaw closed the Report Book and nodded at Sergeant Dobbs.

'That all seems in order,' he said, as the sergeant

replaced the book on the shelf beneath the desk. 'Did anything come of that trespassing complaint? The children who were using a private passage as a thoroughfare on their way home from school?'

'The parents were spoken to, sir,' Dobbs said. 'And the children have been told they've got to go the long way round in future. There shouldn't be any more bother.'

'Very good.' Oakenshaw glanced around the small lobby and sniffed. His nose wrinkled. 'There's a smell in here.'

'Yes, I know, sir,' Dobbs sighed. 'It's from when the lavatories flooded. I've had the cleaning lady go round with the disinfectant several times, but she can't seem to get rid of the smell. The Records room is the same.'

'Ah, yes, the Records Room.' Oakenshaw grimaced. 'Were any of the files recoverable?'

'They've all dried out, but some of them are ruined where the ink has run. Fortunately, most of those were the archived materials.'

'That's something, I suppose. What about the—' Oakenshaw broke off as the telephone on the front desk rang.

'Excuse me, sir,' Dobbs said, and picked up the receiver. 'Foxhall Green Police Station... Slow down, please. I can't—'

Oakenshaw, who had been running a finger along the windowsill testing for dust, turned back to Dobbs, frowning as the sergeant's expression turned from one of confusion to horror. 'What is it?' he mouthed.

'Just a moment, please,' Dobbs said to the caller and put a hand over the mouthpiece. 'It's the ticket lady at the Regal Picture Palace, sir. She says someone has been shooting in the auditorium and people are hurt.'

'Is this some sort of joke?' Oakenshaw demanded irritably.

'I don't think so, sir.'

Oakenshaw snatched the receiver from Dobb's hand. 'This is Inspector Oakenshaw. What do you say has happened?' The creases in his forehead grew deeper as he listened. His eyes widened in horror. 'I'll send officers straight away.' He thrust the receiver back at Dobbs. 'Get all our men to the cinema at once.'

Barnes fell down into his chair. 'He's still asleep, you know?' He jerked his head at the inspectors' office, where Lund could be seen through the partition window, slouched in his chair, head back, mouth open.

'I know,' Denham said. 'He woke up to go over the pub for lunch, came back and went straight to sleep again. He must have had quite a few in there if the way he smelt when he walked past me was anything to go by.'

'Oh, he did,' Barnes nodded. 'I popped to the pub myself to give Frank the money I owed him and Lund was in there with three empty glasses on the table before him. As we were both there, I thought I'd ask if I could leave early tonight and he bit my head off. You'd think I ask all the time, the way he went on at me.'

'What do you want to leave early for?'

'I want to take Judy dancing,' Barnes smiled sheepishly, a little embarrassed to talk about his new sweetheart.

'Poor Judy. I've seen you dance.'

'I'm not that bad,' Barnes protested, then got hurriedly to his feet as Mullinger rushed in. 'Afternoon, sir.'

'Gather round. Gather round,' Mullinger panted, trying to catch his breath. The junior detectives obeyed, and the superintendent opened his mouth to begin when he spied the sleeping Lund. He strode over to the office and flung open the door. 'Lund!' he roared, and the portly detective snorted awake. 'Come out here. Now!'

Mullinger returned to the main office, and the junior detectives, now all on their feet, looked uneasily at one another, expecting a showdown between the inspector and Old Mouldy.

Lund shuffled in, rubbing his eyes. 'Where's the fire?' he asked, seemingly unconcerned at being caught napping.

'I've just had a telephone call from Inspector Oakenshaw at Foxhall Green,' Mullinger said. 'They've got a major incident at the cinema on their high street and they need all the hands they can get. I've already ordered our Uniform over there, but he seems to think CID will be needed. Foxhall Green doesn't have a CID, so any investigation will be down to us. I want you to get over there straightaway and render any assistance necessary.' None of the detectives moved. 'Come on, come on,' he said irritably, clapping his hands. 'There's no time to waste. This is an emergency. All of you over to Foxhall Green now.' Mullinger grabbed Rudd's sleeve as the detectives hurried out. 'Not you.'

'Sir?' Rudd asked, worried he was in trouble.

'I want you to fetch Stannard.'

'But the inspector's on leave this weekend. He's moving into his new flat.'

'I don't give a damn what he's doing. I promised Inspector Oakenshaw I would let him have all our men until the situation is under control and I don't intend to let a fellow officer down. So, you find Stannard and get him over to Foxhall Green as fast as you can.'

Dickie Waite pulled out the sheet of paper from his typewriter and set it down with a sigh. There, he was done for the day.

Pushing away from his desk, Dickie rose, groaning as he

arched his back and felt the muscles straining. He glanced up at the wall clock as he put his hands to the small of his back and rubbed the ache away. Ben should arrive any minute, so he could take off and leave whatever came in to him.

Not that Dickie was eager to leave. He wasn't looking forward to the afternoon his wife had planned for them. Emma had declared they needed a new bed, complaining their old one was ready to fall apart, and no assertions that he could fix it would persuade her otherwise. Emma was determined. They were having a new bed and he was going with her to choose one, whether he liked it or not.

Dickie heard footsteps on the stairs outside and looked expectantly towards the door as it burst open and Ben Riley entered. Whatever young Ben did, he always seemed to do it at a run. Dickie eyed him disapprovingly, wishing the young man would learn to slow down.

'Here I am, Mr Waite,' Ben said. 'Not late, am I?'

Dickie shook his head. 'You're right on time, and I'm off.' He reached for his coat and scarf on the hatstand.

'Hang on a minute. I just need a Jimmy Riddle.'

Dickie rolled his eyes as Ben rushed out to use the lavatory at the end of the corridor. *Every time*, he thought with a shake of his head. *The boy can never just arrive and get straight down to work. There's always something he has to do first.* If it wasn't a need to use the lavvie, it was that he had to call someone or make himself a cup of tea. Still, Ben was a nicer lad than Teddy Welch had turned out to be. Dickie would never have thought when the newspaper had taken Teddy on that he would become such a ruthless little sod in pursuit of a story. His unscrupulousness had nearly done for Matthew a few months earlier when he was writing stories for the newspaper in which he painted the detective as a policeman using his celebrity and position to satisfy his carnal desires and prey on respectable women, an accusation that couldn't have been further from the truth. Dickie was glad he'd been able to put the story straight about that nasty little scandal.

Dickie checked the clock again as the minutes ticked by. *Come on, Ben*, he mentally urged. *How long does it take to pee?* He'd never hear the end of it from Emma if he was late.

His telephone rang. Dickie considered not answering it, then walked back to his desk and snatched it up. 'The *Chronicle*,' he barked into the mouthpiece. 'Dickie Waite speaking.' His eyes widened as the caller spoke and he listened without interrupting. 'We'll send someone straight away,' he declared, and hung up the receiver as Ben came back into the office.

'Sorry I was so long, Mr Waite.' Ben nodded at the telephone. 'Was that something I should know about?'

Dickie stared at the young man for a long moment, considering. By rights, he shouldn't still be in the office. Had he left when he was supposed to, he wouldn't have been there to take the call. Ben would have answered the telephone, and it would be young Ben Riley, junior reporter for *The Chronicle*, who would be off to cover the story, a story that sounded like it might be an absolute belter. But Emma was waiting...

'No,' Dickie said, grabbing his notebook from his desk and stuffing it into his pocket. 'It was something for me. I'm heading over to Foxhall Green.'

'But I thought you were off this afternoon,' Ben protested. 'Don't you have to go shopping with your wife?'

'No, that's all off,' Dickie said with a wave of his hand. 'Stay by the telephone. I may have something big to call in.' He headed for the door.

'All right, Mr Waite. But what do I tell your wife if she calls?'

They'd broken off from unpacking boxes to have a late lunch. Pat came into the sitting room with a plate of sandwiches and yet another round of tea. She handed Matthew a mug.

Georgie came in with Bella in his arms. He dropped her onto the settee beside Matthew and helped himself to a sandwich.

'This is a nice place, Mattie,' Georgie said, taking a bite.

Pat agreed. 'You've got a nice view out of the window with that park just over the road. But it must be costing you a bit.'

'A fair bit,' Matthew nodded. He was in a better mood now the hard work had been done, and he was pleased with Georgie and Pat's approval of his new flat. 'But it's worth it.'

'If you say so. And it's not as if you've got anything else to spend your money on. You happy?'

'Why wouldn't I be?'

'I don't know,' Pat shrugged. 'It's a big change and I know you don't like change.'

'Well, I like this one.' Matthew smiled at Bella as he tickled her under her chin. She purred appreciatively and rolled over for him to stroke her belly.

'She's got chubby,' Georgie said.

'That's what I said,' Pat declared. 'He's feeding her too much.' She broke off and frowned. 'Was that a knock?'

'Maybe it's the porter,' Georgie said. 'I'll go.'

'It might be the GPO,' Matthew called after him. He turned to Pat. 'Did I tell you I've got my own telephone?'

'Yes, you told me,' Pat replied with a mocking smile. 'Who was it?' she asked as Georgie came back.

Georgie jerked his thumb at the man who had followed him into the sitting room. 'Someone to see you, Mattie.'

'Rudd?' Matthew said, getting to his feet. 'What are you doing here?'

'I'm very sorry to disturb you, sir,' Rudd said, awkward in the presence of Pat and Georgie. 'I know you're on leave, but—'

'Oh, don't tell me,' Pat cried.

'Quiet, Pat,' Matthew said sharply. 'What is it, Rudd? What's happened?'

'There's been an incident in Foxhall Green. It sounds serious and the station there needs our help. Uniform and CID. All the others are already on their way – they should be there by now – but Mr Mullinger sent me to fetch you. I reminded him you were on leave, but he was adamant. I am really sorry, sir, but you've got to come.'

5

Matthew climbed out of the car, his eyes fixed on the crowd that occupied the pavement and most of the road outside the Regal Picture Palace, and which the uniformed constables were struggling to control. He wasn't surprised the Foxhall Green constabulary had appealed to Craynebrook for help if this was what they were having to deal with.

A narrow gap had been left between the crowd and the cinema. Matthew, with Rudd two steps behind, made for this gap, showing his warrant card to the constable on guard at the cinema doors. The constable nodded them through, his expression grim.

Matthew and Rudd stepped into the foyer. At first glance, there was nothing amiss. There was no sign of a disturbance; the doors to the auditorium were closed and the foyer empty. Something glinted in the corner of Matthew's eye, and he turned to the ticket booth to see a shiny sixpence catching the sun on the counter. He took a step towards it, but then a door to the left marked 'Gentlemen' opened, and Denham stepped out, wiping his mouth with the back of his hand.

'Denham!' Matthew called, and the sergeant looked up

with a start. His face was grey and shiny with sweat. 'Are you all right?'

'Yes, sir,' Denham said. 'I just had to—' He gestured at the toilet door.

'What's happened?' Matthew asked, understanding the sergeant had vomited.

'There's been a shooting.' Denham pointed at the double doors of the auditorium. 'It was the Saturday matinee. Fortunately, it wasn't all that busy, but there are several dead and others injured. There were some kids in there.'

Matthew stared at Denham, wondering if this was some sick hoax, but the sergeant wasn't playacting his distress. 'Where's Inspector Lund?' he asked.

Denham pointed to the double doors of the auditorium. 'He's in there with Inspector Oakenshaw from the Foxhall Green station.'

Matthew headed for the doors and reached for one of the large brass handles. He hesitated. 'Have these been dusted?'

'There's no point,' Denham said. 'They've been touched by just about everyone here.'

Matthew nodded and grabbed the right-hand handle and pulled open the door. His breath caught in his throat at the sight that greeted him. Bodies littered the aisle, pulled away to the sides to make a channel down the middle of the steps.

'Stannard?'

Matthew tore his eyes away from the bodies to the bottom of the aisle steps, where Lund stood opposite a grey-haired man in a police uniform.

'What are you doing here?' Lund demanded.

'Mr Mullinger sent for me.'

'What for?'

'I suppose he thought you could do with my help.' He gestured at the bodies. 'I'd say he was right.'

'Would you?' Lund sneered. 'Well, come down here, then.'

Matthew obeyed and Lund introduced the uniformed officer. 'This is Inspector Oakenshaw.'

'Can you believe this?' Oakenshaw said, shaking his head. 'What kind of maniac could do something like this?'

'I count eleven bodies,' Matthew said. 'Three men, five women, and,' he swallowed uneasily, 'three children. How many wounded?'

'Five,' Lund said. 'Two women and three kids. They've been taken to hospital.'

Oakenshaw muttered something and turned away, rubbing his forehead.

'The crowd outside is very agitated,' Matthew said to Lund. 'Have they been told what's happened?'

'They saw the injured being taken out, so they know something pretty bad.'

'What about the parents of those boys?' Matthew pointed at the three small bodies in the fifth row.

'We don't know who they are yet.'

'So, no one has told the crowd what's happened?' Matthew repeated, incredulous.

'We haven't had time,' Oakenshaw said angrily.

'You haven't had time? Oakenshaw, there may be parents in the crowd, wondering if their children are dead in here. They're frantic. You should make identifying the boys a priority so you can let their parents know and calm everyone else down. That'll take the pressure off your men.'

'I should tell them?' Oakenshaw cried indignantly. 'It's my understanding Craynebrook CID is in charge here.'

'That's right,' Lund nodded, glaring at Matthew. 'I'm in

charge. And I don't need you telling me what I should be doing, Stannard.'

'Someone obviously needs to,' Matthew retorted. 'How would you feel if you thought your girls had been in here?'

'Don't you bring my girls into this. And stop sticking your nose in.'

'Mullinger wanted me here!'

'Mullinger can go and—'

'I don't believe you!'

All three men turned towards the auditorium doorway. Denham was there, shaking his head at them.

'How can you be arguing over who's in charge when you're surrounded by all this?'

Shame flooded through Matthew. Denham was right; their behaviour in this slaughterhouse was despicable. 'I'm sorry, Denham,' he said. 'We should know better.' He glanced at Lund.

Lund's jaw was tight as he nodded back, not meeting Matthew's eye. 'We'll find out who the boys are. Denham, ask the staff. Find out if they know their names.'

Denham, still angry, nodded and left.

There was a long, embarrassed silence, which Matthew broke. 'I take it your men moved the bodies, Oakenshaw?'

'Yes,' Oakenshaw said. 'We had to get the injured to the hospital.'

'So, there's no point taking photographs of the bodies. The scene's been disturbed.'

'The scene?' Lund cried. 'Are you really worried about where they were when they died?'

'I'm worried about losing evidence, Lund.'

'Oh, for God's sake,' Lund muttered. He turned to Oakenshaw and jerked his head at Matthew. 'He's always going on about evidence. Just ignore him.'

Matthew took a deep breath, resisting the urge to punch

Lund on the nose. 'Are you going to tell me what happened or do I have to guess?'

Lund didn't answer. He lit a cigarette instead.

Oakenshaw looked from Lund to Matthew, then cleared his throat and began. 'We received an emergency call from the ticket lady here, a Mrs Rita Amstell. She told us people were injured. She and the doorman had been in the staffroom when they heard screams and shots. By the time they got to the auditorium doors, the screams had stopped but they heard one more shot. We think it was the gunman shooting the lock out of that side door.' He pointed to the wall where a door was ajar. 'It opens onto a narrow alley between the cinema and the pub next door and leads onto the high street. The manager keeps the bins there. That's how the gunman got out. One of my men was on patrol on the high street and he got here after Mrs Amstell's call came in. He did a quick sweep of the high street, but he didn't come across anyone suspicious.'

Matthew pointed at Lund's feet, where brass casings littered the carpet. 'Those are rifle casings, aren't they?'

Lund nodded. 'That's right.'

'And that?' Matthew pointed to a black metal box angled at the bottom.

'That's a box magazine,' Oakenshaw said. 'Each one holds ten bullets. It's a fast way of loading the rifle. We used them in the war.'

'Are they easy to get hold of?'

'In civilian life? I couldn't say.'

'Sixteen casings,' Matthew said, crouching to count them. He looked over towards the side door. 'And one more there. That makes one bullet for each victim and one for the door.'

'So what?' Lund said irritably. 'There are seventeen casings. What are you getting at, Stannard?'

'I'd say he shot with purpose. Not wasting any bullets. That box is for quick loading, you say? So, he shot quickly and managed to hit every person in this cinema. That makes him a good shot, don't you think? And he must have been calm about it, too. He used up that box magazine and presumably put another in and carried on shooting. He knew what he was doing. Do you know who was shot first?'

'I have no idea.' Oakenshaw said. 'But what does that matter?'

'Because if we knew who was shot first, it might suggest the gunman had an intended target. As it is, we don't know if there was a specific victim or he shot indiscriminately.'

'Of course he shot indiscriminately,' Lund said. 'What reason could he have for shooting all these people?'

'There's nothing to connect them?'

'Not as far as I know,' Oakenshaw shook his head.

'Those three boys,' Matthew pointed, 'are in Scout uniforms.'

'Women and girls were also shot,' Lund said. 'So, the Scouts can't have anything to do with it. Now, if you've finished asking questions, I'd like to get on with my investigation.'

'Fine,' Matthew said. 'What do you want me to do?'

'Well, as you're here,' Lund said with an edge to his words, 'you can deal with the bodies. We've had word from the mortuary that they can't spare their vans for an hour or so to take them away and I don't want them lying here all that time. Find somewhere they can be laid out and you can get them identified.'

'There's the church hall,' Oakenshaw suggested. 'It's just across the road.'

Lund nodded. 'That'll do. You sort that out, Stannard. Get their names and addresses and bring the list to me at the station.'

'Which one?' Matthew asked. 'Craynebrook or here?'

'We'll set up here for the time being. And while you're getting on with that, I'll talk to the staff.' He walked up the steps to the foyer and disappeared off to the left.

'I'll arrange the church hall,' Oakenshaw said, and followed up the steps.

'We're going to need stretchers and sheets or blankets,' Matthew called after him, and Oakenshaw called back that he'd tell his men. As he left, Barnes and Rudd appeared in the auditorium doorway. Matthew called to Barnes. 'Has the photographer been called?'

'He's just arrived, sir.'

'Tell him we want pictures of the side door, the alley, and everything in the foyer. There's no point photographing the bodies. They're not in situ.'

Denham came to the door, keeping his eyes at head level to avoid looking at the bodies. 'The staff reckon one of the boys is a Frankie Ashe, sir. They don't know the names of the others.'

'All right,' Matthew nodded. 'Thank you.'

Denham left without another word as two uniformed constables appeared in the foyer bearing a stretcher with a grey blanket folded up on it. Matthew told them to get the bodies over to the church hall and they set the stretcher down and lifted the nearest body onto it. He followed as they went back the way they had come, and saw the crowd surge forward as the constables emerged onto the pavement, pushing against the other uniformed officers who were only just managing to hold them back.

Matthew shook his head and turned to Barnes and Rudd. 'This is going to take too long with just those two. Go along the high street and see what you can find to serve as stretchers. Then come back here. You'll have to help with moving the bodies.'

The two detective constables hurried out, leaving Matthew to return to the auditorium alone.

Standing there, amongst the dead, Matthew felt a desperate need for a smoke. He patted his pockets in search of his cigarettes before remembering he had left his packet on his new kitchen counter. 'Wonderful,' he muttered, and turned towards the side door, intending to take a look at the alley. But before he could take more than a few steps, he heard something that made him stop and turn back. He listened but heard nothing. Telling himself he must have imagined the sound, he turned back towards the side door.

He whirled around. There it was again! A sniffing, a whimper. His first thought was that a survivor had been missed, and he bent down to the bodies, listening and looking for any sign of life. But then there was another sniff, and he realised it was coming from the rows of seats.

'Hello?' he called, moving back up the steps. His call was answered by a sharp, stifled cry. Matthew saw that four of the seats in one row were still in the downward position. Dropping to his knees, he peered beneath them.

'It's all right,' he said to the small face that stared out at him. 'I'm a policeman. You're safe now. You can come out.' Matthew held out his hand but the boy didn't move. 'Come on. You can't stay there. You've got to come out.'

The boy shook his head.

'He's gone now. He can't hurt you. I promise. Now, you know you can trust a policeman, don't you?'

The boy nodded.

'So, you'll be safe with me.' Matthew held out his hand again. 'Please. Come out.'

The boy stared at Matthew's hand for a long moment, then he took hold of it and Matthew pulled him out. Struggling to get to his feet, Matthew clamped him to his chest and covered the boy's eyes with his hand. The boy stiffened, but Matthew said, 'You don't want to see. Trust me.'

Rudd and Barnes appeared in the doorway, both bearing armfuls of blankets. They stared at the boy in Matthew's arms in surprise. He mouthed at them to be quiet and strode into the foyer.

'It's all right now,' he said, taking his hand away. The boy lifted his head and looked at him with puffy, terrified eyes. 'What's your name?'

'Timmy Lane,' he whispered.

'I'm Matthew. Are you hurt, Timmy?'

Timmy shook his head.

'That's good. Now, we're going to look after you. You see this man here?' He pointed at Rudd. 'His name's Sam and he's going to take you for a ride in a police car. You'd like that, wouldn't you?'

Timmy gave the smallest of nods and Matthew transferred him to Rudd's arms.

'Take him to the hospital,' Matthew told Rudd. 'Get a doctor to take a look at him, just in case.'

'Yes, sir.' Rudd left with Timmy's face pressed against his neck.

'Where was he?' Barnes asked Matthew.

'Hiding under his seat.'

'Poor kid.'

Matthew nodded and looked through the windows at the crowd. 'Uniform's not going to be able to hold them much longer,' he said, and cursed Oakenshaw and Lund under his breath. With a resigned sigh, he went out and held up his hands.

'Ladies and gentlemen. Can I have your attention, please? Thank you. I'm Detective Inspector Matthew Stannard from Craynebrook CID. As I'm sure you've realised, a very serious incident has occurred in the cinema this afternoon. There has been a shooting. The injured have been taken to hospital, but there have also been casualties.'

'My wife was in there,' a man called out.

'If she wasn't taken to hospital, then I'm very sorry, sir, but she may be one of the casualties.' The man stared at Matthew, his face fixed in a stare of disbelief. Matthew hurried on. 'The casualties will be moved to the church hall until they can be taken to a more suitable place. If you think someone you know was in the cinema this afternoon and hasn't already been taken to the hospital, please make your way to the church hall. Thank you.'

Some of the crowd broke off at once and marched across the road. As the crowd thinned, Matthew saw Dickie's face staring out at him and he gave his friend a perfunctory nod before heading towards the church.

Dickie had arrived in Foxhall Green just in time to see Matthew and Rudd disappearing into the cinema.

He merged with the crowd, listening for tidbits of information, but learned little he hadn't already been told. That something terrible had happened was clear, that some people had been injured and taken to hospital was certain, but what was still going on inside the cinema was a mystery to all until the first stretcher was borne out and Matthew addressed the crowd.

Dickie had stayed back, knowing his friend wouldn't tell him anything, whether off the record or on at this stage. Afterwards, when Matthew had followed the stretchered bodies across the road, so too had Dickie, at a discreet distance, and waited outside the church hall, eliciting from the constable guarding the door what little information he could. He lingered for perhaps twenty minutes, hoping Matthew would come out, but when he didn't, Dickie decided it was time to call in what he knew, knowing he would have to speculate quite a lot about what he didn't.

Ben answered the telephone on the first ring. 'Ben Riley. *The Chronicle*.'

'Ben. It's Dickie. Get your pencil and notebook ready. I've got a story for you... Yes, it's big... That's right. A Stop Press. You ready?... Right. Take this down. A tragedy occurred at the Regal Picture Palace cinema in Foxhall Green this afternoon. A Saturday matinee turned into a scene of horror as a gunman opened fire on the unsuspecting cinemagoers. Several people were wounded and more were killed by the gunman's deadly aim. The wounded, which included children, were taken to hospital while the dead were removed to the local church hall where relatives were called upon to identify their loved ones. The motive for the massacre is as yet unknown, as is the identity of the gunman. The case is being investigated by the renowned detective, Inspector Matthew Stannard. DI Stannard has been responsible for bringing several killers to justice, including the Marsh Murderer and the Craynebrook Strangler.... Did you get all that?... Good. Get it done as soon as you can... No, I'm not coming back just yet. I'm going to see if I can talk to a few more people. I might try the local vicar. See what he has to say about all this... I'll see you later.' He was about to hang up when Ben shouted down the line at him. 'What?... Oh, did she? What did you tell her?... No, that's all right, Ben. I'll give her a bell.'

He hung up and dug into his pocket for another coin. Dickie told the operator the number he wanted, and waited impatiently for his call to be answered. As soon as the line connected, and before his wife could say a word, Dickie said, 'Emma, let me explain.'

6

Matthew settled into Oakenshaw's office at the Foxhall Green police station and was typing up the list of the dead when Sergeant Dobbs brought him in a cup of tea and a plate of biscuits. The sergeant had already furnished him with a couple of cigarettes.

'Do you have any idea who did it, sir?' Dobbs asked.

'It's too early to say,' Matthew said, biting into a biscuit.

'It's got to be a nutter, though, hasn't it? I mean, no sane man's going to walk into a cinema and just kill people like that, are they?'

'You'd be surprised what people are capable of, sergeant.'

'I suppose,' Dobbs nodded glumly. 'Is there anything else I can get you, sir?'

'Yes. You can bring me your gun register.'

'The register, sir?'

'It was a shooting, sergeant. A rifle was used. It makes sense to check who has a rifle hereabouts, wouldn't you say?'

'Yes, I suppose it does.' But the sergeant didn't move.

Matthew looked over at him. 'Is there a problem?'

Dobbs made a face. 'We had a spot of bother a month

or so back, sir. Our lavatories flooded and with the Records room being right underneath... well, everything got waterlogged. All the papers have dried out now, but the ink run in some of them, so...' He shrugged helplessly.

'Is there a copy of the register anywhere?'

'I don't think so, sir.'

'So, we have no way of knowing who's registered a rifle locally?' Matthew said, throwing up his hands.

'I wouldn't say that,' Dobbs said a little indignantly. 'I reckon I can remember most of the names. There weren't that many.'

'If you could try, please, sergeant.'

Dobbs went out as Lund, Denham and Rudd came in.

'You've got them all identified?' Lund said, dropping into a chair.

Matthew pulled the sheet of paper from the typewriter and held it out to him. 'A list of the names and addresses. And all the next of kin, if they didn't know already, have been informed.'

'Good.' Lund helped himself to Matthew's biscuits.

Oakenshaw came in, looking a little put out to find his office occupied. 'Well? What now?' he asked Matthew.

Matthew glanced over at Lund, seeing his fellow detective bristle at the assumption he was giving the orders. 'Lund?' he asked pointedly.

'Oakenshaw,' Lund said, crumbs tumbling down his shirt front. 'I want your men knocking on doors along the high street and the surrounding residential streets. Someone must have seen something and I want to know what. We'll get some of our lads to give you a hand. What's that?' he asked as Dobbs came back into the room and handed Matthew a sheet of paper.

'It's the names I can remember,' Dobbs said, and cast an

apologetic look at Oakenshaw. 'The gun register, sir. I've explained the problem to Mr Stannard.'

'What's this about a gun register?' Lund demanded.

'I asked for it,' Matthew said, reading the names.

'It'll be a waste of time,' Lund muttered, snatching the paper from Matthew's hand. 'Our gunman's unlikely to have used a registered gun.'

'We've still got to check.'

'I know that,' Lund snapped, and handed the paper to Oakenshaw. 'Get one of your men checking those names.'

Oakenshaw turned to Dobbs. 'As you already know the names, you can handle that.'

'Will do, sir,' Dobbs said and left the office.

'Did you get anything out of the staff?' Matthew asked Lund.

'Not much,' he said. 'Just a lot about screaming and gunshots.'

'Let's hope the boy can tell us what happened, then.'

Lund stared at Matthew. 'What boy?'

Matthew suddenly realised Lund didn't know about Timmy Lane. 'I found a boy hiding beneath a seat in the cinema,' he explained. 'He wasn't hurt. Just scared.'

'And when were you going to tell me about him?'

Matthew glanced at Rudd, who looked away sheepishly, knowing he should have informed the inspector. 'I'm sorry, Lund. I should have let you know earlier.'

'Planning to keep it to yourself, were you?'

'Of course I wasn't,' Matthew retorted. 'Why would I do that?'

'Because you want to take over. You can't stand me being in charge, can you? You've got to stick your oar in.'

'You're talking rubbish.'

'What are you even doing here?' Lund went on. 'You're supposed to be on leave.'

'I told you, Mullinger sent for me.'

'Well, he shouldn't have. I don't need you. You can go.'

Matthew stared at him, uncomfortably aware of the junior detectives nervously watching. 'You're not serious?'

'Oh, I am, sunshine,' Lund said with feeling. 'After all, you've got court on Monday, haven't you? You can't afford to get bogged down with this. So,' he jerked his head at the door. 'Off you go. Get back to your new flat.'

Matthew stared at Lund and met his eye. Lund was up for a fight, he could tell, and he was damned if he was going to give him the satisfaction.

'Fine,' he said. 'It's all yours.'

Matthew grabbed his hat and coat and left, exiting the station lobby without a word to Dobbs. He thundered down the steps, trying not to let his anger show to the huddle of men and women gathered on the pavement. As soon as they saw him, the reporters amongst them called out, 'What can you tell us about the massacre?' while those that recognised him shouted, 'Inspector? Inspector Stannard?'

Matthew waved them away, pulling his arm angrily out of the tug of one over-eager journalist, and headed for the high street. He heard footsteps behind him.

'I can't comment,' he shouted over his shoulder.

'Slow down a bit, can't you? My legs aren't as young as yours.'

Recognising the voice, Matthew came to a halt. 'Sorry, Dickie. I didn't realise it was you.'

'That's all right,' Dickie said. 'What's the matter? You've got a face like thunder.'

Matthew's usual response would have been to deny there was anything the matter, but he was too angry to keep silent and the words came bursting out before he could stop them. 'Lund has sent me home. He says he doesn't need me.

Can you believe that? A case this big and he doesn't need me.'

He turned to go, but Dickie grabbed his arm. 'Wait a minute. Are you saying you're not in charge?'

Matthew shook his head. 'It's Lund's case. He was first on the scene.'

'But I thought... when I saw you go into the cinema... Well, I'll be blowed. You're not in charge and Lund is. Is he up to it? I mean, he's not the sharpest knife in the drawer at the best of times. Or do you already know who did it?'

Matthew's fury subsided a little. He managed a small smile at his friend's attempt to elicit information. 'Nice try, Dickie.'

'I didn't mean it like that,' Dickie protested. 'What I mean is if you know who did it, then all right, Lund can cope. But if you don't know—'

'It's Lund's case, Dickie,' Matthew cut him off. 'And I'm on leave.'

'Oh, that's right. You're moving into your new flat this weekend, aren't you?'

'I'm supposed to be.' Matthew heaved a sigh. 'Look, I'm sorry for snapping, Dickie. I'm just not in the best of moods. If you want a comment about the case, you'll have to ask Lund.'

'I'll do that,' Dickie said as Matthew walked away. 'And I'll pop round to see your new place. Just let me know when.'

Matthew raised his hand in acknowledgement and made his way to the bus stop.

Matthew almost got on the wrong bus home.

Unable to stop thinking about Lund's accusation that he

wanted to take over, he had waited fifteen minutes at a stop for a bus that would take him to Bethnal Green and his old flat. It was only when the bus came along and he'd put his foot on the step that he'd realised his mistake and waved an apology at the conductor, walking away to wait for the bus that would take him to Halesden.

It was nine-thirty by the time he unlocked his new front door, aware he would have to hang the curtains and make his bed before he could go to sleep and wondering if he could be bothered. Maybe he would just pull a blanket over himself and leave the rest until the morning.

Going into the kitchen to get his cigarettes, he found a bottle of beer, a clean glass and two plates, one upside down on top of the other, on the kitchen counter. Matthew lifted the topmost plate to reveal a ham and cheese sandwich. He opened the kitchen cupboards to find his crockery stacked neatly and his cupboards filled with tins and packets of food that he hadn't bought. He went into his new bedroom and found the curtains had been put up and the bed made.

Matthew smiled, touched by what Pat and Georgie had done for him in his absence. Returning to the kitchen, he took the sandwich and beer back to his bedroom. Kicking off his shoes, he lay back on the bed, balancing the plate on his lap. A moment later, Bella trotted into the room. She looked up at him and he jerked his head for her to jump up onto the bed. She landed on his knees and sniffed at the sandwich. He broke off a piece of ham and fed it to her.

'What a bloody awful day, Bella,' he said as she licked his fingers. Reaching to the bedside cabinet to turn on the light, he saw a folded sheet of paper propped against the lamp. He unfolded it and read.

Mattie,

I've left you something to eat.

I know the plan was we'd come over tomorrow for lunch, but I don't suppose that'll happen now you've been called out. I'll give you a bell around nine in the morning. If you don't answer, I'll assume lunch is off. But it'll be a shame because I've got all the grub and Mum was looking forward to it. She'll moan if she doesn't see you, so please try and make lunch.

Love, Pat

P.S. I've fed Bella. Again!

I can make lunch, Matthew thought bitterly. *Lund doesn't need me.*

He finished the sandwich and beer, then pushed Bella off his lap and went into the hall. Picking up the telephone receiver, checking to make sure it was working, he asked to be connected to the hospital.

'Good evening,' he said when the connection was made, 'I'm sorry it's so late, but I'm Detective Inspector Matthew Stannard... Yes, the shooting... A boy was brought in after the others. He wasn't injured. I wondered what happened to him?... In shock?... Yes, I understand. But is he talking?... No. When do you think... I realise it's difficult to say... Well, thank you, anyway. Good night.'

He hung up, disappointed. If Timmy Lane was in shock and unable to tell them what he'd seen, then they had no idea who they were looking for.

Lund has no idea who he's looking for, he corrected himself. *Not we.*

Matthew's fists clenched at the memory of the scene in Oakenshaw's office. But then Bella rubbed against his legs and meowed, and he forced his irritation away. He wouldn't let it get to him. If Lund thought he could manage without him, then that was fine. He could have it that way. Matthew would not give the shooting another thought.

It was very late by the time Denham got home.

He dragged himself up the stairs, each step feeling heavier than the last, and reached the first-floor landing with a heavy, weary sigh. The bathroom door was open and moonlight fell on the baby clothes hanging over the landing banisters. A lump formed in his throat at the sight of them and he turned towards the box room. Stepping inside, Denham moved to the cot and looked down at his daughter asleep beneath the white wool blanket knitted by his mother.

Denham stared at Ellie for a long time. Then a cry burst from him, and he lifted his daughter from the cot and held her against his chest. He buried his nose in her hair, breathing in the smell of her, and wept, his body shuddering with the strength of his sobs. Ellie wriggled in his hands, protesting at being woken, but he held her tight.

'Justin?'

The sound of Mary's voice startled him, and he choked off his sobs, turning to look at her through his blurry, aching eyes.

She looked at him in alarm, glancing down at their baby, and back up to him. 'What is it? What's wrong?'

In answer, Denham held out his arm to her, and she went to him. He held her tight and she tilted her head to him. 'Tell me what's wrong, please.'

But Denham shook his head. He couldn't tell her. He didn't have the words to explain how he felt. And besides, he didn't want her to imagine the horror he had witnessed that day. All he wanted to do was hold his daughter and know she was safe.

7

Sunday, 19th October 1930

Denham left home before six the next morning, leaving Mary and Ellie asleep in their bed, and gone to work, thinking he would be the first to arrive in CID. But when he walked in, DS Stanley Bissett was already sitting at his desk, the telephone receiver clamped to his ear. Barnes and Rudd arrived a few minutes later. There was none of the usual cheery greetings, no wasting time chatting over tea and biscuits. They were there to work, and they got right down to it. Only Lund let the side down, not turning up until half-past eight and greeting them with a grunt and a demand for tea and a bacon roll which Rudd, as the new boy, had to fetch. Lund went into his office and slammed the door.

An hour later, Denham hung up his receiver and rubbed his reddened ear. The telephones hadn't stopped ringing. There had been call after call, mostly from members of the public claiming to have seen someone suspicious or suggesting candidates for the gunman. Denham knew most of the leads were nonsense, but they all had to be looked into.

'This is going to take days,' Barnes muttered as he dropped his receiver into the cradle. 'I must have two dozen names here. What about you?'

'The same.' Denham ran his pencil down the list he had made. 'Anyone we know?'

'A few.' Barnes gave him the names. 'What do you reckon?'

'I don't think they're likely. They don't have a history of violence or guns. But tell the inspector about them, just in case.'

'Should I tell him about this?' Rudd asked. 'Foxhall Green nick says they've had a vagrant hanging around the high street for the past two weeks, but he hasn't been seen since Saturday morning. Apparently, he's an old soldier, so he'd know how to use a rifle.'

'So would anyone who served in the war,' Denham said. 'But you better add him to the list to tell the inspector.'

'Tell me what?' Lund had come out of his office, unnoticed. He headed for the filing cabinet behind Denham and took the lid off the biscuit tin.

'Foxhall Green has put a name forward as a possible suspect, sir,' Rudd said.

Lund shoved a whole digestive into his mouth. 'Who?' he asked, spraying crumbs.

'A vagrant who's been haunting Foxhall Green for a week or two. Name of Sergeant Ambrose Brock. They tried moving him on, but he kept coming back and some residents lodged complaints. But the thing is, he hasn't been seen since yesterday morning.'

'Bingo! He's our gunman, then. Oh, come on,' Lund said as the junior detectives looked at each other doubtfully. 'A pain in the backside tramp. Refuses to move on. Gets up the noses of all the locals. Harsh words are exchanged. Threats made. And he gets all worked up and has his revenge. Does the shooting before leaving the area. Stands to reason. Get on and find him.' He slid the biscuit tin off the filing cabinet and took it back to his office.

'What do you think?' Barnes asked as Lund shut his door.

'You don't want to know what I think,' Denham said, glaring at Lund through the office partition window as the inspector worked his way through the biscuits in the tin.

Laing's lips twitched in pleasure as he stood at the oak doors to welcome the people coming into his church. So many more than previous Sundays; how very gratifying. It was such a pity so much blood had had to be shed to achieve it.

He fixed a suitably sombre expression on his face as he saw the newest influx was wearing a great deal of black. He chivvied the other parishioners along to clear the way.

Laing clasped hands, expressed his regrets, and guided fragile souls to the front pews reserved for the mourners. He had told Dennis he wanted them all in one place, as that would make it easier for him to address them during his sermon.

When everyone was in and the doors were closed, Laing looked over his church and saw with a swell of pleasure, and not some little pride, that all the pews were filled. There were the usual familiar faces, the Sullivans, the Redmans, the Fairleys, the Wildsmiths, but there were many he had never seen before as well. And there were also reporters, he noticed with interest, casting his eyes towards the back of the church where the members of the Press had gathered. He was glad he'd worked so hard on his sermon the previous evening. If his sermon would be reported in the newspapers, and he hoped it would be, then it had to be powerful.

Laing began his service, following its routine course. He wanted the reading of the lesson to mark the first reference to the massacre. He'd asked Herbert Wildsmith to perform the reading, Herod's Slaughter of the Innocents, knowing his monotonous voice would suit perfectly the solemnity of the occasion. Laing had been worried the Slaughter was too obvious a passage to use, but he had come to the conclusion it was not a day for subtlety. His message needed to be clear if he was going to get through to these blockheads.

As the reading progressed, Laing became annoyed by the sniffs and muffled cries coming from the front pews. The rest of the congregation became distracted as people whispered to each other and craned their necks to see who was making the pitiful noises. They wouldn't do that when he spoke, Laing decided. He'd make them sit up and take notice when he delivered his sermon.

Herbert concluded the reading and returned to his pew, taking his seat between Lydia and Lewis. Laing climbed into the pulpit, put both hands on the lectern and looked out over his congregation.

'Yesterday,' he began, 'was the most terrible of days. We might have been forgiven for believing that the slaughter at the Regal Picture Palace only happened on battlefields, but yesterday taught us that is not so. Evil exists all around us and it is up to us, we good Christians, to make sure it does not triumph. It triumphed yesterday, but,' Laing's right hand clenched into a fist and banged down on the lectern, 'never again!' He leaned back, surveying his audience, making sure he had their complete attention before gripping the lectern again and bearing down on his congregation. 'Is this what we have come to? Is England now a place where society has degenerated to such a degree that the indiscriminate killing of innocent people is even contemplated, let alone enacted? Yesterday showed us it is. We have become a nation that produces wanton murderers, men who kill without motive, without the promise of profit from their deeds. Men who kill because the act of killing pleases them.' He shook his head in dismay. 'How have we come to this? you ask. I'll tell you. We have come to this because society has turned its back on God. How do I know this? I know this because ever since I came to serve this parish, this church has never been more than half-full. You have had no need for God, so you thought, why bother to go to church to worship him?

'And then something like yesterday happens, and suddenly, you have a need for God again. Only God, you realise, can offer some explanation for why this terrible tragedy happened. Only God can offer you the consolation you so desperately seek. And yet, here is the irony. If only you had not turned your backs on God in the first place, such a tragedy as the shooting yesterday might never have happened. God has had to remind you that you need him. You want a reason yesterday happened? Here is that reason. You turned your back on God, so God turned his back on you!'

Another pause, another study of his audience, and Laing continued, this time with a kindly smile on his face. 'But you needn't despair. God is forgiveness. Take Him back and He will take you to his bosom and keep you safe. I grieve with the men and women here today who have lost their loved ones to this terrible act. But know this.' Laing spread his arms wide and beamed down on the faces looking up at him. 'Here you will find peace.'

He finished, certain he had had the congregation in the palm of his hand. No one had fidgeted, no one had whispered in their neighbour's ear. Eyes had been fixed upon him throughout his sermon. Now, the reporters had their eyes fixed on their laps where, no doubt, they were scribbling down his words in their notebooks, ready to be turned into copy for their newspapers.

Yes, it was all very gratifying.

Herbert picked up his hat from the pew beside him and waited for Lydia to gather her things. He had not wanted to read the Slaughter of the Innocents and wished he'd said no to Reverend Laing when he asked. The problem with Laing was that his requests were always phrased more as an order and no matter how one said no, he never seemed to accept a refusal. Besides, what excuse could Herbert have given for refusing when he had said yes so many times before?

'Do hurry up, Lewis,' Lydia said irritably as the young man dawdled over pulling on his coat. She looked around uneasily as her fellow churchgoers made their way towards the doors. 'We shouldn't have come today,' she whispered to Herbert.

'It would have looked bad if we didn't,' he whispered back.

'What's the matter?' Lewis asked.

'Nothing, darling,' Lydia said, forcing a smile. 'I just want to get home.' She grabbed his elbow to encourage him, but Lewis had spotted Dennis.

'Hello, Mr Hillman,' he said as Dennis came over. 'It was a good sermon, wasn't it?'

Dennis frowned at him. 'No, Lewis, I don't think it was. It was in rather bad taste, in my opinion.' He looked over his shoulder towards Laing, who had made his way down the central aisle to talk to the reporters. 'I actually think he's enjoying all this.'

'Well, I thought it was smashing,' Lewis grinned. 'I wish all those people hadn't been crying all through Daddy's reading, though. They were annoying.'

'Those were the grieving relatives, Lewis,' Herbert chided. 'They were entitled to cry.'

'I don't know what for,' Lewis said, buttoning up his coat. 'So what if they're dead?'

'Lewis!' Lydia gasped. 'Keep your voice down. People will hear you.'

'I don't care,' he shrugged. 'I'm glad Frankie Ashe is dead. And so is Reverend Laing and so is Mr Hillman. Aren't you, Mr Hillman?'

Dennis swallowed uneasily. 'Of course I'm not glad, Lewis.'

'Yes, you are,' Lewis insisted. 'Frankie was ruining the Scouts, and you know it. Now he's dead, we can go back to how things were, like we talked about yesterday.'

Dennis opened his mouth to speak, but just then, a middle-aged couple passed them by. Both were dressed in black. The woman was crying, walking almost blindly, a sodden handkerchief to her eyes, as she was led by her husband to the church door.

'The Simpsons,' Dennis said in a low voice. 'They're very upset.'

'Good,' Lewis said with venom. 'I'm glad Lucy's dead too.'

Herbert raised his hand and pointed a finger at Lewis's nose. 'That's enough, Lewis. Be quiet.'

Lewis's mouth tightened, and he stared at the tip of his father's finger mutinously.

'Do you hear me?' Herbert said angrily.

Lewis nodded.

Lydia pushed Herbert's hand away, widening her eyes at him in a silent reproach. 'All right, dear. You've made your point. Come on. Let's go home.'

She gave Dennis a weak smile in farewell, took her son's arm and gently guided him towards the doors.

8

'So,' Matthew said as he brought his mother back to the sitting room after a tour of his new flat. 'Do you like it?'

'Oh, Mattie,' Amanda gasped, her hands pressed to her cheeks. 'It's lovely. Are you pleased with it?'

'Yes, I am,' Matthew said, trying not to smile too much.

He was more than pleased; he was delighted with his new flat. He'd awoken that morning actually warm. He'd had hot water for a bath, and he'd wallowed in it, knowing there would be no Mr Levitt banging on the door demanding he hurry up. He'd opened his curtains to see the view of the park Pat had praised rather than looking out onto another row of dreary tenements. But most of all, he loved it because it proved he was definitely on the up. All his hard work over the years was finally paying off.

'I'm so glad,' Amanda said. 'You deserve it.' She turned to Georgie. 'Bring it in, Georgie.'

'Bring what in?' Matthew asked as Georgie went out into the hall. He glanced over at Pat, who had an excited smile on her face.

'You'll see,' Amanda said.

Georgie returned with a large cardboard box. He set it down on the settee and stepped back.

'Open it,' Amanda told Matthew.

He peeled back the flap and gasped. 'Mum, you haven't?' he said, and delving inside, lifted out a brand new wireless. Georgie whipped the box away so Matthew could set it back down on the settee.

'You like it, don't you?' Amanda asked anxiously.

Matthew ran his hand over the sleek, shiny wood. 'Of course I do. But it must have cost you a fortune. How much was it?'

'You don't ask questions like that,' Pat said. 'It's a present for your new flat.'

'From all of you?'

'No. It's just from Mum. She picked it out herself. Didn't you, Mum?'

Amanda nodded. 'The man in the shop told me it was a good one. I said I had to have the best for you.'

Matthew had a lump in his throat as he put his arm around his mother's shoulder and kissed her cheek. 'It's lovely, Mum. Thank you.'

Pat declared she would find the right spot for the wireless and enlisted Georgie to help her. Matthew settled his mother down with the Sunday newspapers and Bella on her lap, and went off into the kitchen to cook the lunch.

His sister came in as he filled a saucepan with water and set it on the gas. 'Do you want a hand?'

'No. You're a guest. Go and sit down.'

'Don't be daft. Let me do something.'

'No,' Matthew said, peeling a potato. 'I'm cooking as a thank you for helping me with the move.'

'You don't have to thank us. And besides, since when do you know how to cook?'

'I've cooked before.'

'Not a roast dinner, you haven't.'

'How hard can it be? Go and sit down with Mum and Georgie.'

'Oh, I talk to them every day,' she said, leaning back against the counter and folding her arms over her chest.

'So, you're going to watch me, are you?'

'If you won't let me help, yes.'

Matthew turned to her, and with a quick glance at the door, lowered his voice to ask, 'How much was that radio?'

'I told you—'

'I know what you told me, but Mum doesn't have that kind of money to waste on me.'

'You said you liked the wireless.'

'I do like it, but it's too expensive.'

'So what are you going to do? Tell her to take it back?'

'No. I'm going to give you the money for it, so she doesn't know. How much was it?'

'I'm not telling you.'

'Pat, listen to me—'

'No,' she snapped, wagging a finger at him. 'You listen to me. Mum wanted to give you a present. She enjoyed going to the shop and picking out that wireless. She was excited all last night thinking about how pleased you would be when she gave it to you. It's made her happy, so don't spoil it for her. And if you must know, she got it for a good price. The shopkeeper's a friend of Fred's. So, shut up and peel your potatoes.'

Matthew's mouth twitched in amusement as his sister glared at him. He did as he was told and resumed his peeling, feeling her eyes upon his back.

'So, what was that all about yesterday?' she asked. 'Why did you get called out?'

'You didn't hear about it on the news?'

'When do I have time to listen to the news? Especially on a Saturday night.'

'There was a shooting in a cinema over in Foxhall Green. A gunman walked in and shot sixteen people. Some of them were children.'

'Oh, my gawd,' Pat cried. 'What for?'

Matthew shrugged as he dug the eye out of a potato. 'I've no idea.'

'But didn't he tell you why he did it when you questioned him?'

'To question him, we'd have to catch him first.'

Pat frowned. 'But if this gunman hasn't been caught, why aren't you at work looking for him?'

Matthew cut a potato into four and threw it into the pan of boiling water. 'Because Lund didn't want me there.'

'I don't understand. Why did he send that young lad round if he didn't want you?'

'He didn't send Rudd. That was Superintendent Mullinger. Lund thought I was there so I could take over the case, and he wasn't having that, so he sent me away.'

'And were you?'

'Was I what?'

'Trying to take over?'

Matthew rounded on her. 'Of course I wasn't. How can you even ask that?'

Pat shrugged. 'Because you do like to be in charge, Mattie. You know you do.'

They looked at each other for a long moment, then Matthew turned back to the chopping board and grabbed another potato.

'Well, that explains why you've got the hump,' Pat went on, opening the oven door to put the beef joint in.

'I haven't got the hump,' Matthew said. 'It's just that it's a big case and Lund needs all the men working on it he can get. It makes no sense to send me away.'

'Oh, Mattie, can't you just be pleased you've got some time off for once?' Pat sighed. 'Or that someone else has got the responsibility of solving a murder for a change? Haven't you had your fill this year?'

Matthew picked up another potato and peeled it savagely. 'I suppose so,' he muttered.

Laing closed the vestry door and turned to Dickie sitting by his desk. 'What newspaper did you say you worked for?'

'*The Chronicle.*' Dickie took out his notebook and rested it on his knee, pencil poised over the page.

'So, this article won't appear in a national newspaper?'

Was that disappointment he heard in Laing's voice? Dickie wondered, as the vicar pulled out his chair and sat down. 'It's possible a national might pick it up, but no. This will be for local distribution.'

'I see. Well, what can I tell you, Mr Waite?'

'I would say your thoughts on the massacre, but you made those quite clear in your sermon. So, tell me about yourself. I got the impression you have something you want people to hear, and heard by a much wider audience than your usual Sunday congregation. Or am I wrong?'

'No, you're quite right. It pleases me that my sermon was heard by so many, and with the aid of the Press, will be read by many more. My only concern is that it will soon be forgotten and people will revert to their old ways. It was very gratifying to have so many people in my church this morning, but I'm sorry to say, it isn't usual.'

'So, the massacre has filled your church?'

'That's one way of putting it,' Laing said, his smile thinning. He gestured at Dickie's notebook. 'This will be a profile piece, then?'

'Of sorts, yes. As I see it, you're the vicar of Foxhall Green and, as such, you could be considered the lynchpin of the community. After a tragedy like the cinema shooting, it's only natural the grieving relatives, and indeed, all the residents of Foxhall Green, turn to you for solace.' Dickie crossed his legs and rubbed his chin thoughtfully. 'Which makes me wonder if that is a role you're willing to perform?'

Laing frowned. 'Who else could perform it?'

'Well, you'll have to forgive me, reverend, but to my ears, your sermon offered little in the way of solace. To me, it sounded a lot more like criticism.'

'It was intended as criticism,' Laing said sharply. 'One should tell people what they need to hear, not what they want to hear. And the truth, uncomfortable though it may be, is that England has become a godless nation, and as a result, our country, our very society, is suffering. It is, however, a great pity, as I said in my sermon, that it takes a tragedy of this nature to bring that home to people and make them remedy their ways.'

'Is that how you see the shooting, then? As a remedy for society's ills?'

'I do. It is my hope changes will come from this.'

'What kind of changes?'

'That public house opening times are reduced and become less well-attended. That public dances are regulated, so nothing unseemly takes place. That the cinema shows only improving, educational motion pictures and, ideally, that an age bar is placed upon attendance. Children are too impressionable to be exposed to the filth Hollywood dishes up in the name of so-called entertainment. Just think, Mr Waite, if there had been an age bar, those children wouldn't have been in the cinema to be killed.' Laing tapped a pile of paper on his desk. 'In fact, these are sentiments I have been espousing for several years now and which form the basis of my book.'

Dickie pointed at the papers. 'You're writing a book?'

'I am,' Laing smiled proudly. 'I've only been working on it since coming to Foxhall Green, but it contains ideas and beliefs I have held for far longer.'

'When will it be published?'

The smile faltered. 'It isn't finished.'

'But you do have a publisher?' Dickie couldn't resist asking, realising Laing's prevarication meant he didn't.

'I will have,' Laing insisted. 'Once it's finished.'

Dickie nodded. 'One final question. Do you have any idea who might have done the shooting?'

Laing brushed fluff from his trouser leg. 'The shooting was obviously the work of a lunatic or a degenerate. Someone who doesn't have a place amongst decent people. A vagrant, for example.'

'A tramp?'

Laing nodded. 'There has been a tramp loitering around here for the past few weeks. A filthy individual who reeks of alcohol and looks as if he hasn't had a bath for years. He's taken to sleeping in the church grounds despite my best attempts to have him removed.'

'And you think this tramp might be the gunman?'

'I'd say it's a distinct possibility. He's a very dubious character. I told Inspector Oakenshaw yesterday evening the police ought to investigate him.'

'And what did Inspector Oakenshaw say?'

'He was grateful for the information and said he would pass it on to Inspector Lund of Craynebrook CID, who I understand is in charge of the investigation.'

'But what if this tramp had nothing to do with the

shooting? You could be pointing the finger of blame at an innocent man.'

'If he is innocent, then he will be proved to be so, and no harm done.'

'No harm done?' Dickie said. 'You really believe that?'

Laing opened his mouth to reply when there was a knock on the vestry door. Giving Dickie a disdainful look, he rose and opened it to find Sergeant Dobbs on the doorstep.

'Sorry to bother you, Reverend Laing,' Dobbs said, 'but I need Mr Hillman here,' he gestured at Dennis standing behind him, 'to show me the Boy Scout rifles.'

Laing glanced at Dickie. 'It's not convenient, sergeant.' He made to close the door.

But Dobbs put his foot in the gap, preventing him. 'I'm afraid I'm going to have to insist.' He gave the door a gentle nudge.

Laing's mouth pursed, but he nodded and opened the door, allowing Dobbs and Dennis to enter.

'They're in the storeroom,' Dennis muttered, and pointed to the cupboard door.

'Let's have a look at them, then,' Dobbs said encouragingly.

'Why are you checking the Scout rifles?' Laing asked as Dennis went into the storeroom.

'It's just routine, reverend,' Dobbs said.

Dickie rose and went over to the door, watching as Dennis took the key to the trunk down from its hook. 'Are you contacting all the local rifle owners, sergeant?' he asked.

'That's right, sir,' Dobbs said, frowning as he also watched Dennis. 'Is that where the key's always kept, Mr Hillman?' he asked, jerking his head at the hook on the shelving.

'Yes,' Dennis said nervously as he unlocked the trunk and threw back the lid.

'It's not very secure there. Anyone could take the key.'

'Hardly, sergeant,' Laing said scornfully. 'Very few people have access to the vestry.'

'And you'd have to know the key was there to take it,' Dennis protested. 'It's quite out of sight.'

'Be that as it may, sir,' Dobbs said, unconvinced, and moved to the trunk. He pulled on a pair of leather gloves and lifted the rifles out, one by one. 'When were these last used, Mr Hillman?'

'Not for a month or so,' Dennis said. 'I haven't done a marksmanship class for a while.'

'And there's nothing amiss here? All rifles present and correct?'

Dennis looked down at the rifles by the sergeant's feet. 'Yes,' he said. 'All there.'

'I'm going to have to take these away with me,' Dobbs said, gathering the rifles into his arms.

'Take them away?' Dennis cried. 'No, but—'

'Is that absolutely necessary, sergeant?' Laing asked. 'You can't believe these rifles were used in the shooting?'

'They have to be tested,' Dickie said before Dobbs could answer.

'These rifles are in my vestry,' Laing said. 'It is insulting to believe one of them was the rifle used. If it were to get out you had taken them from my church, who knows what people might think? I can't allow it. I know your superior officer, sergeant, and Inspector Oakenshaw—'

'Would be pleased to know you're helping the police in any way you can,' Dickie interjected with a smile. 'After all, I'm sure you wouldn't want people to think you were getting special treatment from the police, reverend?'

Laing's eyes blazed at Dickie. 'Of course not,' he said sharply and turned away to his desk.

Dobbs nodded his thanks to Dickie. He turned to Dennis. 'I'll also need to take your fingerprints, Mr Hillman. Just for elimination purposes. So, if you could come back to the station with me, we'll get those done straightaway.'

Dennis nodded unhappily.

'Well, good day, gentlemen,' Dobbs said with a smile to Laing and Dickie. 'Sorry to have bothered you.'

When they had gone, Laing picked up Dickie's notebook from his desk and handed it to him. 'That's all the time I can spare you, Mr Waite. I'm sure you have enough for your article.'

Dickie tucked his notebook away in his coat pocket, then looked pointedly at the storeroom door. He met Laing's eye. 'Thank you for your time, reverend. It's been very interesting.'

9

Inspector Oakenshaw hung up the telephone receiver with a groan. How many more of these calls would he have to take? Ever since he'd sat down at his desk that morning, the telephone hadn't stopped ringing. If it wasn't worried parents asking if it was safe for their children to go to school or even be let out of the house alone, it was members of the Press wanting to know how the investigation was going. He hadn't known what to say to either group. How was he supposed to know if it was safe for children to be let out? And didn't the Press realise he wasn't in charge of the investigation?

Sergeant Dobbs came into his office and deposited a cup of coffee on the blotter. 'The lads have come back, sir. All the house to house enquiries have been done.'

'Very good,' Oakenshaw said. 'Make sure you update Craynebrook with the results. Was there anything of interest?'

'I don't think so. It seems this fella got away without anyone seeing him. You wouldn't credit it, would you?'

'You certainly wouldn't. Considering it was broad daylight.' Oakenshaw took a mouthful of coffee. 'I've had a

99

telephone call from DC Rudd at Craynebrook. Inspector Lund thinks this vagrant we told them about sounds a prime candidate for the gunman and he wants us to find him. So, let the lads have a cup of tea and something to eat and then send them back out. And if they don't have any luck, get on to the local stations and get them to keep an eye out for him.'

'Yes, sir.'

'Have you got anywhere with the names that would have been in the gun register?'

Dobbs nodded. 'I contacted the manager of the local shooting club and got his rifles, and he gave me the names and addresses of those members who have their own guns. I've spoken with them and they're bringing their rifles in now. I also got the five rifles from the chap who runs the Boy Scouts. And I've checked. None of the owners have a criminal record, so I really don't think the gun used will turn out to be any of theirs.'

'No problems getting these men to hand over the rifles?'

'No, sir. Most of them were only too willing to help. The Boy Scout chap got a bit het up. I think he thought I was accusing him of being the gunman.' Dobbs chuckled. 'Nervous chap. Wouldn't say boo to a goose. I can't see him knowing one end of a gun from another.'

'It was always going to be a long shot,' Oakenshaw said. 'If the gunman has any sense, he would have got rid of the rifle immediately after the shooting.' He looked up at Dobbs. 'You are sure those were all the names in the register?'

'I'm sure, sir,' Dobbs said with a confident nod.

'That's something, I suppose. I won't pretend it didn't make us look very bad to admit the register was damaged. I just hope the Press doesn't get hold of it. They would have a field day.'

'I'm sure it won't get out, sir.'

Oakenshaw grunted, not at all as certain as his sergeant.

'Are you sure we should do this, sir?' Denham asked as he and Lund strode down the hospital corridor. 'The doctor didn't seem that happy about letting us talk to him.'

'I don't give a toss about the doctor,' Lund said. 'We need to find out what that boy saw.' He came to a halt outside a pair of doors and looked up at the name painted above. 'This is it, isn't it? Peachcroft Ward?'

'Yes, this is the one,' Denham nodded unhappily. 'But if the boy is still in shock—'

Lund threw open the door and headed inside. He stopped a passing nurse and asked for Timmy Lane. A little bewildered by his brusqueness, the nurse pointed to a bed at the far end of the ward. Lund marched off.

Denham reluctantly followed. 'You'll need to be gentle with him, sir,' he said.

'Will I?' Lund shot back, and came to a halt at the foot of Timmy's bed.

Timmy took up barely a third of the bed, and his body looked unbearably frail in the blue and white striped pyjamas he wore. His parents sat on either side and they looked over at the two policemen warily.

'I'm Inspector Lund, Craynebrook CID,' Lund said. 'This is DS Denham. We need to talk to your son.'

'You can't,' Mrs Lane said. 'He's still very upset.'

'He looks all right to me.' Lund tossed his hat onto the mattress and hitched himself up on the bed. 'Now then, Timmy. What happened in the cinema?'

Timmy sank lower in the bed and pulled the blankets up to his chin.

Lund sighed. 'Come on, boy. Tell me what you saw.'

Timmy shook his head.

'He doesn't want to talk to you, inspector,' Mr Lane said.

'And the doctor said—,' Mrs Lane began, but Lund cut her off.

'I don't care what the doctor says. I'm investigating a mass murder and I don't have the time to wait for your son to pull himself together. So, come on, Timmy. Talk to me.'

'Do something,' Mrs Lane appealed to her husband.

Mr Lane rose and grabbed hold of Lund's arm. 'I can't allow this.'

Lund shrugged him off and leaned over Timmy. 'You're going to tell me exactly what you saw in the cinema yesterday. A man came in with a gun, yes? What did he look like?'

Timmy tried to get away from Lund, drawing his knees up to his chin and pulling the blanket higher.

But Lund tugged the blanket away. 'Don't play the idiot with me, boy. I'm too bloody tired to put up with it. So, come on, tell me what you saw. What did he look like? Did he say anything?'

'Inspector, I must insist you leave our boy alone,' Mr Lane declared.

'I'm getting angry now, Timmy,' Lund said, ignoring Mr Lane.

'Sir,' Denham said, 'I really think—'

'You shut your face, sergeant, or I'll shut it for you.'

Denham looked helplessly at Mr Lane, who suddenly stormed off down the ward.

'You can't make him talk to you,' Mrs Lane cried, trying to push Lund off the bed.

'I reckon I can,' Lund said menacingly. 'I reckon Timmy will talk to me if I threaten to take him down the station and put him in a cell.'

'Sir!' Denham cried.

'Do you think I'm joking, son?' Lund went on. 'Well,

I'm not. If you don't tell me what happened in the cinema, I'll lock you up and—'

'Inspector! Stop this at once!'

The man's voice, loud and authoritative, did what neither Mrs Lane nor Denham had managed to do. Lund turned. So did Denham, who was relieved to see a man in a white coat standing beside the bed. Mr Lane had fetched the doctor.

'This is outrageous,' the doctor said. 'How dare you come into my hospital and bully my patients in this way?'

'I'm doing what I have to do to find a killer,' Lund declared. 'You mind your own business, doc.'

'This is my business. And I will not be spoken to in this way. You will leave, inspector, before I have you thrown out.'

Lund held the doctor's gaze for a long moment, as if trying to work out how far he could push him. Denham watched him, wondering what the hell he would do if Lund didn't back down. But Lund looked down at Timmy, saw the boy crying in his mother's arms, and grabbed his hat.

'Probably couldn't tell us anything, anyway,' he muttered. He put his hat on his head, gave the doctor another hard stare, then pushed past him and strode off towards the exit.

'I'm so sorry,' Denham said to the Lanes before hurrying after him.

Superintendent Mullinger sighed silently as the voice at the other end of the line droned on. What a windbag Oakenshaw was. Mullinger wished he had listened to his wife and not gone into the station today. It was almost unheard of for him to venture into work on a Sunday, but he had thought it his duty, considering the seriousness of the case, to show his face and make sure his men had everything under control. But no sooner had he sat down at his desk than he had Oakenshaw on the telephone, complaining about Lund.

'I'm sure the doctor exaggerates,' Mullinger said when Oakenshaw paused for breath. 'Lund has to press for information. But I will have a word with him, yes. We don't want any more complaints.'

He got rid of Oakenshaw, dropping the receiver into the cradle with another sigh. This was all he needed. As if it wasn't enough to have the Press clamouring for information and Headquarters wanting to be kept updated, he had an inspector moaning to him about one of his men. *Trust Stannard to be on leave at a time like this*, Mullinger thought. *I wouldn't be getting telephone calls like this if he was in charge.* He tapped his pen on the desktop as he wondered what to do about Lund.

There came a knock at the door. 'Come in,' he called, and the door opened. 'Yes, Denham. What is it?'

'I need to talk to you about Inspector Lund, sir.'

What now? Mullinger thought irritably. He waved Denham in. 'What about him?'

'I don't think he's fit to lead the investigation,' Denham said. 'We were at the hospital earlier. The inspector wanted to question the Lane boy even though the doctor warned us he was still very upset. Just one look at the kid and you could see he was still suffering, but that didn't stop the inspector. He threatened to lock him in a cell if he didn't tell him what he saw. The boy was terrified. After what he'd been through yesterday, it wasn't fair on him.'

Mullinger glanced at his telephone. So, there was something in what Oakenshaw had said after all. 'We all know Lund can be a little rough in his manner,' he said dismissively. 'It's his way. That doesn't make him unfit.' *Though,* he reminded himself, *hadn't that been what the barrister had said about Lund on Friday? That he'd been unfit to stand in the witness box?*

'But he upset him for nothing,' Denham persisted. 'He didn't get any information out of the boy. All he did was scare him so much he's probably clammed up for good. And I can't help thinking that DI Stannard would have handled the boy better. If he was leading the inves—'

'That's quite enough, Denham,' Mullinger cut him off sharply, annoyed the sergeant was thinking along the same lines as him. 'I'm surprised at you, coming to me like this to complain about a superior officer. Where's your sense of loyalty, man?'

'Sir—' Denham protested.

'No. Enough. I won't have this. Inspector Lund is in charge of the case and you must show him all due respect. This is too important a case to have this kind of dissension in the ranks. It looks very bad to the junior officers. Regardless of your personal feelings, Denham, I expect you to do your duty by Inspector Lund. Now, get back to work.'

He waved Denham towards the door. For a moment, he thought Denham wouldn't go – the sergeant's fists were clenched at his side and his jaw was set hard – and he had already decided he would put Denham on report if he refused. He wouldn't stand for any of that nonsense.

But Denham didn't argue. In fact, he didn't say another word, just headed for the door and left the superintendent's office, very nearly, but not quite, slamming the door behind him.

Mullinger leant back in his chair and swore under his breath. His wife had been right. He should have stayed at home.

10

Matthew pulled the curtains, switched on the lamp, turned on the wireless and settled into his armchair, patting his lap for Bella to jump up. He stroked her until she curled up, then reached for the sandwich he had made and opened the *Wisden Almanack* he had not yet had a chance to read.

He was pleased with how the lunch had gone; the beef had been a little overdone for his liking, Pat insisting it needed longer in the oven, but the roast potatoes had been crispy, and he hadn't boiled the vegetables to mush as his sister usually did. The Yorkshire puddings hadn't risen as much as he would have liked, but they had tasted fine. Amanda had said it was the best meal she'd ever had, making Pat silently fume because their mother never praised her cooking, Matthew knew. He'd enjoyed playing host, but he'd been glad too when Pat said she needed to get back to the pub to help Fred and they left. It was nice to have the flat all to himself.

The dance tune playing on the wireless ended and the news came on. Matthew set down his *Wisden* and turned the volume up.

"A female victim of the massacre that took place

yesterday afternoon at The Regal Picture Palace in Foxhall Green, East London, has died from her wounds," the newsreader said. "Mrs Emily Watts, twenty-nine, was being cared for at the local hospital for a gunshot wound to the chest when her condition suddenly deteriorated earlier today. She died a short while later. The police have not yet identified the gunman but are interested in talking with a vagrant who had been seen in the Foxhall Green area and who has since vanished. Mrs Watts leaves behind a husband and nine-year-old daughter. The daughter was also at the cinema and was wounded, but is expected to make a full recovery."

So, that makes twelve dead, Matthew thought as the newsreader moved on to the second item. Would there be any more? *Stop wondering*, he told himself angrily, reaching for his book as the doorbell rang. Groaning, Matthew lifted Bella off his lap and rose to answer it.

'I know I should have waited for an invitation,' Dickie said when Matthew opened the door, 'but with you, that could take forever, so I thought I'd come round, anyway. And you'll let me in because I come bearing gifts.' He held up both hands. In the left was a small cake tin. 'This is from Emma,' he said, 'and this,' he waggled the bottle of whisky in his right hand, 'is from me.'

'You didn't need to bring anything,' Matthew said, gesturing for him to step inside.

'Try telling my wife that. Well, let's have a look at your new place, shall we? Emma will want a full report.'

Matthew showed him around the flat, not believing for one minute that Dickie had come just to see his new home.

'Very nice,' Dickie declared when they finished in the sitting room. 'A big improvement on your old place.' He pointed at the wireless. 'Is that new?'

'A present from my mother.'

'Who's a lucky boy, then?' Dickie said. 'You going to open that whisky I brought or not?'

Matthew fetched two glasses from the kitchen, grabbing a knife and two plates for the cake he knew would be in the tin from Dickie's wife. He returned to the sitting room, gave Dickie the knife so he could cut the cake, and poured two generous measures of whisky. Dickie handed him a plate with a slice of fruit cake.

Matthew took a bite and waited, knowing Dickie would get to the reason for his visit soon enough.

'I was in Foxhall Green today,' Dickie said. 'I didn't see any of your lot. Just the local bobbies.'

'Lund must be working out of Craynebrook.' Matthew took a mouthful of whisky and another bite of the cake.

'Well, aren't you going to ask me what I found out?' Dickie cried in exasperation.

'I'm not interested.'

'Don't give me that.'

'It's not my case, Dickie.'

'Well, I'm going to tell you, anyway. I interviewed the vicar of Foxhall Green. Reverend Bertram Laing. Now, there's a nasty piece of work for you. It made my skin crawl just being in the same room as him. You should have heard his sermon this morning. Just picture this. He's got a church full of grieving relatives and instead of saying comforting things about how their loved ones are in heaven and all that, he has a go at them for not going to church and practically blaming them for the shooting.'

'I don't imagine that went down well?'

'That was just it! Everyone sat there as meek as mice. Not a single voice of protest or outrage. That's not right, is it? Someone should have told him what a callous bleeder he was being.'

'So, write about him in your 'paper if you're that bothered.'

'Oh, I'm going to. Don't you worry. You know, I could swear Laing's glad the shooting happened because it's given him material for his book. And there's another thing.' Dickie poured more whisky into his glass. 'Laing wasn't anywhere to be found on Saturday afternoon. I went looking for him, thinking to get a quote about the shooting, but I couldn't find him anywhere. And the Boy Scout rifles are stored in his vestry cupboard, where he could take one any time he wanted.'

'You can't accuse this vicar of being the gunman just because you don't like him, Dickie,' Matthew said.

'Why not?' Dickie said indignantly. 'That's exactly what Laing's done. He's put your lot onto a tramp he didn't like the look of it.'

'I heard about that on the wireless.'

'All Laing's doing, and you know what I reckon that is? Diversionary tactics. He's getting your lot to look the other way. But I can just picture him talking aim at all those poor sods in the cinema as if they were no more than sitting ducks. If you ask me, Reverend Laing should be number one on your suspect list.'

Matthew sighed. 'I don't have a suspect list. Tell Lund. Not me.'

'Lund won't listen to me.' Dickie pointed at Matthew. 'But he might to you.'

'I'm not getting involved. Lund's made it clear he doesn't want me anywhere near this case.'

'Lund's making a pig's ear of it.'

'You don't know that.'

'I do know that, if what I've heard is true.'

Matthew knew Dickie was dangling bait before him.

But he couldn't help himself. He had to bite. 'What have you heard?'

Dickie popped the last bit of cake in his mouth and leaned towards Matthew. 'That there's been a complaint made against him by a doctor and one of the victim's parents. Something about Lund bullying this kid at the hospital.'

'And who did you hear that from?'

Dickie shook his head. 'That's confidential.'

'If one of us is talking—'

'I never said I heard it from a copper. Anyway, it's not important who told me. What is important is catching this killer and those relatives should have better than Lund heading the investigation.'

'Don't say it, Dickie.'

'You should be in charge.'

'I'm on leave,' Matthew said angrily. 'The first leave I've had in months and I'd really like to enjoy the few hours I've got left, Dickie. And I was enjoying them until you turned up. I had the wireless on, my cat on my lap, and a *Wisden* to read. I was perfectly happy.'

Dickie gave him a look that suggested he didn't believe a word.

Pete Ashe pushed open the door of the pub and looked around for his regular drinking companions. He found them standing at the bar and made his way over.

Benny Cross was laughing, but as he turned to see who had joined him and his friends, the grin froze on his face. 'Pete!' he said, casting a wary glance at Keith and Scott. 'We didn't expect to see you tonight.'

'I had to get out of the house,' Pete said. 'The wife won't

stop crying. It was doing my head in. You going to get me a drink or what?'

'Yeah. Course.' Benny signalled to the barmaid. 'Pint of bitter over here, love.' The pint came up and Benny passed it to Pete.

'We were really sorry to hear about Frankie,' Keith said when the silence went on a little too long.

'I heard they think a tramp did it,' Scott said. 'That's what they said on the wireless, anyway.'

'What tramp?' Pete asked.

Scott shrugged. 'The bloke in the newsagent told me a tramp's been hanging around the high street the last few weeks. Big bloke. Old soldier, he reckoned. Only he ain't been seen since Saturday.'

'I think I've seen him,' Keith said thoughtfully. 'Wears a big overcoat. Dirty old geezer.'

'When the police catch him, they better string him up,' Benny said.

'If they catch him,' Scott said. 'If you ask me, they ain't got a clue how to find him. They'd have had him by now if they did.'

'Yeah, and I tell you something,' Keith said. 'If they do catch him, he'll probably get off because some smart arse solicitor will claim he's not right in the head.'

'Why wouldn't he be right in the head?' Scott wondered.

'Old soldier, ain't he?' Keith shrugged. 'There'll be a load of guff about the war making him mad. I mean, it stands to reason. You've got to be off your head to kill all those people.'

'They better not let him get away with it,' Benny said. 'If he killed Pete's boy, then he's got to be made to pay. That's right, ain't it?' He looked around at the others. 'If he comes back here, we've got to get him?'

Keith and Scott exchanged another glance and didn't answer.

Benny scowled at them. 'Call yourself men? Look at him.' He pointed to Pete, who was staring glumly into his pint. 'He's your mate and you're going to do nothing to get the bastard what did for his boy?'

Pete turned his head to Keith and Scott, the same question in his eyes.

'All right, Benny,' Keith said. 'Keep your hair on. You know we'll get him with you. Won't we, Scott?'

'Yeah,' Scott said, not meeting Benny's fierce glare. 'You know we will.'

'Right. That's decided, then. If we see him, he's for it.' Benny banged his empty glass down on the counter and jabbed his elbow into Keith's ribs. 'Get 'em in, old son.'

11

Monday, 20th October 1930

Only Denham was in the office when Matthew walked into CID at half-past eight on Monday morning. The sergeant had the telephone to his ear and nodded a greeting as Matthew entered.

'Yes,' Denham said into the receiver. 'I'll tell him. Thanks.' He hung up. 'Morning, sir.'

'Morning,' Matthew returned. 'Where is everyone?'

'Rudd's looking into a lead over in Graydon Heath. Bissett's over in Colmbridge and Barnes is at the mortuary.' He looked away. 'For the post-mortems.'

Matthew glanced over at his office. 'And Inspector Lund?'

'I don't know,' Denham said. 'I haven't seen him this morning.'

Matthew said nothing, but wondered at the criticism he'd seen in the sergeant's eyes. He moved to the tea urn and poured himself a mug. 'I heard one of the wounded died yesterday.'

'That's right. Mrs Watts fell into a coma and didn't

wake up. Her husband and daughter didn't even get to say goodbye. Can you imagine that?'

'I don't have a wife or kids,' Matthew said with a shake of his head. 'So, no. I can't.'

'I do have a wife and daughter,' Denham said, 'and I can imagine it. This killer has to be caught. He can't get away with it.'

'He won't. You'll catch him.'

'I wish I could be sure of that,' Denham said savagely.

'It's been less than two days since the shooting, Denham,' Matthew said, a little taken aback by how angry the sergeant was. 'You know these things can take time.'

'And you know, sir, the longer the investigation goes on, the less likely we are to catch the killer. And with Lund in charge, this investigation could go on forever.'

'That's Inspector Lund, Denham,' Matthew reminded him.

'You sound like the Super,' Denham said sourly. 'He thinks I'm being disloyal and disrespectful. But it's difficult to have respect for a superior officer when he's acting the way he is. You don't know what he did yesterday at the hospital to Timmy Lane. The doctor threw us out.'

Matthew narrowed his eyes at Denham. Was this where Dickie had got his information about Lund's complaint? 'Have you been talking to the Press, Denham?'

Denham glared at him. 'No, I have not been talking to the Press, sir. I'm not Gary Pinder.'

'I hope not. Because we've had enough of that here, wouldn't you say?'

Denham jumped up from his chair. 'Forget the Press. Why won't you listen? Lund isn't going to catch this gunman. You have to do something, sir.'

'There's nothing I can do,' Matthew shot back angrily.

First Dickie, now Denham. 'You have to let Lund do his job.'

'But he's not doing it. We've made no progress since Saturday. None at all. We've got no idea who we're looking for.' He grabbed his notebook and waved it at Matthew. 'All these leads that have come in. They'll come to nothing.'

'What about this vagrant?' Matthew asked. 'Is he a strong suspect?'

The question pricked Denham's anger and he fell back into his chair with a heavy sigh. He rooted through the paperwork on his desk to find the notes on the tramp. 'I wouldn't say strong. Just convenient, if you want my opinion.' He held out a sheet of paper with what little was known of Sergeant Ambrose Brock.

Matthew reached to take it as Lund walked in.

'What's that?' Lund pointed at the paper.

'It's what we have on the tramp,' Denham said.

Lund snatched it out of his hand. 'Then it's not for him, is it?' He turned to Matthew. 'I thought you were in court this morning.'

'Not until ten,' Matthew said, following Lund into their office. He closed the door, then wished he hadn't, as the enclosed space made the odour emanating from Lund even more potent. Lund hadn't shaved and was wearing the same shirt he'd worn on Saturday.

Matthew opened the window, then took out his cigarettes and lit one. 'Is everything all right?' he asked.

'Marvellous,' Lund said, slamming one desk drawer shut and opening another. He swore and drove the drawer back in, making the desk shudder. 'Give me one of your fags. I'm all out.'

Matthew tossed his packet to Lund. 'Keep it. I'll get some more.'

Lund lit one and pocketed the packet. 'How did the move go?'

'Fine. I'm all settled in. I had my family round for lunch yesterday.'

'How nice for you.'

Matthew ignored the sarcasm. 'I hear you've got a suspect.'

'That's right. A tramp that was stinking up the high street. Upset a lot of the locals. Oakenshaw's got his lads out looking for him.'

'Did any of the locals report he had a rifle?'

'Not that I know of.'

'They why is he a suspect?'

'Because he is.'

'You mean because he's a tramp and you haven't got anyone else?' Matthew said.

Lund slammed his hand on the desk. 'What did I tell you the other night, Stannard? This isn't your case. Keep your nose out of my business.' Denham knocked on the door and Lund barked, 'What do you want?'

Denham entered. 'Barnes just called in,' he said. 'Dr Wallace has completed the post-mortem on the usherette, Lucy Simpson.'

'So what? He's got plenty of them to do. I don't need to know every time he finishes one.'

Denham's jaw tightened. 'He thought you'd want to know what he found. But if you don't...' He backed out of the door.

'Get back in here,' Lund said irritably. 'What did he find?'

'She was pregnant.'

'Oh, blimey. Is that all?'

Denham glanced at Matthew. *See what I mean?* his eyes said.

Matthew blew out a plume of smoke. 'I expect Dr Wallace, knowing Lucy Simpson wasn't married, thought her being pregnant out of wedlock might be a motive for killing her.'

'Yes, sir,' Denham said to Lund. 'That is what Dr Wallace suggested.'

'So, now I've got pathologists telling me how to run this investigation,' Lund said, glowering at Matthew. 'I wish everyone would mind their own business.'

'It's something we've got to look into, sir,' Denham protested.

'I decide what we look into, Denham,' Lund said.

Matthew saw Denham's anger returning. 'Why don't you let Denham follow it up?' he suggested to Lund with a shrug. 'If there's nothing in it, Denham will be able to tell soon enough.'

'I can do that,' Denham agreed.

Lund rose, looking from one to the other. 'I'll look into it,' he growled. 'If only to shut you two up.'

Herbert cast a glance around the small canteen and unfolded his newspaper. He didn't normally take *The Chronicle*, but he'd seen the headline in the newsagent's that morning and decided he had to find out what the article said. KILLER STILL AT LARGE, the headline blared, and he read the first paragraph as he dropped two cubes of sugar into his tea. A few minutes later, his tea slopped into the saucer as Dennis dropped into the chair opposite and banged against the table.

'I'm so sorry,' Dennis muttered as Herbert tipped the tea back into the cup. 'I'm rather clumsy today.'

Herbert banged the cup down on the saucer. 'You look tired,' he observed, and returned his gaze to the newspaper.

'I am,' Dennis groaned. 'I've hardly had a wink for the past three nights.'

'I thought your doctor prescribed sleeping draughts for you?'

'He did, but I don't like taking them all the time. They make me groggy. And I feel I rather need my wits about me at the moment.'

This last remark intrigued Herbert. He looked up from the newspaper and frowned. 'Why would you need your wits about you?'

Dennis looked around the canteen, then leaned towards Herbert. 'The police came to see me yesterday after church. They took the Scout rifles away for testing. And,' he lowered his voice, 'they took my fingerprints. The policeman said it was for elimination purposes, but if that was the case, why only take mine? After all, I'm not the only one who's handled the rifles. All the boys have used them during my marksmanship classes, so the police should have taken all theirs, shouldn't they? And anyway, it's ridiculous. As if you're going to put the rifle back after the shooting? You'd get rid of it, wouldn't you?'

'Would you?' Herbert wondered.

'Well, of course you would,' Dennis cried. 'You'd be stupid to leave the gun where the police would find it.'

'How would you get rid of it?'

'Throw it in the river. Or break it up and bury it. I certainly wouldn't be stupid enough to put it back in the trunk.'

'No, I suppose you wouldn't,' Herbert agreed, narrowing his eyes at Dennis. 'So, what are you worrying about? Presumably, the rifles will be tested and they'll be able to determine they weren't used in the cinema.'

'It's not just the rifles,' Dennis said miserably. 'I'm worried the police will find out about the boy.'

'The boy?'

'Frankie Ashe.'

'What about him?'

'He's dead.'

'I know he is.'

'Well…'

Herbert shook his head. 'I'm sorry, Dennis, you've lost me. Why does Frankie Ashe matter?'

'Oh, come on, Herbert. You know what a brat that boy was to me. All the trouble he caused at Scouts.'

'He caused trouble for a lot of people.'

'Yes, I know, but I've been wondering if I should tell the police about the trouble he caused me. Before anyone else does, I mean. That way, it won't look as if I've been hiding anything. And if Lewis told them what Frankie did to him, then it wouldn't look so bad for me, I wouldn't be the only one, and—'

'I won't have Lewis involved with the police,' Herbert said sharply. Heads turned in their direction, and Herbert lowered his voice. 'And if I were you, Dennis, I wouldn't be in a rush to volunteer information. You may be able to play it down with the police but there's no getting away from the fact that you hated the Ashe boy. I daresay you're even glad he's dead, despite what you said to Lewis in the church the other day.'

'That's not fair, Herbert,' Dennis cried. 'I'm sure I'm not the only one who's glad he's gone.'

'So. you are glad he's dead?'

Dennis's eyes widened in horror. 'I didn't mean that.'

'That's what it sounded like. And do you think the police will believe your protestations of innocence once they know that's how you felt about him and when they hear what you did to him on Saturday? Oh yes. Lewis told me all about that little incident, when you tried to strangle the boy. It wouldn't look good for you if the police heard about that, would it? Think, Dennis. You hated the boy, you'd already tried to kill him once, and you had the rifles to shoot him with.' Herbert shook his head. 'If you go to the police and blab, they'll arrest you before you can blink.'

'Well, I could say the same about Lewis! He hated Frankie just as much as me, and he knows where the rifles are kept. The police could as easily arrest him.'

'How dare you bring Lewis into this!' Herbert said in a shocked voice. 'To try to put the blame onto my son, who's never done you any harm and wouldn't hurt a fly? It's despicable, Dennis. Utterly despicable.'

Dennis's face crumpled. 'I didn't mean it. I'm sorry, Herbert. I don't know what I'm saying.'

Herbert's expression softened a little. 'I daresay it's because you're tired, Dennis. All you need is rest and you'll feel a lot better.'

'But if the police suspect me—'

'It says here in the newspaper they're looking for a tramp,' Herbert said, pointing to a line of text in *The Chronicle*. 'So, they don't suspect you, do they? Please, put it out of your head of telling the police anything. Think of your mother if you end up getting put in prison. What will become of her?'

'I hadn't thought of Mother,' Dennis said miserably.

'Well, you should. I think it will be best for you, best for everyone, if you keep your mouth shut. Don't you agree?'

Dennis nodded. 'You're right. I won't say another word.'

Denham banged the knocker of No. 23 Kildare Road.

The door opened a few minutes later by a man in his shirtsleeves, his dark-blue braces hanging loosely over his sloping shoulders. His sore, tired eyes stared blankly at Lund and Denham.

Denham held up his warrant card. 'We're very sorry to bother you, Mr Simpson. I'm DS Denham and this is DI Lund from Craynebrook CID. We'd like to talk to you about your daughter.'

At the mention of his daughter, Mr Simpson's eyes watered, but he blinked away the incipient tears and nodded for the two detectives to step inside. He gestured them through to the sitting room where Mrs Simpson was slumped on a settee, a handkerchief held to her nose. Her hair was unbrushed and no makeup adorned her face.

'It's the police, Ethel,' Mr Simpson told her.

She said nothing as Lund took a seat without asking. Denham stayed standing by the sitting-room door, notebook at the ready.

Mr Simpson sat down beside his wife. 'We heard on the wireless you think a tramp did it? Is that right?'

Lund nodded. 'He's a suspect, yeah.'

'I can't imagine why a tramp would want to kill Lucy. Or any of those people. Especially children.'

Lund sniffed and wiped his nose with the back of his hand. 'Talking of kids. Did you know your daughter was in the family way?'

Denham winced. Mr and Mrs Simpson stared at Lund.

'That's not true,' Mrs Simpson rasped, her eyes burning into Lund. 'You're lying.'

'Lucy couldn't have been pregnant,' Mr Simpson said. 'You've made a mistake.'

Lund shook his head. 'There's no mistake. Your daughter was four months gone.'

Mrs Simpson grabbed her husband's hand. 'Why didn't she tell us? Who?'

'That's what I want to know,' Lund said. 'Who was she seeing?'

'Lucy wasn't seeing anyone,' Mrs Simpson said.

'She had to be seeing someone,' Lund said impatiently. 'What boys did she know?'

'She didn't bring boys home,' Mr Simpson said, still a little bewildered. 'We never really knew any of her friends. Lucy was always out.'

'Working,' Mrs Simpson said. 'Lucy was always working at the cinema. I told her the morning she was—' She broke off and Mr Simpson took hold of her hand. She gripped his so tight her knuckles turned white. Drawing in a deep, steadying breath, she continued. 'I told her she oughten to work so hard and that she should try for a job at the Majestic over in Craynebrook if she liked working in the cinema so much. If only she'd listened to me...'

'She would still have been at the Regal on Saturday, dear,' Mr Simpson said. 'There's nothing we could have done about that.'

'We should have stopped her from working there in the first place. She could have had that job in the shoe shop at the other end of the high street. She would have been safe there.'

'Look,' Lund sighed impatiently, 'this is all very well and good, but some fella got her pregnant and I need to know who. So, she didn't bring anyone home. Did Lucy talk about any men to you?'

'Lucy was too young for all that,' Mrs Simpson said, her voice becoming shrill. 'She was an innocent.'

Lund snorted. 'Innocent girls don't get themselves pregnant, Mrs Simpson.'

Mrs Simpson glared at him. 'She didn't get herself pregnant. If she was going to have a baby, it wasn't her fault.

Some man must have forced himself upon her and Lucy was too ashamed to tell us.'

'You can kid yourself with that if you like,' Lund shrugged. 'But you'd be surprised at the number of parents I've known who haven't had a clue what their daughters have got up to. And plenty of girls get up to all sorts that they wouldn't want their parents to know. I reckon your Lucy was one of those.'

'How dare you!' Mr Simpson jumped to his feet. 'How dare you talk about our daughter in that way as if she was some kind of... of...' He couldn't bring himself to say the word 'tart'.

'Well, maybe she was,' Lund said.

It happened so fast, Denham didn't see it coming. Mrs Simpson jumped out of her chair and slapped Lund's face. The blow was struck with such force that it sent Lund crashing sideways on the settee.

'Get out,' Mrs Simpson screamed at him. 'Get out of my house.'

'You mad cow,' Lund cried as blood poured from his nose. 'Look what you've done.'

'Get out,' she cried again, and pulled him off the settee.

'We're going, Mrs Simpson,' Denham assured her, grabbing hold of Lund and manoeuvring him into the hall. As he opened the front door, he looked back and saw Mrs Simpson collapsed in the sitting-room doorway, mewling like an animal.

He shoved Lund onto the doorstep and pulled the front door shut. Pressing his own handkerchief into Lund's bloodied hand, he headed for the police car parked at the kerb.

12

Matthew was needed at court for less than two hours, and he returned to Craynebrook to find an empty CID. He sat down at his desk, lit a cigarette, and discovered that in his absence, Lund had filled his In tray with the cases he no longer had the time to look into. Topmost was a case of petty theft Matthew knew Lund had been working on for weeks and getting nowhere. He opened the file with a sigh, knowing he had no choice but to take over the case and all the others Lund had lumbered him with.

He'd been reading through the file for about fifteen minutes when Rudd walked into the outer office. Matthew watched as the detective constable shrugged off his coat and threw it over the back of his chair, kicking at the legs to turn it around before falling into it with a sigh. There was an air of dejection about him Matthew hadn't seen before.

Matthew rose and moved to his office doorway. 'After-noon, Rudd,' he said.

Rudd bolted out of his chair. 'I didn't see you there, sir. You made me jump.'

'Sorry.' Matthew waved him back into his seat. 'I hear you've been over to Graydon Heath.'

'Yes, sir. The local nick thought they had a potential suspect, but he turned out to be just a nutter who likes to walk up and down the high street, swearing at people. But he was in the hospital Saturday afternoon, so he's got the perfect alibi.'

Matthew nodded ruefully. 'Is that all you've got?'

'No. We've got plenty of leads, but most of them are from cranks. I don't understand why people have to muddy the waters by calling us with useless information. Especially in a case like this.'

'Some genuinely think they're being helpful. The rest just like the attention.' Matthew turned towards the door at the sound of footsteps in the corridor. A moment later, Barnes walked in carrying a large cardboard box. 'What have you got there?' he asked as Barnes set the box down on the evidence table.

'Personal effects of the victims from the mortuary,' Barnes said. 'Clothes, mostly. The women's handbags. Keys and wallets. We don't need to keep them, do we?'

'If they've all been checked, they can probably be returned to the next of kin,' Matthew said. 'If they want them, that is. It's up to Inspector Lund.'

'I'll ask him when he gets in,' Barnes said. 'Anyone want a cuppa?'

'I'll have one,' Matthew said, leaning against his door frame and lighting a cigarette. *Anything to keep me from petty theft for a few more minutes,* he thought. There were more footsteps in the corridor outside and Denham walked in.

'You're just in time for tea,' Barnes said with a smile, which fell off his face when he saw his friend's grim expression. 'Something wrong? Where's the inspector?'

'Don't talk to me about him.' Denham dragged out his chair and sat down with a heavy sigh.

'What's happened, Denham?' Matthew asked.

'We went to see the Simpsons,' Denham said. 'You'd think the inspector would be tactful, wouldn't you? Show some compassion, some understanding. But oh no, not him. For starters, the Simpsons can't believe their daughter was pregnant. They think we've got it wrong. Then, when they accept that she was pregnant, they're thinking that some fella forced himself on her, but the inspector laughs off that idea and as good as calls their daughter a prostitute. Well, you can imagine how the Simpsons took that. Mrs Simpson went mad. She slapped the inspector round the face and gave him a nosebleed. The inspector called her a mad cow and Mrs Simpson screams at him to get out. I had to force him out of the house.' He glared at Matthew. 'I knew something like this would happen.'

Matthew held his gaze, knowing Denham was as angry with him as he was with Lund. Maybe he should have done something about Lund as Denham asked. But what could he have done? He couldn't have known Lund would put his size nines in it. And if he'd tried to tell him to behave himself, Lund would have told him to stick his advice where the sun didn't shine.

'Where is the inspector now?' he asked.

'I have no idea,' Denham said in a tone that suggested he didn't care. 'He said he had something to do and that I was to come back here.'

'He's probably gone down the pub,' Barnes said in a low voice as he handed Matthew a mug of tea.

Matthew took it, wondering if he should pop over the pub and see if Lund was indeed there. But what could he do if he was? Grab him by the scruff of the neck and drag him back to CID? What good would that do? Best to leave him be.

'You all know what you should be doing?' he asked the

detectives, feeling someone should be supervising their work.

They nodded and said yes, and Matthew returned to his office to continue with the petty theft case file. *If I was in charge of the massacre,* he thought as he read the list of the stolen items, then stopped himself. He wasn't in charge, and there was no use wishing.

Oakenshaw stepped down onto the doorstep, turned to say goodbye, and Mr Simpson slammed the front door in his face.

His lips pursing in irritation and embarrassment, Oakenshaw strode off down the path, yanking open the rear door of the car and climbing inside. He sank into the leather with a groan. 'Back to the station, Stevens. And be quick about it.'

'I'll have you there in just a couple of minutes,' Stevens said, and cast a glance at Oakenshaw in the rearview mirror as he pulled away from the kerb. 'Is everything all right, sir?'

'No, Stevens. Everything is very far from all right. I've never had to endure such an interview in all my days in the Force.'

'Were the Simpsons complaining no one's been caught yet?'

'No. They were complaining, but only about Inspector Lund.'

'The inspector? Why? What's he done?'

'He was exceedingly rude about their daughter and insulted Mrs Simpson. I won't repeat what they told me he said, and frankly, if it's true, and I have no reason to believe it isn't, I can't blame them for complaining. I didn't know what to say except apologise and assure them I would inform his superior. Again!'

'That's awkward for you, sir. After all, you're not responsible for the Craynebrook lot, are you? But I suppose, in the public's eyes, we're all the same.' Stevens turned the car into the station's road. 'Oh, blimey,' he muttered, and slowed the car.

'What is it?' Oakenshaw leaned forward to look out of the windscreen. He groaned when he saw the huddle of men and women bearing notebooks and cameras. 'The Press. That's all I need.'

Stevens pulled up at the kerb. Oakenshaw got out, hoping to make a dash for the station doors, but the reporters crowded around him and blocked his path.

'Inspector Oakenshaw. Have you made an arrest yet?'

'Have you found the tramp you're looking for?'

'Is he the only suspect?'

'Are you close to catching the killer?'

Oakenshaw pushed them out of his way. 'You'll have to ask Inspector Lund of Craynebrook CID. He's heading the investigation.' He was at the bottom of the station steps. Just a few more seconds and he'd be out of their reach.

'Inspector, inspector!' A woman grabbed hold of his sleeve. 'Is it true a complaint has been made today against Inspector Lund by a doctor at the hospital where the survivors are being treated?'

Trust the Press to get it wrong. And damn this woman for taking hold of him. 'That was yesterday,' Oakenshaw said, pulling his arm out of her grasp. 'The complaint today was made by a victim's parents.'

As soon as the words were out, Oakenshaw knew he had made a mistake. A barrage of questions hit him.

'Which victim?'

'Who were the parents?'

'What's the complaint about?'

Oakenshaw raised his hands. 'No, no,' he pleaded. 'That

was off the record and I have no further comment to make.' He pushed against the station's front door, but it didn't open, the damp weather causing the wood to swell and make it stick. He banged on the glass to get Sergeant Dobbs' attention and gesticulated frantically to be let in.

'Is Inspector Lund's ability to solve the case now in doubt?'

'I have absolute faith in Inspector Lund,' Oakenshaw cried as Dobbs opened the door, and he all but fell inside. 'Shut it,' he gasped, staring through the glass at the excited men and women outside.

Oh God, he thought. *What have I done?*

Mullinger stormed into Matthew's office. 'Where is Lund?' he demanded.

Matthew got to his feet. 'I don't know, sir. I haven't seen him. Is it something I can help with?'

Mullinger tutted in annoyance and paced the small room. 'I've just had Oakenshaw on the telephone. He was called to one of the victims' families an hour ago so they could lodge a complaint against Lund for rudeness. That's the second complaint he's made to me about Lund in as many days.'

Matthew decided not to admit he'd heard about the previous day's complaint, nor of Lund's behaviour with the Simpsons. He kept quiet, eyeing Denham through the partition window, knowing the sergeant was listening attentively.

'What is the matter with the man?' Mullinger went on. 'Doesn't he realise we're in the public eye with this case?'

'I'm sure Inspector Lund didn't mean to be rude.'

'Whether he meant to be rude is neither here nor there, Stannard. He was rude, complaints have been made, and now I have to deal with them. Not only that, but Oaken-shaw, the fool, told the Press about the complaints. This will be all over the newspapers.' He groaned and rubbed his forehead. 'I've also had the DAC on the telephone. With the massacre making the national news and no arrest being made, he's worried it looks as if we're dragging our feet. I explained to him the difficulties we have and that we are doing all we can, but he feels the mood may turn ugly and we need to get the public on our side. So, he wants me to hold a public meeting in Foxhall Green. Allay the public's fears and appeal for information. What do you think? Is it a good idea?'

Matthew was a little taken aback by Mullinger's question. The superintendent had never asked for his opinion before.

'I suppose it couldn't hurt,' he said. 'A public appeal might help, although it might also throw up a lot of false leads. And from what I've heard, we've got plenty of those already.'

'I agree. Personally, I'm not in favour of appealing to the public. It exposes our shortcomings, and with Lund offending every person he comes into contact with...' Mullinger trailed off, shaking his head. 'What progress is being made?'

'I couldn't tell you, sir,' Matthew protested.

'But damn it all, Stannard, I need to know what's happening.'

'Let me get Denham in here.' Matthew called for the sergeant and told him the superintendent wanted an update on the case.

Denham nodded and addressed himself to Mullinger. 'The lab has identified the casings as .303s and the box cartridge as fitting a Lee Enfield SMLE Mk III rifle. There were prints on the casings and on the box cartridge but they don't so far match any prints we have on file. Foxhall Green has recovered all the rifles they know about and they've been sent to the lab for testing. The post-mortem of Lucy Simpson revealed she was pregnant, which we believe might prove a motive for her murder. We haven't yet been able to identify who the father of her child was.' Denham glanced at Matthew, then back to Mullinger. 'The Simpsons were unhappy about talking to us.'

Denham wanted to say more, Matthew could tell, to let Mullinger know what had happened at the Simpsons, unaware the superintendent already knew. But knowing Mullinger had already ticked off the detective sergeant for complaining about Lund, Matthew thought it best if Denham returned to his desk before he got himself put on report, so he thanked Denham and told him he could go.

Mullinger watched Denham return to his desk. 'He's angry,' he said in a thoughtful voice.

'Denham was very upset by what he saw in the cinema,' Matthew said.

'I'm sure he was. You know, he complained to me about Lund after the hospital incident with the Lane boy.' He shook his head. 'I didn't listen. My mistake.'

Matthew didn't know what to say, so he kept quiet.

Mullinger turned back to him. 'I'll call Oakenshaw and tell him to arrange a meeting for tonight. I want everyone there, Stannard, and that includes you.' He glared at Lund's empty desk. 'And tell Lund I want to see him as soon as he gets back.'

Lund didn't return to CID until after five o'clock. He shuffled into the inspectors' office, fell into his chair, and belched loudly.

'Mullinger wants to see you,' Matthew said, noting the

crusted blood around Lund's nostrils and the black bruise across the bridge of his nose. He also didn't miss the smell of beer Lund had brought in with him.

Lund laughed hollowly. 'Oh, I knew that was coming. Let me guess. The Simpsons have made a complaint about me?'

Matthew shrugged. 'I don't know.'

'It's all right, Stannard. You can tell me. I'm a big boy. I'm going to get a carpeting from Old Mouldy, aren't I?'

'Yeah,' Matthew said, meeting Lund's eye. 'I reckon you are.'

'Oh, well. I suppose I might as well get it over with.' Lund slammed his palms down on the desk and pushed himself up. He swayed, then fell back down into his chair.

'How many have you had?' Matthew asked quietly, conscious of the open office door and the several pairs of listening ears.

'Not enough. Not nearly enough.' Lund pushed himself up again and managed this time to stay on his feet. He held his arms out to the side to show Matthew. 'There. Steady as a rock. Don't you worry about me, sunshine.' He headed for the door. 'I'm off to see Old Mouldy. I may be some time.'

13

For once, the station grapevine was silent regarding what happened between Mullinger and Lund. All Matthew knew was that Lund had had no more than a fifteen-minute meeting with the superintendent and that he had then left the station without a word to anyone. Everyone was wondering whether Lund had been suspended, but no word came from Mullinger and when Matthew walked into the Foxhall Green church hall, he saw Lund slouched in a chair by the trestle table set up at the far side, his head resting on his hand, his eyes closed, three chairs down from Oakenshaw, who seemed to be doing his best to ignore him.

Matthew crossed to Denham and Barnes, manoeuvring around the folding wooden chairs that filled most of the floor space and which were rapidly being occupied.

'We won't have to say anything, will we, sir?' Barnes asked, nodding at the growing crowd.

Matthew shook his head. 'I doubt it. Mr Mullinger will do most of the talking, and he'll call on Inspector Lund for anything else that needs to be said.'

'If he can open his mouth without putting his foot in it,' Denham muttered sourly.

Matthew let the comment pass, keeping his eyes on the people taking seats. Many were dressed in black, and he recognised some from the previous Saturday, when he had taken them around the hall to identify the victims. The women were dressed in blacks and dark greys, sombre hats with net veils covering their faces, and many of the men, if they weren't wearing a black suit, were wearing black armbands.

He saw Mullinger enter the hall with a tall man wearing a dog collar and realised this was Laing, the vicar Dickie had told him about. He studied him with interest, trying to see what Dickie had so disliked, but his eyes saw only a middle-aged vicar, a little pompous maybe, but nothing about him to suggest he was a ruthless killer. That Dickie was right about Laing craving attention, however, was made apparent when Matthew saw Laing tap Mullinger on the arm and gesture at the reporters occupying the back row. He pointed to the chairs at the front, but Mullinger shook his head and sliced the air with his hand. It didn't take a genius to work out Laing had wanted the Press at the front and the superintendent had refused. *Good for Mullinger*, Matthew thought.

Matthew watched Mullinger and Laing make their way to the trestle table. Mullinger greeted Oakenshaw with a nod, then took a seat, casting a disapproving look at Lund, who jerked awake and made some little effort to sit up. Laing stood before the empty chair on the superintendent's other side and clapped his hands to get attention. The hall quietened.

'Ladies and gentlemen,' Laing said. 'I'd like to thank you all for coming here this evening. I am glad myself and my church can be of service to the people of Foxhall Green once more. As you know, I am Reverend Laing and I am your vicar here at St Gabriel's.' This was said,

Matthew suspected, purely for the benefit of the reporters, so they'd put his name in their newspapers. 'This is Inspector Oakenshaw,' he gestured to Oakenshaw on his right, 'who runs the station here in Foxhall Green. And this,' he waved a hand to his left, 'is Superintendent Mullinger of Craynebrook Police. And at the end is Detective Inspector Lund, who is leading the murder investigation. Superintendent?'

'Thank you, Reverend Laing,' Mullinger said, rising as the vicar took his seat. 'I would like to begin by expressing my sincere condolences for all your losses.' A murmuring of sad approval greeted this remark. 'It is the purpose of this meeting to answer any questions you may have and for us to appeal to you to search your memories for any information that may be helpful to us in our enquiries. I cannot stress enough that no detail is too small to bring to our attention.'

A man in the back row jumped to his feet, a notebook and pencil in his hand. 'What progress has been made so far, Superintendent?'

'I'm afraid I can't give you details of our investigation—'

'Is it true a tramp is your prime suspect?'

Mullinger nodded. 'A vagrant is of interest to the investigation but to say he is our prime suspect would be to overstate the matter. We are following up several leads.'

Another reporter got to her feet. 'What was the killer's motive for the massacre?'

'It is impossible to say what motivated this terrible crime as we won't know until we've caught the killer and asked him why he did it. And this is why it is so important that if anyone has information that can help us catch this man—'

'Does that mean you've no chance of catching the killer without more information?'

'Absolutely not,' Mullinger declared indignantly. 'Inspector Lund is confident an arrest will be made—'

The first reporter held up his hand. 'But isn't it true Inspector Lund has never led a murder investigation?'

This question brought a loud murmuring of surprise, as well as disapproval, from the audience.

'No,' Mullinger said, looking a little flustered by the question. 'Inspector Lund has worked on several murders—'

'But never heading up the case,' the reporter persisted. 'Should a case as serious as the cinema massacre be entrusted to a man with no experience of leading a murder investigation?'

Another reporter stood up. 'Is it also true two complaints have been made against Inspector Lund?'

Mullinger's mouth opened and closed a few times as he struggled to find a response before saying. 'Those are not matters for this meeting—'

'Superintendent Mullinger,' another voice called out, cutting him off, and Matthew started as he recognised Dickie's voice. He hadn't noticed he was there. 'With all due respect to Inspector Lund – I know he is a very capable detective – but in view of the complaints that have been made, and regarding the seriousness of the incident, would it not make more sense to entrust the investigation to an officer with considerably more experience in catching murderers? Inspector Stannard, for instance?'

Dickie, what the hell are you doing? Matthew met Dickie's eyes and his friend held his gaze for a long moment before turning back to Mullinger. Matthew looked over at Mullinger, who seemed to be on the point of refusing to answer, then glanced at Lund. Lund's eyes were downcast and Matthew could have sworn there was the faintest hint of a smile on his lips.

The public quickly realised who Dickie was talking about and Matthew became the focus of attention. Voices were raised and fingers pointed. He felt himself growing red and kept his eyes on his feet.

Mullinger banged the table for quiet. 'It is not for members of the Press to decide which officers should lead an investigation and I will not entertain any further comment on this matter. I will return to my main point and that is our need for information—'

'Isn't an appeal for information a sign of desperation, Superintendent?'

'That is not the case at all,' Mullinger said, holding his hand up to halt the various murmurs of agreement. 'We are doing our best—'

A woman in one of the front rows leapt to her feet. 'Your best isn't good enough. If he's no good,' she pointed at Lund, 'then put him,' she waved her arm at Matthew, 'in charge.'

'It's all going off now,' Barnes muttered under his breath.

He was right. Many people echoed the woman's words, and reporters called out to Matthew for a comment. He wondered desperately what to do. Should he support Lund and say he was perfectly capable of finding the killer? Or should he just keep his head down and say nothing?

Laing took the decision away from him. The vicar got to his feet and spread his arms wide. 'Quiet,' he roared, and the hubbub died down. Some of the spectators resumed their seats. Others remained standing. Laing continued, his eyes blazing. 'Behave yourselves. It is not for you to question the decisions of the police.'

'We have a right,' a man insisted. 'It was our loved ones who were killed.'

Laing ignored him. 'I will bring this meeting to an end by repeating the police's request for information. Police officers will remain behind to talk with anyone who can help.

Make yourself known to them if you can tell them anything.' He fell onto his chair and shook his head in disgust at Oakenshaw, who nodded back in equal disapproval.

'What do we do, sir?' Barnes asked Matthew as the crowd broke up, some heading straight for the exit, others lingering to talk to one another.

'We stay here for the time being,' Matthew said, trying not to meet any of the staring eyes in the crowd. He saw Dickie scribbling in his notebook, unperturbed, acting as if he hadn't just caused the most almighty ruckus. He glanced over at Lund. Lund was still at the table, staring blankly over the hall.

'I'm going out for a smoke,' Matthew said. 'It looks like some of these people want to talk to us, so make yourselves approachable. Take full details of anything you're told and who told you. Got it?'

'Got it, sir,' Denham said.

Matthew made his way over to the table, going around the back. He ducked down on Lund's left side, out of Mullinger's line of sight. 'You all right?' he asked.

Lund ran his hand over his face and Matthew heard the rasp of his stubble. 'Did you arrange that?'

'What? No, of course not.'

'Dickie Waite's a friend of yours, isn't he?'

'Lund, I swear, I had nothing to do with it. In fact, I'm going to give him a piece of my mind. He had no right to say what he did.'

'Well, it will have done the trick.' Lund shifted in his chair to face Matthew and turn his back to Mullinger. 'You can bet Old Mouldy will take me off the case and put you on it now.'

'I'll refuse,' Matthew declared.

Lund snorted. 'No, you won't. You've been itching to

take over. And quite frankly, old chum, you're welcome to it.'

'You're not off the case, Lund.'

'I will be.' Lund dug into his jacket pocket, pulled out his cigarettes, and lit one. 'If I'm honest, Stannard, I'm glad. I knew I was out of my depth as soon as I saw those bodies piled up. They deserve better than me. I'm not up to the job of catching this fella.'

'You are up to it,' Matthew insisted. 'Or you would be if you kept off the booze.'

Lund gave him a weary smile. 'It's all right. Being taken off this case is the least of my worries. And besides, you should worry about yourself, not me.'

'Why should I be worried?'

'Because you've got a reputation, sunshine. Everyone expects you to catch this killer because you've done it so often before. So, you better catch him, hadn't you? Because if you don't, I expect Old Mouldy will throw you to the dogs.'

A heavy feeling landed in Matthew's stomach at these words. He rose, feeling he needed a smoke more than ever and left Lund to go outside to the back of the church hall where no one would see him. He lit a cigarette and took a few deep drags before craning his neck back and closing his eyes.

'What are you doing out here?'

Matthew straightened and opened his eyes. 'What the hell did you think you were doing in there, Dickie?' he asked, glaring at his friend.

'What are you talking about?' Dickie protested. 'I just did you a favour.'

'How was that a favour?'

'Because you'll be leading the investigation now, won't you? Lund can't carry on. Not now.'

'No. Not now you've publicly humiliated him.'

'I didn't enjoy it, Matthew, believe me, but it had to be done. I won't apologise for it. This killer needs to be found and Lund's not the man to find him. You are, Matthew, and you know it.'

'And what if I don't catch him?' Matthew said. 'Because we've got nothing, Dickie. We don't know what he looked like, where he came from, where he went or why he did it. Nothing.'

'If that's right, then you have nothing because Lund was in charge of the investigation. Can you honestly say he's been doing a good job?'

Matthew took a final drag, not wanting to admit Dickie was right. He dropped his cigarette on the ground and crushed it beneath his shoe. 'I should get back in there,' he said, pushing away from the wall.

'Yeah,' Dickie nodded. 'I reckon you should.'

14

Sergeant Ambrose Brock pushed at the loose slat on the fence and wriggled his body through the gap, tugging at the skirts of his heavy overcoat where it had become snagged on a nail. He heard a rip and sighed in resignation. Just another tear to add to all the others. Nothing to get upset about.

Brock had been away for a few days, thinking it better to get out of Foxhall Green while the natives were so worked up about him being there. He'd grown tired of the name-calling and the poking with broom handles and taken himself off to Colmbridge to try his luck there. But the people of Colmbridge were no better and he hadn't liked the town as much, so he headed back to Foxhall Green and his preferred sleeping spot, a wooden bench near the church's south-side porch. It was sheltered there, an important consideration now the nights were drawing in.

Settling on the bench, Brock drew his legs up, not without effort, for his aged bones didn't move as smoothly as they had when he'd been a sergeant in the Guards, and lay down on the hard wooden slats. He shifted a few times to get into a comfortable position, tugged his overcoat over his knees, and closed his weary eyes.

Brock was drifting off when he heard voices and recognised the tenor of men who had drunk too much. Throwouts from the pub across the road, he supposed. He lifted his head, ears pricked, hoping they weren't coming closer. Too often had he been the victim of a group of drunks who thought it would be fun to beat seven shades out of a man less fortunate than themselves.

The voices were coming near, and he sat up, peering into the darkness to make the figures out. He saw the brief flare of a match being struck, the flame pausing in mid-air to light the end of a cigarette. There were four of them and they were loud and boisterous. Brock knew the type; knew they would be looking for sport. Keen not to offer himself up, he clambered off the bench and shuffled away into a clump of bushes, hoping he'd moved fast enough to avoid being seen.

'There he is!' a voice yelled, and Brock groaned. He had been too slow.

Another asked, 'Where?'

'There. Let's get him.'

Brock shuffled backwards until his rear knocked against the fence and he realised with dismay he'd cornered himself, put himself in an indefensible position when he should have got out into the open. At least then, he might have had a chance of getting away.

They were only a few feet away now, two of them bending down to stare into the bush.

'It is him,' one of them told the others. 'I can smell him from here.'

'Get him out of there,' another growled.

Should he beg? Brock wondered. Twenty years ago, nothing in the world could have made him beg, but that had been before, when he had had a position, a wife who loved him, children who respected him, and when he could afford to be dignified.

Brock was still deciding on his next course of action when hands reached into the bush and clamped around his wrists. He was dragged out and dropped on the ground, his face hitting the dirt. They turned him over onto his back and he floundered like a fish thrown onto a bank, holding up his hands in protestation and pacification.

'Please,' he croaked, decision made, but it didn't work. The blows still came. He curled himself up into a ball, knowing from bitter experience there was nothing else he could do but take the punishment. But punishment for what? he wondered as his ribs took the kicks, as his hands took the stamp of boots.

At last, the blows stopped. Brock lay still, holding his breath, not only because it hurt to breathe but to play dead.

'That's done for him,' one said.

'Serves him right,' said another.

'Come on, let's go,' said a third, and they left, congratulating themselves on a job well done.

Brock tried to move, but all he got for the effort was a fresh wave of pain. So he stopped trying and gave himself up to the night, his body stiffening as the air turned colder, and until God showed some mercy and allowed him to drift into sleep.

15

Tuesday, 21st October 1930

Matthew took the stairs to the second floor two at a time, knowing he should feel a little guilty about being given the Regal Picture Palace case. At least, he hoped he was going to be given the case; he didn't know for sure. All Mullinger had said to him the night before was for Matthew to see him in his office first thing in the morning.

Matthew reached the top landing and gave the secretary sitting at her desk his best smile. 'Good morning, Miss Halliwell. Mr Mullinger wants to see me.'

Miss Halliwell beamed at him. 'Good morning, inspector. Mr Mullinger told me you'd be up and that you were to go straight in.' Glancing at Mullinger's office door, she leaned forward and said, 'I hear you're taking over the investigation?'

Matthew, a little distracted by the gaping neckline of the secretary's blouse, wondered how to answer, but before he could reply, Miss Halliwell went on.

'I heard what happened last night. Poor Inspector Lund. But between you and me, I think it's for the best.

After all, that man who killed all those people has to be caught, and if anyone can catch him, you can.'

The intercom on Miss Halliwell's desk buzzed. 'Miss Halliwell?' came Mullinger's voice through the speaker. 'Stop flirting with Stannard and send him in.'

Miss Halliwell blushed a deep crimson. 'Yes, Mr Mullinger. Go in,' she said to Matthew with a soft groan and busied herself with the typewriter.

Matthew rapped on Mullinger's door and entered. 'Good morning, sir.'

'I'd be obliged, Stannard, if you'd not encourage my secretary,' Mullinger said, pointing Matthew to the visitor's chair by his desk.

'I wasn't—' Matthew began to protest, then realised there wasn't any point and sat down. 'You wanted to see me, sir.'

Mullinger took off his spectacles and rubbed the bridge of his nose. 'I'm sure you know what I'm going to say to you. It's unfortunate, but there it is. You're taking over the Regal Picture Palace case.'

'Yes, sir,' Matthew said, trying not to grin. 'And Inspector Lund?'

'Lund is on two weeks' leave. In view of the complaints and the public's demands last night, I really had no other choice.' Mullinger replaced his spectacles. 'I read the case file yesterday afternoon before the meeting, and I must say, there's not much to go on. The witness statements from the cinema staff reveal very little. The physical evidence is no better.'

'I agree,' Matthew nodded. Lund had given him the case file before leaving the previous night, and Matthew had read it through several times in bed, dismayed by how little information it contained. 'I'll need to thoroughly review the case with the others and decide where to take it from there.'

Mullinger's expression became pained. 'That sounds rather vague, Stannard. I had rather expected you to take the bull by the horns, as it were.'

What the hell does that mean? Matthew wondered. *Does he expect me to magic the killer out of a top hat?* 'My top priority will be to question Timmy Lane,' he said.

'Ah, now that's a delicate area. Lund's treatment of the boy—'

'I understand, sir, but it's vital we find out exactly what happened in the auditorium.'

'But Lund was of the opinion the boy could tell him nothing. I don't really want the parents complaining that we're harassing them.'

'I'll tread carefully, sir. There won't be any more complaints.'

'I'm very glad to hear it. Very well. If that's what you think best. Get to it.'

'Yes, sir.' Matthew rose and headed for the door.

'And Stannard!

Matthew turned back. 'Sir?'

'I want this case cleared up as quickly as possible. I trust I make myself clear?'

Lund's words came back to Matthew. *Old Mouldy will throw you to the dogs.* 'Yes, sir,' he nodded. 'Very clear.'

The breakfast-room door opened, and the maid came in with the newspaper. Laing held out his hand and the maid deposited it into his eager palm.

'Will there be anything else, madam?' she asked, turning to her mistress.

'No, that's all,' Violet said. 'I'll ring when you can clear.' The maid went out and Violet raised her coffee cup to her lips, looking over the rim at her husband. 'You're unusually interested in the newspaper this morning, my dear.'

Laing flicked through the pages. 'I'm looking for something very particular. Ah, here it is. Letters to the Editor.' He fell silent as he read.

Violet set her cup on the saucer. 'Well, what is it?' she said impatiently. 'Don't keep me in suspense.'

Her husband grinned at her, folded the newspaper and passed it across the breakfast table. 'Read it for yourself, my dear.'

She took the newspaper and read where he pointed. When she had finished, she looked up, admiration shining in her eyes. 'Oh, Bertram. They've printed your letter.'

'Indeed, they have.' Laing reached for the marmalade and deposited a large dollop on his plate. 'And they haven't cut it at all. Every word I wrote is there in print. It's highly satisfactory.'

She handed the newspaper back to him. 'And you've mentioned your book. I didn't think you wanted anyone to know until it was complete?'

'I know it's not finished yet, but it will be soon, and you can never start too early when it comes to publicity, Violet. In commercial terms, you needs to whip up an interest if you want your product to sell.'

'What a very odd way to describe your book,' she said, pouring him more coffee. 'It's not a product. It's an education. And I would have thought there will be plenty of interest when the time comes and it's published.'

'Perhaps you are right, my dear, and I have rather put the cart before the horse in regards to my book, but it was too good an opportunity to pass up. The massacre has aroused people's interest in the state of society and I must take advantage.' He tapped a pile of envelopes on the windowsill beside him. 'These are all about my sermon on

Sunday. People who weren't even in the congregation but who read about it in the newspaper have written to congratulate me on what I said.'

'And for having the courage to say it, Bertram. We knew your sermon might offend some people, but still, you had the courage of your convictions and you gave it, knowing too that your words might be committed to print. It was a very brave thing to do, especially when one considers your past experience with the Press.'

Laing nodded. 'I know, Violet, but you can't deny newspapers have their uses. Their printing my letter, especially in full, will bring a great deal of attention my way.'

'And what do you hope all this publicity will bring you, Bertram? It's not just book sales, I hope?'

'No, indeed, my dear. The massacre has put Foxhall Green on the map, and my sermon and letters have done the same for me, in a manner of speaking. I have been noticed.'

'You've been noticed before,' Violet said with a raise of her eyebrow. 'I trust it won't be like that again?'

'Certainly not,' he said sharply. 'This time, the attention will all be for the good and will convince my superiors in the Church that I am fitted for so much more than this dreadful little town. I need a larger parish. Perhaps a cathedral town.'

'Canterbury?' she suggested with a smile.

'Why not? I don't consider Canterbury beyond me. Not now.'

'I would say nothing's beyond you, Bertram, when you put your mind to something.' She dabbed her lips with her napkin. 'You did say we wouldn't be here any longer than we could help, and I can't pretend I won't be glad to leave. Foxhall Green is such a common little place.'

'Then let us hope that we shall be on the move very soon.' Bertram raised his coffee cup in a salute.

<h1 style="text-align:center">16</h1>

Matthew strode into CID and the junior detectives' conversation came to an abrupt halt. They looked up at him expectantly and he gestured for them to gather around.

'As I'm sure you know, I've been with Mr Mullinger,' he began. 'Inspector Lund is on two weeks' leave starting today, which means I'm taking over the Regal Picture Palace investigation.'

He waited for the inevitable questions: was this change of leadership because of the comments made at the previous night's meeting or because of the complaints? Was Lund really on leave or had he been suspended? But to Matthew's surprise, the junior detectives stayed silent. Perhaps they already knew about Lund and didn't need to ask. Or perhaps they just didn't care. Denham, he couldn't help noticing, looked pleased.

'Obviously,' he went on, 'I'm not as well informed as you about this case, so I want to start by going over what we know. We know a gunman walked into the cinema between 1.55 p.m. and 2.10 p.m. on Saturday and opened fire with a Lee Enfield Mk III rifle. He shot seventeen times, sixteen times at the victims, once into the side door. He left behind eleven dead and five wounded. He escaped via the side alley that led back onto the high street.'

Matthew paused, taken aback by how quickly he had come to the known facts of the incident. Was that really all they knew? *Forget the gunman for the moment*, he told himself. *Move onto the others.*

'The cinema staff,' he said. 'Rita Amstell, the ticket lady, and George Cordell, the doorman, were together in the staffroom from around 1.40 p.m. until the shooting was almost over. Roy Grainger, the manager, was in his office at the top of the building, and Ivor Topling was in the projection room.'

'Hiding,' Denham muttered.

'What was that?' Matthew asked.

'I said Topling was hiding in the projection room. The coward. He didn't come down until it was all over.'

'So, all the staff are accounted for at the time of the shooting. Moving on to the victims.' Matthew pointed to the mortuary photographs pinned to the corkboard. 'David and Rose Colley, both in their sixties. Stanley and Lillian Balshaw, the same. Margaret Thornton, thirty-six. Mother of Kitty Thornton, nine, who was wounded. Joan Faket, twenty-nine. Mother of Alison Faket, eight, wounded. Emily Watts, twenty-eight, wounded. Died Sunday from her wounds. Mother of Dorothy Watts, six, wounded. David Meers, twenty-four. Katherine Lowe, twenty-six, wounded. Lucy Simpson, eighteen. Paul Beale, twelve. Martin Comer, twelve. Frankie Ashe, twelve.'

He came to the end and there was silence as the detectives contemplated the death toll, especially the last three names. Matthew glanced at Denham. He was doodling in his notebook, but the marks he was making were tearing the paper.

'Right,' Matthew said loudly to regain their attention. 'Motives. What do we have? Barnes?'

'The Colleys and Balshaws were your typical elderly couples,' he said. 'Well liked by their neighbours. No one had a bad word to say about them.'

'Margaret Thornton,' Bissett said, 'was a housewife. Her husband seemed genuinely cut up by her death. She did complain to the butcher earlier in the week about a joint he sold her which she claimed had too much gristle in it, but that's it. She'd taken her daughter to the pictures.'

'So had Joan Faket,' Denham said. 'No arguments with neighbours or the like. Marriage all right. No reason to kill her.'

'Emily Watts,' Barnes said. 'She and her husband had money problems. She was talking about getting a job, but he didn't want her to. They had a few rows about it, but nothing too terrible.'

'He admitted the rows?' Matthew asked.

Barnes nodded. 'He was very upset about them. Wished he hadn't argued with her. Guilt, you know, sir?'

'I know. David Meers?'

'Bank clerk,' Denham said. 'Bit of a loudmouth, according to the manager, and one with an eye for the girls.'

'Did he upset any boyfriends?' Matthew suggested.

'He got into one or two fights over girls,' Denham nodded, 'but that was a while ago. Nothing recent.'

'Katherine Lowe,' Rudd said. 'Single. Works at the flower shop. Good worker. Nothing bad about her at all.'

'Which brings us to the children,' Matthew said, pointing at the photographs of the three boys. 'They were all wearing Scout uniforms.'

'Like Timmy Lane,' Rudd pointed out.

'Like Timmy Lane,' Matthew agreed.

'They'd been to a Scout meeting that morning,' Barnes

said. 'They were friends. The manager, Mr Grainger, said they were among a group of kids who had been sneaking in for free through the side door a month or so ago. He ordered the side door to be locked and that put a stop to it. They weren't any trouble since.'

'The boys being in the Scouts is interesting, though,' Matthew said. 'The Scouts have rifles.'

Bissett piped up. 'Sergeant Dobbs got the rifles from the Scout master, Mr Dennis Hillman. They're at the lab now for testing to see if the marks on the casings match any of the rifle barrels. Mr Hillman's fingerprints were checked against the prints on the casings and the box cartridge left at the cinema but they're not a match.'

'Where was Mr Hillman on Saturday afternoon?' Matthew asked.

'He was at home. His mother confirmed it.'

'Was Mr Hillman questioned about the three dead boys?'

'Sergeant Dobbs said he asked if Mr Hillman had had any trouble with them and he said no, they were a nice bunch of boys.'

'It is a bit of a coincidence, though, isn't it, sir?' Rudd said. 'Three Boy Scouts, four if you count Timmy Lane, in the cinema, and the Scouts have rifles for marksmanship practice?'

'A bit too obvious, don't you think?' Barnes said. 'I mean, if you were going to kill all those people, would you use a rifle everyone knows you've got?'

Rudd shrugged, embarrassed his idea had been ridiculed.

'Sometimes,' Matthew said, feeling for the young man, 'the most obvious answer is the right one, Barnes. But I've been told the rifles are kept in the vestry cupboard where several people could have access to them. The vicar, for one.'

The detectives stared at him.

'Reverend Laing?' Bissett asked disbelievingly. 'You're not serious, sir?'

'I'm not going to discount him just because he's a man of the cloth, Bissett,' Matthew said. 'But no, there's no reason so far to suppose the vicar had anything to do with this.' He turned back to the corkboard and studied the photograph of Lucy Simpson. 'Her pregnancy is interesting. Perhaps she wanted the father to marry her and he couldn't because he was already married, or he just didn't want to. Killing her was the only way to get rid of her. It's been done before.'

'But not like this, surely?' Denham protested. 'I agree a bloke might want to get rid of a woman who's putting the screws on to marry her, but to kill all those other people as well? That's mad.'

'I agree,' Matthew said. 'But there are plenty of mad people out there, Denham.'

'What about the tramp?' Rudd said. 'Inspector Lund thought he had a motive, the way he was treated by the locals.'

'Tramps are always badly treated,' Matthew said with a shake of his head. 'I agree he's someone we want to talk to, but as far as I'm concerned, that's to eliminate him as a suspect. There is no evidence against him.'

'But he was in the area, sir, and he hasn't been seen since Saturday.'

'That doesn't make him guilty, Barnes. From the house-to-house reports I've read, he wasn't seen at all Saturday. For all we know, he could have left the area earlier. On the Friday, perhaps. I don't want us putting all our eggs in one basket and thinking this tramp is our only suspect. Now, did anything come out of the public meeting last night? Any new information?'

Denham consulted his notebook. 'We got a few more names of suspicious characters. We're looking into those this morning.'

'Anything that jumps out at you?'

'No, sir. I don't recognise any of the names. But I've still got plenty of other nicks to check with.'

Barnes raised his hand. 'Sir, are we working on the idea that these killings were premeditated? It had to be planned, didn't it? No one takes a rifle to a cinema just because they feel like it.'

'That's a very good question,' Matthew said. 'But if it was planned, then he was taking a hell of a chance of being seen.'

'Unless he knew there would be no one in the foyer when he arrived,' Rudd suggested. 'The manager said Mrs Amstell and Mr Cordell were always leaving the foyer unattended when the pictures were running. He moaned about it.'

'Then that's interesting,' Matthew said. 'Could the killer have been a regular at the cinema who knew the staff habits? Did they report anyone acting suspiciously? Any disgruntled customers?'

Denham shook his head. 'The staff said they had no idea who the killer could have been.'

Matthew sighed. It felt as if he was getting nowhere. 'What about the other rifles?' he asked Bissett.

'Sergeant Dobbs collected six from the shooting club members and private owners. They're at the lab. None of their prints matched those on the casings.'

'And their whereabouts on Saturday? I didn't see their statements in the case file.'

Bissett swallowed nervously. 'I don't believe there are any statements from them, sir. At least, I haven't seen them.'

'Do you mean you don't know whether Dobbs questioned those other owners?"

'I expect he did question them, sir, and he would have said if any of them were dodgy. He did say they were all decent chaps.'

'Decent chaps?' Matthew repeated disbelievingly, making Bissett colour in embarrassment. 'Get those statements, Bissett. If Dobbs didn't establish their whereabouts for Saturday afternoon, then make sure you do. And while I think of it, I didn't see any prints in the case file.'

'I've got them, sir,' Bissett said. He glanced down at his messy desk. 'Somewhere,' he added in an undertone.

'You should either be working off the photographic copy or returning the original to the case file when you've finished,' Matthew said as Bissett searched for the cards. 'I won't have vital information being misplaced.'

'No, sir,' Bissett said. 'Sorry, sir.'

'And while we're on the subject of missing papers from the case file, who's got the plan of the cinema?' Matthew asked, looking around. The detectives glanced at each other. 'A plan was made of the cinema, wasn't it? And it was searched?'

'Inspector Lund left the search to the Foxhall Green Uniform, sir,' Denham said.

'And where's their report?'

No one answered. Matthew's jaw tightened and he forced himself not to lose his temper in front of the men. He took a deep breath and looked at all of them. 'You don't need me to tell you this investigation hasn't been handled properly,' he said. 'And I'll be blunt. You can't blame it all on Inspector Lund. Most of you are experienced enough to know what's required of you in a murder investigation and shouldn't have to be told to follow up on statements and suchlike. This is the only time I'm going to mention what's gone before. From this point on, I expect you to do better. Is that understood?'

The detectives murmured, 'Yes, sir,' all of them too shamefaced to meet Matthew's eye.

The telephone on Bissett's desk rang. He received a nod from Matthew that he was to answer it and snatched up the receiver. 'Craynebrook CID. DS Bissett speaking.' His eyes widened and met Matthew's. 'Thanks. I'll tell him.' He hung up. 'That was Foxhall Green station, sir. They've found the tramp.'

'They've got him in custody?'

'Not exactly. He was found in the church grounds this morning beaten to a pulp. He's been taken to the hospital.'

17

Matthew stood at the end of the bed and looked down at the man beneath the blankets.

Brock's face was a mass of purple and black bruises. There were ragged cuts across the cheeks and his left eyebrow and bottom lip were split. The fingers on the hands lying on the blanket were bandaged together to hold the broken bones straight. More bruises ran down the vein-streaked hands to the wrists, running off beneath the pyjama sleeves. Whoever had beaten him had certainly done a number on the old man.

'Mr Brock?' Matthew asked quietly, unsure if he was awake.

A tongue moistened the cracked lips. 'Sergeant Brock,' came the growl of a reply.

'I'm sorry. Sergeant Brock. Do you know where you are?'

The eyes struggled open. 'In hospital. Who are you?'

'DI Matthew Stannard.' Matthew moved to the chair beside the bed. 'Who did this to you?'

'The usual. Men who didn't like the look of me.'

'You didn't provoke them in any way?'

There was a pained snort of derision from the man in the bed. 'I didn't do anything.'

Matthew felt ashamed for asking the question. He knew people like Brock were often the target for men who enjoyed a good punch-up. 'Could you identify the men who attacked you?'

'Like you care.'

'You've been the victim of an assault. It's my job to care.'

'First copper I've met who thinks that. Most of your lot just want to get rid of me.' Brock sighed. 'I can't tell you anything about them. They were just men in the dark.'

Matthew nodded, knowing the men were unlikely to be caught. 'Do you know we've been wanting to talk to you?'

'What about?'

'There was a shooting at the Foxhall Green cinema on Saturday. Twelve people were killed, including children. Others were wounded. You were put forward as a potential suspect.'

'Who by?' Brock demanded.

'Reverend Laing.'

'That sod? He was always trying to get rid of me.'

'And it was claimed you hadn't been seen in Foxhall Green since the shooting.'

'When did it happen?'

'Saturday afternoon around two o'clock.'

'I weren't in Foxhall Green then. I'd gone to Colmbridge early Saturday morning.'

'Can anyone confirm that?'

Brock considered for a moment. 'The tobacconist. I asked him for a little bit of baccy around that time. He told me to scarper and we got into a row.'

'I can check on that. Why did you return to Foxhall Green?'

'I liked it better than Colmbridge. I wish I'd stayed

away.' He lifted his head and frowned at Matthew. 'Is that why those fellas did this to me? They thought I'd killed those people?'

'I expect so,' Matthew nodded. 'As an army man, I assume you know how to use a rifle?'

'Of course I do. I wasn't the best shot in the regiment, but I could always hit a Hun if I had to.'

'Do you own a rifle?'

'I carry everything I own on my back and that ain't much.' He nodded at the bedside cabinet and told Matthew to take a look.

Matthew opened the cupboard door and took out Brock's overcoat and his flat cap. He felt in the pockets and took out a row of medals.

'Those are the only things I've got left,' Brock said sadly. 'They're of no value to anyone but me.'

Matthew put the medals back in the pocket and returned the coat and cap to the cupboard. 'Is there no one you could go to for help? You don't have any family?'

'None that would own me.' Brock groaned and his face creased in pain.

'Shall I call the nurse over?' Matthew asked.

Brock shook his head. 'I'm all right. So, are you going to charge me for this shooting?'

'Only if you did it.'

'You said children were hurt. You think I'd hurt kiddies?'

'I don't know. I need to confirm your alibi.'

'Now you sound like a copper.' Brock sniffed and Matthew saw tears leaking from his eyes. 'I wish they had finished me off.'

'You shouldn't say things like that.'

'Why not? If I was dead, it would make it easy for you, wouldn't it? You could have blamed it all on me.'

'I'm not in the habit of making innocent people scapegoats.'

'You think I'm innocent, then?'

Matthew did think Brock was innocent, but he wasn't ready to admit it. 'I'm reserving judgement for the time being. I want to catch the killer, and if you're him, then I won't hesitate to put the cuffs on. But I don't approve of people taking the law into their own hands. So, if there's anything you remember about the men who attacked you, you let me know. I'll see they get what's coming to them.'

'All right, son. If I remember anything, I'll tell you.' Brock's eyes closed.

Matthew left the sergeant sleeping and made his way to Peachcroft Ward, finding Rudd hovering outside the door.

'How is he, sir?' Rudd asked.

'Pretty bad,' Matthew said. 'He says he was in Colm-bridge on Saturday. We need to check on that, but I don't think he's our gunman.' He nodded at the ward doors. 'You've told the Lanes I want to talk to Timmy?'

'Yes, sir. I can't say they were too happy about it.'

'I don't expect they were.'

'But I told them you were the man who found Timmy and that you wouldn't be like Inspector Lund.' Rudd reddened as he realised he had said something he probably shouldn't.

'Let's get in there,' Matthew said, trying not to smile.

Mr and Mrs Lane looked at Matthew and Rudd with undisguised suspicion as they approached Timmy's bed. Matthew gave them both his best smile and introduced himself.

'This young man has assured us you won't be as rude as your colleague,' Mr Lane said as Matthew took a seat by the bed.

'I won't be rude at all, Mr Lane,' Matthew promised. 'I just need to talk to Timmy.'

Mr Lane considered him for a moment, then said, 'Very well. But if he gets upset, I insist you stop.'

'Of course.' Matthew turned his attention to Timmy, who, he was pleased to note, was looking a lot more like a little boy without a care in the world should look. 'Do you remember me?' he asked.

Timmy nodded. 'You found me in the cinema.'

'That's right. And you remember Sam?' Matthew said, pointing at Rudd beside him.

'He took me in the police car,' Timmy said, and his eyes brightened a little.

'Maybe we'll take you out in the car again when you're feeling better,' Matthew said.

The boy sat up. 'I'm better now,' he said eagerly.

Matthew grinned. 'We'll do it another day. And I'll even get Sam to put the bells on for you. How does that sound?'

Timmy nodded enthusiastically, and Matthew saw Mrs Lane's expression soften at her son's pleasure.

'Timmy,' he said carefully, 'I need your help. I need to know what you saw at the cinema.'

The smile disappeared from the boy's face. 'You want to know about the man who came in?'

'Yes, I do. What can you tell me about him?'

Timmy looked at his father, who gave him a nod of encouragement, then back at Matthew. 'He came in after the film had started. He went to the bottom of the steps, near the screen, then turned around and opened his coat. He took out—' he broke off, tears brimming in his eyes.

'It's all right, Timmy,' his mother said, stroking his hair.

'I know it's difficult,' Matthew said, 'but I need to know everything.'

Timmy nodded. 'I didn't know what it was at first, but then he held it up to his shoulder like this.' He lifted his arms and positioned his hands as if he was holding a rifle. 'Then he started shooting and I got under the seat.'

'Thank God you did,' Mr Lane said. 'If he'd seen you—'

'Oh, don't, Arthur,' Mrs Lane said, grabbing Timmy and kissing him fiercely. Timmy jerked away and wiped his cheek, embarrassed by his mother's show of affection in front of Matthew and Rudd.

'Can you tell me what this man looked like?' Matthew asked.

Timmy shook his head. 'It was so dark in there and he had his back to the screen, so I couldn't see his face. He had a hat on and it was pulled down low. The collar on his coat was up as well, so I couldn't see anything.'

'Was he fat or thin?'

'Thin.'

'Short or tall?'

'Tall.'

'How tall?' Matthew gestured for Rudd to stand up. 'As tall as Sam?'

Timmy frowned at Rudd. 'I don't know. Maybe.'

'And you said he was wearing a hat. What kind of hat?'

Timmy's eyes flicked to Matthew's trilby. 'Like yours.'

'What colour was it?'

'I couldn't tell. It was too dark.'

'What about the coat? How long was it?'

'It came to below his knees, I think. I don't know what colour that was either.'

'That's all right. That's very helpful, Timmy. Now, I need to know about when he started shooting. When the man lifted the gun to his shoulder, was he aiming it at anyone?'

Timmy's pale brow furrowed. 'I don't know. He swung it around a bit.'

Matthew leaned forward. 'Before he started shooting, he moved the gun around? As if he was picking people out?'

'Maybe. He sort of pointed the gun at Frankie.'

'Frankie Ashe?'

'He was near the front with Martin and Paul.'

'You weren't sitting with them. Why was that?'

'They weren't my friends,' Timmy said, making a face. 'They were rotten to me.'

'They bullied you?'

'Sometimes. Not all the time. It was mostly Frankie.'

'He was bullying you?' Mrs Lane cried. 'Why didn't you tell us?'

'So,' Matthew interrupted, not wanting Timmy to be distracted, 'do you think the man was aiming for Frankie?'

'I don't know. He might have been.'

'You say he swung the gun around?'

'Only for a bit. He stopped when the lady screamed.'

'When which lady screamed?'

'The usherette. She screamed and jumped up and he shot her. She made a funny noise and fell down.'

'Was she the first person he shot?'

'Yes.'

'Did you see who he shot next?'

'Frankie. That's when I got under the seat.'

'Did you see or hear anything once you were under the seat?'

'Not really. I shut my eyes. There was a lot of screaming, and a lot of shots. I put my hands over my ears, but I could still hear them.' The tears finally fell and Mrs Lane drew him to her breast.

'Can't you leave him alone now, inspector?' she pleaded.

Matthew nodded at her. He didn't want to push the boy and he thought Timmy had told him everything he could. He thanked Timmy and his parents, and he and Rudd left.

'Poor boy,' Rudd said as they walked back to the car. 'To go through all that.'

'At least he survived,' Matthew pointed out. 'And now we know the kind of man we're looking for.'

'Do we? I didn't think it was much of a description.' Rudd opened the rear door for Matthew. 'A man in an overcoat and a hat? That could have been anyone.'

'A thin man, maybe as tall as you, in a calf-length overcoat and trilby,' Matthew corrected. 'If nothing else, that crosses Sergeant Brock off our suspect list. He's not thin or tall and he wears a cap. And we know more than we knew an hour ago. We have another potential intended victim. Frankie Ashe.'

'But the gunman shot Lucy Simpson first.'

'Maybe he was getting his aim in with Frankie, then Lucy screamed, alarming him and changing his plan. Maybe he shot her to shut her up. Maybe he only meant to shoot Frankie.'

Maybe, maybe, maybe, Matthew thought as he climbed into the back of the car. *Too many damn maybes.*

'So, are we thinking Frankie Ashe was the target and not Lucy Simpson now?' Rudd asked as he got in the front.

Matthew considered. 'I still think Lucy is the more likely.' He checked his watch and made a face. The interviews with Brock and Timmy had taken far longer than he had expected, and time was moving on. 'We still have to question the Simpsons and search the cinema. I don't want to get distracted with Frankie Ashe just yet. Let's find a telephone, Rudd. I want to call in.'

18

Denham put down his pencil and rubbed his eyes. His vision was going blurry staring at the prints in the files and comparing them with the prints taken from the crime scene. Nothing had turned up so far, and he was doubting anything would. If the gunman didn't have a criminal record, if he'd never had his prints taken, they weren't going to find him this way.

'You look like you could do with a break,' Barnes said as he came into the office.

'We don't have time for breaks,' Denham said. 'You heard the inspector. We have to do better.'

'Even so, take a rest. Five minutes won't kill—' Barnes broke off as his telephone rang. 'DC Barnes,' he said into the mouthpiece. 'Yes, sir. He's here. I'll pass you over. It's the inspector for you,' he said, holding out the receiver to Denham.

Denham took it. 'Yes, sir?' He fell silent as Matthew talked. 'I'll get over there right away. Yes, sir. I know what to ask.'

'What's that about?' Barnes asked as Denham hung up.

166

'The inspector got Timmy Lane to talk,' Denham said, stuffing his notebook in his pocket. 'He said the gunman may have been aiming for Frankie Ashe, so he wants me to question the parents.'

'He reckons Frankie Ashe was who the gunman wanted to kill?'

'He says it's a possibility. But Timmy Lane also said Lucy Simpson was the first to be shot and he's still keen on her being the prime target. He and Rudd are going to interview the Simpsons before they go on to the cinema.'

Barnes nodded. 'Do you want me to come with you?'

'No. I need you to carry on checking these prints.' Denham passed Barnes the stack of files he had been working through. 'And he also wants Sergeant Brock's alibi confirmed. Brock claims he had a row with the tobacconist in Colmbridge around two o'clock.'

'So, the tramp's off the suspect list, is he?' Barnes said, scribbling these instructions down.

'Looks like it. He doesn't match the description of the gunman Timmy Lane gave.' Denham patted his pockets to make sure he had everything. 'Right. I'm off. If anything comes in for me, you know where I am.'

'Nice to be finally getting somewhere with this case, isn't it?' Barnes called as Denham headed for the door.

Denham turned back to him. 'It's nothing to be glad about, Si. It should have happened sooner.'

Denham held up his warrant card as the door opened. 'DS Denham. Craynebrook CID. Mrs Ashe?' The woman nodded mutely. Her red-rimmed eyes stared blankly at Denham. 'Can I come in?'

'Why?' she said, leaning against the door.

'I need to ask you about your son.'

Her face crumpled. 'He's dead.'

'I know. I'm very sorry. Can I come in?'

'I suppose so.' She turned away, leaving the door open for him.

Denham stepped inside and closed it, following her into the front room. Mrs Ashe fell onto the settee and poured gin into a dirty glass as he took a seat on a rickety dining chair. 'Is your husband home?' he asked.

She closed her eyes and shook her head. 'I don't know where he is. Down the pub, probably.'

And left you here, alone, like this? Denham thought sadly. 'About Frankie,' he prompted.

Mrs Ashe took a mouthful of gin. 'What about him?'

'We're looking into the possibility he was an intended target for the gunman,' Denham said, hating the way he'd phrased it. So cold, so impersonal. But Mrs Ashe didn't seem to notice.

She frowned, trying to understand. 'You mean someone meant to kill my Frankie? Just him?'

'It's something we're considering. So, do you know if there was anyone who had a grudge against your son?'

'Huh,' Mrs Ashe said, tipping the gin bottle upside down and grimacing as nothing came out. Pushing herself up from the settee, she shuffled over to the sideboard and took out another bottle, this one labelled sweet sherry. Mrs Ashe sat back down and pulled out the cork. 'Everyone had it in for my boy,' she said as she filled her glass.

'Who's everyone?' Denham asked, his interest roused.

'People round here. The school. The vicar. They all hated my Frankie. Said he was a wrong 'un. That's what the school called him. A wrong 'un.' She shook her head. 'Frankie weren't an angel, I know, but then boys ain't supposed to be, are they? They're supposed to get into trouble.'

'What kind of trouble did he get into?'

'The school said he was a bully. Made me go in and see the headmaster about him, but it was just boys being boys. Then it was people round here complaining about him. He was playing Knock Down Ginger, that's all. All the kids do it, but they've always had it in for us, so Frankie got the blame. They complained to your lot and we had coppers round here, telling us to keep him under control.'

'The neighbours made a complaint to the police?'

Mrs Ashe nodded. 'So did the vicar. Reverend High-and-Mighty Laing. Frankie broke one of his windows. He didn't mean to do it. It was an accident. But would he listen? Oh no, according to him, Frankie did it on purpose. And then he came on our ear'ole, writing to us to demand we pay for the damage. As if we've got the money for that. Pete soon saw him off.'

'Pete?'

'My husband. Frankie's dad.'

'Do you still have the letter from Reverend Laing?'

She shook her head. 'Pete threw it away.'

'Did you ever receive any threats about Frankie? Anyone threaten to do him harm?'

'No, nothing like that.' She drained her glass and rested her head on the back of the settee, eyes closed. 'I don't want to talk about Frankie anymore. It hurts too much.'

Denham put his notebook away and rose. 'Thank you, Mrs Ashe.' He headed for the door, not wanting to stay to witness the poor woman's sorrow.

'I miss my boy,' she called after him.

He turned back to her. Mrs Ashe's face had crumpled and tears were flowing down her cheeks. Denham's throat tightened. 'We're doing everything we can to catch the man who did this, Mrs Ashe.'

'It won't bring my Frankie back, will it?' She fell face down onto the seat, her sobs muffled by the upholstery.

Denham couldn't bear it any longer. He hurried out of the house.

19

Mr Simpson hadn't been at all pleased to see policemen on his doorstep again and had only reluctantly allowed them to enter when Matthew explained he had taken over the case and that Lund was no longer involved.

Mrs Simpson eyed them angrily as her husband conducted them into the sitting room and Matthew flashed Rudd a probably unnecessary warning to be on his very best behaviour.

'I'd like to apologise for my colleague's behaviour yesterday,' Matthew began without preamble. 'I'm very grateful you've agreed to speak with me today.'

'My husband's agreed,' Mrs Simpson said. 'He's more forgiving than I am.'

Matthew accepted Mr Simpson's invitation to take a seat. Rudd remained standing by the door, trying to be as inconspicuous as possible.

'How can we help you, inspector?' Mr Simpson asked as he sat down next to his wife.

'By talking to me about Lucy. I'm trying to find out if there was an intended victim at the cinema or whether the gunman just shot randomly. I realise this is a difficult subject for you, but I need to ask you about your daughter's pregnancy. We're considering it as a possible motive for her murder.'

Mr Simpson turned to his wife. 'We must talk about it, Ethel. There's no point burying our heads in the sand.'

She held his gaze for a long moment, then, biting her lip, nodded. Mr Simpson turned back to Matthew. 'We've been wracking our brains trying to work out who the father could have been, inspector, and we just can't think of anyone.'

'I understand you thought she may have been forced or taken advantage of?'

'We did at first, but now we're not so sure. If something like that had happened to Lucy, she would have been upset and we would have noticed. But she wasn't upset. She was actually very happy of late.'

'Was Lucy courting?'

'Not as far as we know. But then,' he said sadly, 'we've come to realise we didn't really know our daughter at all. We thought we'd brought her up properly, that she wasn't the kind of girl who would get herself pregnant before she was married.'

Mrs Simpson sniffed and crossed her arms over her chest. 'Someone told the Press she was having a baby. Was that you?'

'I assure you, Mrs Simpson, it didn't come from us.' It could only have been someone at the mortuary and he made a mental note to have a word with Dr Wallace when the case was solved.

'God knows what everyone's saying,' she went on, staring out of the window. 'She's done nothing but brought shame on us.'

'Ethel, don't start again,' Mr Simpson said, putting a warning hand on her arm. He smiled feebly at Matthew. 'Is there anything else you want to know?'

'You say Lucy was happy? She hadn't received any threats, written or otherwise? She didn't say there was someone who was angry with her?'

'No, nothing like that.'

Matthew was disappointed. 'I wonder if I could look around Lucy's bedroom?'

'Why?' Mrs Simpson asked. 'What do you expect to find?'

'I really don't know, Mrs Simpson,' Matthew admitted.

'You can look if you think it will be of help, inspector,' Mr Simpson said. 'It's the second door on the left at the top of the stairs. I won't come up with you, if you don't mind. We haven't been in there since...'

'That's fine,' Matthew assured him, glad he wouldn't have Mr Simpson peering over his shoulder as he searched. 'DC Rudd will stay down here with you. If you can think of anything else that might be helpful, please let him know.'

Matthew gave Rudd a nod, a silent instruction to keep the Simpsons talking, and left the sitting room to climb the stairs to the first floor.

Lucy's bedroom seemed very feminine to Matthew's inexperienced eyes. The walls were decorated in a pink floral wallpaper and the single bed was covered with a dark pink bedspread. A chest of drawers occupied the far wall, a wardrobe stood on the wall inside the door. A dressing table was beneath the window.

Matthew moved around the bed, probing beneath the mattress, hoping to find a diary that would tell him everything he needed to know, but he came away empty-handed. *That would be too much to hope for*, he told himself, as he shoved his hand up the chimney of the small fireplace in the corner, again finding nothing. He rocked on the floorboards to see if any weren't fixed in place, but none of them moved beneath his feet. If Lucy had had a hiding place, he hadn't found it yet.

Matthew moved to the dressing table. Sitting in a cranberry-coloured glass tray was a bottle of perfume. He took the top off and sniffed. It was heady, musky, expensive smelling. Not the kind of scent he would have expected a young girl of eighteen to be able to afford. This bottle was of the kind to be found in a department store. Surely her money would have only stretched so far as Woolworths or Boots the Chemist?

Matthew opened the drawers, finding a writing folio in one. He felt inside the secretarial pocket and drew out several bank notes. His eyebrow rose as he counted ninety-five pounds. Where had Lucy got that much money? He ran his fingers over the blank page of the writing pad, hoping to feel the indentations of a pen or pencil, but the paper was smooth to his touch.

The wardrobe was next. Lucy hadn't had many clothes; three dresses, two skirts and four blouses hung on the rail. He searched the shelf above and found two woollen scarves, a pair of leather gloves and a woolly hat. On the bottom of the wardrobe, behind three pairs of shoes, was a stack of jumpers. These looked old and very well worn, and as he poked them, they toppled over to reveal three shoeboxes. It seemed as if the jumpers had been deliberately placed to hide the boxes. Matthew lifted the boxes out of the wardrobe and carried them to the bed.

Lifting the lid off the first box, Matthew found two more bottles of the same perfume as that on the dressing table. If one bottle had been expensive, how had Lucy had the money to buy three at once? He set the perfume aside and took out five packets of brand new silk stockings. He frowned; there was something very odd here. Taking the lid off the second box, he found a paper-wrapped carton marked NAAFI STORES FOR HM FORCES. Inside were twenty packs of cigarettes.

Matthew gathered up the boxes and left the bedroom. Mr Simpson was waiting at the bottom of the stairs.

'What have you got there?' he asked, staring at the boxes.

'Tell me, Mr Simpson,' Matthew said, sidestepping the question. 'Did Lucy smoke? Or know anyone in the NAAFI?'

'I don't think so.'

'Or anyone in a department store?'

'No. Why?'

'It doesn't matter.' He nodded at the boxes. 'I'll be taking these with me.'

'Have you found something? A clue?'

'Possibly.' Matthew saw Rudd hovering in the sitting-room doorway. The young detective discretely waved his notebook, suggesting he had something to report. 'Well, thank you for your time, Mr Simpson. We'll be off now.'

'What have you got?' he asked Rudd as they walked to the car.

'The name of a friend of Lucy's. A Miss Jenny Taylor. Mrs Simpson reckoned if anyone knows who got Lucy pregnant, it will be her.'

20

Jenny Taylor was at home when Matthew and Rudd called. Her mother showed them into the sitting room where Jenny was stretched out on the settee, a blanket over her legs, and a collection of soggy handkerchiefs on the table beside her. She looked up at Matthew and Rudd through dull, tired eyes as her mother introduced him.

'Please, don't get up.' Matthew put out a hand to stop Jenny. 'We're sorry to disturb you when you're not well.'

'It's just a cold,' Jenny said with a sniff. 'Are you here about Lucy?'

'Yes,' Matthew said, taking a seat in an armchair and feeling a broken spring poke his backside. 'We were just with her parents and her mother told us you and Lucy were friends. Did Lucy tell you she was having a baby?'

'No. I read about it in the newspaper.'

'Do you know who the father could have been? Was she seeing anyone four or five months ago?'

'Lucy never told me about the men she was seeing.'

'The men?' Matthew glanced at Rudd. 'She was seeing more than one?'

'Probably dozens,' Jenny said savagely. 'Lucy was such a trollop.'

Matthew frowned. 'Forgive me, Miss Taylor, but you don't sound that friendly towards Lucy.'

Jenny tugged at the handkerchief in her hand. 'We used to be friends until last year. Lucy changed when she started working at the cinema. She was all right before then. I mean, we weren't as close as we had been, but we still went out quite a bit. And we were doing the correspondence course together.'

'What course was that?'

'A typing course. We were both learning to type because we were going to be secretaries. Well, that was the idea, anyway, until we had the row.'

'What did you argue about?'

'Oh, it was silly, really,' she said with a careless shrug. 'We were here, practising our typing. Lucy broke a nail on a key and she got annoyed about it. The way she went on, you'd have thought she'd broken her finger. Anyway, she said she'd had enough and was going to pack the typing in. I thought she was joking at first, but she was serious, and so I said she was being selfish because her parents had paid a lot for the course and she had to learn to type and get her speed up if she wanted to be a secretary. I can do forty-five words a minute, but Lucy could barely manage twenty-five, even though she had had more practice than me. But Lucy said she didn't want to be a secretary, that she was going to do something better. I said there was nothing better, and she laughed and said being a secretary might be good enough for me, but it wasn't for her. Well, that gave me the pip, her saying she was better than me, and I gave her a piece of my mind. We had a row and she stormed out. That was back in May. We didn't speak again.'

May would have been just before Lucy got pregnant.

Was she seeing the father then? Matthew wondered. 'She didn't say what she was going to do that was better than being a secretary?'

Jenny shook her head. 'I don't know what she was getting at.' She looked into the corner of the room where a black case was propped against the wall. 'She left her typewriter here that day. I thought she might come back for it and we would make it up, but she never did. You couldn't take it back to her parents, could you? I don't want it here and I can't face them.'

Matthew nodded to Rudd to take the typewriter case. As Rudd picked up the case, a shopping bag stuffed behind it fell to the floor.

'That as well,' Jenny said. 'It's got pens and pencils and things in it. And the manuscript Lucy was typing up for Reverend Laing.'

Matthew's eyebrows rose. 'Reverend Laing? Lucy knew him?'

Jenny wiped her nose. 'She sang in the choir a year or so ago, not that she had much of a voice. And when he knew she was doing the typing course, he said Lucy could type up his manuscript for practice, if she wanted.'

'When was this?'

'I'm not sure. In spring, early summer, maybe. I do know she'd only just started working on his book when she packed the typing in.'

'Did she get on well with Reverend Laing?'

'I couldn't say. She never talked about him. She didn't tell me anything.' She closed her eyes and groaned quietly.

Seeing the girl was suffering, Matthew thanked her for her time, wished her better, and he and Rudd left, taking the typewriter and bag with them.

'Could the vicar be the man who got Lucy pregnant?'

Rudd asked as they clambered back into the car. 'The timing's about right.'

'Yes, it is,' Matthew agreed thoughtfully, but he wasn't convinced. If Timmy's description was accurate, the gunman had been tall and thin, and Laing was neither. If Timmy's description was accurate.

Rudd banged his door shut and turned to Matthew. 'Where next, sir?'

'The scene of the crime, Rudd,' Matthew said. 'Let's get over to the cinema.'

Laing stared into the fire, feeling highly satisfied.

The invitation to take tea with Bishop Lancey had come as a surprise, but the more Laing reflected on it, he realised he shouldn't have been surprised at all. His sermon on the cinema massacre, his interview in *The Chronicle*, his letter in *The Times* and the correspondence from his parishioners were all proof that Bertram Laing was a churchman worth listening to and that was a rarity in the Church. It was only right his superiors would want to talk to him.

The door opened and Bishop Lancey came in. He sat down in the armchair opposite with a squeak of the red leather. 'Sorry about that,' he said, propping his slippered feet on the fender. 'I had to take a call from the palace.'

Laing's interest piqued. The bishop had been talking to Lambeth Palace! Could he have been the subject of their conversation? 'Not at all,' he said with an understanding smile. 'God's work must come first.'

'God's work. Yes,' Lancey said thoughtfully. 'A tricky thing in this day and age.'

Laing took a sip of his tea. Was this the moment to tell the bishop his ideas? he wondered. But the bishop carried on before he could decide.

'You've been very voluble these past few days, Bertram. I heard your sermon on Sunday was quite something. You had an interview printed in a local newspaper yesterday and a letter in *The Times* this morning.'

'I did.' Laing swelled with pride. 'This is such a splendid opportunity to remind people of where they've been going wrong. The response I've had from my parish has been very encouraging. People have been looking for leadership from the Church—' He broke off as he noted the bishop's disapproving expression. It wasn't tactful to criticise the lack of leadership in the Church to the bishop. 'But as you say, God's work is not always easy in this day and age.'

'Indeed.' Lancey said. 'But I wonder if you have not been rather too voluble? You see, your words, provoked as they were by the tragedy in Foxhall Green, have, in their turn, provoked comment.'

'That is what I was hoping, Your Grace. To start a public debate, to—'

'I meant comment among our brethren,' Lancey interrupted. 'I have spoken with several of them since Sunday who believe your remarks have made it appear as if the Church is exploiting the tragedy at the cinema.'

'It's not exploitation. The cinema shooting was the spur the public needed,' Laing protested irritably. 'Without that, there would be no appetite for the debate my sermon, my interview and my letter have already created. One only has to read the newspapers to see that the shooting has got the nation talking about the problems with society because of a lack of faith. The nation is talking about Christianity once more. Your Grace, surely you would agree the shooting was a gift from God? I would even go so far as to say the gunman was performing an act of God.'

Lancey stared at him in horror. 'The slaughter of innocent people an act of God?'

'They weren't all innocent,' Laing snorted. 'There was one young woman amongst the slain who was no innocent at all, I can assure you.'

'But children were killed, Bertram.'

Laing made a noise of impatience. 'Brats, Your Grace. That's all they were. I knew those boys and I can tell you, they were nothing but unruly little criminals in the making. Their parents are slatterns and drunks who didn't even try to discipline them. The worst examples of the working classes. Loutish. Vulgar. You know, I've long thought it a pity the war ended when it did. After all, there's nothing like a war for culling a sick herd. In fact, I think I may write another letter to *The Times* on that very subject.'

His mind wandered to his vestry office, to the words he would write on his best writing paper. Good words, powerful. Even more powerful than his letter already printed. Laing glanced over at the bishop and frowned. The bishop was looking at him with a most peculiar expression on his face.

'Bearing in mind your history, Bertram,' Lancey said, 'I would have thought you would want to keep a low profile rather than seek to raise it.'

'My history, Your Grace?' Laing asked uneasily.

'I don't want to dredge that business up again, but I'm afraid mud always sticks. Were I you, I wouldn't want to put myself in a position where more mud could be slung at me.'

'But I am doing God's work. You surely cannot object to that?'

'I'm afraid I do object,' Lancey said. 'I can't order you to cease in your current vein, of course, but I do advise against continuing. If I were you, I would do all I could now to distance myself from the massacre. If it was thought you were making capital out of it, it may not go down so well with those who have authority over us. And bearing in mind your ambitions...' He raised his eyebrows meaningfully. 'Your future may depend on how you act now.'

A chill settled over Laing. The interview was not going at all the way he had expected. His hopes, expressed over the breakfast table with Violet that morning of regaining something of his former prestige, had been destroyed by a few words from the bishop.

As he put his cup and saucer down on the side table with a trembling hand, he realised everything he had done over the past few days may have done him more harm than good.

21

The police car pulled up outside the Regal Picture Palace and Matthew reflected how different the scene was from when he had last been on this spot. There was no crowd outside now, just a police constable from Foxhall Green guarding the doors.

Rudd opened the door for Matthew and he climbed out of the car. He looked up and down the high street. Something was bothering him.

'What is it, sir?' Rudd asked.

Matthew checked his wristwatch. It read a quarter past two. 'It's fairly busy along here, wouldn't you say?'

Rudd studied the high street. 'Yes, sir,' he said, the tone of his voice suggesting he had no idea what Matthew was getting at.

'And this is a weekday. On Saturday, this would have been even busier.'

'I suppose.'

'So, how can a man walk into the cinema with a rifle, shoot everyone in there, and come out of that gate there with no one seeing him?' He shook his head, unable to understand it. 'Nothing came out of the enquiries made along here?'

'No, sir. No one reported seeing anything. It is odd,' Rudd agreed.

'Bloody odd,' Matthew muttered, then shook the worry away to think about later. 'All right. Let's get in there.'

Rudd instructed the constable to open the door and they stepped inside. Matthew looked around the foyer, noting the door to the right marked Private, which led to the staffroom, and the stairs to the left, which led up to the manager's office and the projection room. He stared at the stairs. Something else was bothering him now.

'Have you made notes on the cinema staff statements?' he asked Rudd, knowing the young man invariably wrote everything down in mind-numbing detail.

'Yes, sir.' Rudd took out his notebook and flicked the pages. 'Which statement are you after?'

'The ticket lady's.'

A few more flicks. 'Got it, sir.' Rudd looked at Matthew expectantly.

'Stop me if I get this wrong,' Matthew said. 'Rita Amstell said she was standing in the entrance doorway there, when Ivor Topling spoke to her, making her jump because she hadn't see him behind her. Yes?'

Rudd checked his notes. 'Yes, sir.'

'So, she's standing here, inside the doors, looking towards the auditorium. If Topling had been hiding in the projection room during the shooting, as he claims, and only came down once the shooting stopped, he would have been in the foyer in front of her.'

Rudd looked around the foyer. 'You're right, sir. He would have come down there.' He pointed to the bottom of the stairs. 'He should have been in plain view. What does that mean, sir?'

'I'm not sure yet,' Matthew said. 'I want to see the projection room.' He crossed to the stairs and Rudd followed him up.

'I've never been in one of these,' Rudd said as they entered the projection room. 'I've always wondered what they're like.' He went over to the two projectors and peered at their workings before putting his face to one of the small square windows. 'It's not as good a view of the auditorium as I thought it would be.'

Matthew looked out of the other window. 'But you can see the bottom of the aisle steps from here. So, he would have seen the gunman if he'd looked out.' He turned back to study the room. 'There's nowhere to hide if the gunman had come up here. No lock on the door. Nothing you could move quickly and unaided to barricade yourself in. How safe would you have felt up here?'

'Not very,' Rudd said. 'And he would have had plenty of time to run out. That's what I would have done. I wouldn't have wanted to be a sitting duck up here. I'd have run.'

Matthew nodded. 'And if Topling was that scared, he would have stayed up here until the police came to get him, don't you think? A coward would have stayed where he was until he was sure it was all over.'

'You think he's lying about where he was, sir?' Rudd asked. 'But if he wasn't up here, where was he?' A thought occurred to him. 'In the auditorium?'

Matthew said nothing, but he was wondering the same thing. He moved to the metal racking where the reels of films were kept. He flicked through them, recognising the titles of some of the recent films, then saw a cardboard box stuffed behind the racking in the corner. He dragged it out and opened the flaps. Three more film tins greeted him. He took the topmost one out and his eyebrows rose as he read the label bearing the film's title. '*The Master and the Governess*,' he said, showing Rudd. He picked up the second tin. '*Cleopatra and Her Lovers*.' He took out the third. '*The Naked Bridge Party*.'

'Are those what I think they are?'

Matthew pulled out a section of film and held it up to the light. 'I'd say so. Take a look.' He passed the reel to Rudd.

Rudd too held the film up to the light. 'Blimey. They don't leave much to the imagination, do they?'

'And look at these.' Matthew took a carton out of the box. 'NAAFI cigarettes. The same as I found in Lucy Simpson's wardrobe. And the same stockings and perfume.'

'So, there's a connection between Topling and Lucy?' Rudd said excitedly.

'There always was. They worked together.'

'I know, but those,' Rudd pointed to the stockings, cigarettes and perfume, 'prove there was a lot more going on between them, doesn't it?'

'Put those tins back and we'll take the box with us. Now, let's go down and take a look around the auditorium and side alley.'

Rudd followed Matthew down the stairs to the auditorium, leaving the box in the foyer. There was nothing alarming about the auditorium now; all that remained were a few red stains on the carpet to remind Matthew and Rudd of the terrible event that had happened there.

'Lucy was shot here,' Matthew said, standing beside the row where he remembered seeing Lucy's stockinged leg.

'And Frankie Ashe was here.' Rudd pointed to a row near the front. 'Most of the other victims had time to get out of their seats and make for the doors.'

'That tallies with Lucy and Frankie being the first two shot.' Matthew moved to where the casings had littered the carpet and looked back up over the auditorium. He put an imaginary rifle to his shoulder and pulled the trigger, again and again, shooting an imaginary Lucy first, then Frankie, then the others. It wasn't pleasant to reenact the shooting, and he dropped his arms and turned to the side door. A plank of wood had been nailed to the frame to secure it. 'Can you get that off?'

Rudd tugged and tugged, and with a groan, wrenched the plank from the frame, splintering it. He threw it on the floor. 'Inspector Oakenshaw won't be pleased,' he said wryly.

'He can complain to me,' Matthew said, putting his hand into the hole where the lock had been and pulling the door open. Stepping into the alley, he moved to the rear wall where rotting wooden doors and planks were stacked and other rubbish littered the ground. The doors and planks were at a severe angle, so severe Matthew was surprised they still stood upright. He peered behind them.

'There's a door here,' he cried in surprise. Matthew shoved at the wood, moving it a few inches, enough to expose the door he had found. He tried the handle. It turned easily, and he pulled it open, putting his head in the gap. 'There's another alley running down the back. It must go on for a hundred yards or more.'

'That would take it down this section of high street.'

It all made sense now. 'This is how he got away,' Matthew declared. 'That's why no one saw him coming out of the side gate back onto the high street. Come on.' He angled his body through the gap and stepped into the back alley.

Rudd joined him. 'I wonder who knows this is here.'

'Grainger must know of it,' Matthew said, setting off down the alley, Rudd at his heels. 'And the owners of these shops must know it's here.'

'Our suspect list might just have got bigger, then, sir. If it isn't Topling, that is.'

They carried on down the alley, both detectives keeping an eye out for anything that would tell them the gunman had come this way. But after a sharp, right-handed turn at the end of the alley, they had spotted nothing and emerged onto the street.

Matthew took a few steps towards the pavement and looked back down the high street. 'That bush entirely covers the exit from the high street. He could have come out there and no one would have seen him.' He snatched off his hat and ran his hand through his hair. 'All the shop owners and residents at this end of the high street will have to be questioned if they haven't been already. And I want the rears of all these shops that back onto the alley searched.' He put his hat back on his head with a groan. 'God, but this case! We take one step forward and two steps back.'

'We do have a new lead, sir,' Rudd pointed out.

Matthew nodded. 'That's something, at least. Let's get back to the cinema and pick up that box. Then we'll drop in on Oakenshaw and tell him he's going to have to do a search and house-to-house enquiries again.'

'And then what, sir?' Rudd hurrying to keep up with Matthew as he set off down the high street.

'And then,' Matthew said, 'I want to speak with Rita Amstell and Ivor Topling.'

Rita Amstell was up to her elbows in flour when Matthew and Rudd knocked on her front door. She wore no makeup and her hair was wrapped in a patterned turban. Conscious of her drab appearance, she showed Matthew and Rudd into her front room, told them she wouldn't be a minute, and returned in ten, wearing a cream blouse and green skirt, her hair pinned back, a light dusting of face powder and a smear of bright red lipstick.

'I don't know what more you think I can tell you,' she said, plumping down on the settee and smoothing her skirt over her knees. 'I told that other policeman everything I know.'

'There are a few things I'd like to hear for myself,' Matthew said, giving her his best smile. 'Please tell me what happened on Saturday.'

Rita's expression became pained. 'It was all so horrible. I was in the staffroom having a cup of tea with George while the picture was on. We'd been in there for about fifteen minutes when we heard what sounded like shots being fired. At first, we didn't think anything of it because it was a Western showing and we thought it was just the cowboys shooting at the Indians, even though it sounded a lot louder than normal. But then we heard screaming, and I knew that wasn't in the film, so I said to George we ought to go and have a look. George opened the doors and... well, I've never seen anything like it. All the people were lying there on the floor. I just stood there, shocked, until Mr Grainger came down and told me to call the police. Am I doing all right?' she asked Matthew anxiously.

'You're doing fine,' he assured her. Everything she had said tallied with what she'd told Lund. 'I need to ask you about something you said in your statement. You said Mr Topling gave you quite a fright when he spoke to you because you hadn't realised he was there.'

'That's right. Made me jump out of my skin, he did.'

'Where were you standing when he made you jump?'

'In the doorway.'

'The front doors? Looking into the foyer.'

'That's right.'

'And where was Mr Topling when he made you jump?'

'Behind me.'

'Did you see him come down the stairs from the projection room?'

Rita opened her mouth to reply, then halted and narrowed her eyes at Matthew. 'No,' she said at last. 'I didn't. But no... that can't be right. That would mean he wasn't up there at all.'

'Tell me, Mrs Amstell,' Matthew said. 'Do you know if there was anything going on between Ivor Topling and Lucy Simpson?'

'You're asking because Lucy was pregnant, aren't you?' Rita reached for her cigarettes. 'I can't say I was surprised when I read it in the newspaper this morning.'

'Was there something between her and Topling?' Matthew asked.

Rita lit her cigarette and tossed the match into an ashtray. 'Well, men always try it on, don't they? But Lucy wasn't having any of that from Ivor and he soon got the message. It made him be a bit nasty about her, actually. He said horrible things about her behind her back.'

'What sort of things?'

'Oh, just that she wasn't as pretty as she liked to think she was. How she thought she was better than the rest of us. And the other week, I said something about Lucy not having the brains to do my job. She wasn't very good with money, always short-changing the customers when they bought the chocolate and cigarettes. Ivor laughed when I said that, not a very nice laugh, and said I didn't know the half of it. And then he...' Her mouth pursed and she looked away.

'Then he what, Mrs Amstell?' Matthew pressed.

Rita drew herself up a little primly. 'Well, you'll have to excuse my French, inspector, but Ivor said Lucy was a scheming little bitch.'

Matthew glanced over at Rudd. The young detective was looking excited, confident they may have made a breakthrough in the case and got their first good suspect. Matthew wasn't sure about that, but what Rita had told him was enough to make him hope.

'Thank you, Mrs Amstell,' he said, rising. 'We won't take up any more of your time.'

'Well, if you're sure,' Rita said, a little disappointed. 'I'll see you out.' She opened the door and Matthew and Rudd stepped out onto the front path.

'Oh,' Matthew said, halting her as she was about to shut the door. 'There is just one more thing. Did you tidy up the ticket booth before you and Mr Cordell went into the staffroom?'

'Yes, of course.'

'You wouldn't have left any money out?'

'No. Why are you asking?'

'There was a brand new sixpence lying on the counter. I wondered if you'd left it there.'

Rita shook her head. 'There would have been hell to pay if Mr Grainger caught me leaving money lying around, even if it was only a sixpence. Whoever left it there, inspector, it wasn't me.'

Ivor Topling's front door was opened by a woman with a pink net around her hair and curlers poking out the front.

Rudd showed her his warrant card. 'Craynebrook CID. Are you Mrs Topling?'

'Yes,' she said. 'What do you want?'

'We'd like to talk to your husband. He in?'

'If it's about the shooting,' Mrs Topling said, 'he's told your lot everything already.'

Matthew, standing behind Rudd, saw the net curtain at the window twitch. Ivor was in, all right. 'We can talk to him here or down the station, Mrs Topling,' he said, in no mood to pussyfoot around. 'Which is it to be?'

It didn't take her long to work out which she preferred. Mrs Topling opened the door. 'All right,' she said. 'I don't like letting just anybody in, you know?'

'We're not anybody.' Matthew stepped into the small hall and turned into the front room.

Ivor was standing by the window. 'What's this?' he asked, forcing a nervous smile as Matthew and Rudd entered. 'Police?'

'That's right,' Matthew nodded. 'I'm DI Stannard. This is DC Rudd. We'd like to talk to you about Lucy Simpson.'

Ivor swallowed, then glanced over at his wife hovering in the doorway. 'Why don't you make some tea, love?'

Mrs Topling went out, eyeing her husband suspiciously, and Ivor closed the door quietly behind her. 'What about Lucy?' he said, settling into an armchair.

Matthew took a seat. 'How well did you know her?'

'Not well. She was downstairs. I was up.'

'Did you two get along?'

'Yeah. Course we did.'

'How well?'

Ivor frowned. 'What you getting at?'

'I think you know what I'm getting at, Mr Topling. Lucy was a very pretty girl.'

Ivor made a face. 'Not that pretty.'

'But pretty enough. You tried it on with her.'

'Who says I did?'

'Rita Amstell.'

Ivor glanced at the closed sitting-room door. 'Well, girls like you to try it on with 'em. They get the hump if you don't.'

'I'm sure you've read in the newspapers that Lucy was pregnant when she died, Mr Topling,' Matthew said. 'Was the baby yours?'

'Now, you wait just a minute,' Ivor said, pointing a nicotine-stained finger at Matthew. 'I never touched her, not like that. The furthest I ever got was pinching her backside, and I got a slap for it, so don't give me any of this about a baby. That was nothing to do with me.'

'So, why did you give her perfume and stockings and cigarettes?'

Ivor's mouth fell open. 'I didn't. I didn't give her nothing.'

The door suddenly burst open and Mrs Topling came flying in. Ivor jumped out of his chair and backed away into the bay window.

'You were having it off with that tart,' she screeched as she slapped at him, again and again. 'All those nights you told me you was working, you were out with her.' Blow after blow rained down upon Ivor as he raised his hands over his head to fend off his wife.

Matthew glanced at Rudd and jerked his head at husband and wife. Rudd, understanding, moved quickly, grabbing hold of Mrs Topling's arms and pinning them to her sides.

'Get off me!' she screamed at him.

'Calm down, Mrs Topling,' Matthew told her.

'Don't you tell me to calm down! He's been giving a tart presents when I'm struggling to put food on the table.'

'I haven't, Vera,' Ivor protested. 'It's not what you think.'

'Not what I think? All those nights staying late at the cinema. You were with her, weren't you?' With a renewed burst of energy, Mrs Topling broke free of Rudd's grasp and threw herself at her husband once more.

'Stop it,' Ivor cried as she pummelled him. ''ere, copper!'

'Yes, Mr Topling?' Matthew replied coolly.

'Get me out of here, will ya?'

22

Dickie heaved himself onto the stool and leant both elbows on the counter.

'What can I get you?' the barmaid asked.

'I'll have a stout, please,' Dickie said and glanced around the pub. A group of four men were over at a far table, huddled over their pints; a middle-aged couple were at another table; a young man was sitting alone reading a newspaper and two men were playing darts. 'Not busy today?'

'It is a bit quiet,' the barmaid agreed, putting the stout in front of him and holding her hand out for payment. 'It's been that way since Saturday.'

'Why's that, do you think? Are people afraid to come out?'

'Could be,' she nodded. 'I mean, something like that makes you wonder if you're safe anywhere.'

It was the same sentiment Dickie had heard expressed a dozen times since Saturday, and which he had already included several times in his copy for *The Chronicle*. He needed something new, some new angle. The police were being very tight-lipped about the investigation, giving nothing away, and so Dickie was haunting the pubs and talking to strangers on the street in the hope he would find something of interest to put in his article for the morning's edition.

'I haven't seen you in here before,' the barmaid said, wiping a glass with a tea towel.

'It's not my local,' Dickie said. 'I'm here for work.'

'Oh yes? What do you do?'

'I'm a reporter for *The Chronicle*.'

'You're here because of the shooting?'

'That's right. I need a story for tomorrow's 'paper.'

'What kind of story?'

'Like the police have caught the killer,' Dickie said, smiling at the unlikelihood of that happening in the next few hours.

The barmaid shook her head. 'If you ask me, I don't think the police know what they're doing. Not if all that stuff about the detective in charge is true.'

'He's been replaced,' Dickie said, taking a mouthful of his stout. There had been one short statement from Mullinger first thing that morning announcing Matthew had taken over the investigation. 'DI Stannard is in charge now. He'll find the killer.'

'You sound very sure.'

'I am sure. He knows what he's doing.'

A blast of cold air hit Dickie's back and he turned on the stool to see a middle-aged, heavy-set man come in and head for the bar. He rubbed his hands together and smiling at the barmaid, said, 'Give us something to warm us up, Babs.'

The barmaid put a brandy on the counter before him. 'How are you, George?'

'Oh, not too bad,' George said, lifting the glass to his lips. 'Considering.'

'I said to Bert just this morning, you were lucky you

weren't shot. Just think, if you'd been at the door when he walked in, you'd have copped it too.'

'I know. Makes my blood run cold to think of it.'

The penny dropped in Dickie's brain. This was George Cordell, the doorman at the Regal. What a stroke of luck!

'Are you George Cordell?' he asked.

George's eyes narrowed at him. 'Yeah. Who are you?'

Dickie held out his hand. 'Dickie Waite.'

'He's a reporter, George,' the barmaid said.

'Reporter, eh?'

'That's right. *The Chronicle*. I'm here in Foxhall Green to cover the story. I'd like to have a chat with you, if that's all right?'

George shook his head. 'The police said I wasn't to talk to reporters about what happened. Said it could harm the investigation.'

Bugger, Dickie thought, and tried a different tack. 'Did you see the tramp the police are looking for? Did he ever come into the cinema?'

'I saw him,' George nodded. 'Not in the cinema, mind. On the high street. I gave him a bob, actually. I've always got time for old soldiers.'

'Why did he do it, do you think?' the barmaid wondered.

'If you ask me, he didn't. I reckon the police are barking up the wrong tree looking for him.'

'Why do you say that?' Dickie asked.

'He didn't seem the type to do that sort of thing. Give him a wash, put him in some decent clothes and he'd be quite respectable. And I tell you something else. His hands shook something rotten. I don't see how he could have held a rifle straight, let alone shoot one and hit someone every time.'

'Who do you think the police should be looking for, then?' Dickie said.

George swirled the remains of his brandy in his glass thoughtfully. 'I could tell you, but I don't know if I ought to.'

'Tell us what, George?' the barmaid asked eagerly.

George looked from her to Dickie, a smug smile playing on his lips. He leaned forward conspiratorially. 'The police have been asking questions about Ivor.'

The barmaid gasped. 'Ivor?'

'Ivor Topling?' Dickie said. 'The projectionist at the Regal?'

George nodded. 'Rita called me not half an hour ago saying she'd had detectives round hers asking about Ivor and Lucy. She was all excited because she said talking to them had made her realise Ivor couldn't have been where he told the police he was during the shooting.'

'Where was he, then?' the barmaid asked.

'We don't know. He told the police he was hiding in the projection room. So, why did he lie? What's he got to hide?' George raised his eyebrows and nodded knowingly.

'He shot all those people?' the barmaid said, shaking her head in disbelief.

'Now, I'm not saying that,' George said, holding up his hands and casting a wary look at Dickie. 'All I'm saying is the police have been asking questions about him and they've taken him to the station.'

'How do you know that?' Dickie asked.

'Because I passed his house on the way here and his missus was out the front, having a go at the neighbours for gawping at her husband being carted off by the police. So there must be something in it, mustn't there?'

'I can hardly believe it,' the barmaid said, shaking her head. 'I was talking to Ivor only the other day. He was sitting where you are now.' She nodded at Dickie. 'And all the time, he was thinking of doing that...'

'Makes you think, don't it?' George said. 'You never can tell with some people.'

'But that means—' The barmaid broke off and turned her head towards the two men playing darts. 'I wonder what Pete will say when he hears about this.'

'Oh blimey, is he over there?' George said, alarmed. 'Don't say anything, Babs.'

'But he's got a right to know, George.'

'Well, don't say it came from me. I don't want any trouble. You know what him and his friends are like. They'll think, because I worked with Ivor, that I had something to do with it.'

'Course they won't,' she chided. 'They know you.'

'They know Ivor, too. Do you think that'll stop them? Don't say anything, Babs. Please.'

Her expression became pained. 'They're looking over here,' she said under her breath.

'I'm off,' George said, and hurried towards the door, looking over his shoulder as he yanked it open and went out.

Dickie stared at the swinging door, wondering what had worried the doorman so much, when a voice at his elbow said, 'Where's George off to in such a hurry?' He turned to see that one of the men had come over.

'Oh, he had to get back, Benny,' the barmaid said with a shrug.

'He didn't give his condolences to Pete,' Benny said accusingly.

'I don't expect he saw him. I'm sure he would have done if he'd seen Pete over there.'

Dickie could see Benny wasn't convinced.

'Has he heard anything?' Benny asked. 'Does he know what's going on?'

'I don't think so,' she said, wiping the counter vigorously with the tea towel.

Benny's eyes narrowed at her. 'I heard you talking about Ivor.'

'It was nothing, Benny,' she said, and Dickie saw the anxiety on her face. What was she so worried about?

'What about Ivor?' Benny said, leaning closer.

The barmaid glanced over at the other man by the dartboard, who was watching them with interest. She licked her dry lips, glanced unhappily at Dickie, then said, 'George said the police have taken Ivor in for questioning. But that's all he knows, Benny. Honest.'

'Right,' Benny said, and slunk back to the dartboard. Dickie watched him talking to the other man.

'Are you all right, love?' Dickie asked the barmaid quietly.

She nodded unhappily, looking out of the corners of her eyes at the two men.

'Who are they?'

'The one who came over is Benny Cross. The other man is Pete Ashe. His boy was one of the kids that were killed. I'm not sure if I should have told them about Ivor.' She twisted the tea towel and groaned. 'Oh, I do hope there won't be any trouble.'

'You haven't told me how your tea with the bishop went, Bertram,' Violet scolded as she sat down in the armchair opposite her husband and took out her embroidery. 'Did he ask after me?'

Laing stared moodily into the fire. 'No, he didn't. It wasn't really that kind of meeting.'

Violet frowned. 'I thought it was a social occasion. Weren't there other churchmen there?'

'No, it was just me. It turned out he summoned me so he could have a word.'

'A word about what?' she asked.

Laing drew in a deep breath and swirled the brandy around in his glass. It was his third that evening and still the pain of his interview with the bishop had not yet dulled. 'I received a ticking-off, Violet,' he said, unable to keep the anger out of his voice.

'A ticking-off for what?'

'For speaking my mind. The bishop doesn't approve. He accused me of exploiting the death of innocents for my own ends. He said I was making it look as if the Church was profiting from murder.'

'That's ridiculous. What you've done is bring attention to the depravities of society. You've done a great service to the Church.'

'You try explaining that to the bishop. I've been told to desist, Violet. To stop. That's what the invitation to tea was all about. Not to congratulate me at all but to tell me to behave.'

'How dare he!' Violet said, her eyes flashing with indignation. 'Well, I don't think you should stop, Bertram. In fact, I think you should ignore him and do more. Give more interviews. Write more letters. Show the bishop how wrong he is.'

Laing shook his head. 'There's more to it than that, my dear. The bishop indicated that any hopes of my being promoted out of Foxhall Green would be quashed if I continue to speak my mind. I even got the impression I would be punished were I not to heed his warning.'

'He threatened you?' Violet was aghast.

'No, of course not. His warning was delivered as advice, but the meaning was clear. If I want to be promoted out of this backwater, I need to keep my mouth shut.' He kicked at a log sticking out of the grate, sending sparks flying. 'When I think of all I've done to get to this point, it makes my blood boil. Why can't the bishop realise what an opportunity I've provided for the Church? The massacre has done in a few days what the Church hasn't managed in ten years. I've roused the interest of the public. I've got reporters ready to print my every word. But because the bishop is squeamish, I'm told to stop. It's all been for nothing.'

'You still have your book, Bertram,' she reminded him.

He shook his head. 'I fear that will never see the light of day now, Violet. I may as well throw it on the fire.'

'No, don't do that,' she said, putting her hand on his knee. 'Perhaps the Church isn't ready for you and your ideas for a clean, decent society. But there will come a day when it is, and when that day comes, you'll be ready to answer the call. Your conscience is clear, Bertram. Remember that. Despite what anyone says, you've done nothing wrong.'

23

Ivor was in the only interview room Foxhall Green station had, sitting across the table from Rudd. Matthew entered, took a seat next to Rudd and lit a cigarette.

'Ready to talk, Mr Topling?' he asked.

'I ain't got nothing to say to you,' Ivor muttered. 'I just wanted to get out of the house before Vera killed me. That's your fault, you know? Saying all that about Lucy.'

Matthew set his cigarettes and matches to one side and leaned back in his chair. 'What was the nature of your relationship with Lucy Simpson?'

'I didn't have a relationship with her,' Ivor said. 'We worked together, that was all.'

'So, just work colleagues, is that it?'

'Yeah. That's right.'

'No problems? Arguments?'

'No.'

Matthew took a drag of his cigarette and narrowed his eyes at Ivor. 'Then why did you call Lucy a scheming little bitch?'

Ivor looked a little taken aback. 'I didn't.'

'Mrs Amstell says you did. She also said you got quite

203

nasty about Lucy. DC Rudd, read out what Mrs Amstell told us Mr Topling said about Lucy and money.'

Rudd flipped to a page in his notebook. 'She said Lucy wasn't very good with money, always short-changing customers, and that Mr Topling laughed unpleasantly and said she, Mrs Amstell, didn't know the half of it.'

'So, what was the half Mrs Amstell didn't know?' Matthew asked.

'I don't know what she's talking about. I didn't say that.'

'Why would Mrs Amstell lie?'

'Why do women do anything?' Ivor said sourly, and asked Matthew for a cigarette.

Matthew gave him one, lighting it for him. 'We searched your projection room earlier today. What do you think we found?'

Ivor blew out a plume of smoke and shrugged. 'I don't know.'

But Matthew had seen the flicker of alarm in Ivor's eyes. 'We found a cardboard box with bottles of perfume, brand new stockings and cartons of cigarettes in it. The same cigarettes, the same stockings, and the same perfume Lucy Simpson had in her bedroom.'

Ivor's expression brightened. 'Then it must have been her box. I don't know nothing about it.'

'We also found films in the box. Films, I doubt, are standard fare at the Regal Picture Palace. You know the films I mean, don't you? *The Naked Bridge Party. Cleopatra and Her Lovers.* Ring any bells? Or are you going to say those films were Lucy's, too?'

Ivor snorted. 'You think she was such a little innocent, don't you?'

'Actually, I don't,' Matthew said. 'Innocent girls don't get themselves pregnant before they're married. Nor do they have affairs with married men.'

'I wasn't having an affair with Lucy. I didn't knock her up.'

'So, who did?'

'I don't know,' Ivor said angrily. 'If she was having a baby, it was nothing to do with me. Why won't you listen?'

'All right, Mr Topling,' Matthew nodded. 'Let's forget about Lucy and the films and the box in the projection room for a minute. Let's talk about Saturday afternoon and the shooting. In your statement, you claimed you hid in the projection room during the shooting and came down only once it was all over.'

'That's right.'

'And yet, you couldn't tell Inspector Lund what happened in the auditorium?'

'Because I didn't see anything.'

'You didn't look through the window to see what was going on?'

'No. I didn't want the gunman seeing me and shooting at me.'

'It's very unlikely he would have noticed you. It's a small window, and with the light shining in his eyes, he would have been blinded.'

'I didn't know that. For all I knew, he could have seen me, so I stayed out of sight.'

'It didn't occur to you to get help?'

Ivor licked his dry lips. 'I was scared. And besides, what could I do against a madman with a gun? I didn't want to get my head shot off.' He looked from Matthew to Rudd and back again. 'Look, I know it don't make me look good, me hiding like that, but it's the truth. I was too scared to move, so I stayed up in the projection room and I didn't come down till the shooting stopped.'

'I could understand that,' Matthew said. 'Not everyone's cut out to be a hero. But you see, what you said in your statement doesn't make sense. Not when it's compared to Mrs Amstell's statement. She made no mention of you being in the foyer until after the police constable came in from the high street, which is several minutes after the shooting stopped. In fact, she didn't see you come down the stairs from the projection room at all. She told us the first time she saw you was when she turned around and saw you standing behind her in the doorway. Now, given there isn't an exit from the projection room onto the street, I can't work out how you could have been there if, as you claim, you'd been hiding in the projection room all that time.'

Ivor said nothing, and Matthew went on.

'Shall I tell you what I'm wondering? I'm wondering if you came in from the street because you'd come out of the side alley after shooting all those people?'

Ivor's eyes widened and he shifted forward to the edge of his seat. 'Now you wait just a minute. I had nothing to do with that. I never shot nobody. I had no reason to.'

'I think you had a very good reason to kill Lucy if she was carrying your child and making a fuss about it. You could stand to lose quite a lot if she started telling people. Your job, your marriage. That's reason enough to want to keep her quiet.'

'I wasn't having an affair with Lucy.'

'You gave her perfume and stockings and cigarettes.'

'It wasn't like that. They weren't presents.'

'What were they, then?'

Ivor put his head in his hands and sighed.

'You might as well tell us, Mr Topling,' Matthew said. 'We'll find out sooner or later. And it will go better for you if—'

'All right,' Ivor growled. 'I'll tell you.' He fell back into his chair and looked at Matthew wearily. 'Those films you found. I show them after hours, when the cinema's shut up and everyone's gone home. I charge an entrance fee for men who like those kind of pictures. There's all that equipment just sitting there, and I thought I might as well put it to good use and make a bit on the side. So, I show the films and sell the cigarettes and any other stuff I can get my hands on to the punters. I weren't doing no harm.'

'So, how does Lucy fit into this little sideline of yours?' Matthew asked.

'Lucy found out about the film shows. She threatened to tell Grainger. The perfume, the stockings, the fags. They were all Lucy's cut.'

Matthew stared at him. 'She was blackmailing you?' he asked in astonishment.

Ivor nodded. 'She came back to the cinema one night after hours to pick up something she'd forgotten. She saw a film playing and men in the seats and came up to me in the projection room. Gave me the shock of my life, she did. I thought she would be disgusted, but she was all excited and wanted to know what I was up to. Like a bloody idiot, I told her all about the films and the stuff I sold the punters. This is before I knew what she was like, you see. And then she comes back with a demand to be cut in on the deals, fifty fifty. If I said no, she'd tell Grainger and that would be that. I had no choice but to go along with her.'

'That must have been very annoying..' Matthew said, the bank notes he'd found in Lucy's writing folio now making sense. 'Having to share so much of your profits.'

'Well, I weren't best pleased about it.'

'I expect you would have done anything to be rid of her.'

Ivor took a drag of his cigarette. 'I didn't kill her. I'll admit, Lucy was a pain in the rear end, but it was only money. I was making enough.'

'You would have made a lot more if Lucy wasn't taking a fifty per cent cut.'

'You think I killed her for fifty per cent?'

'Men have killed for a lot less.'

'For God's sake, I didn't do it. Why would I kill her? I was on to a good thing. So was Lucy. And having her involved meant the takings went up.'

'How do you mean?'

Ivor sighed. 'The punters liked having a woman there while the films were on. They got a kick out of it. Some of them even paid her to sit with them.'

Matthew stared at him. 'Do you mean to say Lucy was in the auditorium while the films were playing?'

Ivor smiled at the shock on Matthew's face. 'You've really got the wrong idea about Lucy. Yeah, she stayed and watched some of the films. She got a taste for them. And she got a taste for money, too. She put the prices up for entry and the goodies, and the punters were willing to pay because of her. Lucy could get money out of anyone.' He grinned. 'Rita says Lucy had no brains for handling money because she was always shortchanging the customers? Lucy weren't shortchanging them because she couldn't add up. She shortchanged them on purpose so she could keep the money, and you'd be surprised how many men let her get away with it. If they made a fuss, she let them put their hand up her skirt, and then they wouldn't say a word. Believe me. I know what I'm talking about. I saw her do it often enough.'

Matthew was stunned. An eighteen-year-old girl from a good family behaving like that! 'Did any of your punters have a problem with Lucy? Threaten her?'

'Nah, nothing like that.' Ivor sat up, suddenly realising what Matthew was getting at. 'Oh, what? You mean, would one of them have wanted to kill her?' He thought about it, then shrugged. 'I dunno. As far as I could tell, she got on all right with them.'

'I need to know the names of these punters of yours,' Matthew said.

'Ah, sorry. Can't help you there. First rule in that line of business. Don't get names.'

'So, how did you acquire your punters? How did men find out about your out-of-hours film shows?'

Ivor shrugged. 'You get talking to a fella in a pub. They talk to someone else, other interested parties. Word gets around.'

'Would you recognise any of these men who came to the cinema?'

'Yeah, if I saw them again.'

Matthew stubbed out his cigarette in the ashtray. 'All right, Mr Topling. You've told us about your illegal film shows. Let's go back to last Saturday. You weren't in the projection room during the shooting, were you?'

Ivor sighed and shook his head. 'I was over the road doing a deal with the fella who gets me the goodies.'

'By goodies, you mean...?'

'Fags. Stockings. Perfume. Cigars. Chocolates. Alcohol. Whatever he can lay his hands on.'

'And I assume these goodies are off the back of a lorry?'

'I suppose so. I don't ask and he don't tell me.'

'What about the films? Does he get those for you as well?'

Ivor nodded.

'So, you were over the road...?'

'Round the back of the church. That's where we do our deals.'

'When was this?'

'It was just after I changed the second reel, so that was around a quarter to two. I'd arranged to meet him at two o'clock. I was going to get over there, do the deal and be back before I had to change the third reel.'

'And you did the deal?'

'Yeah. I met him. He showed me what he had and I gave him the cash.'

'What did you get off him?'

'More cigarettes. A couple of boxes of cigars.'

'And you took them back to the cinema?'

'No, I hid them under a bush at the church. I was planning to get them later.'

'So, they'll still be there?'

Ivor shook his head. 'I picked them up on Sunday night. They're in my shed at home.' He leaned forward. 'Look. I've told you everything, right? I wasn't in the cinema when all those people were killed. I was over the road. I had nothing to do with it. I swear.'

Matthew studied Ivor's face for a long moment. 'All right, Mr Topling. You give us the name of the man you get your goods from and where we can find him, and we'll find out if you were where you say you were. In the meantime, you'll be charged with the showing of obscene material under the Obscene Publications Act and receiving stolen goods. I'll also need you to sign a new statement confirming everything you've told us. You'll stay with us until all that's done.'

Ivor fell back in the chair. 'That's all right with me. I'm in no rush to get home.'

Matthew saw Ivor put into a cell, then made his way to the lobby, meaning to update Oakenshaw. As he drew near, he heard voices.

'I'm sorry, sir, but I can't tell you that,' he heard Sergeant Dobbs say.

'Just tell me if he's here. That's all I'm asking.'

Matthew knew that voice. He turned the corner that

brought him out to the front desk and cried, 'Dickie! What are you doing here?'

Dickie shot Sergeant Dobbs an exasperated glance. 'Looking for you.'

Dobbs turned to Matthew. 'I did tell Mr Waite you were busy, sir.'

'It's all right, sergeant,' Matthew said. 'I know Mr Waite.' He moved around the front desk and into the lobby, taking hold of Dickie's elbow and drawing him aside. 'What are you doing here, Dickie?' he asked again.

'I've heard a rumour you've arrested the projectionist from the Regal,' Dickie said. 'Is that right?'

Matthew didn't bother to ask where Dickie had heard the rumour. 'He's helping with our enquiries. And before you ask, that's as much as I'm telling you.'

'I'm not here for the 'paper,' Dickie said irritably. 'I heard about the projectionist from George Cordell, the doorman at the Regal. He'd heard it from Rita Amstell.'

'I can't stop people talking,' Matthew said. 'I only wish I could.'

'My point is this conversation was overheard by a couple of men, one of whom had a boy killed in the shooting. Once Cordell realised they were there, he was very keen to get away. He came over all anxious and so did the barmaid. One of the men got it out of her that you'd taken Topling away and when he'd gone, she said to me she hoped there wasn't going to be any trouble. Now, I don't know about you, but that sounds like she was worried these fellas were going to cut up rough.'

'With Ivor Topling?'

'If they can get hold of him,' Dickie nodded. 'But if you've got him in here, they won't be able to, so who do you think they'll go after instead?'

Matthew understood. 'You think his family may be in danger?'

Dickie shrugged. 'I've seen it before. I'm sure you have too. Revenge attacks. Of course, I might be wrong. Nothing was actually said. It's just a feeling, but I've talked to a lot of people over the last few days, and I'm sure you don't need me to tell you, there's a lot of anger about. I just thought your lot would want to know what I heard.'

'I appreciate the warning, Dickie,' Matthew said, 'but unless a crime is committed, there's nothing I can do.'

'There must be something. Can't you have a word with them? Let them know you're watching or something like that?'

'Who were these men?'

'The barmaid said they were Pete Ashe and Benny Cross.'

Matthew considered, then shook his head, mindful of Mullinger's warning about complaints. 'It could make matters worse if the police paid them a visit. A grieving father being hounded by the police, that sort of thing. In fact, the sort of thing a newspaper like yours would love. Is that it? You want to stir up a story?'

'What do you take me for, Matthew?' Dickie snapped. 'All right. So, you're not going to do anything. But I've done my bit. My conscience is clear.' He shoved his hands in his pockets and raised his eyebrows at Matthew. 'As I am here, what can you tell me about this projectionist?'

'Nothing,' Matthew said firmly.

'Come on, give me something. I need a story for the morning edition.'

'If you want a story, then write about the attack on Sergeant Brock. I'm sure you've heard about that?'

'The tramp? He got beaten up.'

'Probably because it was all over the news that we wanted to speak to him.'

'You think the attack on Sergeant Brock was an act of vigilantism?'

Matthew nodded. 'I think it's likely. So, you can print we're taking the attack on Sergeant Brock very seriously, that we're pursuing his attackers and are confident they will be caught and punished. Also, put in that the police advise the public not to take matters into their own hands.'

'All right. I will. I take it as you've got Topling in that you don't think the tramp did it?'

'Off the record?'

Dickie nodded.

'I'm still waiting for his alibi to be checked, but I'm fairly confident Brock's innocent,' Matthew said.

'Lund thought he did it,' Dickie reminded him.

'I think Lund was wrong.'

'It wouldn't be the first time. How is he?'

'Why are you asking? Feeling guilty?'

'A bit,' Dickie admitted.

'I haven't seen him since last night. Officially, he's on two-weeks' leave.'

'Maybe that's what he needs. Time off to get himself straight.'

'Maybe,' Matthew checked his watch. 'I've got to get on, Dickie.'

'Yeah, all right. I'll see you, Matthew.'

Matthew saw Dickie out, then went to Oakenshaw's office.

'Have you charged this Topling yet?' Oakenshaw asked as Matthew entered.

'No,' Matthew said, taking a seat. He told him about Ivor's interview. 'I've got Rudd checking his alibi, but I have a feeling he's telling the truth.'

'Pity. I thought you had your man.'

'So did I,' Matthew admitted ruefully. 'Listen, I've just been told it's got out that we've brought Topling in for questioning. In view of the beating Sergeant Brock took, I think it would be a good idea to keep an eye out for anyone causing trouble, taking the law into their own hands.'

'Vigilantism?' Oakenshaw scoffed. 'This is Foxhall Green, Stannard, not the Deep South of America. We don't have vigilantes here.'

'I don't know how long we're going to have to keep Topling in here. I think it would be sensible to keep an eye on his family,' Matthew insisted. 'What happened to Sergeant Brock—'

'What happened to Brock is par for the course for men like him. Tramps are never welcome and are always encouraged to move on.'

'What was done to him was more than encouragement to get out of town,' Matthew snapped. 'He was almost killed. Now, I've told a reporter to print that we're taking the attack seriously and any similar incidents will not be tolerated, but let's try to prevent them rather than having to deal with the aftermath, yes?'

'Don't lecture me, Stannard,' Oakenshaw said. 'I've heard you'll do anything to get your name in the 'papers, but making such a fuss over a tramp is really going too far. And as for keeping an eye on the Toplings. Exactly how am I supposed to do that? Where am I supposed to magic these extra men from? Or are these the same men I've got re-doing house-to-house enquiries and searching the rear of shops for you? I don't think you realise how few men I have. We're stretched thin as it is.'

'I really don't want an argument, Oakenshaw,' Matthew said wearily, feeling the familiar ache in his skull where Gadd had clobbered him. 'Please, just do what you can.'

'Oh, very well.' Oakenshaw waved irritably at the door. Matthew took his cue and left.

<h1 style="text-align:center">24</h1>

It took a few hours for Rudd to find Ivor's shady dealer, who reluctantly confirmed he and Ivor met in the church grounds in Foxhall Green at two o'clock on Saturday. Rudd returned to Foxhall Green to tell Matthew, and Ivor was released. It had gone eight o'clock before Matthew and Rudd returned to Craynebrook.

The detectives were at their desk, heads bent over paperwork, when they walked into CID. Without a word, Barnes jerked a thumb behind him where Mullinger was studying the investigation corkboard. Matthew went over to him.

'Good evening, sir.'

The superintendent turned to him. 'Good evening, Stannard. I heard you've released this Topling fellow?'

'Yes, sir. He's got an alibi for the time of the shooting, but we have charged him with other offences.'

'Oakenshaw told me.' Mullinger frowned. 'He also told me you've asked him to conduct more house-to-house enquiries and to keep a watch on Topling's house. He's concerned he doesn't have the manpower.'

'I didn't ask for a constant watch,' Matthew explained.

'Just an occasional patrol. It's a precaution, sir, nothing more. I have explained this to Inspector Oakenshaw.'

'Oakenshaw can be awkward.' Mullinger picked up a newspaper from a nearby desk and handed it to Matthew. 'I wonder if you've seen this?'

It was that morning's copy of *The Times*, turned to the Letters to the Editor page. Laing's letter had been circled in red and Matthew read it while Mullinger waited.

'This is written by the vicar from Foxhall Green,' Matthew said when he'd finished. 'He expressed similar sentiments in an interview he gave to *The Chronicle*.'

'Yes. I saw it. I found it a rather unpleasant read.' Mullinger frowned and scratched his temple. 'A year ago, I would never have even contemplated saying this, but tell me, Stannard. Have you considered Reverend Laing as a suspect?' Matthew was astonished, and it must have shown on his face, because Mullinger nodded and sighed. 'I know it sounds ridiculous, but experience has taught me we can't afford to ignore any possibility, no matter how ridiculous it seems. Now, don't misunderstand me. I'm not saying Laing was the gunman. But perhaps he knows the gunman and influenced him in some way? Filled his head with his rather extreme ideas and the gunman decided to do something about it? A member of his congregation, perhaps. After all, Reverend Laing is certainly making capital out of the shooting.'

'I agree it seems so, sir,' Matthew said. 'And I've discovered today Laing knew Lucy Simpson. He's the wrong build for the gunman himself, but as someone who might have put the gunman up to it? I hadn't considered that. I'll certainly bear what you've said in mind.'

'Very good. Well, I'll leave you to it.' Mullinger bid the detectives a good evening and left CID.

'He might be right about the vicar, sir,' Denham said, as

Barnes handed Matthew a mug of tea. 'I spoke to Mrs Ashe as you said, and she told me a number of people had made complaints about Frankie, including Reverend Laing.' He reached back to his desk and snatched up a file. 'This is the complaints file. The one from Laing is in there, along with the others made by various residents. You said the vicar had a connection with Lucy Simpson?'

'Lucy was typing up Laing's manuscript,' Matthew said as he read the complaints. 'It was around the time Lucy must have got pregnant.'

'You think he was the father of her child?'

'It's possible.'

'Then let's go and question him,' Denham said.

'I need to go through these complaints first,' Matthew said. 'I'll review these and then decide what we're doing in the morning. It's been a long day. Go home. Get some rest.'

'Are you sure you don't want to question him tonight, sir? Get him on the hop?'

'I don't want to rush into an interview without knowing all the facts,' Matthew said, wearied by the ache in his head and Denham's angry enthusiasm. 'Good work on this, but go home.'

Before Denham could protest further, Matthew made his way to his office and rooted in his drawer for the aspirin bottle he kept there. Washing two pills down with his tea, he watched the detectives depart.

Matthew had planned to spend no more than half an hour reading the report Denham had left on his desk of his interview with Mrs Ashe and going through the other paperwork, but when he next looked up, it was ten past ten. He stretched his arms out wide and yawned, then rose and took down his hat and coat from the stand. Walking through the main office, he bid DC Tapper, who was covering the night shift, good night and was halfway out of the door when the telephone rang. He paused while Tapper answered it.

'Sir,' Tapper said, putting his hand over the mouthpiece. 'It's the night sergeant from Foxhall Green. He said you would want to know this.'

'Know what?' Matthew asked.

'It's about Ivor Topling, sir. His house has been set on fire.'

The police car screeched to a halt at the kerbside. Matthew threw open the door and scrambled out, spotting Oakenshaw on the pavement, staring up at the house with smoke billowing from its windows.

'Oakenshaw!' Matthew shouted, hurrying towards him. 'Is anyone hurt?'

The Foxhall Green inspector wasn't pleased to see him. 'No. The family all got out. They're over there.'

He pointed behind him at the open doors of an ambulance where Ivor, his wife and their two children were huddled. A young girl was leaning against Ivor, both of them staring at the house, while a boy had his face buried in his mother's bosom.

'Was it arson?' Matthew asked.

'We don't know yet.'

'Did they see anything?'

'Look, Stannard,' Oakenshaw turned on him angrily. 'I don't know what you're doing here, but if you're so interested, you ask Topling.' He waved him away.

Matthew, biting his tongue, hurried over to Ivor.

Ivor saw him coming. 'Look what you've done,' he yelled, gesturing at his house. 'We're lucky to be alive.'

'I'm very sorry,' Matthew said. 'What happened?'

Ivor shook his head, still angry, but he gave his daughter

to her mother and wiped his mouth with the back of his hand, leaving a streak of soot around his lips. 'The missus had put the kids to bed, and we were in the kitchen having a cup of tea. We heard glass breaking in the hall and I went out to see what it was. The side window had been shattered and the carpet around the bottom of the stairs was on fire. So, I rushed up to get the kids. She was screaming,' he says, nodding at his wife, 'terrified for the little 'uns, and the kids start crying when they see all the smoke and the flames. But the fire had got onto the stairs by now, so I couldn't get them back down. I shouted at the missus to get out the back door while I dropped the kids out of the window and climbed out after them.'

'Did you see who did it?'

'I didn't see a thing. I was too busy trying to save my kids' lives.'

'I'm very sorry,' Matthew said again, knowing how worthless his apology was. 'Why don't you let the ambulance take you and your family to the hospital? Get your children looked at?'

'We're all right. I've just got to work out where we're going to stay tonight.'

'I'll talk to Mr Oakenshaw. See what he can do.' Matthew walked back to the inspector. 'They're going to need somewhere to stay. Can you arrange that?'

'I'm not running a hotel, Stannard,' Oakenshaw said. 'They must have friends or family who can put them up.'

'You're all heart, Oakenshaw,' Matthew said with a disgusted shake of his head. 'I take it the patrols didn't see anything?' Oakenshaw didn't answer, just glared at Matthew out of the corner of his eyes, and Matthew understood. 'You didn't order any patrols, did you?'

Oakenshaw rounded on him. 'I told you I don't have the manpower. What do you expect me to do? This,' he thrust his hand at the smoking house, 'is down to you. You shouldn't have made such a show of bringing Topling in.'

Matthew turned away, too angry to trust himself to speak further with his fellow inspector. His headache had started up again, and his eyes were sore from the smoke in the air. He looked around the street, full now of neighbours come out of their homes to watch the show, all of them still in their nightclothes.

Matthew frowned. No, not all of them. There was someone standing at the far end of the pavement in trousers and a short jacket, the peak of a cap casting his face into shadow. Curiosity mounting, Matthew started towards him.

He was twenty feet away when he saw the man's head turn in his direction. A second later, the man had spun on his heel and was running away.

Without stopping to think, Matthew ran after him. The man was fast, and Matthew was tired, but he was determined to catch him, certain the man he pursued was involved in the fire, for why else would he run?

He followed him down street after street, not realising how many turns he had taken until the street lamps ran out and darkness surrounded him. But he could hear the other man, could hear his footsteps slowing just a little ahead of him. Heard them coming to a stop. He had him.

Matthew turned the corner and skidded to a halt. The man was before him, maybe ten feet away, his back to Matthew as he stared at the brick wall in front of him. He'd run into a dead end. *Gotcha!* Matthew thought, bending and putting his hands on his knees as he tried to catch his breath.

And then the man turned to Matthew, and a painful memory flashed into his mind, an image of a man raising his arm to deliver a killing blow. His heart banged against his ribs, sweat broke out all over his body, and his chest tightened so he couldn't breathe. The man came towards him. Matthew, his legs giving way, tried to move away, and succeeded only in falling onto his backside. He shuffled backwards until he felt the wall press against him. He closed his eyes, waiting for the blow he knew was coming.

'Inspector Stannard?' someone called, and the man halted, lifting his head like a dog sniffing the air.

Matthew's eyes opened. He tried to call out, but no sound came.

'Inspector?'

The man ran past him, out of sight. Matthew drew his knees up and clutched them to his chest. Closing his eyes, he willed himself to breathe.

Footsteps came closer, and Matthew looked up to see the familiar police helmet outlined against the sky.

'Inspector Stannard?' the policeman asked. 'Are you all right?'

Tell him you're fine, Matthew told himself, but still he couldn't speak.

The policeman bent down, and Matthew heard the creaking of his boots. A hand was put on his arm. 'Inspector? Did he get you?'

'No,' Matthew croaked, finding his voice at last. 'I just...' He broke off and took several deep breaths, filling his lungs.

'Come on. Let's get you up.'

Matthew felt himself pulled to his feet. He hoped his legs would support him, that he wouldn't go down on his backside again and embarrass himself more than he already had.

'What happened, sir?' the policeman asked. 'I saw you take off after that fella and thought I ought to follow.'

'He looked suspicious. I cornered him here, but he got away.'

'Did you get a good look at him?'

Matthew shook his head. 'It was too dark.'

'Shame, but never mind. Well done for trying to catch him, but maybe you should leave that sort of thing to Uniform in future. That's what we're good at. Now, what say we get back, sir, and I get your driver to take you home?'

25

Wednesday, 22nd October 1930

'Morning, sir,' Denham said as Matthew walked into CID. He peered into Matthew's face. 'Are you all right?'

Matthew nodded. 'I'm fine,' he said, understanding why Denham had asked.

The police driver had dropped him off at the entrance to his block the previous night, and he'd forced a smile at the night porter in the lobby, wincing at the squeal of the lift's metal gate as he pulled it shut. His head pounding as he fitted his key into his front door lock, he'd fumbled to turn the light switch on before daring to step foot into his flat.

Calling for Bella, Matthew had waited for the comforting sound of her claws clipping on the linoleum. He'd held his breath as he waited, fearful she wouldn't come, but then Bella trotted out into the hall and he'd grabbed her, crushing her against his chest as he buried his face in her fur. Before he knew it, he was wetting her fur with his tears, and she'd meowed in protest. He'd apologised, smiling to himself as he imagined what Pat would say if she caught him saying sorry to a cat, and carried Bella into the kitchen. Putting her on the worktop, he'd opened a can of tuna and left her to eat while he poured himself a very large whisky.

Matthew turned every light on in his flat and checked every corner before he finally conceded he was alone and could go to bed. He had lain awake for hours, and when he did eventually sleep, it was broken with bad dreams. When he awoke around six a.m., Matthew felt half dead.

'I read your report and the complaints file last night,' he said to Denham, 'and I want you to follow them up.'

'The vicar and the residents?' Denham asked eagerly.

'No. I'll talk to the vicar. I need to question him about Lucy Simpson as well as the Ashe boy. You talk to the residents who made the complaints.' He nodded towards Rudd, who was frantically searching in the evidence table boxes. 'What's up with him?'

Rudd heard the question and turned. 'It's the victims' personal effects, sir. I returned them all, but I've had two complaints from the relatives that some items are missing.'

'Have you checked with the mortuary for them?'

'I have and they're adamant everything they had was sent on to us.'

'So, what's missing?'

'A Scout scarf and the usherette's cap. I don't know what I'm going to tell the parents.'

'Lucy Simpson's cap?' Matthew said, moving over to look into the box Rudd had been searching. 'That's not here?'

'No, sir. Nor is Frankie Ashe's Scout scarf.'

'Is anything else missing?'

'Not as far as I know,' Rudd said.

'That can't be a coincidence. Items belonging to the two people we think may have been the intended victims are missing.'

'What are you thinking, sir?'

Matthew forced his tired brain to work. 'That the gunman took them.'

Rudd frowned. 'Why would he do that?'

'I don't know, but we keep the fact that some personal items are missing to ourselves. They may prove useful evidence against this killer. If we ever find him,' Matthew added miserably.

'So, what do I tell the relatives?'

'You can tell them they're being kept back as evidence.'

'What about Lucy Simpson's typewriter?' Rudd pointed to the black case on the far edge of the evidence table and the shopping bag lying on top of it. 'Can I send that back to her parents?'

Matthew had forgotten about the typewriter. 'Have you checked it? And the bag?'

'Er, no, sir,' Rudd admitted awkwardly. 'I haven't got round to it yet.'

Matthew dragged the typewriter case over. He lifted the lid to reveal a shiny Remington Portable typewriter. He replaced the lid and opened the bag. He took out a small brown envelope and put it on the table before delving into the bottom of the bag where he encountered several pencils, a cheap fountain pen and a pencil sharpener. Then his fingers closed around a square cardboard box. He drew it out.

'What's that, sir?' Rudd asked.

Matthew opened the flap and took out the metal reel. 'It's a film.'

'That's a lot smaller than the films at the cinema.'

Matthew pulled out a length of the celluloid and held it up to the light. 'I think this is the sort of film that goes in a handheld camera. Can you make the pictures out?' He handed it to Rudd and delved into the bag again. He brought out another cardboard box containing a film.

'I think there's a figure in this one,' Rudd said, pointing to one frame.

Matthew glanced at it and nodded. He set the film box down and picked up the envelope. Opening it, he drew out the contents. His eyes widened. 'Blimey.'

'Sir?'

Matthew replaced the items in the envelope and took back the film from Rudd. 'Don't give these back to the Simpsons just yet,' he said, gesturing at the bag and typewriter case. 'I need to see what's on these films.'

Rudd shook his head. 'I don't think the machines at the cinema will take film that size.'

Matthew nodded. 'We need someone with a smaller machine. And I think I know who might have one.'

Denham rang the doorbell of No. 14 Clarence Road. The door opened and a woman peered out at him.

'Mrs Lydia Wildsmith?' he asked, introducing himself and showing her his warrant card.

'Yes,' Lydia said. 'Is something wrong? Lewis is all right, isn't he?'

'I'm here about the shooting,' Denham explained.

'What about it?'

'Frankie Ashe was one of the victims. You made a complaint about him to the police.'

'I did. But what does my complaint have to do with him being killed?'

'That's what we're trying to find out. Can I come in?' he asked irritably, tired of her questions.

Lydia bristled at his tone but stepped back, opening the door for him to enter. 'Go through to the sitting room.'

'Thank you. I assume your husband is at work?' Denham asked as he took a seat.

'Yes, he is. You don't need to speak to him, do you?'

'It shouldn't be necessary. I'm sure you'll be able to answer my questions.'

'And what questions do you have?'

'I need to know the problems you had with Frankie Ashe. What led you to make the complaint to the police?'

Lydia settled herself in an armchair and smoothed her skirt over her knees. 'The boy was a nuisance. He would walk up and down the street with a stick, banging it on the fences and gates and breaking them. He threw stones at our front doors and windows. I even saw him throw a stone at next-door's cat once.' Lydia tutted and shook her head. 'I saw him putting rubbish through the letterbox of the door over the road. And then he would ring the doorbells along the street and run away. I know that's a game children play,' she added, 'but he did it all the time. It was really very provoking.'

Provoking enough for someone to kill him? Denham wondered as he made a note of Lydia's words in his notebook. So far, she hadn't told him anything that hadn't been in her official complaint, and he couldn't help but feel a little disappointed. He glanced up and his eyes settled on the mantelpiece, which was littered with framed photographs. Lydia with a man, presumably her husband, and a boy. The boy and his father. Lydia and the boy. The boy on his own. In none of the photographs was the boy smiling.

'We've been told that Frankie Ashe bullied other children.' He pointed at the photograph of Lewis standing alone. 'Did he bully your son?'

Lydia looked over at the photograph. Denham saw her face soften.

'I'm afraid he did. He would call Lewis names. Play tricks on him. The usual things ignorant boys like Frankie Ashe do.'

'Did you talk to the school about it? Or the boy's parents?'

Lydia made a face. 'Talking to the parents was a waste of time. My husband did try to reason with them, but they're not reasonable people, inspector. The mother was extremely rude. That's why I made the complaint. I thought complaining to the police would stop the boy's antics, but it didn't.'

'And yet you didn't complain to the police again?'

'Well,' she shrugged, 'there didn't seem any point. Complaining the first time had made no difference. The boy still came round here, making a nuisance of himself. And he continued to be very unkind to Lewis.'

'I'm sorry to hear that,' Denham said. 'Did you or your husband know any of the other victims of the massacre? Lucy Simpson, for example? She lived in the next street.'

Lydia reached over to the side table and adjusted the figurine that sat there. 'No. I didn't know her.' She looked at her wristwatch. 'Is that all? Only I do have to go out.'

'Just one last question,' Denham said. 'Can you tell me where your husband was on Saturday afternoon?'

Lydia stiffened. 'Why do you want to know that?'

'It's just routine. We need to know the whereabouts of all men who have a connection with the victims, however slight.'

'I see. Well, Herbert was at his allotment all afternoon from just after lunch until around six o'clock when he came home for tea.'

'And can anyone confirm that?'

'I expect so,' Lydia said. 'There are usually other men at the allotment on a Saturday afternoon. But I really don't see why confirmation is necessary. I'm not in the habit of lying, Sergeant Denham.'

'I'm sure you're not. As I said, it's purely routine. I think that's all, Mrs Wildsmith,' Denham said, putting his note-book away and getting to his feet. 'Thank you for your time.'

Lydia saw him to the door. 'Are you close to catching the man who did it?' she asked as Denham stepped out onto the path.

Denham wished he could answer in the affirmative. He had told Mary when he got home the previous evening that Matthew had taken over the case and he had been pleased, hopeful, and yet, for all that, they didn't seem any further along. First, the tramp's alibi had been confirmed and then Topling's. They seemed to get suspects only to have them slip through their fingers.

'I really can't comment on the investigation, madam,' Denham said.

Her eyes narrowed at him before she nodded a goodbye and closed the door.

26

'Inspector,' Bill Edwards hallooed Matthew as he entered *The Chronicle*'s office. 'This is a surprise. What brings Craynebrook's finest to our door?'

'I need to ask a favour,' Matthew said, turning to Dickie as he rose from his desk and came over. 'You have a small projector machine thing here, don't you? I remember you telling me about it.'

'Yes, we have a projector,' Edwards said, answering for Dickie. 'It was one of the toys Teddy Welch said I should buy. A complete waste of money. We've never used it.'

'I wonder if I could use it now?' Matthew asked. 'I need to view some film.'

'Of course,' Edwards nodded. 'Anything to help the police, providing we get something in return.'

'I can't promise you anything, Mr Edwards.'

'Then I can't—' Edwards began, but Dickie gave him a gentle thump on the arm.

'Come off it, Bill,' he said. 'Mr Stannard's investigating the shooting of women and kids. You don't bargain when it's something like that.'

Edwards looked from Dickie to Matthew, his already

florid face flushing a shade darker. 'All right, Dickie. You can show him.' He shooed them away with an embarrassed wave of his arm.

'Thanks for that,' Matthew said, as he followed Dickie into the dark room.

'Don't mention it.' Dickie closed the door. 'So, what have you got there?'

'I'm not sure. Can you set these up for me?' Matthew held out the film boxes.

Dickie took them and put them on the side. He took a small projector out of a cupboard and set it down on the worktop. Opening the first cardboard box, he loaded the film. 'Am I staying to watch these or have I got to leave you to it? These machines can be tricky if you don't know what you're doing.'

Matthew looked at the projector doubtfully. He would have preferred Dickie to leave, but he had no idea how to work the machine, so he agreed he could stay. 'But you can't talk or write about what you see in these films, Dickie. You have to promise me.'

Dickie looked wistfully at the film coiled around the machine. 'All right,' he said. 'Though you're ruining my career, you know that?'

'What career?' Matthew said with a grin and gestured for Dickie to start the machine.

Dickie flicked a switch, and the machine ratcheted into life, casting the film onto the blank wall opposite.

Is that—? Dickie began, then glanced at Matthew.

'Yes,' Matthew nodded grimly. 'That's Lucy Simpson.'

'Wasn't shy, was she?' Dickie quipped as he watched Lucy push her slip down over her hips, letting it fall to the ground before hooking it over her toes to flick it towards the camera with a coquettish smile. 'Where did you get these?'

'A friend of hers gave them to me,' Matthew said as Lucy stood naked before them.

'Lucy was only eighteen, wasn't she? Where did she learn to do this sort of thing?'

Matthew thought of the films Ivor had shown after hours at the cinema and which Lucy had stayed to watch. Was this why she'd stayed? So she could emulate the women in them? He and Dickie watched the rest of the film for a few more minutes in silence. Lucy struck poses, some fairly innocent, others more provocative, before the film ran out.

'You want me to run the second one?' Dickie asked.

Matthew nodded, and Dickie threaded the film through the machine. He flicked the switch, and the film played.

'It's the same place,' Matthew said as Lucy walked into the frame, this time wearing her usherette uniform. 'Where do you reckon that is?'

Dickie shook his head. 'I don't know. But those are wooden planks, I think. A hut or a shed, maybe. Oh, here she goes again.'

Lucy was undressing. There was a little more polish to her movements this time. She seemed more confident, surer of her movements. She teased, making the viewer wait. But the teasing was too much for whoever had been filming, for a hand suddenly entered the frame and waved impatiently for her to get on with it. Lucy laughed, held up a finger and waved it in mock reproof.

'Whose hand was that?' Dickie asked.

'No idea,' Matthew said, annoyed he'd seen no ring or mark by which he could identify the hand.

Lucy was naked again, save for the cap on her head. She left it on as she struck a pose, one that made both Dickie and Matthew shake their heads in disgust.

'Do her parents know she was doing this sort of thing?'
Dickie asked.

'I don't think her parents had any idea what she was
up to,' Matthew said. The film ended, and the strip
slapped against the worktop. 'Put it back in the box,
Dickie.' He took the photographs out of the envelope.
'Were these taken in the same place as the films, do you
think?'

Dickie handed Matthew the boxes with one hand and
took the photographs with the other. 'The background is out
of focus,' he said, flicking through them. 'But it looks like
wooden planks again, so I reckon it's the same place.' He
handed them back. 'You've no idea who was holding the
camera?'

'None at all. Tell me something. How expensive is that
projector machine?'

'I don't remember, exactly, but it was a fair bit. I know
Edwards baulked at forking out for it.'

'And the camera that would have filmed these? That
would be expensive too?'

'I expect so. And not easy to get either. Those kinds of
cameras are American. They're not made over here.'

'Ordered from abroad, then?' Matthew asked hopefully,
thinking they might be able to trace the sale.

But Dickie shook his head. 'I don't know about that. We
got ours from a shop in London.' He put the projector back
in the cupboard and turned to Matthew. He raised his
eyebrows. 'So, there's been an arson attack on Topling's
house?'

Matthew nodded.

'I warned you.'

'Yes, you did. And I asked Oakenshaw to keep an eye on
the house. He didn't bother.'

'Bloody Oakenshaw,' Dickie muttered, shaking his

head. 'He's lucky the family were all right, otherwise I'd do a right number on him in the 'paper.'

'What good would that do?'

'It would make me feel better.' Dickie dug into his pocket for his pipe. He put it in the corner of his mouth and lit it. 'So, Ivor Topling's innocent. Who else is on your list?'

'I'm looking into Reverend Laing.' Matthew grinned at Dickie's expression. 'I knew you'd be pleased.'

'I am,' Dickie nodded. 'But why? What have you got on him that's made you change your mind?'

'I haven't changed my mind,' Matthew said. 'I just wasn't about to suspect him on your say-so.'

'All right, all right,' Dickie said, rolling his eyes. 'So, what have you got?'

'Well, as it turns out, you're not the only one who thinks Laing might be dodgy. This'll surprise you. Mr Mullinger has told me I should look into him as being involved.'

Dickie's face was a picture. 'You're kidding? Why?'

'He doesn't like what Laing's been saying in the newspapers. Thinks he's exploiting the shooting for his own ends.'

'Well, well. There's a turn-up for the books. I never thought I'd be in agreement with Superintendent Mullinger.'

'Ah, but he thinks differently from you,' Matthew said. 'He thinks Laing may have influenced someone to do the shooting, not done it himself.'

Dickie sucked on the pipe stem. 'It's possible, I suppose. Laing finds some impressionable young man who swallows his rhetoric hook, line and sinker. So, what have you found out about him?'

'This is still off the record?'

'Yes, of course.'

'Laing has a connection with both Lucy Simpson and

Frankie Ashe. He made a complaint against Frankie to the police and Lucy was typing his manuscript for him around the time she got pregnant.'

'You're thinking he's the father, are you? Interesting. Do you want to know what I've found about him?'

'Go on, then. Tell me.'

'Before he came to Foxhall Green, Bertram Laing was the treasurer at Salisbury Cathedral. A post with a great deal of responsibility.'

'The vicar of Foxhall Green's a bit of a comedown, then,' Matthew said. 'Why the move?'

'It wasn't his choice. There was a scandal.'

'Fiddling the books?'

Dickie shook his head. 'A woman.'

Matthew straightened. 'Really?'

'Ah, now you're interested, aren't you?' Dickie said gleefully. 'The story goes Laing was performing a service in the cathedral, and this woman of his turns up in the middle of it, screeching at him about broken promises and what a liar he is, how he's ruined her. All sorts of things.'

'She was his mistress?'

'Laing denied it. Tried to pass her off as a highly strung parishioner or some such rot. Nobody believed it. There was a little bit of a public outcry and he was given the elbow sharpish.'

'Where'd you get all this?'

'From staff at the church and the local rag,' Dickie said, puffing on his pipe.

Matthew considered. 'Maybe she was just a mad parishioner.'

'If that's all she was, why did Laing buy a house for her over in Colmbridge?'

'He did?'

Dickie nodded. 'It makes me sick. There he is, going on

about morals and degenerates and he's carrying on with a woman and installing her nearby so he can have his way with her whenever he feels like it.' He took out his notebook and tore out a page. 'That's her name and address if you want to look into her.'

Matthew pocketed the slip of paper. 'Thanks.'

'And,' Dickie went on eagerly, 'if he has an eye for one woman, there's no reason why he wouldn't have an eye for more. And younger ones, at that.' He pointed at the film boxes. 'Well, that is what you're thinking, isn't it?'

'It might be,' Matthew admitted.

'And remember, Laing wasn't anywhere to be found Saturday afternoon. So, where was he, eh?'

'He could have been anywhere.'

'Yes, he could be. You need to ask him and don't let him fob you off with how he's beyond reproach and that kind of rubbish.'

'I don't need you to tell me how to do my job, Dickie.'

'Don't be so touchy, Matthew. I'm just saying, don't discount him because he's a man of the cloth.'

'When have I ever done that?' Matthew demanded. 'I just want to be sure of my facts before I go charging in and accusing a vicar of murder. I made that mistake before.'

'You mean Stephen Pettifer?' Dickie said, referring to the vicar Matthew had briefly thought might be the killer of Josiah Clough during his investigation of the Blackbird Farm murder.

'There are some people who think I hounded Pettifer out of Craynebrook.'

'And they don't know what they're talking about. Don't let that incident cloud your judgement about Laing. He's quite a different kettle of fish, I promise you. Have you met him yet?'

'Not yet. He was at the public meeting but I didn't speak to him.'

'Well, when you do, you'll see what I mean.'

Lydia rapped on the office door and entered. Herbert looked up from his account ledger and frowned.

'What are you doing here?' he asked.

'Lewis forgot his sandwiches.' She took a greaseproof-wrapped parcel from her shopping bag.

Herbert tutted. 'That boy would forget his head if it wasn't screwed on. You can leave them here. I'll see he gets them.'

Lydia deposited the sandwiches on the edge of Herbert's desk. 'Herbert,' she said thoughtfully. He murmured in response, his attention on the account ledger. 'I had a policeman at the house this morning.'

Herbert stared up at her. 'What did he want?'

'He was asking about the complaint I made about the Ashe boy. He wanted to know what the boy did.'

'What did you tell him?'

'I told him about the damage he caused and the games he played. And then he asked if he bullied Lewis. I said he had.'

'You told him that?'

'I didn't know what else to say. But I think it's all right. He didn't go on about it.'

'What else did he say?'

'He asked where you were on Saturday afternoon. I told him you were at the allotment and he asked if anyone would confirm that. I think he's going to check on you. That's all right, isn't it?'

Herbert frowned. 'Eamonn was there,' he remembered. 'He'll vouch for me. There's no need to worry, Lydia.'

'I do worry. Not about you, but what if the police want to talk to Lewis about the bullying?'

'We'll tell them they can't.'

'But if they insist? You know what he's like when he talks about that boy. He gets so het up and angry. It will make the police wonder.'

'We'll just have to keep him away from them, that's all.'

'Do you think we should get a solicitor for him, just in case?'

'In case of what?'

'In case they take him in for questioning or whatever it is they do.' She leant over the desk and whispered, 'Or arrest him. A solicitor will make sure he doesn't say anything he shouldn't.'

'I'm sure it won't come to that. Lewis hasn't done anything wrong, Lydia. And besides, do you have any idea how much a solicitor costs?'

'You would put money before your own son's welfare?' she cried indignantly.

'Don't be so melodramatic,' he snapped. 'Lewis will be fine. Now, Lydia, you really must go. I'm very busy.'

'You will see he gets his sandwiches, won't you?' she asked, heading for the door. 'I don't want him going hungry.'

'Yes, my dear. I'll see he gets them,' Herbert sighed, keeping his head down until he heard her heels on the staircase. Then he gnawed at his bottom lip and stared thoughtfully at the sandwiches on the edge of his desk.

27

Matthew opened the door to the church hall and stepped inside. His footsteps echoed in the empty hall as he moved to the centre and took out the brown envelope containing the photographs of Lucy.

He flicked through them, looking for one that was the least blurry. Finding one, he held it up, comparing the background in the photograph with the wooden plank walls of the hall. There was a similarity, to be sure, but Matthew was unable to discern any marks, knotholes or peculiar grains that provided a definite match.

'What are you doing in here?'

Matthew turned at the voice to see Laing standing in the doorway. 'It's DI Stannard, Reverend Laing. I was just checking something.'

'Oh yes? What were you checking?' Laing said, coming into the hall and eyeing Matthew with suspicion.

Not ready to go into Lucy's pictures just yet, Matthew put the photographs away in the envelope. 'I was coming to see you, actually,' he said. ' I wanted to talk to you about two of the victims of the shooting.' He studied the older man's face for any sign of apprehension. He didn't see any.

'Which two?' Laing asked.

'Frankie Ashe and Lucy Simpson. You made a complaint about Frankie Ashe to the police.'

'Yes. The boy broke one of the stained glass windows in my church.'

'You wanted the parents to pay for the damage. They refused.'

'They didn't refuse, inspector. They didn't have the courtesy to reply to my letters asking that they pay. But one can't expect good manners from people of that class.'

'That must have been very frustrating.'

'It was. The window is still boarded up. The church has not the funds to replace it with stained glass, so it shall probably have to be glazed with ordinary glass.' Laing shook his head in dismay.

'Was that the only problem you had with Frankie Ashe?'

'Certainly not. The boy was a troublemaker, inspector. A nuisance to all decent people. Foul-mouthed. Ill-disciplined.'

'No great loss, then?'

Laing eyed him narrowly. 'I wouldn't say so, no.'

'Would you say the same about Lucy Simpson?'

'Lucy Simpson was a very unpleasant young woman, inspector. I daresay her parents are sorry for her loss, but I have no opinion on the matter.'

'You must have got along with her at one time,' Matthew said, pulling Lucy's typed pages out of his pocket. 'These are yours, aren't they?'

Laing took the sheets of paper and flicked through them. 'Where did you get these?'

'From a friend of Lucy's. They are yours?'

'Yes, they're pages from an early draft of my manuscript. I'd quite forgotten about them. I gave them to

Lucy to improve her typing speed. I needed my draft typed and she needed the practice. It seemed like a good idea at the time.'

Matthew held his hand out for the pages and Laing reluctantly returned them. 'That suggests it didn't turn out to be such a good idea?'

'What little typing Lucy did for me was of very poor quality, the pages she bothered to return, that is. I would give her pages to type and she would keep me waiting for them, often not doing them until I pressed her. I told her that if she wasn't interested in doing the typing, I wouldn't give her any more.'

'And what did she say to that?'

'I didn't speak with her again.'

'When was the last time you spoke with her?'

'Several months ago. I can't remember the exact date.'

Matthew waved the sheets of paper at him. 'You didn't need these pages back?'

'No. As I said, they were an early draft. My book has changed quite considerably since then and those pages are no longer of any use.'

'I see. Do you own a camera, reverend?'

Laing looked taken aback by the question. 'A camera?'

'Yes. An ordinary camera or a moving picture camera? Or both?'

'I have a camera that takes photographs. Why?'

Matthew took out the envelope containing the photographs featuring Lucy. He selected one of the less provocative ones and passed it to Laing. 'Have you seen this photograph before?'

Laing took it and his neck flushed purple. He glared at Matthew and shoved the photograph back at him. 'How dare you show me that filth?'

'You know who it is in the picture?'

'Of course I know.' His eyes blazed as he realised what Matthew was asking. 'You don't think I took that picture, do you?'

'I don't know who took it, reverend. You don't seem surprised that Lucy Simpson would have posed for a photograph like that.'

Laing straightened and breathed deeply. 'Nothing that young woman did would surprise me. She was a wanton. As proven by her being with child out of wedlock.'

'She would have got pregnant around June,' Matthew said. 'That was roundabout the time she was typing for you, wasn't it?'

Laing drew himself up. 'Are you suggesting...?' He broke off, unable to say the words.

'I'm asking if your relationship ended because she became pregnant?'

'It had nothing to do with that. And to imagine I would fornicate with that girl! It's disgusting.'

'Fornication is abhorrent to you, reverend?'

'It is a sin, inspector.'

'But you have a mistress, don't you?' Matthew said. 'A Mrs Roberta Wincott? Lives over in Colmbridge? She was why you had to leave Salisbury and come to Foxhall Green, wasn't she?'

Laing stared at Matthew in astonishment. 'How dare you bring Roberta into this!'

'Where were you last Saturday afternoon, reverend?'

'That is none of your business.'

'It is my business. And I need an answer.'

'Are you accusing me of having something to do with the shooting?'

'I know you weren't here in the church that afternoon,' Matthew shrugged.

'That is correct, I wasn't. I wasn't in Foxhall Green at all when the shooting occurred. That is all you need to know.'

'I need to know more. Were you having an affair with Lucy Simpson?'

'For the last time, no. I will not stand here and listen to these vile accusations—'

'Bertram?'

Both men turned towards the doorway. Violet was there, smiling sweetly.

'I heard raised voices,' she said, entering the hall. She smiled at Matthew. 'And who are you?'

'DI Stannard, Craynebrook CID,' Matthew said. 'And you are?'

'This is my wife, inspector,' Laing said.

'Violet Laing,' she said, holding out her hand to Matthew, forcing him to take it. 'I believe you were asking my husband if he fornicated with Lucy Simpson and whether he has a mistress in Colmbridge?'

Matthew reddened. 'I have to ask these questions, Mrs Laing.'

'Oh, yes. I quite understand. Allow me to help you. My husband does not have a mistress, inspector. He has never had a mistress. The lady you referred to, Mrs Roberta Wincott, is in fact, a very old friend of my husband's. When they were both young, Bertram asked her to marry him, but she refused him and married another man. It was her misfortune. Mr Wincott mistreated her, so much so that she suffered a nervous breakdown and has never recovered. My husband retains a deep affection for her and does what he can to see she is cared for. He helps with her financial affairs, ensures she receives medical attention and arranged the employment of a lady companion so Mrs Wincott is never alone. Last Saturday, the companion telephoned to ask my husband to visit, as Mrs Wincott was having one of her bad days. That is where he was last Saturday afternoon, inspector. Not at the cinema murdering people.'

Matthew felt as if he was back in school being told off by the headmistress. 'And the companion will confirm that?' he asked.

'If you require confirmation, I'm sure she shall.'

'What about Lucy—?'

'Oh yes, Lucy Simpson,' she cut Matthew off with a wave of her gloved hand. 'She was not my husband's mistress, either. In fact, Bertram found her a most disagreeable young woman once he discovered her true nature. He caught her half naked and cavorting with a young man in his church one day. The girl was quite shameless.'

'Who was the young man?'

'Lewis Wildsmith. The young man was not to blame, of course, for the incident. It was all Lucy's fault.'

'And now you have insisted on poking your nose into my private affairs, inspector,' Laing said stiffly, 'you may as well know that Lewis Wildsmith is in the Scouts, the same group as Frankie Ashe. And he hated the boy. In fact, I even heard him once wish Frankie Ashe was dead.'

'So,' Violet said with a girlish shrug and simpering smile, 'if you are looking for the father of Lucy Simpson's child, inspector, and you want to know who has a motive for killing both her and the Ashe boy, rather than harassing my husband, you would do far better to speak with Lewis Wildsmith.'

Matthew hurried up the stairs to CID.

'Denham!' he called, and the sergeant looked up from his desk, his expression changing to consternation as he realised Matthew was not in the best of moods. 'Did Mrs Ashe say anything about a Lewis Wildsmith to you?'

'No, sir,' Denham said, getting to his feet. 'But I talked to a Mrs Lydia Wildsmith. Lewis is her son.'

'And you questioned him?'

'No, sir. He would have been at school.'

'At school?' Matthew frowned. 'How old is he?'

Denham shrugged. 'The same age as Frankie, I suppose. Eleven or twelve.'

'He can't be. Reverend Laing's wife has just told me her husband caught Lucy Simpson and this Lewis Wildsmith half naked together in the church and that Lewis is probably the father of her child. The vicar also told me Lewis has often said he wished Frankie Ashe was dead.'

Denham stared at him. 'The pictures on the mantelpiece were of a young boy, and the way his mother talked about him, he sounded like a kid. I just assumed the son was the same age as the boys who were killed.'

'What have I always said, Denham?'

'Never assume, sir. I know. I should have checked on the boy's age.'

'Yes, you should,' Matthew said. 'Do I have to do everything myself?' He knew he was being hard on Denham, but because of him, the Laings had made him look a fool and that was something he couldn't easily forgive. 'I want to talk to Mrs Wildsmith,' he said. 'Denham, you're with me. You can fill me in on what Mrs Wildsmith said to you in the car. Come on.'

The police car pulled up at the kerb outside No. 14 Clarence Road. The net curtain at the front window fell back into place as Matthew and Denham walked up the path and banged on the door.

Lydia opened it, a wary look in her eyes. 'Yes?' she asked.

'You remember me, Mrs Wildsmith?' Denham said. 'I called earlier. This is DI Stannard. We'd like to talk to you about your son.'

'Lewis hasn't done anything,' she burst out.

'Can we come in, please?' Denham said.

'No. You can't.' Lydia went to close the door.

'Mrs Wildsmith,' Matthew said. 'If you don't let us in, we're going to have to take you down the station.'

Lydia's mouth opened. 'Me? You're arresting me?'

'We just want to talk to you. We can do that inside.'

She hesitated only a moment longer before opening the door and waving them inside. 'Go into the sitting room,' she ordered, and followed them in.

As Matthew took a seat on the settee, he glanced at the mantelpiece and saw the photographs of the Wildsmith family. There were no pictures of the son older than about ten and he understood how Denham had made his mistake.

'How old is your son, Mrs Wildsmith?' Matthew asked.

'Lewis is eighteen,' Lydia said.

'I understand he's in the Scouts? I would have thought he was too old for that.'

'He's the Scout leader's deputy. Lewis used to be in the Cubs, and he loved it so much, Dennis found a way for him to stay on.'

'Dennis?'

'Dennis Hillman. He's the Scout leader.'

'And where is Lewis now?'

'He's at work. He works at the biscuit factory over in Graydon Heath.'

'Bradley's Biscuits?' Denham asked.

Lydia nodded and watched as he wrote the name down in his notebook. 'He hasn't done anything,' she repeated plaintively.

'You told my sergeant,' Matthew went on, 'that you didn't know Lucy Simpson.'

Lydia's face hardened. 'I don't.'

'But there was an incident with Lewis and Lucy at the church a few months ago.'

'That was nothing,' she said, fiddling with a loose thread on her skirt.

'So, you did know Lucy?' Matthew pressed.

'Well, what if I did?' she snapped. 'My knowing her has nothing to do with your investigation.'

'It may do, Mrs Wildsmith, and I'm curious why you lied.' She said nothing and Matthew continued. 'It has been suggested that Lewis was the father of Lucy's child.'

Lydia's eyes widened. 'That's nonsense. Lewis never touched that creature.'

'They were found half naked in the church together.'

'That was all her doing. Lucy toyed with Lewis, that's all. Reverend Laing found them before they did... that.'

'How do you know?'

She glared at Matthew. 'Because Lewis told us. My husband talked to him and found out exactly what they had done, and I can assure you, inspector, they didn't go that far. Lewis didn't understand what Lucy was doing.'

'What do you mean he didn't understand? He's eighteen. Surely he knows about the birds and the bees?'

'Lewis may be eighteen in years, but not up here.' Lydia tapped her temple. 'He's not backward, I won't have you thinking that. Just young for his age. Lucy took advantage of Lewis to satisfy her cruel sense of humour. She thought teasing him was terribly funny.'

'Did they continue to see each other after the church incident?'

'Certainly not. My husband told Lucy to stay away from Lewis and I told Lewis to keep away from her.'

'And he obeyed you?'

'Of course he did. Lewis is a good boy, inspector. Now, if that's all?' She rose and gestured them towards the door.

'Not quite all,' Matthew said, and waited for her to resume her seat. 'You told Sergeant Denham that Frankie Ashe bullied Lewis. Did Lewis ever talk about Frankie?'

'No, never.'

'He never said he wished Frankie was dead?'

Lydia's chest heaved. 'I know what you're doing,' she said. 'You're trying to make out Lewis killed him and Lucy and all those other people, aren't you? Well, I won't have it. Lewis wouldn't hurt a fly. You leave him alone. Now, I've answered your questions and I'd like you to leave my house.'

'We have a few more—' Matthew began.

'I don't care what you have,' she cut him off, getting to her feet once more. 'You can arrest me if you like but I refuse to answer any more questions. I want you to go. Please leave.'

Matthew nodded at Denham and both men rose. Matthew thanked Lydia for her time and they left.

'To the factory, sir?' Denham asked.

'Yes, Denham,' Matthew said. 'To the factory.'

28

Matthew and Denham were shown onto the factory floor by a bespectacled, middle-aged woman in a tweed skirt suit who led them to a tall, thin man in a brown coat. 'The police to see you, Mr Hillman,' she said.

Matthew introduced himself and Denham. 'You're Mr Hillman, the Leader of the Boy Scouts?'

'Yes. Is this about the shooting?'

'That's right.'

'Well, why on earth do you want to see me?' Dennis asked, his eyes widening in alarm. 'I haven't done anything.'

'We're actually here to see Lewis Wildsmith,' Matthew explained, wondering why Dennis was so nervous.

'Lewis?' Dennis said in surprise, relaxing a little. 'Why do you want to talk to Lewis? He hasn't done anything wrong, has he?'

'We've been told Frankie Ashe bullied Lewis. Did you see any of that during Scout meetings?'

Dennis's expression became pained. 'There was a bit of that, yes. Lewis tried not to have anything to do with Frankie, but that wasn't always possible, of course, and there were incidents.'

'Such as?'

'The usual things, I suppose,' Dennis said with a shrug. 'Name calling. A bit of pushing and shoving. Boys will be boys, you know.'

'And how did Lewis respond to this bullying?'

'Not particularly well. Lewis being the way he is means he gets upset very easily. You do know Lewis is not quite right?'

'His mother told us,' Matthew nodded. 'You didn't ever hear Lewis threaten Frankie?'

'Only the usual taunts. Nothing to be taken seriously. Shall I take you to Lewis?' he asked hopefully.

'Please do,' Matthew said, and Dennis gestured for them to follow him. 'You use rifles in the Scouts, don't you?'

'Yes,' Dennis said over his shoulder. 'For marksmanship practice so the boys can get their badges. A sergeant came round and took ours away.'

'The sergeant said the rifles were locked in a trunk in the vestry, but that the key was easily accessible. Is that right?'

Dennis came to an abrupt halt and rounded on Matthew. 'Not that again. The rifles were perfectly secure, inspector. It's a church, for heaven's sake. The key to the trunk is kept on a hook at the back of the racking. You'd have to know it was there to find it.'

'Does Lewis know the key's there?'

'Of course. He unlocked the trunk when he helped me put the First Aid equipment away on—' Dennis broke off, his eyes darting from Matthew to Denham.

'On, Mr Hillman?' Matthew pressed.

'The last time we did First Aid Instruction.'

'And when was that?'

Dennis swallowed. 'Saturday morning.'

Matthew's heart beat a little faster. 'Lewis put the rifles away on Saturday morning? Before the shooting?'

Dennis nodded. 'Wait here,' he said. 'I'll bring Lewis over.'

'What do you think, sir?' Denham asked as Dennis hurried away.

'I think we may be on to something,' Matthew said, watching as Dennis approached a young man. 'If that's Lewis, I'd describe him as tall and thin, wouldn't you?'

'I would, sir,' Denham agreed. 'I wonder if he has an overcoat and trilby.'

Dennis returned with Lewis. 'These are the men who want to talk to you, Lewis,' he said, gesturing at Matthew and Denham.

'Hello,' Lewis said eagerly. 'You're the police, aren't you?'

'Yes, we are.' Matthew nodded at Dennis. 'We won't be needing you, Mr Hillman. You can get about your business now.'

'I see. Well, if you're sure.' Dennis walked away, looking back nervously over his shoulder.

'Mr Hillman said you wanted to talk to me about Frankie Ashe,' Lewis said. 'He's dead, you know?'

Matthew was a little taken aback by the glee with which Lewis said this. 'Yes, we know. He was killed in the shooting at the cinema.'

'So, what do you want to ask me?'

'I'd like to know how you got along with Frankie?'

Lewis shrugged. 'I didn't like him. He was horrible to me. But he's gone now, so that's all right.'

'It's all right?'

Lewis nodded. 'He can't bully anyone now, can he? So, it's all right.'

Matthew saw Denham's eyebrows rise in astonishment

at such blatant pleasure. It was a little unsettling. 'You also knew Lucy Simpson, I'm told?'

Lewis's cheeks coloured. 'Mummy says I'm not to talk about her.'

'Were you and Lucy friends?'

'We were. But that was before.'

'Before what?'

'I told you, I'm not supposed to talk about it. You mustn't try and make me. Mummy will be cross. If that's what you want to talk about, I'm going back to work.'

'All right, Lewis,' Matthew said, as Denham put out a hand to stop him. 'I'll ask you something else. About rifles.'

Lewis's eyes lit up. 'What about them?'

'You know how to use a rifle?'

'Do I?' he cried. 'I'm the best shot in the group. I always hit the target. You ask Mr Hillman. I got my marksmanship badge when I was twelve, long before anyone else.'

'That's very impressive,' Matthew agreed. 'And do you have your own rifle?'

Lewis shook his head. 'I wish I did. I will do one day. But at the moment, I have to use the Scout rifles.'

'They're kept in a trunk in the church vestry, aren't they?'

'That's right.'

'And you can take them out when you want?'

'I'm not supposed to, but I know where Mr Hillman keeps the key. You won't tell him I take them, will you?'

Matthew glanced at Denham. 'No, I won't tell him. One more thing, Lewis. Where were you last Saturday afternoon?'

'STOP! STOP AT ONCE!' a voice called out.

Matthew turned to see a man hurrying towards them. 'Who are you, sir?'

'I'm Herbert Wildsmith, Lewis's father. And I absolutely forbid you to talk to him.'

'I'm afraid you don't have the authority to prevent me.'

'You don't understand. You can't question Lewis. He isn't capable.'

'He's eighteen years old, Mr Wildsmith. He's an adult.'

'Daddy?' Lewis said. 'What's going on?'

'Nothing, Lewis. Don't worry.'

'I am going to question your son, sir,' Matthew said. 'Either here or at the police station.'

'You can't treat him like a criminal. He had nothing to do with the shooting.'

'Daddy?' Lewis called urgently.

Herbert ignored him. 'Lewis was here Saturday afternoon. He was working.'

'Do you have proof of that?' Matthew asked, a sinking feeling in his stomach.

Herbert turned to Dennis. 'Show him the roster for Saturday, Dennis.'

'Daddy!' Lewis called again. 'Don't.'

But Dennis had taken down a wooden clipboard from the wall and was flicking through the paperwork, looking for Saturday's roster. Matthew glanced at Lewis and saw the look of panic on the young man's face as he shook his head at his father. His father was frowning, not understanding his distress.

'Here it is,' Dennis said, and handed a sheet of paper to Matthew.

Matthew studied the roster. His heart skipped a beat. He looked up at Herbert. 'According to this, Mr Wildsmith, Lewis didn't clock on last Saturday. He's not down here as working at all that day.'

'What?' Herbert snatched the roster from Matthew's

hand. 'This is wrong,' he declared. 'It just hasn't been filled in correctly.'

Matthew turned to Lewis. 'Were you here last Saturday?'

Lewis looked from Matthew to his father, terror in his expression. He started to back away until Denham stood behind him and blocked his retreat. 'Daddy?' he cried. 'What do I say?'

'You were here, Lewis,' Herbert said. 'You know you were.'

'Lewis?' Matthew asked again. 'Where were you?'

Lewis took a few deep breaths and Matthew saw his hands curling into fists at his sides. He raised them and took a step towards Matthew before shouting at him, 'I went to the cinema, all right?'

29

A stunned silence had greeted Lewis's statement until Matthew pulled himself together and told the young man he was arresting him on suspicion of murder.

Matthew used the receptionist's telephone to call the CID and tell Barnes and Rudd to get over to Foxhall Green and search the Wildsmith house before making his way to the police car. Denham was in the back with Lewis, so Matthew climbed into the front seat.

'Where are we going?' Lewis asked as the driver started up the engine.

'Foxhall Green police station,' Matthew said, as the car pulled out onto the road.

'Why are we going there?'

'Because we need to talk about Saturday, Lewis.'

'But I've already told you where I was.'

Matthew said nothing. He was working out how he was going to handle the interview. That Lewis was subnormal was obvious and he would have to be careful how he questioned him. If it turned out Lewis was the gunman, then he didn't want a defence barrister claiming at trial that the police had put words in Lewis's mouth.

'Does Daddy know where we're going?'

'Yes,' Matthew nodded, keeping his eyes on the road ahead. 'He knows you're with us.'

'Is he angry with me?'

'I don't think so.'

'Will you tell Mummy where I'll be? She'll be worried if I'm not home for tea.'

'I'm sure your father will tell her.'

Lewis prattled on, wondering whether he would be paid for the rest of the afternoon, whether Mr Hillman could manage without him on the machine, whether the other workers would pack his biscuits in the boxes properly. Matthew, meanwhile, wondered whether the childlike Lewis really could have killed all those people in the cinema.

'I've never been to a police station before,' Lewis said, when his wonderings had run out. 'Is it far?'

'We're almost there,' Matthew said. 'It's just round this corner.'

The car turned the corner, and the driver cried out, 'Bloody hell,' as he slammed on the brakes. Matthew was thrown forward, only avoiding banging his head on the windscreen by bracing himself against the dashboard.

There was a crowd outside the station, and the police car had been seen. Someone shouted and pointed at the car, and the crowd surged towards them with a roar.

'Reverse! Reverse!' Matthew ordered, and the driver yanked at the gearstick. It made a harsh, grinding noise, but the car didn't move. He locked his door. 'Are your doors locked?' he yelled at Denham.

Denham slammed his hands down on both locks. 'Yes, sir.'

'What's happening?' Lewis wailed, his hands gripping the driver's seat as he rocked back and forth.

'Get us moving!' Matthew yelled as the car was surrounded and a man tried to open his door.

'I'm trying,' the driver cried, grinding the gearstick again. But he hadn't locked his door and it was yanked open. Hands reached in and grabbed him. He yelled for help as he was dragged from the car.

Matthew reacted fast. He climbed into the now vacant driver's seat and threw a punch at the face that presented itself through the open door. He winced in pain as his knuckles connected with a cheekbone, but his punch had sent the man stumbling backwards, and Matthew tugged the door close, slamming down the lock.

He cranked the gear as the mob pounded on the car's bodywork and he felt the car sway as some of the men rocked it from side to side. Mercifully, the car came to life. He sounded the horn, and it surprised some of the mob into jumping away from the car, clearing the road ahead. Matthew floored the accelerator, and the car sped off, leaving the mob behind.

'Are you all right?' he shouted over his shoulder as the houses on either side flashed by. 'Denham?'

'Yes, all right,' Denham shouted back. 'Where the hell was Uniform?'

Matthew slowed the car down and willed his heart to do the same. He caught sight of Lewis's panic-stricken face in the rearview mirror and felt a pang of pity for the young man.

'We'll take him to Craynebrook,' he said. 'He should be safe there.'

Matthew slammed the receiver into the cradle and swore loudly.

He'd called Oakenshaw as soon as they got back to

Craynebrook and demanded to know why the hell he'd allowed the mob outside the police station to go unchecked. Oakenshaw had been on the defensive, affirming his men had done all they could to control the crowd, but if Matthew hadn't bothered to warn him he was bringing in a suspect and that he hadn't been discreet about the arrest, then he should have expected an unpleasant welcome like a baying mob.

Matthew took a mouthful of the coffee that had gone cold while Oakenshaw had ranted, then lit a cigarette, inhaling deeply to let the nicotine work its magic. He felt the familiar throb at the side of his head and opened his desk drawer to take out the aspirin bottle he kept there. Shaking two pills into his palm, he washed them down with the cold coffee as Denham came into the office.

'Wildsmith's been booked in and put in a cell. Do we know if Bill's all right?' he said, asking after their driver.

'Oakenshaw said he's fine. A bit shaken up. How's Lewis?'

Denham shrugged. 'He was crying when I left him.'

'Tell Copley to keep an eye on him.'

'We shouldn't nursemaid him, sir. He doesn't deserve special treatment.'

'You're assuming he's guilty?'

'Well, don't you think he is?' Denham frowned at Matthew. 'You heard him, sir. He boasted about how good a shot he is and said he hated both Lucy and Frankie. And he's not right in the head. We all said only a nutter could have done the shooting.'

Matthew was about to tell Denham they should treat Lewis as any other suspect, innocent until they could prove he was guilty, when he saw Mullinger enter the main office. He got to his feet as the superintendent headed his way.

'This is excellent news, Stannard,' the superintendent

said cheerfully as Denham left to answer the telephone that was ringing on his desk. 'Has this fellow you've brought in confessed to the shooting?'

'Not yet, sir. I'm waiting on the results of the house search before I interview him.'

Mullinger nodded. 'Yes, let's get all we can on him. Give him no opportunity to wriggle out of it. Tell me, Stannard. What's all this I've heard about a mob outside the Foxhall Green station?'

Matthew told him what had happened. 'Someone at the factory must have talked.'

'How quickly word gets around. But you acted well, Stannard. If it wasn't for your quick thinking, that could have turned very nasty indeed.'

'Thank you, sir,' Matthew said, astonished by the compliment. What had come over Mullinger lately?

'Was this mob anything to do with the attack on Topling?'

'I imagine the arsonist was in the crowd somewhere.'

'Well, hopefully, all this hysteria will die down now the culprit's been caught.'

'Suspected culprit, sir,' Matthew corrected. 'Wildsmith hasn't confessed.'

'Oh, I'm sure you'll get a confession out of him, Stannard,' Mullinger said with a wave of his hand. 'So, carry on. Keep me informed.' The superintendent left as quickly as he had arrived.

Denham came back in. 'Message from the front desk, sir. Mrs Wildsmith is downstairs, demanding to see you. She's creating quite a fuss, apparently.'

'She's all I need,' Matthew muttered and stubbed out his half-smoked cigarette. He rose and headed for the door, then turned back and told Denham to check Lewis's prints against the prints from the rifle casings and box cartridge taken from the cinema. Then he made his way down to the lobby and Lydia rushed at him.

'I want to see my son,' she screeched. 'You have no right to arrest Lewis. He's done nothing wrong.'

Matthew held up his hands. 'Please calm down, Mrs Wildsmith.'

'Don't you dare tell me to calm down. You dragged my son away from his work, humiliated him in front of every-one. You lock him up in a filthy cell and all for no reason.'

'Not for no reason. He's admitted to being at the cinema on Saturday afternoon.'

'I don't care what he said to you. You can't pay any attention to him. Where is he? I want to see him.'

'That's not possible.'

'I want to see him. You have no right to keep a mother from her son.'

'I've every right, Mrs Wildsmith. Your son has been arrested on suspicion of a very serious offence.'

'It's absolutely ridiculous to think Lewis had anything to do with the shooting. Lewis wouldn't hurt a fly.'

'Mrs Wildsmith,' Matthew sighed, 'I suggest you go home. Your son is going to be here for a while.'

'Go home?' she cried. 'How can I go home with Lewis in here? And that's another thing. You've got policemen in my house, searching through all our private things. How dare you! I mean, what do you expect to find?'

'It's usual procedure following an arrest,' Matthew explained. 'Now, please. For your own comfort, Mrs Wild-smith. Go home.'

'I'm not going anywhere without my son,' she said, planting herself on the bench beneath the noticeboard. She glared at Matthew, daring him to force her out of the police station.

Matthew wasn't about to insist she leave. If Lydia

wanted to spend several uncomfortable hours in the station lobby, then she could for all he cared. He turned to Turkel, standing behind the front desk. 'Get Mrs Wildsmith a cup of tea, would you, sergeant?'

30

Maurice Cousins picked up the appointments book from his secretary's desk and ran his fingers down the lines. He knew he shouldn't be pleased, and he wouldn't dare show that he was, but the shooting had, if he was honest, been good for business. The appointment book had four new entries, all relatives of the victims. Cousins and Son Funeral Directors were going to be busy.

His secretary came in, carrying two mugs of tea. They only bothered with cups and saucers when clients were present. 'The police are searching all the shops, Mr Cousins,' she said. 'They'll be here in a minute.'

'Searching for what, Mrs Fraikes?'

'I don't know. They haven't told anyone. But it must have something to do with the shooting, mustn't it?'

He nodded thoughtfully, then looked down at the ledger. 'I was just looking at the appointments for today.'

'We have a busy day again.'

'Yes. I hope the police won't get in the way. The last thing we need is the clients seeing them.' He glanced down at the tray. 'Do we have any biscuits?'

'You're supposed to be cutting down,' she said reproachfully.

'You sound like my wife.' He turned as the door opened, his suitably sombre expression already fixed in place. 'Oh! Good morning, constable.'

'Morning, sir,' the constable returned. 'Need to have a look in your backyard.'

'Yes, Mrs Fraikes said you've been searching. What for, may I ask?'

'Whatever we can find, sir. Through there, is it?' He gestured at a door at the back of the shop.

'Yes. I'll take you through.' Mr Cousins set his mug down and led the constable to the backyard. 'We have our workshop out here, as you can see,' he said, gesturing at the large shed. Raindrops spattered his bald head, and he hurried across the yard to open the rickety wooden door. He stepped inside and the constable followed.

'A bit grisly, isn't it, sir?' the constable said, indicating the coffins filling the shed.

'It's my business, constable,' Cousins said stiffly. 'I don't find it grisly at all. I provide a very necessary service.'

'Yes, sir. I didn't mean anything by it.' The constable moved around the shed, peering over coffins, toeing through layers of sawdust, and peering into tool cabinets. He sighed as he stood in the centre of the shed and put his hands on his hips, then pointed at the back wall. 'You've got a broken window there, sir.'

'How the devil did that happen?' Cousins said irritably, moving to the window with its large weblike cracks.

'When was the last time you were in here, sir?' the constable asked, joining him by the window.

'A week or so ago. It looks like a branch did it. See there.'

The constable squinted at where Cousins was pointing.

'Is that a branch?' he asked doubtfully, then hurried out of the shed.

Cousins followed. 'What is it, constable?' he said, his neck retreating into his collar as the rain came down.

The constable had put his face to the gap between the wall of the shed and the brick wall separating the alley beyond. 'Blimey,' Cousins heard him mutter, then saw him put his arm in the gap and give something a tug.

'What is it?' Cousins asked again, his eyes widening as the constable's arm was withdrawn. 'Oh, my God. Is that—'

'Yes, sir,' the constable said, holding the rifle at each end with a finger. 'I think it is.'

'Sir,' Denham said excitedly as Matthew walked back into CID. 'Lewis's prints match those on the casings and box cartridge.'

'You're sure?' Matthew said, taking the cards Denham had thrust at him. Denham had circled in red pencil the identical markings on the inked copies of Lewis's fingerprints.

'I'm sure, sir, and there's more. Foxhall Green called in while you were downstairs. They've found the rifle. It was thrown over the back of the funeral directors on the high street. And,' he grinned, 'if you needed more proof, the rifle has 'Property of Foxhall Green Boy Scouts' scratched into the butt. It's got to be him, sir. It's just got to be.'

Thank God, Matthew thought. *I could have this case closed by nightfall.*

'Were there any prints on the rifle?'

'No. He'd wiped it clean.'

'He wiped that clean but left his prints on the ammunition?'

His words pricked Denham's elation. 'He forgot to wear gloves when he loaded the rifle. That's all.'

'Maybe,' Matthew said. 'Get the rifle sent over to the lab straight away.'

'Yes, sir. Shall I put Wildsmith in an interview room?'

'A little patience, Denham,' Matthew said. 'Any news from the house search?'

'Barnes and Rudd are on their way back.'

'And?' Matthew pressed.

'They didn't find anything,' Denham said reluctantly. 'No cap. No scarf. No camera. But Barnes said Lewis's walls are covered in film posters and articles torn out of magazines. They're all about gangsters and crime. He had a whole bookcase full of detective novels.'

'So does half the country,' Matthew said. 'You don't really expect me to declare a man guilty of murder just because of the kind of books he reads, do you?'

'How much more proof do you need?' Denham cried. 'He hated both Lucy and Frankie. He had access to rifles. He's an excellent shot. His prints are on the casings. And he said he was at the cinema.'

'He's also a young man of subnormal intellect, Denham,' Matthew shot back. 'For all her protestations, his mother's right. People like that may not realise what they're saying. So we have to go carefully.'

'You're going to let him get away with it, aren't you?' Denham said, his jaw hardening. 'Just because he's an idiot.'

'It's not up to me, sergeant. It's our job to gather evidence and get a confession, if we can. What happens to him once he's in court is up to the lawyers. We'll have done our bit.'

'So, let's get a confession. What are we waiting for?'

'Denham—'

'You do remember what he did, don't you, sir?' Denham burst out. 'All those people dead. Three of them kids.'

'I do remember.'

'But you weren't there to pull the bodies aside, trying to find the living amongst them. Having women with blood pouring out of them asking if their children were all right. You weren't there for that.'

'That's enough, Denham,' Matthew yelled, casting a glance at Bissett, who was watching the encounter between the two detectives in astonishment. 'Now, I know this whole thing has upset you, but I won't have you speaking to me like this. If you can't calm down, if you can't take my orders, then I don't want you here. I will put you on report and advise Mr Mullinger to suspend you. Is that clear?'

Denham glared at him.

'Is it clear?' Matthew asked again.

'Yes, sir,' Denham said, and turned away as Barnes and Rudd walked in.

They must have heard the raised voices, for they entered warily and stared at Matthew and Denham.

'I heard you didn't find anything,' Matthew said, determined to keep his temper under control.

'No, sir. Nothing,' Barnes said.

'It's possible Lewis has other hiding places. Denham.'

Denham turned back to face him.

'I want you to conduct a search of the factory.'

'We can do that, sir,' Barnes offered, gesturing at Rudd.

'No. I want Rudd in on the interview with me,' Matthew said. 'You can go with Denham to the factory.'

Denham dragged his coat from the back of his chair and walked out of CID without a backward glance.

'Go with him, Barnes,' Matthew ordered, and Barnes hurried out. When their footsteps had faded, he turned to

Rudd. 'Get Lewis in an interview room. It's time we had a chat.'

31

Lewis was picking at his nails when Matthew and Rudd entered the interview room, and he looked up at them with curiosity rather than alarm as they pulled out chairs opposite and sat down. His eyes were slightly puffy where he had been crying, but he seemed to have pulled himself together. The young man watched as Matthew took out his packet of cigarettes and lit one, tossing the match into the ashtray on the table. Matthew set the packet and the box of matches down on the table between them and Lewis snatched them up, examining the designs on the covers.

'You can have one if you want,' Matthew said.

Lewis opened the cigarette packet and looked inside. 'Mummy says I mustn't smoke. She doesn't like it.'

Matthew sucked on his cigarette and blew out a plume of smoke. 'Do you know why you're here, Lewis?' he asked.

'Something to do with Lucy and Frankie,' Lewis shrugged.

'Do you understand you're under arrest?'

'I know that's what you said, but I don't know what it means.'

'I arrested you on suspicion of murder, Lewis. Now, you

know what murder is, don't you?' Matthew received a nod. 'So, you understand how serious this is?' Another nod. 'You're in here so I can ask you questions about the shooting at the cinema last Saturday, and so you can give me truthful answers.'

'So, it's like a quiz?' Lewis asked eagerly.

'Sort of like a quiz. So, my first question is, did you shoot all those people in the cinema?'

Lewis looked from Matthew to Rudd and back again. 'What if I say I did?'

'Then the quiz is over,' Matthew said, his heart beating fast. Was it really going to be this easy? 'You'll sign a statement saying you did it and that will be that.'

'And if I say I didn't?'

'Then I ask you another question.'

Lewis played with the cigarette packet and matches, his eyes narrowing as he looked at Matthew. Irritated, Matthew snatched the boxes out of Lewis's hands and put them away in his pocket.

'What's your answer, Lewis?'

Lewis drummed his fingers on the table. 'Don't know,' he said, biting his bottom lip.

Matthew sighed silently. It wasn't going to be that easy. 'All right. Let's try another question. Where were you last Saturday afternoon between 1.50 p.m. and 2.15 p.m.?'

'I told you that,' Lewis said brightly. 'I was at the cinema.'

'What were you doing at the cinema?'

He laughed. 'That's a silly question. I went to see *Underworld*. That's what you do at cinemas, you know? You see films.'

'But that's not what happened at the cinema last Saturday, was it? At the cinema last Saturday, a lot of people were killed.'

'I know,' Lewis sighed. 'It's all everyone talks about.'

'You sound as if you're bored by all the talk.'

'Well, why does everyone have to go on about it? So what if they got killed?'

'You don't care about those people?'

'Why should I?' Lewis said angrily. 'I didn't know most of them, and those I did, I didn't like.'

'Who didn't you like?'

Lewis picked at his nails again and said nothing.

'Frankie Ashe?' Matthew suggested.

'I didn't like him,' Lewis said, nodding vigorously. 'He was a pig.'

'Why didn't you like him?'

'He used to bully me. I'm glad he's dead.'

Rudd cleared his throat and Matthew could tell the young man's blunt words had unsettled him. 'What about Lucy? You liked her at one time, didn't you?'

'Mummy says I'm not to talk about Lucy.'

'You and Lucy were friends, weren't you?'

'She was my girl,' Lewis said with a shy smile.

'Your girl? So, you and Lucy were courting?'

Lewis frowned, as if he didn't understand the word.

'Were you going to get married?' Matthew asked.

'I don't know,' Lewis shrugged.

'You don't know? But Reverend Laing found you and Lucy in the church without your clothes on? Do you do that with girls you're not planning to marry, Lewis?'

Lewis's cheeks flushed red. 'Mummy says I'm not to talk about that time. She said it was naughty what Lucy made me do and that I'd get into trouble if I told anyone about it. So, don't make me talk about it. Mummy won't like it.'

'Did you break up with Lucy after Reverend Laing threw you out of the church?'

'Lucy said she didn't want to see me anymore.' His fists

clenched. 'I told her she was being mean to me and that I'd tell Mummy how mean she was. She laughed and said I was a mummy's boy.' He banged his fists on the table. 'She said she'd just been playing with me.'

'That must have hurt.'

Lewis shrugged as if he didn't care. Then he grinned. 'Anyway, she can't laugh now, can she? She's dead, so there.'

'Did you want her to die?'

'She deserved to. She shouldn't have laughed at me.'

'And what about Frankie? Did he deserve to die too?'

'I expect so.'

'Did you kill them, Lewis?'

Lewis's eyes narrowed at Matthew, but he said nothing.

'We found the rifle,' Matthew went on. 'You had the sense to wipe it clean of your fingerprints, but you didn't think to wear gloves when you loaded the box cartridge. You left your prints on the casings, Lewis. So, we've got the rifle. We've got your prints on the casings. And you've told us you were at the cinema Saturday afternoon. So, why don't you tell us why you did it? Why did you kill all those people?'

Lewis drummed his fingers on the table as he stared at Matthew. *Come on, Lewis,* Matthew mentally begged. *Tell us everything.*

'I'm not playing this game anymore,' Lewis said. 'I want to go home.'

32

Matthew pushed open the door of The Fiddler's Retreat and made his way over to the bar.

Fred was pulling a pint, and he did a double take when he saw his brother-in-law. 'What are you doing here?'

'I fancied a drink,' Matthew said. 'Thought I'd pop in.'

'Ruby,' Fred called to the barmaid a little further along the counter. 'Get Matt a whisky.'

Ruby looked over at Matthew, flashed him a smile, then pushed a glass against the optic of a whisky bottle. 'Hello, stranger,' she said, handing him the glass.

'Hello, Ruby,' he said and drained it. The whisky burned as it flowed down his throat. Matthew waited for Ruby to start up her usual flirtation, but she gave him a quick wave and moved away. Where was the suggestion they go out sometime? The invitation to walk her home one night? He looked to Fred for an explanation.

'She's got a new fella,' Fred said. 'So, you've lost your chance there, Matt. You going up or you having another?'

'One's enough. Is Pat upstairs?'

'Yeah. You want to talk to her? Nothing wrong, is there?'

'No,' Matthew said, as Fred lifted the flap in the bar counter for him to pass through to the back. 'I've just come round for a chat. See you later.' He passed beyond the bar and climbed the stairs, making his way to the kitchen where Pat stood at the sink washing up, her back to him. He leant against the doorframe and put his hands in his trouser pockets. 'You missed a bit.'

Pat gasped and spun around, a hand to her heart. 'Don't do that,' she chided. 'You'll give me a heart attack, creeping up on me like that. What are you doing here?'

'That's what Fred said. Do I have to wait for an invitation?'

'It's not like you to turn up unannounced,' Pat said, drying her hands on a tea towel. 'You come to see Mum? Only she's having a lie down.'

'No, I just thought I'd drop by.' Matthew turned and went into the sitting room, flouncing down on the settee, stretching out his legs, and making himself comfortable.

Pat came to the doorway and looked at him quizzically. 'What's up?' she asked.

'Nothing's up,' he said as nonchalantly as he could manage. 'Why?'

'Because we're not on your way home, Mattie. Something's up or you wouldn't be here. So, spit it out.'

'We caught the gunman,' Matthew said with a shrug. 'At least, I think we did.'

'You think?'

'I'm not sure. He's an eighteen-year-old with the mental ability of... I don't know... a twelve-year-old. I'm not even sure he really understands why we arrested him or if he knew what he was saying to us. But he had a motive for killing two of the victims, victims we think were the primary targets. He had access to a rifle. And,' he sighed, 'he said he was at the cinema last Saturday.'

'Well, then!' Pat cried. 'What are you getting your knickers in a twist about? If he says he was there, he did it.'

'I know, but what if he's just telling us what we want to hear? You should hear how he talks, Pat. Mummy says I'm not to smoke. Mummy says I mustn't do this, mustn't do that. Does that sound like someone who can take a rifle and kill a roomful of strangers to you?'

'There's no knowing with some people, Mattie, especially those that aren't right in the head.'

'But the gunman was calm. Calculating. He had the sense to wipe the rifle clean of his prints and to make his escape, so no one saw him. I just don't see this boy Lewis having the sense to do that.'

'What evidence do you have against him?'

'His fingerprints were on the bullet casings.'

'Well, then, that means he did it, doesn't it?'

'I don't think his fingerprints being there are that conclusive. The bullets came from the Boy Scouts. He's the deputy Scout leader. He could have handled those bullets any time.'

'Sounds to me like you're making excuses for him, Mattie.'

'I don't mean to. I hope he is the gunman, then I can close this case. But these things are niggling me.'

Pat sat down beside him. 'What did you come here for tonight, Mattie?' she asked, taking his hand. 'Be honest.'

What had he come for? He studied her hand in his. 'Reassurance that I'm doing the right thing. I could go in tomorrow and charge him on the evidence we've got and his admission that he was at the cinema. If he's found guilty at trial, he could hang, or at the very least, spend the rest of his life in Broadmoor. I'm just worried he doesn't realise what he's saying. I mean, he probably didn't even know he could have a solicitor in the interview. I should have told him he could.'

'You don't have to do that, Mattie.'

'I know I don't, but I should have.'

'Has he got family?'

'Parents.'

'Then it's up to them to get a solicitor for him. That's not your job.'

'I know,' he muttered.

'You want reassurance?' she said. 'Then I'll give you reassurance. You always do the right thing, Mattie. I'm not a copper, so I don't know all the ins and outs of your work, but I know you won't let an innocent man be hanged. So, if you're not sure yet, take your time until you are sure. Forget what everyone else is telling you to do. You work it out for yourself. Right?' Matthew nodded and she patted his hand. 'Now, tell me. Have you had any more of those funny turns?'

'No more funny turns,' he lied, not about to tell Pat of his encounter with the man he chased the night of the arson attack. That really would put the tin hat on it and have her marching him to a doctor. 'And don't go on about that, Pat. I told you I don't want to talk about it.'

'I was only asking, you touchy sod. You hungry? I'll do you something to eat.' She got up and headed for the kitchen. 'What do you want?'

'Whatever you've got.'

'Bacon sandwich all right?'

'Fine.' Matthew pulled out the newspaper he'd found stuffed down the side of the settee. With a wry smile, he saw it was *The Chronicle*, probably his mother's copy. Amanda had been buying *The Chronicle* ever since he was posted to Craynebrook, firmly believing Matthew would be featured in every edition.

It was an old copy, dated the previous Friday. He flicked through the pages with only a desultory interest until he came to the advertisement section and an advert for a new cat food caught his eye.

'Do you want your bacon crispy?' Pat called.

'No. Just done,' he replied, a little distractedly, as his eyes moved further down the page. He frowned as he read the film listings for the Majestic, the Craynebrook cinema. The gangster film *Underworld* had been showing for the Saturday, billed as a one-day-only showing because it was an old film. The title rang a bell...

Pat came back into the sitting-room and handed him a plate with a bacon sandwich on it, brown sauce oozing out the sides. 'What's the face for?' she asked, staring at him.

He looked up at her, a memory worming its way to the front of his brain. '*The Virginian*,' he cried.

'The what?'

'It was *The Virginian* that was showing at the cinema in Foxhall Green last Saturday. Not *Underworld*.'

'So what are you getting at, Mattie?'

Matthew stared back down at the newspaper and the advertisement for the films. 'I think Lewis Wildsmith was talking about a different cinema.'

Barnes rapped on Denham's desk. 'Coming down the pub, Just?'

Denham shook his head, keeping his eyes on the transcript of Lewis's interview he was reading. 'Not tonight.'

'I thought you said Mary was at her mother's tonight.'

'She is.'

'So, while the cat's away...' Barnes grinned, but his face dropped at Denham's unchanging expression. 'Come on, Just. The inspector told us to call it a night. He wants us fresh in the morning so we can start again with Wildsmith. Besides, we could all do with relaxing for an hour or so.'

'I just want to finish up a few things,' Denham said, wishing Barnes would shut up and go away.

'Suit yourself. You're coming over the pub, aren't you, Sam?' Barnes asked hopefully as Rudd pulled on his coat.

Rudd shook his head. 'Not tonight, Si. I want to get home.'

'Well, I'm not going over on my tod,' Barnes said sulkily. 'I might as well go home as well. I'll walk out with you, Sam. See you tomorrow, Just.'

Denham waited until their footsteps had died away, then picked up his telephone and called home, hoping Mary would be back by now. He wanted to tell her about Lewis and, if he was honest, to vent his anger at Matthew to someone who wouldn't defend him. But the line rang and rang, and Denham hung up with a curse. He made himself a black coffee and stared for a full ten minutes at the corkboard, hoping he would see something, some clue, some important detail, he hadn't seen before that would prove Lewis guilty and convince Matthew. But nothing came to him and he checked his watch, deciding he would try home again. He picked up the telephone receiver and listened despairingly as the line continued to ring. But then, just as he was about to hang up, the line connected and Mary's breathless voice said, 'Hello?'

'Mary?'

'Justin?'

'Yes, it's me. Why are you out of breath?'

'I've just come in. I had to hurry to answer the telephone. Are you calling from work?'

'Yes, I'm still here. I wanted to tell you we've got someone for the shooting,'

'You've caught him? Who is it?'

'A man who works at a local biscuit factory. He's eighteen.'

'Is that all he is?' she said, and Denham could sense her shaking her head. 'Why did he do it?'

'He was being bullied by one of the boys and he got the usherette pregnant.'

'So, the inspector's charged him?'

'No. He hasn't confessed yet.'

'Oh,' she sighed. 'Then you're going to be very late. How long will it take for Mr Stannard to get him to confess?'

'Stannard's gone home,' Denham said, his jaw tightening in frustration. 'He's going easy on him. He even sent me away to do a search Uniform could have done just because I was pushing him to charge him.'

'You're not in trouble, are you?' Mary asked worriedly.

'I don't think so. He gave me a warning, though.'

'Oh, Justin.'

'Don't moan at me, Mary,' he snapped. 'I've had enough today.'

'Then come home.'

'Not yet. I want to go through the case file, try to find something that will convince the inspector this bastard's guilty.'

'Language, Justin.'

'Sorry,' he muttered. 'You sound tired. You should go to bed.'

'I was going to. I'm exhausted and Ellie's fallen asleep in the pram.'

'Put the telephone next to her so I can listen.' Mary went quiet and Denham hoped she wasn't wondering if he'd gone mad. How could he explain why he wanted to hear his daughter breathing? But the next moment he heard faint, measured breaths and knew his wife had done as he'd asked without wanting to know why. He closed his eyes and listened.

'Justin! Are you all right?' came Mary's worried voice down the line.

'Yes, I'm fine,' he croaked, trying to swallow down the lump in his throat. 'Get to bed. I've got to go.' He dropped the receiver into the cradle. 'Soppy sod,' he chided himself as he wiped his eyes.

He returned to the transcript, and read Lewis's words, *So what if they got killed?* And to think Lewis was down-stairs in a cell, probably sleeping like a baby. It wasn't right.

Denham pushed away from his desk and strode out of CID.

It was nearly eleven o'clock by the time Matthew got back to the station. He'd had to wait for a night bus and the journey had been frustratingly slow.

As he sat by himself on the nearly empty bus, Matthew replayed the interview with Lewis in his head. The more he went over it, the more he realised what a poor interview he had conducted. He'd gone in, believing Lewis was the gunman, and he'd asked questions in such a way that, inno-cent or not, Lewis would give guilty-sounding answers. When he finally climbed off the bus in Craynebrook, he hurried through the park and ran up the station steps.

''ere,' PS Bowden, the front desk sergeant, cried as Matthew burst into the lobby. 'What's the idea? Oh, it's you, sir. Everything all right?'

Matthew heard movement behind him and turned to see Lydia blinking at him, her bleary eyes evidence she had been dozing. He'd forgotten she was encamped in the lobby, and he cursed inwardly that he hadn't gone round the back of the station.

'I want to see my son,' she declared.

'Bear with me, Mrs Wildsmith,' Matthew pleaded, and fled up the stairs to CID before she could utter another word.

DC Tapper got to his feet in surprise at Matthew's entrance. 'I thought you'd gone for the night, sir,' he said as Matthew rifled through the paperwork on Rudd's desk.

'I had,' Matthew muttered.

'What are you looking for, sir?'

'The transcript of Lewis's interview.'

'Denham had that last. It's on his desk.'

Matthew moved to Denham's desk and found the transcript on the sergeant's blotter. He snatched it up and scanned the text. 'Got it,' he said under his breath and ran out of CID, heading for the police cells.

'Open up number two for me,' Matthew said to Hitchens, the night custody sergeant.

'Again? Denham was only in there half an hour ago.'

'Denham? Why was he in there?'

'He said he wanted to check on him. Nothing wrong, is there, sir?' Hitchens asked nervously.

'Was Denham alone with him?'

'Yes, sir.'

'Open up the cell,' Matthew ordered, worry creeping over him as he followed Hitchens to the cells. He watched impatiently, a sick feeling in his stomach, as Hitchens unlocked the cell door and turned on the light.

The door swung open. Matthew stepped inside and saw Lewis lying on the bench, a grey woollen blanket covering his body. Lewis raised his head and blinked sleepily at Matthew.

Matthew relaxed. Denham hadn't touched him.

'Can you wake up, please, Lewis?' he asked.

Lewis propped himself up on an elbow and rubbed his eyes. 'What is it?' he mumbled.

'I need to ask you something about the cinema. Do you remember saying to me you wanted to see the film *Underworld*?'

Lewis nodded. 'But don't tell Mummy because she doesn't like me watching gangster films.'

'Did you see the film?'

'I told you I did.'

Matthew remembered. When he asked what Lewis had done at the cinema, Lewis had replied he had watched a film because that's what you did at a cinema. How could he have missed that?

'When you said you were at the cinema last Saturday,' he said, 'which cinema did you mean?'

'The Majestic.'

'The Majestic here in Craynebrook?'

'Yes.'

'Lewis, this is very important. Did you go to the Regal Picture Palace last Saturday?' Matthew asked, holding his breath as he waited for the answer.

Lewis shook his head and fell back down onto the pillow. 'No. It was showing a Western and I wanted to see a gangster film. Please don't tell Mummy.'

33

Thursday, 23rd October 1930

Agnes Hillman opened her eyes, blinking a few times to dislodge the crusts of sleep in her eyelashes. She stared at the closed curtains. The sun was bleeding strongly through them, too strong for seven o'clock. She lifted her head from the pillow and squinted at the clock on her bedside. Her myopic eyes could just make out the position of the hands: half-past eight or thereabouts.

So late. What was Dennis playing at? Had he gone to work without waking her?

Agnes sat up in bed. 'Dennis,' she called and waited for his reply. None came, and she called again. Silence again met her call.

Her bladder full to bursting, Agnes threw back the covers and rose from the bed, grunting with the effort. Shuffling across the hall, she closed the bathroom door and fell onto the lavatory to relieve herself. When she was done, she returned to the hall and called, 'Dennis, are you home?'

Still no answer came, and she tutted as she went into the kitchen. Fancy going off and not telling her. He hadn't even made her a cup of tea before he went. She put the kettle on before returning to the hall and crossing to Dennis's bedroom, wondering if he'd even bothered to make his bed.

Agnes pushed the door open and started. 'You are here!' she cried. 'Why are you still in bed? You not well?'

But Dennis didn't answer her, nor did he move. Agnes moved to the bed and poked his shoulder. 'Dennis?' she queried and put her hand to his forehead. She gasped and snatched it away. 'Oh, Dennis,' she moaned and stroked his head. Pulling herself together, she returned to the hall and picked up the telephone.

'Doctor?' she said when the line connected. 'It's Agnes Hillman. I'm sorry to bother you so early, but it's Dennis... No, it's not that again. I think... No, I'm sure he's dead.'

Matthew accepted a mug of tea from Rudd and told the junior detectives to gather round. Denham wasn't among them and he asked where he was.

'Sleeping in, sir?' Barnes suggested. 'He was working late last night.'

Don't I know it? Matthew thought sourly. 'Well, we're not waiting for him. There have been developments in the case. Lewis Wildsmith is no longer considered a suspect and has been released.'

The detectives all began speaking at once.

'Why?' Barnes cried.

'You're kidding,' Rudd gasped.

'But he said—,' Bissett began, breaking off as Denham burst into the office.

'Where's Wildsmith gone?' he demanded.

'You're late, Denham,' Matthew said.

'I've been down to the cells. Wildsmith's not there.'

'I know he's not. I released him last night.'

Denham stared at him, 'But he confessed. I put his statement on your desk.'

'I read it. In my office, Denham. Now.'

The other detectives stared in bewilderment as Denham followed Matthew into his office and closed the door.

'Sir, I don't understand,' Denham said.

'Nor do I,' Matthew said. 'Explain to me what you were doing questioning Wildsmith last night in his cell, without my knowledge and without another officer present?'

'I was getting a confession, sir,' Denham said. He pointed to the statement on Matthew's blotter. 'Wildsmith's signed it. He's admitted he did the shooting.'

'I can see that, but what I don't see written there is what you said to him. For example, did you tell him the only way he could go home was by confessing to the shooting? I'm waiting, Denham,' Matthew added when the sergeant didn't speak.

'I may have said something like that,' Denham said with a shrug. 'But only to get him to talk.'

'To make a false confession. Because that's what his statement is, Denham.'

'No, sir,' Denham insisted. 'Wildsmith said he was at the cinema.'

'Yes, he did say that, and he was at the cinema. But he was at the Majestic here in Craynebrook, not the Regal Picture Palace in Foxhall Green.'

Denham stared at him. 'I don't believe it.'

'I've had it confirmed. An usherette at the Majestic remembers Lewis being at the cinema at the time of the shooting because he kept calling out and clapping during the film and she had to tell him to be quiet.'

'Sir, I...' Denham shook his head. 'I don't know what to say.'

'You could try saying you regret coercing a suspect to confess. You could promise me it would never happen again.'

Denham nodded. 'I *am* sorry, sir, and it won't happen again.'

'I'm glad to hear it. Get rid of this.' Matthew handed Denham the statement. 'And we'll say no more about it.'

Barnes suddenly rapped on the office door. Matthew waved him in.

'Sorry to interrupt, sir,' Barnes said, glancing uneasily at Denham. 'But I've just had Sergeant Dobbs on the line. Foxhall Green has had a call out to the house of Dennis Hillman.'

'What's happened?' Matthew asked, fearing another arson attack.

'He's dead,' Barnes said. 'His mother found his body this morning. Sergeant Dobbs says it looks like Mr Hillman killed himself.'

34

Matthew showed his warrant card to the constable guarding the door of the Hillman bungalow and he and Rudd were nodded through into the hall.

Oakenshaw came out of a doorway on the left. 'Ah, Stannard. There you are. He's in here.' He waved Matthew to follow.

Matthew entered the bedroom and his eyes immediately fell on the body in the bed. Dennis lay on his back, the blankets pulled up under his armpits. His head was turned to the left, his eyes were closed.

'His mother found him?' Matthew asked Oakenshaw.

'Yes. She called the doctor. The doctor called us.'

'Cause of death?'

'He took an overdose,' a voice behind Matthew said.

He turned to see a grey-haired, middle-aged man in a navy blue suit standing in the doorway. 'And you are?'

'Doctor Molland. I'm the Hillmans' GP. How do you do?'

Matthew took the hand he offered. 'An overdose of what?'

'Sleeping draughts.' Molland pointed to a glass tumbler

on the bedside cabinet. At the bottom of the glass was a white powder residue. 'I prescribed them,' he added ruefully.

'Why did he need sleeping draughts?'

'Mr Hillman was in a very heightened state of anxiety. He was attacked a few months ago, hit over the head and robbed, and it affected him badly. His nerves were shot to pieces, and his sleep was affected.'

'Was he suicidal?'

'I didn't think so, but it's not always obvious, I'm afraid. I daresay his mother could tell you more.'

'He left a note, Stannard,' Oakenshaw said, handing Matthew an envelope.

Matthew frowned at the marks on it. 'This has been trod on.'

'That was me,' Molland said apologetically. 'It was on the doormat and I trod on it as I came in.'

'His suicide note was on the doormat?' Matthew asked incredulously.

Molland nodded. 'It must have fallen from the hall table and his mother didn't see it. I hope I haven't damaged evidence?'

'It's perfectly all right, doctor,' Oakenshaw assured him.

Matthew took out the note. 'It's typed,' he said in surprise.

Oakenshaw shrugged. 'Maybe his handwriting was poor and he was worried it would be illegible.'

'"I can't live with what I've done",' Matthew read. '"I didn't mean to get Lewis into trouble. I'm taking the only way out."'

'He couldn't live with himself after killing all those people,' Oakenshaw said. 'So, it looks like you were wrong about that young man you arrested yesterday. It goes to show even Craynebrook's finest can't be right all the time.'

'I knew Lewis Wildsmith wasn't the gunman late last night. I've already released him.' Matthew said, refusing to rise to Oakenshaw's jibe. He turned back to Molland. 'You're certain it was suicide? There's no sign of a struggle? No bruises?'

Molland frowned. 'No, nothing at all. What are you suggesting, inspector?'

'What are you up to now, Stannard?' Oakenshaw muttered.

'I spoke with Mr Hillman yesterday,' Matthew said. 'He was nervous, certainly, but I wouldn't have taken him for suicidal.'

'As I've told you, inspector,' Molland said, 'the signs are not always obvious.'

'He's left a note, Stannard,' Oakenshaw said irritably. 'What more do you want?'

Matthew ignored him. 'I want to talk to the mother.'

'She's in the sitting room across the hall.'

Matthew found Agnes sitting on the settee, her chin resting on her hand as she stared blankly at the patterned carpet.

'Mrs Hillman?' Matthew said, and Agnes looked up. 'I'm DI Matthew Stannard. I'm very sorry about your son.'

'I don't know why he did it,' she said, shaking her head. 'Things were looking up.'

Matthew took a seat beside her and nodded at Rudd to take notes. 'I know this is difficult, but I need to ask you some questions. When did you last see your son?'

'Last night when I went to bed. That was about nine o'clock.'

'And how was he last night?'

'Dennis was upset. He told me about the police arresting Lewis at the factory. He thought you'd come for him. He was worried you suspected him of being the gunman.'

'Why was he worried we thought that?'

'Oh, it didn't take much to worry Dennis. Just your lot asking him questions did that. But I think it was mostly because of the rifles. I don't suppose it matters if I tell you. Not now.' Agnes sighed. 'Dennis had six rifles for the Scouts, but he told your lot he only had five because he never got the sixth registered. He thought the sixth rifle was the one the gunman used and you'd find that out and be after him for it. I suppose he thought that boy would tell you there were six and then you'd know he'd lied.'

Matthew glanced at Rudd to make sure he'd got all her words down. Rudd nodded, and Matthew turned back to Agnes. 'Dennis left a note. He wrote that he couldn't live with what he'd done. Do you know what he was referring to?'

She frowned at him. 'With what he'd done? Dennis hadn't done anything. What are you trying to say?'

'It might mean,' Matthew said carefully, not wanting to upset her more than she was already, 'he was the gunman.'

Agnes's expression hardened. 'He didn't kill all those people. Not my Dennis. No.'

'I understand Dennis had been feeling under the weather lately?'

'He hadn't been right ever since he was robbed,' she nodded. 'Dennis was never the same after that, always jumping at shadows. He thought the fella that hit him was going to get him again.'

Matthew nodded, knowing the feeling well.

Agnes went on. 'The doctor prescribed Dennis sleeping powders to help him sleep, but they didn't stop the night-mares. Dennis might have been all right if that fella who hit him had been locked up. But it wasn't just that. Things were getting on top of Dennis. At work and the Scouts.'

'The Scouts?'

'There was a boy, a nasty little brat, who played Dennis up all the time. It got so bad Dennis was talking about leaving as Scout leader.'

'Do you know the name of the boy?' Matthew asked.

'Yes. It was Frankie Ashe.'

It was all making sense. Matthew had to acknowledge that. 'Did Dennis have any lady friends?'

'Dennis? He wasn't interested in girls. He was too shy. To be honest, I don't think he ever really grew up. That's why he loved the Scouts.'

'He never mentioned a Lucy Simpson?'

Agnes shook her head and pulled a crumpled handkerchief out of her sleeve to blow her nose.

'What was the problem at work?' Matthew asked.

'Oh,' she sighed as she stuffed the handkerchief back up her sleeve. 'The factory is opening a new head office in Enfield. There was talk for a while of the Graydon Heath factory closing down and a bigger one opening up out in Essex. Dennis was worried he was going to be made redundant, but it turned out all right. The factory's staying open. It's just the office staff that are going. Dennis's job was safe.'

'I have just one more question, Mrs Hillman. Do you know where Dennis was last Saturday at two o'clock?'

'He was out in the shed.' She pointed through the back window at the garden. 'Pottering, like he always does.'

'So, you weren't actually with him? You didn't see him in the shed?'

'I was having my afternoon nap. But he would have told me if he was going out.'

The tears were coming and Matthew knew it was time

to leave her be. 'Is there anyone who can sit with you, Mrs Hillman?' he asked.

Agnes shook her head. 'I only had Dennis,' she said, and she burst out crying, covering her face with both hands.

Matthew jerked his head at Rudd. Rudd put his notebook away and hurried over. 'Take her to her room,' Matthew said in a low tone to Rudd. 'Ask the doctor to take a look at her.'

'Yes, sir,' Rudd said, and bent to put a hand under Agnes's arm. 'Mrs Hillman,' he said kindly as he encouraged her to rise. 'Let's get you to your room so you can have a nice lie down.'

Agnes went with him. Matthew took out his cigarettes and lit one as Oakenshaw came into the sitting room.

'What did she say?' he asked.

'She can't understand why he killed himself, but she said he had a problem with Frankie Ashe.'

'There you go, then,' Oakenshaw said. 'He did the shooting and couldn't live with himself when he thought Lewis Wildsmith was going to hang for it. That settles it.'

'I wouldn't say that,' Matthew said thoughtfully, moving to the sideboard. He opened the left-hand sliding door to reveal a few bottles of alcohol: sweet sherry, gin, brandy and whisky. There were five crystal tumblers, the sixth presumably the one on Dennis's bedside cabinet. A wastebin stood beside the sideboard, and Matthew examined its contents.

'Why don't you think it's settled?' Oakenshaw asked irritably as Matthew brushed past him and found the door to the bathroom. He followed as Matthew rooted in the bathroom cabinet and took out a cardboard box. 'It seems cut and dried to me. What have you got there?'

'The sleeping powders Dr Molland prescribed.' Matthew read the label. 'This box contained ten sachets. There are four empty sachets in the sitting-room bin.'

'So? He took four sachets to overdose himself. Four would have done it, I'm sure.'

'Yes. But why are the empty sachets in the sitting-room bin?'

'Because that's where he mixed them with his drink.'

'What drink did he have?'

'It smelt like whisky. He probably mixed it with water.'

'Have you dusted for prints?'

Oakenshaw made a noise of impatience. 'It's suicide, Stannard. What are you trying to do? Make a murder out of it?'

Matthew sighed, knowing Oakenshaw, for once, was probably right and Dennis Hillman had killed himself for no better reason than life had got too much for him. He'd seen it before, people ending their lives when they simply couldn't cope. There didn't always have to be some big reason for it.

'You're right,' he sighed dejectedly. 'You can get the body over to the mortuary. Rudd, let's get back to the station.'

35

'So, it was this Scout leader,' Mullinger said, passing a cup of coffee across the desk to Matthew. 'Well, well. And his target was the boy, Frankie Ashe, with all the other victims simply caught up in the shooting? It seems incredible.'

Matthew took a sip of coffee and winced. Too hot. He set the cup back in the saucer. 'Dennis Hillman was in a very nervous state according to both his doctor and mother. He possibly lost control in the auditorium.'

'A case of the red mists? Yes, I suppose that would explain it. And he killed himself out of remorse.'

'It seems so, although the note he left was rather vague.'

Mullinger noticed Matthew's frown. 'Something's worrying you, Stannard.'

Matthew nodded. 'Several things, sir. The suicide note was found on the doormat in the hall. The doctor stepped on it when he came in. The idea is that it fell down from the hall table and went unnoticed by the mother. If that's right, the hall table seems an odd place to put a suicide note. Surely, it would make more sense to put it by the bedside? Or under the mother's bedroom door? Then there's the fact

294

the note was typed rather than handwritten, but we didn't find any typewriter in the house. And it also wasn't signed.'

'Yes, well—' Mullinger began, but Matthew wasn't to be stopped now.

'And the empty sachets of sleeping powders were in the sitting-room bin when I would have expected to find them in the bin in the bathroom or bedroom. And going back to the note. By all accounts, Dennis Hillman was devoted to his mother and yet, he didn't mention her. No apology for putting her through his suicide. No asking for her to be looked after.'

Mullinger shook his head. 'I think you're reading too much into it. The man was obviously in a state of despair. You can't expect him to act in a rational, reasonable manner. Thinking of his mother at such a time – well, it probably never entered his head. As for the absence of a typewriter, I daresay he typed it up at his place of work.'

'It's possible,' Matthew agreed. 'Although he worked on the factory floor, not in the office. There's also no trace of Lucy Simpson's cap or Frankie Ashe's scarf. Of course, it is just a guess the gunman took them, but—'

'No, Stannard,' Mullinger held up a warning finger. 'No buts. I've left you alone so far in this enquiry, but enough's enough. This fellow left a note saying he couldn't live with what he had done. He had access to the rifles and lied about how many he had. He hated the boy. His doctor confirmed he was a bundle of nerves, and the alibi his mother gave him doesn't hold up. He was guilty. We should be grateful he killed himself and saved the taxpayer the cost of a trial. I shall make a statement to the Press that the gunman has been caught.' He leaned back in his chair and folded his hands over his stomach. 'Well, Stannard, it's been a busy week, hasn't it?'

'It has, sir,' Matthew said.

'And I'm mindful your leave was interrupted. Unfortunately, with Lund away, I can't let you go straight away, but as soon as he's back, you'll have what's owing to you.'

'Thank you, sir,' Matthew said, doing his best to keep the surprise out of his voice. He wasn't sure he liked this newly solicitous Mullinger. 'Well, I should be getting on and writing my report.' He excused himself and made his way to his office.

Hitching himself up onto the windowsill, Matthew lit a cigarette and blew the smoke out of the window, the air chilly on his skin. It was over. The case was solved. He should be happy, and yet...

He thought ruefully of Pat. If she were in his office, she would have told him to stop being an idiot, agreeing with Oakenshaw and Mullinger that it was all cut and dried, and to stop making things difficult for himself.

Matthew finished his cigarette, then sat down at his desk. He opened the case file, flicking through the cinema staff statements, the post-mortem reports, the lab results. There was nothing he hadn't read a dozen times before and which could shed any light on Dennis Hillman and his suicide. With a sigh, he took out the crime scene photographs and laid them out, side by side.

There were several pictures of the bodies. Two of the spent casings. One of the damage done to the side door. And one of the ticket counter, where Matthew had spotted the sixpence.

He frowned. The sixpence still bothered him. Why was it there? Rita Amstell had made it clear she wouldn't have left any money out on the counter, which suggested to Matthew it had been left there by someone else, and the only person he thought could have left it was the gunman. But why? Why would he leave a sixpence?

Matthew lit another cigarette. He was smoking too much, he knew; he would have to cut down. Out of the corner of his eye, Matthew saw Rudd come into the office. He had sent Rudd to the biscuit factory to find the typewriter Dennis's suicide note had been typed on. He called out to him and Rudd hurried into his office.

'Well?' Matthew asked.

'We found the typewriter the suicide note was typed on in the main office,' Rudd said.

'Had anyone seen Hillman up there typing?'

'No, sir. He must have done it after hours.'

Matthew nodded. 'Get your report typed up. I want it for the case file.'

'Will do, sir.'

'You didn't have any trouble at the factory?'

'No. Although people were asking why we were there.'

'What did you tell them?'

'That we were following up on our investigation of yesterday. They seemed to think Lewis Wildsmith was still in custody. His father obviously hadn't said anything.'

'You didn't have any problems with Mr Wildsmith?'

'No. He hovered over me a bit while I tested the typewriter. Asked if we were going to apologise for arresting Lewis when the gunman was under our noses all the time. I said I couldn't comment. That was right, wasn't it, sir?'

'Quite right,' Matthew nodded. 'Did you let Foxhall Green know we'd found the typewriter?'

'I popped in there on my way back.' Rudd reached into his jacket and drew out an envelope. 'Sergeant Dobbs gave me this for you. Mr Simpson brought it in. He took it to Foxhall Green this morning, thinking it might be relevant to the case. Of course, Mr Simpson wouldn't have known about Dennis Hillman and it all being over then. But I said I'd give it to you.'

Matthew took the envelope, seeing that it had already been opened, presumably by Mr Simpson. He took out the letter inside. As he unfolded it, he noted the name on the letterhead: Robertson Adoption Agency. Matthew read the letter, which was confirming the agency would accept Lucy's baby on their books. He set the letter aside, a new niggle working its way to the front of his mind. Matthew went into the main office.

'Rudd,' he said, and the young detective stopped making himself a cup of tea and turned to Matthew. 'Herbert Wildsmith said the gunman was under our noses all the time?'

'Yes, sir,' Rudd said.

'So, he knew Dennis Hillman was dead?'

'The whole factory knew. I think the doctor called them.'

'Do you have the number for Dr Molland?'

Rudd produced it from his notebook, and Matthew snatched up the nearest telephone and asked to be connected. 'Dr Molland?' he said when his ring was answered. 'DI Stannard. Tell me. Did you notify the factory of Dennis Hillman's death?... No, there was no reason why you shouldn't. But did you tell them it was a suicide?... I'm not suggesting you would betray a confidence, doctor. I just need to know what you told them.... So, just that he was dead?.... Thank you.' He hung up.

'What is it, sir?' Rudd asked.

'I'm not sure,' Matthew said, trying to get his jumble of ideas into something that made sense. 'But how did Herbert Wildsmith know the gunman was under our noses? The doctor only told the factory Hillman had died.'

'Perhaps Mrs Hillman told him?' Rudd suggested. 'Lewis was close to Mr Hillman, after all.'

Matthew shook his head. 'The doctor said Mrs Hillman

298

asked him to call the factory and tell them Dennis had died in his sleep. And even if she did speak to Herbert, Mrs Hillman wouldn't have told him Dennis was the gunman. She didn't believe it. It's too early for the Press to know. Mr Mullinger's still drafting a statement. So, how did he know?'

'Do you want me to go back to the factory and ask him, sir?' Rudd offered.

'No,' Matthew said after a moment. 'I don't expect it matters.'

He returned to his office and stared at the photographs on his desk. Leaving the picture of the sixpence on his blotter, he gathered the other images up and put them at the back of the case file. Returning his gaze to the sixpence photograph, he drummed his fingers on the edge of his desk. It was no good; he had to know why it had been left on the counter. Rita Amstell hadn't known anything about the sixpence or why it was there. Would Roy Grainger would be able to enlighten him? Matthew wondered. He would go and see him, he decided, just to satisfy his curiosity. Mullinger need never know.

Matthew glanced at the adoption letter on his desk. Mrs Hillman had said Dennis didn't know Lucy, but mothers didn't always know everything and it was just possible Lucy had mentioned Dennis to the agency if he had been the father of her child. It was a long shot, Matthew admitted to himself, but it was worth asking the question. Tie up a loose end. But Mullinger had wanted him to put the case to bed; he'd told him enough was enough. He really shouldn't go against the superintendent's instructions, but...

To hell with it. Matthew shoved the letter back inside the envelope and placed it in his jacket pocket. Grabbing his hat and coat, he strode out of his office.

'You off out, sir?' Rudd said as Matthew headed for the door. 'Do you want me to come with you? I'll get the car.'

'Not this time, Rudd,' Matthew said, pulling on his coat. He wanted to be on his own, to tie up the loose ends of this damned case without anyone looking over his shoulder. 'I'll take the bus.'

'But where should I say you've gone if anyone asks?' Rudd called down the stairs. He didn't get a reply.

36

'I read about the massacre, of course,' Mrs Bamber said as she poured Matthew a cup of tea. 'Such a terrible thing to have happened. And you say Miss Simpson was one of the victims?'

'She was,' Matthew nodded. 'When did she first come to see you?'

'Oh, let me see.' The adoption agency manageress consulted a ledger. 'The fourth of last month.'

'What can you tell me about that visit?'

'I remember her quite clearly,' Mrs Bamber said, removing her spectacles. 'Most of the unmarried women we get here usually cry throughout the interview. They've got themselves into trouble and realise they have to give up their child and it quite naturally upsets them.' She shook her head. 'Not Miss Simpson. She wasn't at all upset at the prospect of handing her child over to us.'

'I assume you asked why she wasn't keeping the baby?'

'She said the father was a married man. I have no idea if that was true. Many of the girls who come here are free with their favours and when they get pregnant, they make excuses for their behaviour and say the man was married

301

and that they were taken advantage of. I asked whether the father could provide for the child, for then she might be in a position to keep it. I do feel a child is usually best with the mother and there are sometimes ways of getting around objections. A girl can pass the child off as a sibling in a new town where her family isn't known, that sort of thing. But she said she didn't want to be tied to the father for the rest of her life and that a baby would get in her way. "Best it goes to someone who actually wants it, Mrs Bamber," she said. She then told me the father had told her to get rid of the baby and had even given her money to have it done. I'm sure you know what she meant by that, inspector. But she said she wasn't about to risk her life in that way. Not a thought or qualm she would be committing murder by doing such a terrible thing. Just that she would put herself in danger. And she laughed and said she took his money but wasn't going to give it back as a punishment for suggesting it.' She tutted and shook her head.

'You didn't like her?' Matthew observed.

Mrs Bamber drew herself up. 'No, inspector, I did not. She was not a very pleasant young woman. I agreed with her it was best for the child that she didn't keep it. I can only imagine the kind of upbringing it would have had.'

'I don't suppose she told you who the father was?' Matthew asked hopefully.

'Oh yes, she told me. So many girls don't. They want to protect the man who got them in the family way. But Miss Simpson didn't care a jot about him. I have it here.' She put her glasses back on her nose, opened a file on her desk, and took out a piece of paper. 'The father's name was a Mr Wildsmith.'

Matthew nodded, unsurprised. 'Then she was lying about him being a married man. Lewis Wildsmith isn't married.'

'No, inspector,' Mrs Bamber said. 'It wasn't a Lewis Wildsmith she named as the father. It was a Herbert.'

Matthew hurried to Foxhall Green, his brain buzzing with what he'd learnt. Had Lucy told the truth when she named Herbert Wildsmith as the father of her child? Could she really have had an affair with that dull, middle-aged accountant, even while she had been carrying on with his son? And if it was all true, what did it mean for the investigation?

He got off the bus and hurried to the police station. Taking the front steps two at a time, Matthew burst through the station doors, his dramatic entrance causing Dobbs and the man standing at the front desk to turn to him in surprise.

'Ah,' Dobbs grinned at Matthew, 'here's the man who might be able to give you an answer. Inspector Stannard.' He gestured at the man standing before him. 'This is Mr Grainger, manager of the Regal Picture Palace.'

Grainger turned to Matthew. 'I'd like to know when I can reopen the cinema, inspector. We're losing an awful lot of money. Is there any chance of opening for the weekend?'

'It's possible,' Matthew replied, wondering if anyone would want to go to the cinema after what had happened there. 'Actually, it's quite the coincidence you're here, Mr Grainger. I've been wanting to talk to you.'

'Oh? What about?'

'There was a sixpence sitting on the ticket booth counter after the shooting. Mrs Amstell told me she'd locked all the money away before she went into the staffroom. Do you know why there was a sixpence on the counter?'

'I suppose it could have been for a ticket,' Grainger shrugged. 'Sixpence buys the cheapest seat we have. Perhaps a customer put it there? He or she came in late, after the film had started. Rita wasn't in the ticket booth, so they left it on the counter?'

It sounded feasible. Could that latecomer have been the gunman? Matthew wondered. A man prepared to kill all those people yet decent enough to pay for a ticket? It seemed incredible, and yet, from what he'd seen of Herbert...

'Tell me something, Mr Grainger,' Matthew said. 'Do you know a Herbert Wildsmith?'

Grainger laughed. 'Do I know Herbert? Of course I do. We were neighbours until a few years ago when we moved across Foxhall Green. And we were friends before that.' He held up a finger and smiled. 'I can show you.' Delving into his pocket, he drew out his wallet. Flipping it open, he pulled out a creased and faded photograph. 'That will show you how far back Herbert and I go. That's us back in 1915. We enlisted together.'

Matthew took the picture. It showed a much younger Grainger and Herbert in their army uniforms, an arm around each other's shoulder, grinning at the camera.

'Yes,' Grainger went on. 'I like to keep that picture about me to remind me of when I was young. And had more hair,' he grinned, then sighed and shook his head. 'Those were happy days, if that's not too strange a thing to say about the war. I expect Herbert would say the same, especially with all the trouble he's had with Lewis over the years. I did hope that when the boy got older, Herbert's problems with him would stop, but it seems he's heading for even more heartache. I heard what happened outside here yesterday. The mob going for him. Poor Lewis. Of course, if he did kill all those people, then he deserves everything he gets, but what Herbert must be going through...' He shook his head in sympathy.

'Lewis wasn't the gunman,' Matthew said. 'He was released late last night.'

'Oh, I am glad,' Grainger said. 'It must be a great relief to Herbert, especially after all the problems he's had.'

'What problems?'

'His financial difficulties,' Grainger grimaced. 'The poor chap got himself into a bit of an embarrassing position a few months back and asked me for a loan. Unfortunately, I had to say no. My wife wouldn't have allowed it, even if I'd had the money to give him.'

'Did he say what he wanted the money for?' Matthew asked.

'I didn't ask, inspector,' Grainger said in an affronted tone. 'It was none of my business. And anyway, Herbert got through his rough patch. Said he'd found the money and was all right again. Of course, that was before he heard he was about to be made redundant. You see, the biscuit factory is opening a new head office and centralising all the administration. They don't need Herbert, so the poor chap will be out of a job in a few weeks. He asked if I could do anything for him but I have no vacancies at present.'

'Herbert was after a job at the cinema?'

'He was hankering after the projectionist post. Herbert knows a thing or two about cameras, you see, and he reckoned he could pick up the operation of the projectors very easily. But I already have Topling, and despite everything, he's very good at his job. ' Grainger shrugged. 'But I did what I could for him, although I admit it wasn't much.'

'And what was that?'

'Cut-price tickets to the cinema. Anywhere in the house for the lowest ticket price.'

'And the lowest ticket price is sixpence, isn't it, Mr Grainger?' Matthew asked, trying to keep his growing excitement under control.

'Yes, it is,' Grainger said, then frowned as he realised what Matthew was implying. 'You don't think—'

But Matthew cut him off, holding up the photograph and pointing at a blurry mark on Herbert's sleeve. 'What's that?'

Grainger peered at the picture. 'It's an arm badge, inspector.'

'I can see that, but I can't make out the design.'

'It is a bit fuzzy,' Grainger agreed, then drew his finger in a straight line over the badge twice. 'Those are crossed rifles.'

Matthew stared at him. 'Rifles?'

'Herbert was a marksman during the war, inspector,' Grainger said. 'He's really an excellent shot.'

37

Matthew rapped on Oakenshaw's office door and entered without waiting for a reply. Oakenshaw looked up from his desk, his face registering surprise.

'I'm sorry to burst in,' Matthew said, 'but this is important.'

'What is? I'm just writing a few lines for Mr Mullinger to add to his statement to the Press.'

'You might want to hold off on that,' Matthew said, falling into the visitor's chair. 'Dennis Hillman wasn't the gunman.'

'What?' Oakenshaw cried despairingly. 'But the man killed himself.'

'I don't think he did. I think he was murdered.'

'I was joking when I said that, Stannard.'

'I know you were,' Matthew said with a smile. 'Can I use your telephone?' He snatched up the receiver before Oakenshaw could reply and asked the operator to connect him with Craynebrook police station. He ignored Oakenshaw's outraged stare. 'Rudd!' Matthew cried when the line connected. 'I want you to get down to the factory and bring Herbert Wildsmith in for questioning... Yes, Herbert... For murder, Rudd... You heard me... I'll explain later. Just get down there and bring him in.' Matthew hung up.

'Herbert Wildmsith?' Oakenshaw said. 'For murder? What are you playing at, Stannard?'

'I'm not playing at anything,' Matthew assured him. 'Herbert killed Hillman and all the people in the cinema, I'm sure of it.'

'Tell me why you're sure,' Oakenshaw demanded. 'Because I'm having a hard time keeping up with you. First it was Topling. Then Laing. Then Lewis Wildsmith. And now Herbert. And this, despite Hillman saying he did it in his suicide note.'

'He didn't say any such thing,' Matthew said. 'That suicide note was vague to the point of being meaningless. It could have been written by anyone. And the note wasn't signed. If there's one time you're going to put your name to a letter, it's when you're writing your suicide note. Have you ever come across one without a signature?'

'Well, no,' Oakenshaw admitted reluctantly. 'But there's always a first time.'

'There are other odd things about his suicide. The sleeping draught sachets in the sitting-room bin. The lack of concern for his mother. The suicide note being on the doormat.'

'It fell down from the hall table, Stannard. That's all.'

'Or it was posted through the door by the killer.'

Oakenshaw stared at him in disbelief. ''That's ridiculous. Why would anyone do such a thing? Even if Hillman was killed, the killer would leave the note on a table.'

'Not if he couldn't be sure the victim wouldn't see it. Not if the victim was going to take a while to die.'

'All right,' Oakenshaw said, nodding with exasperation. 'Let's say I go along with this little fantasy of yours. Why kill Hillman? What had he done?'

Matthew jumped to his feet, too excited to sit still any longer. His ideas were all jumbled up in his head, and he hadn't yet had a chance to get them in order. 'I don't think he did anything. I think he was a scapegoat. We'd arrested Lewis. Herbert feared his son was going to be charged with murder and, in all probability, he'd hang for it. How could Herbert prevent that from happening? Simple. He gives us the killer. Hillman was perfect. A man with means, motive and opportunity.'

'But what's Herbert's motive for the shooting?'

'Herbert had an affair with Lucy. She named him as the father of her child when she arranged to have it adopted. Whether he was the father or not,' Matthew shrugged, 'there's no way of knowing. But he thought he was and he gave her money to have an abortion. But she didn't have one and kept his money. Maybe she demanded more, threatened to tell his wife about their affair. He had to get rid of her.'

'And what about Frankie Ashe?'

Matthew considered. 'Frankie bullied Lewis. Maybe Herbert thought he could kill two birds with one stone.'

'How did he get the rifle?'

'I don't have all the answers yet,' Matthew said irritably. 'Maybe Lewis told him where they were kept and where the key was. I don't know.'

'So, this is all guesswork,' Oakenshaw said, raising a sceptical eyebrow. 'But assuming you're right, how did he kill Hillman?'

'He must have gone there last night while Lewis was locked up with us and Lydia was waiting at the station. At some point, Herbert laces Dennis's drink with the sleeping powders. He does that in the sitting room, which explains why the sachets are in the sitting-room bin rather than the bathroom bin. He must have typed the suicide note at the factory that afternoon. But he can't leave it where Dennis might see it before he goes to bed. So he waits and posts the suicide note through the letterbox once all the lights are out. That's why it was on the doormat.'

Oakenshaw threw up his hands. 'I don't know what to make of all this.... this speculation, Stannard. Do you have a single shred of evidence against Herbert Wildsmith?'

'No,' Matthew admitted after a moment. 'But if I can borrow a couple of your men, I'm going to try to get some.'

'Borrow my men? What for?'

'According to his wife, Herbert was at his allotment Saturday afternoon. I need to find someone who can confirm he was there, if they can.'

'And if they do confirm he was there?'

Matthew shrugged, not wanting to consider that possibility. 'Can I have some men?'

'You can take Dobbs,' Oakenshaw said, gesturing at the sergeant through the window. 'He's all I can spare.'

38

Herbert wasn't at the factory. He had left for lunch and not come back. Not knowing what else to do and fearing what Matthew would say if he returned without Herbert in custody, Rudd rushed to the Wildsmith house and banged on the door.

It was opened by Lewis with a ham sandwich in his hand. 'You're not here for me, are you?' he asked fearfully.

'Who is it, Lewis?' Lydia called, coming into the hall. She saw Rudd and the uniformed constable behind him and her face blazed red. 'Oh no,' she cried. 'You're not taking him again.' She grabbed the front door and tried to close it.

But Rudd was too fast for her. He put his foot in the door and shoved it back with all his might. Lydia stumbled backwards, falling against Lewis and squashing his sandwich.

'Mummy!' he whined in protest.

'We're not here for Lewis, Mrs Wildsmith,' Rudd said, concerned he had been too rough and reaching out to steady her.

She swatted his hand away. 'Then what are you here

for? This is harassment. My husband says we could have the law on you.'

'We are the law,' Rudd shot back. 'And it's your husband we want.'

'What do you want Daddy for?' Lewis asked, taking a bite of his sandwich.

'Is he here, Mrs Wildsmith?' Rudd asked, ignoring him.

'No, he's not,' Lydia said, her brow creasing in her confusion. 'Lewis has the afternoon off, but Herbert will be at work until six.'

'He's not at work,' Rudd cut her off. 'I've just come from the factory. They haven't seen him since before lunch. So, where is he?'

Lydia stared at him in astonishment. 'He's not...?' She looked at Lewis. 'Do you know where your father is?'

Lewis shook his head and looked at Rudd. 'Is Daddy in trouble?'

'Yes, he is,' Rudd said. 'We need to talk to your father about the shooting at the cinema.'

Lydia's eyes widened. 'You're mad. First, you accuse my son and now my husband. You get out. You get out of my house.' She flapped her hands at Rudd and he backed away onto the front step.

'We'll be waiting for him,' Rudd promised Lydia as she slammed the door in his face.

'What exactly are we doing here, sir?' Dobbs asked as he followed Matthew along a very muddy channel at the allotment.

'According to his wife,' Matthew said, 'Herbert Wild-smith was here Saturday afternoon. We need to find someone who can tell us if they saw him then.'

'But it's all over, isn't it?' Dobbs said. 'I thought Dennis Hillman was the gunman. That's why he killed himself.'

'That's what we were supposed to think.' Matthew stopped as he saw a man coming out of a shed. 'Excuse me, sir!' he called.

The man looked over at him. 'Yes? Can I help you?'

'Were you here last Saturday, sir?' Matthew asked, showing the man his warrant card. 'Last Saturday afternoon?'

'Yes, I was. Why?'

'Can I take your name?'

'Eamonn Whitely.'

'Do you know Herbert Wildsmith?'

'Herbert? Yes, I know him. His plot is over there.' Whitely waved at a patch of ground with a shed about thirty feet away.

'Did you see Mr Wildsmith last Saturday afternoon?'

'I remember you,' Whitely said, pointing a finger at Matthew. 'You were the policeman at the meeting the other night in the church hall.' He glanced over at Herbert's shed. 'Is this about the shooting at the cinema?'

'Did you see him here then?' Matthew asked, wishing the man would just answer the question.

'Yes, I saw Herbert,' Whitely nodded, and Matthew's stomach sank. 'Him and Lewis.'

'Lewis was here? What time was this?'

'Oh, now you're asking.' Whitely raised his face to the sky. 'Let me see. I got here around one o'clock and Herbert was here then. Lewis turned up about fifteen minutes later, and they had quite a to-do.'

'They had a row?'

'Well, that's what it looked like. There was a lot of arm-waving and pointing. I don't think Herbert was pleased to see Lewis.'

'What were they arguing about?' Matthew asked.

'Oh, I couldn't say. They were too far away.'

'And how long were they here?'

'Lewis was only here for five minutes or so.'

'And Herbert?'

'I don't know. I went over to a friend of mine's plot at the far end of the allotment to give him a hand when Lewis went.'

'So, Herbert could have left just after Lewis?'

'I suppose so. Why are you asking about Herbert?'

'It's just routine, Mr Whitely,' Matthew said. 'Thank you. I'll let you get on now.'

Reluctantly, Whitely returned to his shed. Matthew turned to Dobbs. 'See if you can find anyone else who was here last Saturday, Dobbs. I want to be sure Herbert wasn't here.'

'Yes, sir,' Dobbs said, and tramped off.

Matthew headed for Herbert's plot. He knew nothing about gardening, never having had a garden, but he could see the plot was well-maintained and that Herbert had got the ground ready for the coming winter. He tried the door handle of the shed and was pleased when the knob turned and the door opened.

He felt a thrill of satisfaction as soon as he stepped inside and recognised the interior. The shed's wooden plank walls were just like in the photographs of Lucy Simpson, and there, on the far wall, was the lantern from the films.

Matthew stepped further in. The shed was neat and tidy. The workbench on one side had recently been used for seedlings; moist earth dotted the wood. Beneath the workbench were wooden crates. Matthew pulled out each of them, one by one. The first contained sacks. The second, a collection of twine and sticks. The third, seed packets. The fourth had a tarpaulin thrown over it. Matthew pulled it away, and his breath caught in his throat. There in the crate was a red, gold-braided usherette cap and a green Scout scarf. He lifted them out and, as he did so, he revealed the shiny case of a moving picture camera and the familiar brown leather of a Kodak box camera.

A shadow suddenly fell over Matthew. His blood chilled, the hairs on the back of his neck prickled erect. Terror flooding through him, Matthew slowly turned his head to see a tall, thin figure, the light behind him, standing in the doorway. *It's not Gadd*, he told himself, but blood was pounding in his ears and making his head swim. Matthew shut his eyes, willing the dizziness to stop. *Not now*, he pleaded. *Please, God, don't do this to me*. Forcing his eyes open, he watched as the figure stepped forward, and Matthew found himself staring up at Herbert Wildsmith. There was a shovel in Herbert's hands.

Herbert looked at the cap and scarf Matthew held, then at Matthew. Their eyes met, understanding passed between them, and Herbert raised the shovel.

But at that moment, Sergeant Dobbs appeared in the doorway and grabbed Herbert by his pullover and yanked the shovel out of his hands.

'I'll take that, Mr Wildsmith,' he said, and shoved Herbert up against the wall of the shed. Dobbs frowned down at Matthew. 'You all right, sir?'

His whole body shaking, Matthew dropped the cap and scarf back into the box and clambered to his feet. 'I'm fine, Dobbs. Thank you.'

'Snuck up on you, did he?' Dobbs said, giving Herbert a hefty thump on the back, making him grunt in pain. 'There's a coward, if ever I saw one. A heartless killer and a sneak. And just so you know. I found a fella who said he saw Mr Wildsmith here leaving on Saturday just before half past one. So, shall I slap the cuffs on, sir?'

'Please do, sergeant,' Matthew sighed.

39

Herbert was in the Foxhall Green station's only interview room and Matthew was in Oakenshaw's office, still shaking.

Dobbs brought him in a cup of tea, then went over to a filing cabinet in the corner of the office and opened the top drawer. He pulled out a bottle of whisky and poured some into Matthew's tea.

'Drink up, sir,' he said, replacing the bottle. 'Make you feel better.'

Matthew took a mouthful. 'Dobbs,' he said as the sergeant headed for the door. 'I'd be grateful if you didn't mention what happened in the shed to anyone.'

'I didn't see a thing, sir,' Dobbs assured him as Oakenshaw came in.

'Your man Rudd's arrived,' Oakenshaw said, 'and he's in with Wildsmith in the interview room. Mrs Wildsmith has been informed her husband's under arrest. When are you doing the interview?'

'I'll do it now,' Matthew said, finishing his tea. 'Assuming Herbert hasn't asked for a solicitor?'

'Not as far as I know. By the way,' Oakenshaw said as

317

Matthew headed for the door. Matthew turned back. 'We found the arsonist.'

'Who was it? Pete Ashe?'

'No. A friend of his. Benny Cross. My men found paraffin bottle bombs in his shed, already made up for use, presumably, on his next victim. He's confessed to setting fire to Topling's house and to the beating of Sergeant Brock, along with a Keith Baker, Scott Harris and Pete Ashe. They've all been charged with assault.'

'That was quick work,' Matthew said. 'Well done.'

'Thank you,' Oakenshaw preened. 'Well, you better get to the interview room and get a confession. Good luck.'

Herbert was sitting at the table, his arms resting on the tabletop, hands together when Matthew entered the interview room. Rudd was sitting across from Herbert, and he got his notebook ready as Matthew took a seat. He lit a cigarette, pleased to see his hands had stopped shaking.

Herbert took his spectacles off and cleaned them with his handkerchief. 'I suppose you want me to confess?'

'Yes,' Matthew said, taken aback by the question. 'That would certainly make things easier.'

'I don't want to be difficult,' Herbert said, replacing his spectacles on his nose. 'It was me. I was the gunman at the cinema. And I also killed Dennis Hillman.'

Matthew glanced down at Rudd scribbling these words in his notebook. 'I'm going to need some details about these murders. Firstly, your motive for the shooting?'

'I don't think that's important,' Herbert said. 'I did it. That's enough.'

'I'd prefer to know why.'

'And I'd prefer not to say.'

'Then I'm going to tell you what I think this has all been about and you can stop me if I go wrong,' Matthew said. 'You had an affair with Lucy Simpson. You took photographs of her. Explicit pictures. And you shot pornographic films of her. We found the cameras in your shed at the allotment. She became pregnant. You wanted her to have an abortion, but you needed money for that and you didn't have any. So you asked Roy Grainger for a loan. How am I doing so far?'

Herbert said nothing, so Matthew continued.

'But you got the money, and you gave it to Lucy to have the abortion. I don't know where you got the money from—' He broke off, an idea suddenly striking him. 'From Dennis Hillman? Were you the one who robbed him?' There was a flicker in Herbert's eyes, and Matthew knew he'd guessed right. 'You got the money and gave it to Lucy, but she didn't have the abortion. Instead, she made arrangements to have it adopted, but maybe she didn't tell you that. Maybe you thought she was going to tell your wife about your affair unless you kept giving her money and you couldn't risk that. You were about to lose your job. You didn't have any more money to give her.'

He paused, giving Herbert an opportunity to speak. But Herbert stared impassively at Matthew and didn't say a word.

'And then there was Frankie. He bullied your son, made his life a misery, so you had reason to kill him, too. I can only assume you killed all the other people in the cinema because leaving them alive was too big a risk. They might have been able to identify you.'

'I'm sorry about the others,' Herbert said. 'But I really had no choice.'

'What I don't know,' Matthew went on, 'is how you knew Frankie would be at the cinema that afternoon? Lucy worked at the cinema, so you knew she would be there, but Frankie?'

'You're assuming it was planned, inspector.' Herbert shook his head. 'It wasn't. It was serendipity.'

Matthew had no idea what the word meant. 'You're going to have to explain that to me, Mr Wildsmith.'

'Lewis came to the allotment with the rifle. He wanted to do some practice, but he was supposed to be at work. I took the rifle off him and sent him off to the factory. I intended to put the rifle back in the vestry trunk, but when I got there, the door was locked. I didn't feel like going home, so I went to the cinema, thinking I would try the vestry again after the film.'

'You took the rifle with you?'

Herbert nodded. 'I wrapped it in my coat. There was no one in the foyer, so I went into the auditorium and sat in the back row.'

'And what happened then?'

'I watched a little of the film, inspector, and then I saw Lucy with that latest young man of hers.'

'You were jealous?'

'To be jealous, I would have had to be in love with Lucy, and I was never that. But I was put out. When he grabbed her cap and threw it in the aisle...' He shrugged. 'I don't know why that act had such a profound effect on me, but something snapped. I put on my hat and coat, grabbed the rifle and walked down to the bottom of the steps. I think I may have had an idea of frightening her with the gun. But then I saw the Ashe boy there and it all became so clear to me. I could be rid of them both.' He blinked his pale blue eyes at Matthew.

'Why take Lucy's cap and Frankie's scarf?'

'I don't know, really. I just saw them there and...' He shrugged.

'Souvenirs?' Matthew suggested.

'I suppose so. Souvenirs of a job well done.'

Matthew's stomach churned at the callousness. He took a deep drag of his cigarette to hide his distaste. 'And you escaped down the back alley?'

'Yes. I knew I should get rid of the rifle, so I wiped it clean and threw it over the wall.'

'But you forgot about the casings,' Matthew said. 'Lewis's prints were on those.'

'Yes. That didn't occur to me. I should have taken them with me.'

Matthew tapped his cigarette against the ashtray. 'What about Dennis Hillman?'

'You were questioning Lewis. I knew he was innocent, of course, but I also knew he was just as likely to say things that would make him appear guilty. So, I had to do something. I needed a scapegoat, someone you would believe killed all those people. Dennis was a perfect choice. I went to his house while you had Lewis in custody. I knew Lydia would wait at the police station for him, so no one would know I hadn't been home. When I got to the bungalow, Dennis was very distressed, and going on about how his nerves couldn't take much more, that sort of thing. I settled him in the sitting room – he was very willing to be ordered about – then went to the lavatory and took four of his sleeping draughts from the box. I fixed him a drink and added the draughts. I stayed until he'd drunk most of it, then left. I put the note I'd typed up at work through the letterbox once I saw the lights go out.' He drummed his fingers on the tabletop once and narrowed his eyes. 'I thought it was perfect. What did I do wrong to make you suspect me?'

'You knew about us suspecting Hillman of being the gunman before it had been announced,' Matthew said.

'Ah,' Herbert nodded. 'Silly of me. I was feeling boastful, I expect. I was certain I'd got away with it all.'

'You were proud of killing all those people?' Rudd said, aghast. 'All because you got upset when you saw Lucy Simpson with another man?'

'No. It wasn't just that,' Herbert snapped. 'That was just the last straw. Young man, I was tired of being pushed around. Lucy had had her fun with both me and Lewis. Frankie Ashe was a constant thorn in my family's side. And after twenty years of dedicated service, my employer simply said I wasn't needed anymore. I was going to be thrown on the scrapheap. I'd had enough.' He looked across at Matthew. 'Have I told you all you want to know, inspector?'

'I have just one more question,' Matthew said. 'The sixpence left on the ticket booth. What was that about?'

'It was payment for my seat in the cinema,' Herbert said. 'Roy Grainger had told me I could have any seat in the house for the cheapest ticket price. Sixpence.'

40

'Congratulations, sir!' Barnes handed Matthew a tumbler of champagne. 'Sorry we don't have the proper glass.'

'Where'd you get champagne?' Matthew said with a smile.

'Courtesy of Mr Mullinger,' Denham said with an expression that displayed as much surprise as Matthew felt. 'He said we deserved it.'

'What has come over the man?' Matthew said under his breath and took a swig.

'You did it, sir,' Barnes said. 'Again.'

Matthew shook his head. 'We did it.' He raised his glass. 'To all of us.'

'To justice for the victims,' Denham said sombrely.

They all took a drink. The silence that followed felt awkward, and Matthew hurried to fill it.

'Well, as Wildsmith isn't going anywhere until tomorrow, I say we leave all the paperwork until the morning and call it a day.'

The men cheered and drained their glasses. After a few sips, Matthew decided he didn't really like champagne and set his glass down on a desk. As he turned meaning to go into his office, he found Denham standing in his way.

'Sir,' Denham said, staring into his mug, 'I just wanted to apologise again. I was wrong about Lewis and I was out of line doing what I did. It won't happen again.'

'It's in the past, Denham,' Matthew said. 'And I appreciate this case got to you. Let's forget what happened. Yes?'

'Yes,' Denham nodded. 'Thank you, sir.'

'Coming over the pub, sir?' Barnes asked as he pulled on his coat.

'Another time, Barnes,' Matthew said, and gestured for Rudd to come over.

'Yes, sir?'

'I want to ask a favour, Rudd.'

'Of course, sir. Anything I can do.'

'Well, if you don't mind, I'd like you to get over to Timmy Lane's.'

'For an identification of Mr Wildsmith, sir?'

'No. I think we can spare the boy that. But we promised him a ride in a police car, didn't we?'

A grin spread over Rudd's face. 'We did, sir.'

'Let him sit in the front, go as fast as is safe, and make sure you put the bells on,' Matthew said. He dug into his trouser pocket and, pulling out his wallet, handed Rudd his last note. 'And get him some sweets or whatever it is kids like these days. Spoil him. I reckon he deserves it.'

Rudd took the money. 'I'll see to it, sir,' he promised.

Matthew stepped up to the bed, casting a shadow over Sergeant Brock.

Brock looked up from his newspaper. 'Oh, it's you.'

'You're looking better, sergeant,' Matthew said, glad to

see some healthy colour in his cheeks mingling with the black and blue. 'How are you feeling?'

'Better than I was.' Brock tossed the newspaper aside. 'You come to put the cuffs on me, have you? Decided I'm guilty after all?'

'No.' Matthew pointed at the chair and Brock nodded that he could take a seat. 'In fact, we caught the gunman.'

'You got him, did you? Who was it?'

'Just a very ordinary man.'

'Well, I'm glad you've caught him. But why are you here, then? If you've come to ask me if I remember anything about the fellas who did for me, you've had a wasted trip.'

Matthew shook his head. 'I've come to tell you your attackers have been caught. They've been charged and will be prosecuted.'

'You have been busy.'

'Actually, I had nothing to do with it. Foxhall Green police caught them.'

'I'm surprised they bothered,' Brock said. 'But does that mean I'll have to go to court?'

'It may do, but I suppose the court would have to know where you'll be and you don't have a fixed abode. Of course, if you decided to settle down and stay in one place...?'

'It's not something I've got a choice about, son,' Brock said sadly.

'Actually, you do,' Matthew said. 'If you want.'

Brock narrowed his bruised eyes at him. 'What do you mean?'

'I mean that I've spoken with a lady at the Royal British Legion. I told her about you and asked if there was anything the Legion could do to help. She said they can help you find a job and somewhere to live, if you're willing. What do you think?'

'What will they want from me?' Brock asked suspiciously. 'I won't have to take the pledge or get on my knees every morning and pray, will I?'

'I don't know,' Matthew admitted, 'but it's got to be better than sleeping on park benches, don't you think?' He dug into his pocket and pulled out a piece of paper. 'This is the name and number of the woman I spoke with at the Legion. Call her. Go and see her. If you don't like it, you leave. But at least give it a chance.' Matthew rose and put the paper on the bedside cabinet.

'Why are you doing this for me, son?' Brock asked.

'Because I can, sergeant.' Matthew put his hat on his head, gave the old man a kindly smile, and left.

41

Matthew banged the knocker, wondering if this was such a good idea after all. He half hoped his knock wouldn't be answered, but he heard the latch turn and knew then it was too late to walk away.

The door opened, and Lund peered out at him. His face registered surprise. 'What are you doing here?'

'I thought I'd drop by and let you know what's happened.' Matthew was shocked by the way Lund looked. The portly detective was even shabbier than usual, and he had several days' worth of stubble on his grey face.

Lund hesitated, giving an uncertain look over his shoulder, before saying, 'I suppose you better come in.'

Matthew stepped inside, his nose wrinkling at the smell of stale sweat and beer coming off Lund.

Lund told him to go through to the front room. 'It's a bit of a mess,' he said, gathering up a dirty shirt and vest from the settee and tossing them into a corner of the room.

'It's fine,' Matthew said, picking up a dirty plate from the seat so he could sit down.

Lund fell into an armchair opposite. 'So, you've solved the case, have you?'

'Yes,' Matthew said. 'The gunman was—'

Lund waved for him to be quiet. 'You caught him. That's all I need to know.' He reached over to a side table, grabbed a bottle of beer, and poured it into a dirty glass. He waved the empty bottle at Matthew. 'Want one?'

Matthew didn't, but thought it would be rude to refuse. Lund groped behind his armchair and pulled out another bottle. He took off the top and handed it to Matthew, along with a not-so-clean glass.

'You really don't want to know who it was?' Matthew asked, disappointed by Lund's lack of interest.

'I don't care. To be honest, sunshine, I don't care much about anything these days.'

Matthew looked around the room, noting the mess, the dust, felt the absence. 'Where's your wife, Lund?' he asked quietly.

'Gone,' Lund declared. 'Left me and took the girls with her.'

'So, that's why you've been...' Matthew left the sentence unfinished, unsure how to describe Lund's behaviour without being cruel.

'Yeah,' Lund nodded. 'That's why I've been.'

'I'm sorry. Is it just a row or has she gone for good?'

'Well, I thought it was just a row, but it's been over a month now, so it looks like it might be for good.'

'Have you tried to get her back?'

'Of course I've tried. But she says she had enough.'

'Of what?'

'Of me. Of me never being here, which I think is an exaggeration. Of me not paying her enough attention, which is probably true. Of me not caring about the girls, which definitely isn't true.' He shook his head. 'I don't know, Stannard. I thought I was doing right by them, but apparently, my best isn't good enough.'

'She'll come round,' Matthew said.

Lund shook his head wearily. 'You don't know what you're talking about. You haven't been married.' He frowned. 'That's right, isn't it? I mean, I assume you haven't been married.'

'No, I've never been married,' Matthew said. 'I came close once, though.'

'Oh yeah? What happened? Did she realise what a pain in the arse you are and decided she wasn't going to be lumbered with you for life?'

'No.' Matthew took a mouthful of the beer. 'She died.'

'Oh, God.' Lund made a face. 'Me and my big mouth.'

'It's fine,' Matthew assured him, and they both took a drink.

'So,' Lund smacked his knee, 'Stannard's done it again and caught a killer. I bet Old Mouldy's pleased?'

Matthew nodded. 'He gave us champagne.'

'Blimey!' Lund stared at Matthew for a long moment, then shook his head. 'I'm pleased for you, Stannard.'

Matthew laughed, embarrassed. 'How much have you drunk?'

'Too much,' Lund admitted. 'But I mean it. I am pleased for you. You're a good detective. Much better than me.' His face grew serious. 'I don't want everyone at the station knowing my business, Stannard. Don't tell them about this.'

'I won't breathe a word,' Matthew promised. 'Can I help at all? Are you all right for money?' Mullinger had said Lund was officially on leave, but for all Matthew knew, Lund could have been suspended without pay.

'I'm managing.'

'If you're short, I can—' Matthew reached into his jacket pocket for his wallet, but Lund held up his hand.

'I don't need your money, Stannard.'

Matthew let his hand drop. He hadn't meant to offend

Lund. 'Well, I just wanted to let you know about the case. I'll be on my way.' He rose.

'Nah. Don't run off,' Lund said. 'Stay for another beer.'

Matthew had barely touched his first, but there was a note of desperation in Lund's voice that made him sit back down. 'All right,' he said. 'Just one more.'

Matthew dropped his keys on the console table in the hall and kicked his front door shut. He was more than a little drunk. The just one more beer had turned into two and a couple of whiskies because Lund had been eager for company and Matthew by that time had felt no inclination to leave. Only when Lund started talking about his wife, confiding things he would regret when sober, did Matthew feel it was time to go. He said goodbye to Lund, saying he'd see him at work in a few weeks' time.

He paused in the hallway, knowing he was waiting for something, but unsure what. Matthew realised as he kicked the door shut that he hadn't worried there was a man hiding in his flat, waiting to kill him, and he laughed out loud. 'Progress,' he said to the empty hall and laughed again.

But what was it he had been waiting for when he came in? Then it came to him. Bella normally greeted him when he came home, her claws tapping against the floorboards, wanting food and a cuddle. But there was no sign of her.

'Bella?' he called. There was no cry or meow in response. 'Bella?' he cried, a sliver of anxiety piercing his heart. The constant stream of traffic that passed beneath his window had worried him and led to the decision to keep Bella in. Had he left a window open and she'd got out? What if she'd got out and been run over?

She wasn't in the kitchen or the bathroom. She wasn't in

the sitting room. He stumbled into his bedroom, hoping to see her curled up on his pillow. But his cat wasn't there.

'Bella,' he groaned. 'Where are you?'

A feeble mew reached his ears. Matthew looked hurriedly around the bedroom, trying to work out where it had come from. He called again, and he heard another mew. Dropping to his knees, Matthew peered into the space under his bed. Two eyes glinted at him.

'There you are.' He sighed with relief. 'Are you coming out so I can feed you?' The offer of food always worked with Bella, so when she didn't move, Matthew grew worried again. 'What's wrong?' he asked and reached up to grab the lamp on his bedside cabinet. He pulled the cord to turn the light on and thrust it beneath the bed.

'Oh, Bella,' he grinned as his black and white cat mewed once more at him, then licked the head of one of the three kittens curled up against her. 'You clever girl.'

Matthew's next case...

Matthew's had a tough year.

He's investigated four murder cases, suffered a brutal attack and been accused of impropriety. He's weathered them all, but they've taken their toll. He's feeling battered, vulnerable and alone.

It's probably not the best time to have another murder to investigate. But murder doesn't take a holiday, and when a couple are found dead on Christmas morning, it's up to Matthew to find their killer.

It seems an open-and-shut case, just a burglary gone horribly wrong, but when a detective from a provincial force turns up following a lead on a baby-snatching case, and convinced there's a connection with Matthew's murder, the investigation becomes not only complicated, but personal.

Read ***A Killing for Christmas***

Join my newsletter

Get a FREE, UNPUBLISHED scene from
The Empire Club Murders when you join my
newsletter.

Scan the QR code below.

Read every gripping Stannard story

Visit

www.ckharewood.com